BLOOD TIDE

ROBERT F. JONES

Blood Tide

Macdonald

A Macdonald Book

First published in the United States in 1990 by
The Atlantic Monthly Press.
First published in the United Kingdom in 1991 by
Macdonald & Co (Publishers) Ltd,
London & Sydney.

Printed in Great Britain by
BPCC Hazell Books
Aylesbury, Bucks, England
Member of BPCC Ltd.

British Library Cataloguing in Publication Data
Jones, Robert F.
  Blood tide.
  I. Title
  813.54 [F]

  ISBN 0 356 19574 0

Macdonald & Co (Publishers) Ltd
165 Great Dover Street,
London SE1 4YA

A member of Maxwell Macmillan Pergamon Publishing Corporation

For Leslie,
who sails deeper seas

On men reprieved by its disdainful mercy,
the immortal sea confers in its justice
the full privilege of desired unrest.

—JOSEPH CONRAD

Excerpt from *The Philippine Pilot,* vol. IX

15. FLYAWAY ISLANDS

This chapter describes the Islas Efemerales, or Flyaway Islands, marked on some charts as Dampier's Folly. From NE to SW the group includes San Lázaro, Balbal, Moro Armado, and Perniciosa, along with some three dozen islets and atolls that are seasonally inhabited, if at all. Lying in the Sulu Sea midway between Palawan and Mindanao, some seven hundred sea miles southwest of Manila, the group is rarely visited. (See "Caution.")

San Lázaro, the largest island, is about twenty-seven miles long, NE to SW, and seventeen miles wide. The interior is mountainous, heavily wooded, and cut with deep ravines known locally as *laberintos venenosos* for the poisonous snakes, insects, plants, and Negritc headhunters inhabiting them. The highest mountain is an active volcano, Mount Haplit, with an elevation of 2,819 feet. Its smoke plume is often visible at a distance of fifty miles. Close to the coas are many seemingly fertile valleys interspersed with old lava flows and narrow strips of apparently cultivated lowland, from which the mountains rise abruptly. Beaches of red and black sand comprise the leeward shore of the island, supporting lofty, wind-tossed stands of coco palms. Attractive as they appear from the sea, the beaches are infested with hordes of disease-bearing sand fleas (*pulgarenas* in the local dialect) and should be avoided by visitors.

Balbal is similarly mountainous, with 1,699-foot Cerro Corsario rising in pyramid shape from its center, and thickly forested. Formerly a base for Dyak and Tausuq sea raiders, the island is now reportedly occupied only by a small band of animist indigenes related to the "gentle Tasaday" of Mindanao. Rare mouse deer, peacock pheasants, giant carnivorous flying squirrels (the *balbal* for which the island is named), and the small, fierce, V-horned wild buffalo known locally as *tamarau* are also present in delicate balance with the aborigines. To preserve that balance, Philippine President Ferdinand Marcos in 1978 placed Balbal off limits to visiting vessels. The ban, though rarely enforced, remains in effect.

Moro Armado is a hilly, scrub-grown, boomerang-shaped island twelve miles long by four miles wide. Surrounded by abrupt fringing reefs, its most prominent feature is a complex of *salinas,* or salt pans, at the S end into which the tide flows. These *salinas* are diked and controlled by sluice gates to permit the entry, entrapment, and evaporation of seawater, and are mined in rotation for the resulting salt. The labor was performed in the past by indentured *mineros,* who lived in coral-block huts the size of dog kennels. Currently the task falls to political prisoners and hostages whose plaintive cries and work chants can be heard far offshore, especially on a NE wind.

Perniciosa, flat, corralled, and uncharted, is visited only by snake hunters and malaria researchers. A Japanese submarine refueling depot was located here during World War II but abandoned in 1944 due to disease and guerrilla raids.

The sea bottom surrounding the Flyaways is rugged and rapidly variable. A "Dangerous Ground" of reefs, shoals, trenches, shifting sandbars, and submarine ledges (called *putas* in local parlance) girds and interpenetrates the main group, rendering approach hazardous even to the best-equipped vessels.

Wrecks abound.

History. Obscure, violent, mythic, and not yet written.

COLREGS Demarcation Lines. International rules of the road apply.

Vessel Traffic Management. Not applicable.

Anchorages. Variable, dependent upon wind, tide, current, and political developments. A good weather eye and a busy leadsman in the chains afford the best assurance against grounding. All anchors should be buoyed for quick slippage and an anchor watch maintained at all times. (See "Caution.")

Tides. Probably semidiurnal on the South China Sea side of the group, diurnal in the Sulu Sea. Tide tables for these waters have not yet been compiled.

Currents. Little known, though a NW current of twelve to twenty knots may set directly through the islands and their outliers, at least during certain months.

Weather. Mild to severe, year around. The outstanding feature of the marine weather is its unpredictability. Trade winds and monsoons are frequently interrupted by cold fronts that reach the islands from as far away as Tibet and Mongolia. Gale-force winds, though unlikely, can drop with great suddenness from seemingly clear skies. These squalls are known locally as *vientos azores,* or "hawk winds," for the swiftness and ferocity of their descent. Seas in the area usually run about ten feet, but have reached forty feet or more on occasion. Waterspouts are common.

Storm-Warning Displays. These are unknown in the Flyaways.

Pilotage. Unreliable. (See "Caution.")

Towage. Hazardous. (See "Caution.")

Quarantine. Not required. (See "Caution.")

Customs. Ruinous. (See "Caution.")

Immigration. No passport or visa is required of anyone seeking to enter the Flyaways.

Supplies. Bunker fuel, diesel, and gasoline are rarely available. Most fuel sold to visiting mariners has been purposely diluted with water or spiked with corrosives. Sugar is frequently added to gasoline so as to burn pistons and render visiting vessels inoperable. Fresh meat, fruit, and vegetables can be purchased, along with casks of supposedly fresh water, from local pump boats. A frequent, low-cost offering is the native rum, a potent drink called *tuba asesina* (see "Caution"). All such produce should be thoroughly examined, washed, strained, peeled, cooked, or otherwise tested (perhaps on the ship's cat) before human consumption. Ice, yeast, and stationery are sometimes available in the bicycle shop above the Carniceria Cabrónes near Love Boat Wharf at Avenida Putissima.

Repairs. The Vela Vieja Sail Loft at Narr Lagoon on Moro Armado is equipped with a deep-throat (thirty-seven-inch) sewing machine. One-Eyed Balabatchi, a shipwright on San Lázaro, does excellent if expensive work in both wood and fiberglass (ask for him at the Millikan Shipping offices opposite the mosque on Dewey Square in Lázaro City). Though all Flyaway Islanders are competent mechanics, requests from visiting mariners for engine repairs are often construed as invitations for sabotage (see "Caution").

Communications. Roads between principal ports and towns are poor, unpaved, rutted, and beset by bandits. Bridges over the many streams that drain the higher islands are few, flimsy, poorly maintained, and exorbitant in their toll rates. The islands have no air service. Though steamship lines from Manila, Puerto Princesa, and Zamboanga served the islands in years past, the looting and subsequent sinking of a Hong Kong cruise ship at dockside in Lázaro City in 1978 caused termination of passenger service. Only small, interisland vessels called *kumpits* now operate in the Flyaways (see "Caution"). Telephone, telegraph, and radio communications to the outside world have never been available, and probably never will be.

Currency. The monetary unit is hard cash (gold or silver) in any available coinage. No credit cards are accepted. Barter is widespread (see "Caution").

Language. The common language of the Flyaways is a koine, an amalgam of Spanish, English, Tagalog, Dyak, Tausuq, Chinese, Annamese, and Palaweño Negrito. Most of the younger islanders speak English.

Ornithological Note. The Flyaways' reputation for harboring devils, reported from the logs of its earliest visitors, is probably based on the eerie cries of the Barabbas erne, or gallows bird *(Haliäetus galga),* which Duvoisin's *Field Guide to the Raptors of Southeast Asia* describes as thirty-five inches long, dark-backed, black-capped, and hook-billed, one of the world's rarest seabirds. They are known to inhabit only certain small islands off the SW end of Isla Perniciosa, where they come and go at night. They feed on flotsam, including the corpses of the drowned, but have been implicated in attacks on chickens, pigs, and small children. Stiff-winged, they glide low over the water. Silent by day, they are extremely noisy at night, especially when breeding or feeding. The cry is said to be a prolonged and mournful *weep-weep-wak-fungouuu.*

Caution. Mariners are advised that the Flyaways have long been notorious throughout Southeast Asia and indeed the entire western Pacific not only for their myriad navigational hazards but for the ingrained and seemingly irremediable villainy of their inhabitants. The island economy is now and always has been based on piracy, smuggling, wrecking, barratry, mutiny, kidnapping, prostitution, slavery, arms manufacture, forgery, and the cultivation of controlled substances. Few vessels in Flyaway waters show running lights or observe rules of the road. Harbor vessels displaying a white letter *P* on their hulls are not pilot boats but pirates. Even the small, seemingly harmless outriggers of local turtlers and egg hunters should be given a wide berth: the boatmen, regardless of age, sex, or apparent degree of decrepitude, are invariably armed and dangerous.

Local fishermen commonly mark the position of their nets and traps with plastic bleach bottles. Care should be taken to avoid contact with these floating markers as they are often mined with high explosives.

All buoys and lights must be regarded with extreme suspicion.

Anomalous latitude and longitude computations are common in these waters. Mariners who manage to return from the Flyaways inevitably find that all navigational equipment, from the most sophisticated modern electronics to the simplest sextant, requires calibration at the next port of call.

Perhaps the final word of caution concerning the Flyaways should be left to William Dampier (1652–1715), the English freebooter and explorer who visited these islands nearly three centuries ago: "Avoide them at all Costes," he wrote in his *Voyages and Descriptions* (1699). "Onlie a Foole or a Man of suicidall Despairation woulde ever willinglie shape his Course toward the Flyawaie Islandes."

Part One
CULDEE

ONE

~~~~~~~~~

The Culdee place stood on a headland overlooking the fogbound sea.
It was the oldest house on that bleak stretch of the northern
California coast, and its timbers were even older. They had been
salvaged more than a century ago from a vessel caught on the lee
shore and driven aground below the bluff. From the sea, in the oddly
canted light that precedes a storm, the house still resembled a ship,
dismasted and hurled to destruction by conflicting currents, its bows
pointing seaward, captain and crew whirled off in the storm winds
and the hulk itself left derelict at the whim of the surf.

The nautical motif was appropriate, for the Culdees were invet-
erate seafarers. They had captained trading schooners along the
coast since the days of the gold rush, clubbed seals on the ice of the
Chukchi Sea, hunted sea otters in the inshore kelp beds, and
harpooned whales on the blue water from the Line Islands to the
Antarctic. More than a few of them had served in the navy, and
Culdee bones lay encrusted in coral off beaches where palm trees
swayed. Jim Culdee, the last male of the line, had almost added his
bones to the pile. Often, now that he was on the beach, he wished
he were down there with his kinsmen. Instead he lived here, a
derelict, alone except for his daughter, Miranda.

Dogs loped along the beach in the early morning, wild dogs,
skinny in the fog. From the bows of his house the old sailor could see
them ghosting through the mist kicked up by the surf, pausing to
sniff a clump of kelp or a slippery driftwood burl. Some mornings,
especially after a storm, dead things washed up on the beach, half-

buried in the clattering shingle. The dogs ripped them apart and bolted them down in angry, convulsive gulps. Heads buried themselves in a bloated belly, tails waving spastically in the fog, their salt-wet fur matted and dull in the sunrise. They emerged only to gasp for breath. Muzzles dark with blood, they ran off to bury the bones— gone till tomorrow.

When he was younger, Culdee might have felt disgust or outrage at their behavior. Death should have its dignity. But the dogs were fierce in defending their finds, and he would have had to fight them to liberate the carcass. Once, he was almost sure, he had tried. It was the body of a young woman, the victim of a wandering iceberg, or a gale, or perhaps an enemy torpedo. He saw her awash in the surf, turning gracefully toward the rocks, her dark hair spread like a sea fan until the next wave hurled her onto the stones at the high-water mark. Something in the way she moved—the toss of a slim, bare arm, a coquettish twist of her neck—gave him a momentary hope that she might still be alive.

He could save her yet, he thought, carry her up to the house, to the warmth of the fire, spoon brandy down her throat, watch her cold breasts slowly flush with color, her pulse quicken, her eyelids quiver and open . . .

He raced down the stone steps, vaulted the seawall, ran in long, eager strides across the slippery strand. But the dogs were there before him. Bristling, lean, foul smelling as the rot they ate, their black leather lips drawn back from yellow teeth, they growled even louder than the sea itself. Beyond them lay the girl. Already the crabs had broken her eyes.

It is a wild, rank place, he thought, *and there is no flattery in it.*

The house, though, was snug and tight, secure against the sea's cold indifference. In the entry hall yellow oilskins hung over ranks of sea-boots and hip boots clotted with drying marsh mud. Shotguns, rifles, and fishing tackle gleamed from pegs on the wall, dark with oil. Old duck decoys carved from swamp cedar and wayward hatch covers, austere in the flat, primary colors of house paint, lay coiled in their anchor cords—widgeon and gadwalls, shovelers and golden eyes, old-squaws, teal, a pair of harlequin drakes in their winter plumage. Crab pots and fish traps, awaiting new slats or wire, stood neatly stacked in one corner near a scarred and blunt-tined clam rake. All of these were now Miranda's tools, for Culdee rarely went out any more.

The floors inside the hall door were of polished pine, lustrous with wax, the walls lined with books that bore the dog-ears and ripped jackets of heavy reading. There were shelves filled with curios from many forgotten voyages—soapstone sednas from the Beaufort Sea and coral formations from the Paumotus, faded pink conch shells and the fluted calcium of giant tridacnas, medusae, abalones, a chambered nautilus. Weapons from the wars—a kris from the Sulu Sea, a yataghan from the Caspian, a nicked sword stick from the coast above Lamu on the Erythraean Sea, a Zamboangan bolo, an imperial Japanese bayonet. But the muted gleam of brightwork and pewter and delicate china on the other shelves took the edge off this cutlery. Or so it often seemed to the old sailor, who preferred not to remember how his family had come by these weapons.

From the beamed ceilings in every room, turning slowly in random drafts from the many windows and fireplaces, hung the tiny ships that Miranda carved when she wasn't sweeping, or dusting, or polishing, or cooking, or reading, or hunting, or fishing, or pulling the crab pots, or sailing her catboat into town for the mail. Ancient vessels, all of them, which she had found described or pictured in her sea library—nefs and cogs, shallops and gundalows, flutes, naviculas, five-masted barkentines and hermaphrodite brigs, a yard-long replica, complete to the last ratline, of Sir Humphrey Gilbert's pinnace *Squirrel*, hell-bent for doom north of the Azores in 1583. At night, with the lamps turned low and the fires burned down to coals, tiny balls of Saint Elmo's fire seemed to glow in the pinnace's rigging, but Miranda would never say how she achieved that effect.

Some of the models she sold, now and then, along with the surplus fish she caught, to augment their small income. Any cash left over after their meager expenses were taken care of went into a bank account she kept for some undisclosed purpose. The old sailor, as dead to matters of finance as he was to most other things, never asked her about it.

He spent his days in a captain's chair at the prow of the shiplike house, drinking cup after cup of coffee and watching the movements of the sea. Often—too often—the coffee was spiked with rum. When Miranda came into view, he watched her with the same dispassion he spent on the waves. She was a tall, green-eyed girl with a strong face, broken nose, and dark hair that hung clear down to her shoulders, and in the early morning, before the wild dogs appeared to feed along the sea wrack, she danced on the rocks at the base of the headland, with the sea crashing around her. She danced to some music shaped by the waves thudding and rasping on the shingle, odd rhythms of hissing sand, breaking shells, melting mud, and the cries of seabirds overhead. The fulmar fling. The gannet gavotte. The waltz of the terns and petrels. She wore a white nightgown that swirled around her as she spun and swayed, her hair swinging a beat or two behind.

Culdee watched her strong, bare feet grab the rock, thrust from it, grab again, and spin, sure on the wet, black granite. Sometimes she sang as she danced, old chanteys delved from her ancient sea books:

> *Heisa, heisa*
> *vorsa, vorsa*
> *wow, wow*
> *one long draft*
> *more might, more might*
> *young bluid, young bluid*
> *more mude, more mude*
> *false flesh*
> *lie aback, lie aback*
> *long swack, long swack*
> *that, that, that, that*
> *there, there, there, there*

yellow hair, yellow hair
hips bare, hips bare
tell 'em all, tell 'em all
gallows birds all, gallows birds all
great and small, great and small
one an' all, one an' all
heist all, heist all . . .

Down on the beach, the dogs were eating something large and gray. The old sailor did not care any more what it was. He turned his chair from the sea. The fog in his mouth tasted of sea coal.

TWO

~~~~~~~~~

Only at sea could Culdee come really alive. The first clank of the anchor chain through the pawls of the wildcat set his heart to singing. He loved it up on the forepeak then, hosing down the ground tackle as it came aboard, sluicing great gray globs of harbor mud off the links and flukes of the anchor and watching them fall in awkward, heavy splashes that clouded the water. He loved to hear the engine bells ringing from the bridge, a profane Angelus of the sea. The Captain's crisp, dispassionate commands, the helmsman swinging the wheel, the first bite of the rudder when he had the wheel watch—all of these were Culdee's sacraments. It was like taking a cathedral to sea.

The whole ship shuddered as the wake boiled out behind them—bobbing buoys and winking lighthouses, the slowly sinking hotels and banks and spires of the receding shore, wind over the bridge, gulls wheeling and screaming, all hands to quarters for leaving port, harbor seals gaping from the stone of the breakwater and the first taste of salt as a wave blasted the prow, spray sheeting high over the gunwales, as high as the wheelhouse, wetting even the flag bags on the signal bridge, the seawall behind them falling back, sinking like the city into the sea, and only the empty ocean dead ahead . . .

Another cup of coffee gone cold. He sipped it anyway and watched the waves slide ashore through the fog.

Once they had run independently from Japan back to San Francisco, in fog the whole way. A great circle route that took them up to the Aleutians, then back down in a slow arc past Alaska along the Pacific coast. Only once had they seen land—a brief glimpse of Mount Logan, shining pale and solid through the seasmoke; most of the way you couldn't see half a mile from the bridge. They passed no other ships, but in midocean whales sometimes broached and blew close at hand, the rotten-fish reek of their breath drifting through on cool, damp air. Porpoises rode the bow wave, and the ship settled into her working routine as if the fog would never break: they might be steaming in one spot forever. All day the sound of paint scrapers rasped from the steel decks, and the smell of fresh red lead washed back into the fabric of the fog. On the messdecks, they ate as though every dawn brought holiday routine—steak and eggs for breakfast (it was Kōbe beef, tender and juicy, hand-massaged by pretty little Japo farm girls with night soil between their toes; the eggs stayed fresh the whole way across). There wasn't a single fight on deck or in the crew quarters. Not one man was haled to captain's mast—not even tough little baby-faced Reibald, whose father had been a "chopper in the woods" in Oregon and once got his throat cut in a fight over a girl on the Pike in Long Beach but made it back to the ship so the pharmacist's mates could stitch him up and he wouldn't miss movement for WestPac. Even little Reibald, the signalman striker who looked like a choirboy convicted of murder, was full of the milk of human kindness on this cruise. Ed Krueger, the chief electrician and the hairiest man in the navy (except for his bald head; from his lower eyelids down, he was as shaggy as a black bear), raced up the ladder to the bridge one day, spread his arms wide, the fog misting his rimless glasses, and yelled for all to hear, "Every day in the navy's just like Sunday on the farm!"

Now, dead at heart in the captain's chair, Culdee realized it had been the Sunday of his life. But that was long ago.

Now even his tattoos were fading.

9

THREE

~~~~~~~~~~~~

In the end it was the land that killed him, a ratty, mangrove-tangled stretch of it on the beach somewhere north of the Ben Hai River. Culdee had his own command then—a fast, hard-hitting, throaty little Swift boat that could turn thirty knots with her twin diesels two-blocked. Their job, part of Operation Market Time, was to patrol the Vietnamese coast near the DMZ, watching for junks and sampans that might be carrying enemy troops or ammo south. When they found one, it usually meant a fight. But the Swift had twin .50s mounted atop the pilothouse, another machine gun and an 81-mm mortar tube aft, and plenty of maneuverability along with her speed. She looked like a cross between an old World War II PT boat and a pilot boat, and she drew only three feet of water.

That came in handy when they ran SEAL teams into North Vietnam, usually in the dead of night and dark of the moon. In a way, though, it was the boat's shallow draft that lured Culdee to his death. They were running north at dusk, above Quang Tri, just idling along the ten-fathom curve and watching the coastline a thousand yards off the port beam. They were under strict radio silence, and they didn't have to extract the SEALs until dawn the next day. There had been reports of enemy movement along the coast—maybe some NVA units infiltrating toward Con Thien was the word.

"Something's happening in there, Chief," the lookout said. "Back in the mangroves. Could be Charlie."

Culdee looked through his glasses—they were Leitz 9 × 35s, clear and crisp. He'd won them off a West German news photographer in a poker game at Cam Ranh Bay. He focused them and saw the dusty green mangrove leaves snap sharp. There was movement beyond the web of twisted branches—darkness and light; black cloth, pale skin—like a priest dimly glimpsed through the screen of a confessional. The light was fading fast, though, and Culdee saw a string of cormorants angling along just above the tops of the mangroves and the last light shining golden-green on the coconut palms back of the beach. He spun the wheel to port and pointed the bow toward the movement.

Drake, the gunner's mate, was already hunkered behind the twin .50s. Culdee heard him work the retracting handle back; he heard a click, then the second pull to seat the round. He looked astern. Earhart, the young engineman, was at the aft gun mount. The diesels grumbled and farted at low revs, and small waves slapped the fifty-foot hull. They were heading straight into the last of the sunset, and the light on the water couldn't be worse. There was coral all along the coast that could tear your heart out. Culdee kept a sharp eye out for the quick, shy swirls that broke over reefs and niggerheads. The water was shoaling fast.

Then he saw something awash, right in close to the mangroves. At first it looked like the body of a man. Then it looked a lot bigger.

"Could be a crate or something," the lookout said. He was using the twelve-power glasses. "Maybe wrapped in a tarp?" he added.

There was no more movement in the trees, but that didn't mean anything. They were about three hundred yards off the beach now, and it was getting dark fast. There is no twilight in the tropics.

"Hey, Guns," Culdee yelled topside. "Cut me down some of them mangroves."

"Aye, *sir!*"

The .50s slammed; great white flocks of egrets lurched screaming into the dusk. Leaves flew, big chunks of purple and white wood went soaring off crazily, whole stands of trees slowly toppled. There was no answering fire.

"Maybe it was just water buffalo," the lookout said doubtfully. But buffalo would have run, or at least bellowed.

11

Culdee dropped the engines into neutral. The crate, or whatever it was, still lay sloshing in the shallows.

"Put a couple of rounds into that thing," Culdee told the lookout.

There was an M16 racked on the port wing of the bridge. The lookout snapped the selector lever to semi and popped the crate twice, then a third time for good measure. Nothing screamed. Nothing blew up.

"Okay," Culdee said. "I'm going to bring her in so you can grab that thing with the boat hook. Use the handle like a sounding pole, up there in the bow, and yell the depth back to me. Remember, we draw three feet."

The hell of it was they had only the old French charts to go by up here in the North. Even the most recent of them was fourteen years old, and some dated back to the 1930s. A lot of typhoons had blown through since then, a lot of sand had shifted from one spot to another. In waters like these, whole reefs could die and be born again in a new place while your back was turned. It was worse in the delta. Down there, where the alligator navy lived, each monsoon season laid a new grid of channels and shoals over the mouth of the Mekong. They ran PBRs in the delta that drew only a foot and a half of water. Glass-hulled thirty-two-footers that could go like stink once they got up on the step. But they ran on those damned jet motors—Jacuzzis, the white hats called them—and the impellers were constantly jamming with water hyacinth. Up here, at least, the water was clean and clear. In good light you could read a beer-can label on the bottom in ten fathoms. Count your blessings . . .

But Culdee knew he was evading the main issue. He smelled a rat, and the rat's name was Charlie. It could be a setup. Sucker you in to check out whatever Charlie had left in the water, then cut loose with everything they've got. On the other hand, maybe the Swift's appearance had interrupted a resupply mission. Maybe there was a sampan, courtesy of Uncle Ho, tucked away behind the mangroves, in one of the thousands of invisible inlets that notched the coast. He had his orders. If he didn't go in and check it out, he'd be facing the green banana for sure. It he did go in and it was a setup, the only banana he'd face would be the one Charlie'd left for him to skid on. After that, he wouldn't have to face anything.

They eased up toward the shore. The only sounds were the burble of the exhaust, rising now and then to a peevish blat, the croak of a night heron on the hunt, and the whine of mosquitoes, piercing as a dentist's drill. The light was becoming subaquatic.

"Almost four feet," the lookout said. The bottom of the boat-hook pole looked black in the dusk, like a dipstick pulled from a sump of dirty oil.

"Three and a half.

Nothing moved in the mangroves. All the birds seemed to have flown.

"A touch over three . . . I think I can reach it now."

He extended the pole, leaning far out over the bow. A silver comma winked in the gloom—the hook.

"Got it."

As he pulled back on the pole, the crate rolled slightly, sucking in the easy wash. Then the hook slipped. There was something dangling over it—pallid, snaky, angling back into the mangrove roots. Det cord . . .

Oh, fuck! In his mind's eye, Culdee saw Charlie hunkered back in the swamp, the ends of the wires scraped bare, one in each hand. Charlie brought the ends together . . .

"Hey!" the lookout yelled, his voice cracking like a teenager's. "It's a fucking wi—"

Flash.

Culdee was in the water, warm as blood, red as blood. It was blood, blood full of twitching meat. A severed hand sunk through it. A tattoo on the back of the hand—Culdee checked numbly: he still had both of his. The tattoo, he suddenly saw, was a tiger head, fangs dripping blood. Underneath the blood, VUNG TAU '66. The hand turned over as it sank; small fish darted and ripped at the flanges that fanned from the wrist. Drake's hand—he had a tattoo like that . . .

The Swift was down by the bow. There was no bow. Big chunks of it continued to splatter down all around Culdee when he lay in the water far away. No, quite close, actually. No, pretty far away. Lights winked in the mangroves like giant fireflies. It was gunfire, but Culdee couldn't hear it. The roar in his ears was too loud. The stern of the Swift was cocked high against the sky. Culdee saw the muzzle flash of the aft .50 caliber still pumping strings of fire into the mangroves—Earhart. But then the .50 went dark, too. They got him.

Culdee floated. He couldn't move enough even to dog-paddle away into the dark. Something eased out of the solid wall of mangrove roots—a sampan. Low voices chattered in dink. Guys were poling at the high-curved stern. There was a glint of weapons—AKs. A dink up on the bow was leaning on a long, skinny pole . . . with a hook at the end.

At first Culdee thought it was the lookout's boat hook, blown back into the mangroves by the blast of C4 that blew off the bow of the Swift, and the men along with it. But it was a gaff. Culdee'd seen them on the fishing boats he'd interdicted—hand-forged, rusty, spangled with scales and encrusted with dry fish slime, but honed to a bright point at the recurved tip. He thrashed weakly, like a played-out pompano.

The dink leaned over through the darkness and gaffed him through the shoulder.

14

FOUR

~~~~~~~~~~~

That was the end of the good life. For the next six years, like it or not, Culdee pulled shore duty. And he hated shore duty. It was the essence of that quarter of the planet called the Beach—stability, salutes, red tape, mortgages, shopping malls, cars, banks, credit cards, telephones, restaurants. It was shore duty, among other things, that had led to and finally disrupted his marriage. Culdee was stationed at Key West then, soon after Korea wound down. The girl worked in a bank on Duval Street. Her name was Vivian, and she was lovely—dark-haired, blue-eyed, with a wide, white-flashing smile that seemed, in those days at least, as fresh as the sea breeze on Mallory Dock.

Weekends he borrowed a boat from the naval base—a heavy carvel-built double-ender—and they sailed out to the Marquesas, sometimes even as far as the Dry Tortugas. She'd grown up in the Keys and knew boats. They fished for permit and mutton snapper over the wreck at the west end of The Quicksands—"Mutton's better 'n nuttin'," Viv always said. They trolled over Isaac and Rebecca shoals on their way out to the Tortugas. If there were boats tied up at the wharves on Garden Key, they angled over to Bird Key and dropped the hook there. From a distance, wreathed in terns, Fort Jefferson looked as final as the sunset—solid, fierce, its red brick walls the ultimate meaning of shore duty.

But it was in the fresh wash of sunrise, on the parapets of one of those broken walls, that Culdee asked Viv to marry him. They had climbed the rotting stairways in the dark, bringing a blanket and a thermos of orange juice spiked with Cuban rum, to watch the dawn break.

"Keep your eyes peeled for the flash of red," Culdee told the girl.

"The what?"

"You've heard of the green flash at sundown—hell, you've seen it, from Mallory Dock. But there's a sunrise flash, too."

"And it's red?"

"Sure. The green one's the ocean's starboard running light. The red one's on the port side."

She looked down at the cutter, where it rolled at its moorings beside the wharf.

"That means the sea runs south," she said. "And the sun at noon is the masthead light."

"You've got it," he said. They laughed, and he kissed her. Terns circled overhead as they made love, watching curiously with bright black eyes. Viv saw the terns. Culdee, looking down from the parapet, saw a barracuda chasing baitfish in the shallows. Then he proposed to her.

Sadly, for both of them, she accepted.

The joy soon faded. Viv hated being a "dependant"—the official navy designation for wives and children. Still dutiful, though, still loving, she followed him from home port to home port—Norfolk, Boston, Virginia Beach, San Diego, Newport, Long Beach, Treasure Island, even Vallejo, when one of his ships was in the yard at Mare Island. There were no jobs for her in these towns—at least none that counted for anything. No one wanted to hire a navy wife. Her husband might be transferred any minute. She longed to be back at the bank in Key West. Any bank. Any decent job with a chance for advancement, where she was treated as a human being, not a "dependant."

"Why don't they just call us *appendages* and be done with it?" she said.

She took to badgering him, cautiously, obliquely at first, to quit the navy, or least to change his rating to something that would justify more shore duty—he was smart enough to learn electronics, say, or perhaps become an Airdale; he was maybe even smart enough to enter OCS and become a supply designator. That way they could be together more, rather than him being off at sea half the time, three quarters of the time! And if he learned electronics, he could cut loose from the navy and get something that paid real money—maybe his own TV repair business—some day, at least.

So Culdee grew slowly sullen. That's when the drinking started in earnest, and the bar fighting. He began looking forward to long tours at sea—Operational Readiness Training, offshore work as a target ship for submarines honing their torpedo marksmanship, complex landing and minesweeping exercises, especially the nine-month rotations to WestPac. An old navy tradition had it that all marriage vows were null and void once a man had crossed the international date line. At first he resisted. Then he said, Fuck it. And did.

On one of those tours the baby was born. Miranda—he loved her, a bouncing, brown little thing that ran around naked in the backyard of their cracker-box house in Seal Beach, splashing in and out of the small blue plastic wading pool they'd bought her. A savage, feral little rug rat, quick to talk and fight. He called her his cookie crook, his house ape—while Viv bit her tongue in her own sullen silence. Miranda's eyes were green like his, specked with motes of brown—sea eyes, he called them, with islands scattered here and there. She was ten the last time he saw her, just before he left for Vietnam, and he loved her more than the sea. But it wasn't enough.

On another of those WestPac tours Viv went back to school. She studied computers and banking. She was an admirably vital woman, energetic, committed, a ball of fire as they say—a human dynamo. Everyone said so. To housekeeping and child rearing, full-time occupations for most women in those days, she added one activity after another—cooking classes, Planned Parenthood meetings, yoga, modern dance, a history course at a community college, where women gathered at night to drink bitter tea and rewrite the texts that described the nature of their sex. Then she took part in a sit-in. They were back on the East Coast by then—Culdee was in a frigate out of Newport—and Viv went down to the sub base at Groton for an antinuclear demonstration. Culdee's CO called him on the carpet for that.

"Look, sir," Culdee told him, "she's her own woman."

"It doesn't look good, Boats," the skipper said. "I mean, a navy wife—"

"She's a better navy wife than many, sir," Culdee said. "She's no lush, she doesn't fool around, she runs a taut ship at home. I mean, hell, sir, she keeps a lot of balls in the air."

The skipper stared at him. "Yeah," he said. "Yours among them."

There was a long pause.

"Sir," Culdee said. He could feel himself shaking.

The skipper looked away and blushed.

"I'm sorry, Boats," he said. "That was out of line—way out of line. I'm sorry. But please try to talk to her, would you? It was the goddamn FBI blew the whistle on her."

So Viv got a job, at one of the new electronics companies on Route 128 up in Boston. Within a year she was earning double what Culdee made as an E7. When he was transferred back to California in 1963, she stayed in the East. It was better that way. They both agreed. Oh, sure, when he pulled leave, he'd come back to Boston if he could deadhead on some navy or air force plane going that way, and once they rendezvoused in Pensacola and spent two weeks sailing and fishing in the Gulf. Miranda was with them, and already she was a good man in a boat.

"Just like your mommy," Culdee told her.

"And my daddy," she added solemnly.

But it wasn't the same. The marriage was in limbo. They both knew it.

"Why don't you put in for retirement?" Viv asked one night as they lay at anchor off Cedar Key. "We've got plenty of money in the bank. You could get something in Boston, or even out on Cape Cod. Something to do with boats and the sea."

A night heron croaked, hunting along the mangroves of the shore.

"I've still got four years to go on my twenty," Culdee said at last. "And now with this thing in the Tonkin Gulf, the navy might really need me."

"Goddamn the navy," she said. "At least ask for shore duty."

And this was shore duty with a vengeance.

Culdee came to know it—its geography, language, customs, nuances—better than he knew his own homeland. From Dogpatch up near the Chinese border to the cluster of camps in and around Hanoi—Alcatraz, the Zoo, the Plantation House, Skidrow, the Rockpile, Farnsworth, and Camp Hope. He knew the floor plan of the Fiery Furnace—Hoa Lo in Vietnamese, the Hanoi Hilton to the POWs—as well as he knew that of any house or ship he'd ever lived in. Hoa Lo had all the amenities. It was an old French prison from colonial days. Many times he took a sauna and massage in Room 18, more familiarly known to paying guests as the Meathook Room. Many days and nights (indistinguishable from one another) he spent in meditation in the austere decor of the Black Room or the Knobby Room.

He came to know the staff with an intimacy formerly reserved for family members, and not just by face or name, but by the very tread of their sandals and the jangle of their keys. He could not fault them for attentiveness. Often he wished he could. Manager of the entire chain was Major Bui—the Cat to those on conversational terms with the man—slim, soft-spoken, tall for a Vietnamese, well educated, fluent in both French and English. A busy fellow, the Cat, assiduous, serious, totally dedicated to his profession, the consummate military hotelier. Unfortunately, though, he was addicted to quiz shows. A malaise of the times, no doubt. His favorite was a Tonkinese variation on *Truth or Consequences*. If you didn't do well on the questions, Beulah the Buzzer rang, and in came the consequences—Pigeye, Vegetable Vic, Hocus Pocus, or the one they called Puddles. These men were conjurers of great art, adept with leg irons, handcuffs, and the Southeast Asian rope trick. In the wink of an eye they could turn a white man's hands and feet black with dead blood. They were marvels at the vanishing thumbnail gag. In a matter of mere hours they could cause shiny bright scars to encircle a man's arms—"Hanoi bracelets," which were a great rarity Stateside.

The highest-paid masseurs and bone crackers of the Western world had nothing on these practitioners when it came to limbering a man up. By tying his arms—tightly, in Manila rope—behind his back so that the elbows touched, they imparted remarkable elasticity to the rib cage and chest muscles. They were expert as well at tenderizing tough meat. Their skill at evoking a sincere primal scream was unequaled in therapeutic circles.

Puddles in particular seemed fond of his work. At the height of the treatment, with his client enjoying (perhaps for the first time in his life) a total aspiration of the lungs and maximum vibration of the vocal cords, Puddles was wont to step back thoughtfully, a dreamy smile playing about his lips, and perform an act of manual self-therapy—selfish but uncontrollable—the culmination of which earned him his nickname. Or, as Culdee once relayed it in tap code through the camp: "Under the spreading chestnut tree, the village slopehead sat, amusing himself by abusing himself and squirting the juice in his hat."

Most of the prisoners in the Hanoi camps were fly-boys—either brown-shoe navy or air force. Culdee had little in common with them. Now and then, though, a blue-water sailor would fall into the hands of the V, men like Culdee with no state-of-the-art technological or tactical knowledge. He thought at first that because of his ignorance of the big picture he would be spared the quizzes and beatings afforded his superiors—the talking walls reported nightly on these sessions. But the V weren't really after military information. They wanted to break your spirit. They wanted propaganda. They were out to break you, whoever you were, to get you singing the full-dress blues regardless of rank or service. If they could get you talking once, they could teach you how to sing. Writing was even better.

Culdee first caught on to this at a temporary camp near Haiphong Harbor called Brigadune. He'd been out at a place they called Upper Slobbovia, near the Laotian border—the camp must have been used by Russians at one point, because the walls of the huts were plastered with pinups of enormously fat ladies, the Fanny Fullenwiders of the Slavic world—and was suddenly awakened in the night, told to grab his tin cup, bamboo mat, blanket, and spare pajamas and *di-di-mau*. He *di-di'*ed as *mau* as he could after two years of jungle soup, cold rice, sour brussels sprouts, weevily bread, and an occasional piece of pigskin with the hair still on it. The truck bumped and rattled for hours, then they were at Brigadune.

It looked like a navy camp, and you could smell the sea. There were sand flies and mangroves and mosquitoes as loud as A6 Intruders. The commandant was a fat little lieutenant commander of the North Vietnamese Navy with a weedy cookie-duster on his apelike upper lip. The *My*—the Americans—nicknamed him Wimpy. His henchman were Bluto and Swee'pea. The assistant commandant was a two-striper who played good cop to Wimpy's bad cop. This man was known as Olive Oyl.

Culdee spent his first two weeks at Brigadune in solitary, in a stifling, mildewed, ten-by-ten cell called the Chain Locker. His only companions were spiders as big as teacups. In the haste of departure from Upper Slobbovia, he had lost his mosquito net. No replacement was issued. The room, windowless, was lighted by the world's weakest light bulb. Culdee figured it at about fifteen or twenty watts. The diet was nautical—hardtack, *nuoc mam,* smoked shark, the occasional hunk of boiled catfish, but more often, its whiskery head. And rice, of course. But at least there was plenty. No two ways about it. Brigadune was a feeder.

Or at least until the quizzes began. A Quiz:

WIMPY. Cuddy, you tell. What you do U.S. Navy?

21

CULDEE. *Toi khong hieu.* [I don't understand.]

W. What your job—your rating—in American navy?

C. Oh, I thought you were talking Vietnamese.

(*Silence, only the sound of buzzing mosquitoes.*)

W. Cuddy, *You tell! I wait! What you rating?* (*He is angry now, mustache twitching.*)

C. You know that already. Deck Ape.

W. (*Calmer now*). Cuddy, what is deck ape? Same bosum mate, hein?

C. Yeah.

W. (*Getting to the point.*) What equipment you use bosum mate, Cuddy?

(*Silence. This is stupid, Culdee thinks, his balls contracting. This shit heel knows damn well what a boatswain does—same fucking thing he does in any navy. He just wants to break me. Again. If I don't talk—if I follow the code . . .*)

W. You tell, Cuddy, or you receive resolute and severe punish.

(*There it is, Culdee thinks, the operative phrase. They use it at every camp.*)

W. Cuddy, you have bad attitude. You tell!

C. Well, I can't tell you without violating the code of conduct I swore to uphold.

W. You have bad attitude, Cuddy. (*He gestures to* BLUTO *and* SWEE'PEA.)

(*Later.*)

C. (*Hoarsely*). I use the same gear as these guys. (*He looks up at* BLUTO *and* SWEE'PEA.)

22

W. (*Looks over at the torturers, shocked, perhaps a bit fearful.*) What equipment, Cuddy?

C. Ropes. Hooks. Blocks and tackles. Fids—

W. What is fid, Cuddy? (*He pushes over pen, ink, and paper.*) You write down.

C. Well, no. I can't. I can't write it down.

W. Cuddy, you have bad attitude. You will receive reso—

C. Okay, okay, I'll write it down. (*He reaches for the pen and knocks over the inkwell, splattering the soggy gray writing paper. Patiently,* WIMPY *takes more paper from a desk drawer and hands it to* CULDEE. CULDEE *forces his fat, black fingers around the pen, dips it weakly in the ink, writes: "Fid: A long, pointed wooden spike used in the splicing of rope."*)

W. Cuddy, now you have *good* attitude. Now you do for camp! (*He smiles beneath that ratty cookie-duster.* WIMPY'S *got his hamburger at last.*)

That night Olive Oyl dropped by Culdee's cell, armed with a Flit gun. He slunk around, spraying delicately, casting fervid, sidelong glances at the prisoner. He smiled gently. He checked that the guards weren't watching and then reached into his pocket. He handed Culdee a piece of fudge. The fudge had lint on it, and what looked like a curl of pubic hair.

"You are good man, Cuddy," he whispered as he left. "Tomorrow you get roommate."

When the cell door closed, Culdee dropped the piece of fudge into his honey bucket. It sank out of sight in the day's excrement.

FIVE

〜〜〜〜〜

He was moved to a new cell the following morning. Compared with the Chain Locker it was spacious—ten paces wide by five deep. It had a big, iron-barred window that opened onto the beach. There were *sou* trees outside and a few tattered palms, and beyond them he could see the blue water of the Tonkin Gulf. The breeze tasted sweet after his long confinement. The window even had a screen in it to keep out mosquitoes.

There were no leg irons at the foot of the long, wide bunks that stood one over the other on the starboard bulkhead. The bunks were built of hardwood, well joined and smoothly sanded. In the lower bunk lay his new roommate. A blond guy, tall but not cadaverous, and freshly shaved. He grinned and got up with an outstretched hand.

"Hi, Chief. I'm Tim Turner."

Culdee took his hand. No fat fingers on Turner, all fingernails present and accounted for. He had a strong grip for a POW.

"Culdee," he said. "Chief boatswain." He looked around the cell in wonder. "Where's the complimentary basket of fruit and wine?"

Turner laughed. "Hey!" he said. "As a matter of fact I *do* have something for you." He rummaged in his gear, folded neatly at the foot of the lower bunk, and came up with a square of fudge. For a moment Culdee wondered if it was the same piece he'd shit-canned the previous night. He took it anyway.

"What's your rate and rating?" he asked.

"Gunner's mate second," Turner said. "Off the *Hancock*. We

24

were out on Yankee Station when the chaplain got word my mother was sick. I pulled compassionate leave. The plane that was taking me down to Quang Tri splashed—engines crapped out."

"Tough," Culdee said.

"Could be worse," Turner said. "I'm the only one got out of the plane. I guess I'm lucky. A fishing boat spotted me."

Turner had only been in the Dune for a couple of weeks. The *Hancock* had just arrived in the area from Stateside, so he was full of news. Things were bad back there—anti-war protests, sit-ins, draft-card burnings, hippies all over the place. It didn't sound like the same country to Culdee. Bobby Kennedy was dead, shot by some Arab. Martin Luther King, too, by a redneck. LBJ wasn't running again. It looked like Nixon would be the next president. He was making noises about ending the war.

Oddly, the news left Culdee unmoved. It all sounded unreal, as if it were happening in Oz. But then, a few weeks later, Turner said something that stirred him up for the first time since he'd reached the Dune.

"There's PT boats in the basin just south of the cellblock," Turner reported. "I saw them today when I was on work detail. Russian PA-3 types. Old but fast. Forty knots or better. They've got 'em hidden under camo netting, lightly guarded."

Culdee passed the word by tap code to the senior officer, a SEAL lieutenant named Mr. Thomas. Slowly but surely, at Culdee's urging, the escape plan took shape. Turner reported that it was no more than two hundred meters from the southern side of the compound to the boat basin. A low seawall offered cover most of the way. Only a fence of concertina wire lay between the cells and the seawall, maybe some razor wire as well—Turner couldn't be sure. Guards walked the wire day and night with AKs, but they didn't appear especially alert, and there was a ten-minute cycle to their appearance at any given point on the perimeter. The monsoon season was fast approaching—wind, rain, darkness. . . . It looked eminently workable.

Culdee was not picked for the escape party. His shoulder

wound, where the gaff had pierced him, had suddenly flared up again—some sort of deep-seated infection. Neither was Turner. He was too junior—there were men in the Dune who had been POWs for five years. Culdee himself had been in only two. Turner lamented more about Culdee's not going than about his own disqualification.

"It's not right," he said angrily the night before the breakout. "You know these waters better than those SEALs. You ran a Swift boat, you're a boat handler from way back. I don't see why they can't take you along if only to guide them through the channel."

"I'm not a SEAL," Culdee said. "They stick together."

"Well, it's not right."

"They ought to take you," Culdee said. "You're the one who spotted the PTs in the first place. You're the one who mapped out the escape route."

"Well, not really," Turner said. "It was a fluke. Anyone who'd been on that detail would have seen the possibilities. And anyway, you're the one who passed it on to Mr. Thomas."

It almost seemed to Culdee that Turner didn't want to go. For a moment, suspicion flared: could this be some kind of setup? But he dismissed the thought as just another episode of POW paranoia. Turner was a good sailor. He couldn't be slimy. And yet there was something about him. . . . Then it came back strong for a moment. Turner had too much vitality. He moved with a certain snap. His eyes were bright, his tongue uncoated. He smiled too much—not bitterly or ironically, but with a kind of contentment that might almost be mistaken for pride in duty well done. And Turner's wrists were unscarred. No Hanoi bracelets, as if he'd never been handcuffed. How had he remained so healthy, so unscarred if he weren't slimy?

In POW lingo, a man who was slimy was a collaborator.

He stared at Turner long and hard. When Turner caught his eye, he looked away.

The following morning Culdee was haled to Wimpy's office. Bluto and Swee'pea cuffed his hands, bone-tight, behind his back. Wimpy smiled.

"Cuddy," he said, "you have bad attitude." He slapped Culdee hard across the mouth. Culdee tasted blood. "I think you spend some time alone for now. Ponder your sins. Then maybe you get good attitude."

So it was back to the Chain Locker for Culdee, but not without a preliminary massage and manicure from Bluto and the Pea. That night it rained hard, the monsoon winds howling eerily through the bars of the other cells so that they resonated like harp strings, the music reaching even his sealed compartment. The breakout was set for two in the morning. Culdee remained awake all night, listening. Then, during a lull in the storm, he heard it: the slow, hollow chugging of the AKs as they cut down Mr. Thomas, Chief Wysocki, and the three SEAL ratings who went with them.

Later he learned that they hadn't even made it to the seawall. What's more, there never had been any Russian PT boats in the basin. And Turner—cheerful, happy-go-lucky Turner, Culdee's good buddy and roommate, the man who'd looked up to him with such respect—Turner had been released to an American peace delegation in Hanoi a week after the breakout failed.

He'd been slimy all along.

It was another five years before Culdee learned the extent of Turner's betrayal. By then the war was over, at least the American part of it. Culdee returned to the world on the first Starlifter flight of American POWs from Gia Lam Aiport in Hanoi to Clark Field in the Philippines. Each returning POW was met on the hardstand by an officer or enlisted man of equivalent rank or rate, whose job it was to "escort" the returnee through the trauma of reentry. Culdee was met by a lieutenant from the judge advocate general's office and two Marine Corps guards. They hustled him into a small office, and the lieutenant began reading something from a handbook.

"What is this?" Culdee asked.

"Article 31, Uniform Code of Military Justice," the lieutenant said. "I'm reading you your rights."

"My rights?" Culdee was stunned. "What the hell for . . . , sir?"

Culdee stood accused of collaboration with the enemy. Hadn't

he been instrumental in setting up the failed prison break at Brigadune? Hadn't he received special treatment from the camp's second
in command—candy, extra rations, a comfortable cell? Hadn't he
given military information of a sensitive nature to the enemy, in
direct contravention of the code of conduct?

"Yeah," Culdee said. "I told them what a fid was. If you consider
a ten- or twelve-word definition of an implement that's been in use in
the navies and merchant fleets of the world since the days of
Christopher Columbus to be 'military information of a sensitive
nature,' sure. But I doubt it won the war for them."

"So you go on record as believing that the DRVN won the war?"
The lieutenant wrote that down on a legal pad. "Nonetheless, you
gave your captors information beyond that permissible under the
code of conduct—name, rank, serial number, and age. You violated
your oath. Do you admit that freely?"

"No. Yes. I mean, you had to be there. Yes, I broke in a way;
we all broke. But we got stronger later and made them break us
again. We made it as tough for them as we could—"

"All right, moving right along now," the lieutenant said. "What
influence did your ex-wife have in extenuation or mitigation of your
willingness to collaborate? The divorce must have come as something
of a shock to you."

Culdee sat openmouthed. This had to be some kind of nightmare—either that or he'd gone crazy.

"My *ex*-wife? Divorce?"

"Yes, in her letter to you."

"I didn't get any letters from her. Or from anyone, for that
matter. What do you mean, divorce?"

"Oh, come on, Culdee," the lieutenant said wearily. He con-
sulted his folder. "Vivian Culdee began divorce proceedings against
you for desertion four years ago. The decree was granted late last
year. You mean you didn't know any of this?"

"No, sir."

"Well, you may have repressed it, I guess," the lieutenant said, visibly worried now. He flipped through the pages of his folder, stalling for time. Then he focused on Culdee.

"Look, sailor," he said. "The navy doesn't want to make a federal case of this. Bad publicity, a POW with a previously good record suddenly going ratty on his pals. You have twenty-four years in service. We'll retire you as an E7, honorably, to avoid the scandal. Fair's fair. All you have to do is sign the papers."

He flapped the documents on the desk and offered Culdee his ballpoint.

Numbed, the room reeling around him, Culdee signed. There was no sense fighting it. His career was over. All he wanted now was rest.

"Good, that's very good, sailor," said the lieutenant, rising. He smiled a tight little smile. "The marines will show you to your temporary quarters. We'll have you back Stateside day after tomorrow."

Culdee stood up, shaky in the knees.

"Just one question, sir," he said. "Where did you get all this dope about the Dune? Not a word of it is true, not a bit of it."

The lieutenant flipped open the dossier.

"From an Office of Naval Intelligence debriefing," he said. "The subject was a former POW released a few years ago, fellow name of Turner. Timothy N. Turner, gunner's mate second."

So Culdee returned to the land of his birth, a sailor bereft of the sea. Sitting in the captain's chair on the deck of his shiplike house, he watched the surf pound on the hard beach below. For a while the pounding waves said, "Turner, Turner, Turner." But finally even that sound faded.

All he could hear was his sorrow . . .

Then Miranda came back into his life.

Part Two
MIRANDA

SIX

~~~~~~~~~

Smooth sailing can be rough, Miranda realized. It gives a person too much time to think. All morning the wind had blown from the southwest quadrant, ideal for her destination. At dawn the Point Reyes light had flashed good morning from her starboard beam, and since then all she'd had to do was hold a steady course. That and worry about her arrival. Will he be there? And if he is, will he be glad to see me? Will he even remember me? More than sixteen years now, closer to twenty . . .

She eased the starboard sheet to broaden the sail's reach, and the blue-hulled catboat kicked up its heels to the freshening wind. Blowing fifteen knots or better, she calculated, looking up at the faded red telltales whipping from the stays. Squadrons of white horses cantered toward the beach. She smiled wryly at the image: she loved those old-time metaphors of the sea and often repeated them to herself when she was single-handing, bored in the long watches, dredging up from memory whole chapters of the books she'd read as a girl. When the plots failed her, she made up her own. This one even had a title that rhymed: *Miranda Culdee Comes Home from the Sea.* She wondered whether it had a happy ending.

She'd forgotten how ominous this shoreline could feel. Muscular bulges of granite rose sheer from a cold, green surf in places where tentacles of kelp swayed like beckoning yellow arms. Now and then the head of a sea otter popped up through the kelp and gazed at her. The bluffs were crowned with tall, wind-bent firs and crooked encinas that needed only a dangling corpse or two to complete the hanging-

33

tree image. A grim coast all right. Even the houses, few and far between, had a no-nonsense look to them, a New England look out of place in California: solid, white, fretted with obsessively intricate Victorian band-saw work, usually with a flagpole out front and a glider on the porch. Tidy boathouses stood on pilings alongside docks, and bluff-bowed workboats bounced at their moorings.

She'd encountered little traffic since passing Port Albion early that morning—a few squat, square-shouldered salmon trollers dragging their gear astern; a big, heavily laden container ship nearly hull down on the horizon, plugging southeast toward Oakland or San Pedro. She passed close aboard a lobster boat, and the crew waved when they saw a girl at the catboat's tiller. They looked odd in their yellow slickers and Oakland A's baseball caps. She was used to dark brown fishermen who worked shirtless and hatless, except perhaps for a rough wreath of palm fronds around their heads and a red and white pareu to guard their groins from flying hooks. These California fishermen probably took her for some college girl out for a day's adventure in Daddy's toy boat. She laughed. Let them think what they wished. Miranda Culdee had already logged more blue-water miles under her keel than these inshore watermen would see in a lifetime of lobstering.

Culdee blood, she thought. There are tides in it that draw you out to sea, like it or not. And she'd liked it as far back as she could remember. Even in the best of times, before her father disappeared from her life, he was rarely home—he was always at sea. But when he did come back, he was full of stories. Her mother never cared for them; she would listen with a knowing, cynical smirk while he reeled off his tales of storms at sea, monumental brawls ashore, the oddball loners he'd served with in the big, gray navy ships, and the even odder places they'd visited. When there were boats available, he took Miranda sailing—just the two of them, for her mother no longer cared for the movements of the sea—and he taught her the rudiments of seamanship. To tie working knots and the points of sail, to read the weather and dodge the worst of it, to use the currents and tides rather than battle them—he taught her everything from scrimshaw to celestial navigation. Then came Vietnam, and he was gone, a prisoner in the north. Her mother didn't consult her about the divorce, didn't even tell her about it until a month after the papers came through.

Miranda had just turned eighteen then. Her mother wanted her to go to San Diego State for a business degree, then come to work in the bank where she was now a rising star in the loan department. "Money is the lifeblood of the world," her mother said. But Miranda's lifeblood was the sea. She was legally an adult now, free to choose her own course in life. She signed up as a deckhand on a tuna clipper heading down the South American coast.

It was hard work on a cold sea. The captain, a former shipmate of her father's, treated her no better or worse than he did the rest of the crew but saw to it that the men didn't try to mess with her. She swabbed decks, polished brightwork, and mended rigging with the best of them, learned to gut hundred-pound yellowfin tuna with one slash of the knife. Often at night she left her shipmates in the fo'c'sle and climbed the rigging to sit shivering in the tuna tower, watching the moon on the distant snowcaps of the Andes. She could feel the whales blowing out there, the shoals of tuna rolling as they fed, and the bone-dry, far-off mountains. Fish scales whirled off her hands like snowflakes in the wind. She earned her sea legs on that cruise.

In Hawaii, later, she crewed on gypsy charter boats for a while, then signed on a racing yacht as a grinder. A girl on the winches was good public relations for the millionaire who owned the boat. She was strong—nearly six feet tall, as wide-shouldered as most men, with short-cropped black hair bleached at the ends by the sun, and big, hard hands and callused feet. In the tropic heat and rain her face and bare arms had tanned as dark as a Polynesian's. Her eyes, though, were sea green and bright as coral water, with island flecks of brown in them. She had a hawklike profile thanks to a broken nose. Down near Viti Levu in the Fijis, during a transpacific race, a winch exploded on her one night, the boom came across at once, and she caught a glancing blow as she wrestled with the runaway sheet.

The accident left her jobless, in the clinic at Suva with a concussion, and with very little money. The racers sailed on. Down at the docks, once she'd healed, she met a skipper named Taka, a big, dark, grave man from Tongatapu who owned a trading schooner that worked regularly from Samoa down to New Zealand and back. She sailed with him for a year, working her way up to mate. It taught her more of the ways of the working sea, as opposed to the racing one, with all its glitz and glamour. Taka hauled pigs and chickens, copra and gas drums and diesel engines. His canvas sails weighed a ton compared with the light synthetic ones on the yachts. The schooner's wooden hull demanded a lot of care. They holystoned her teak deck once a week with sand and firebricks and sluiced the planks with buckets of seawater until the sun bleached them bone white. They careened the schooner from time to time in shallow lagoons to scrape the barnacles from her hull and slap on antifouling paint to foil the shipworms. They rove new rigging, mended blown sails, fought a nonstop war against verdigris, termites, and cockroaches.

Topside, Miranda became adept with sextant and chronometer, charts and star tables, compass, dividers, and parallel rules. She learned to read the tropical sky and the sea in all their swirling complexities—tides, winds, currents, clouds, set and drift, haze and spindrift and rings around the moon; rocks and shoals, shifting on up through the color spectrum as the keel neared danger, from blue through green and yellow to hull-gutting brown. She learned to tell good holding ground from bad in any anchorage and the places where you had to settle for bad if you didn't want to get eaten alive by sand fleas or mosquitoes. She learned to find a hurricane hole in a hurry when she needed one and, if she couldn't, to ride out the storm at sea. That sort of lesson, once learned, she hoped she'd never have to repeat.

Along the way she saved her wages, and with them, finally, she bought a thirty-six-foot ketch from a broker in Auckland. The ketch was named *Seamark*. It was white-hulled and weatherly, fast on the wind. In her Miranda sailed the web of the central Pacific, from Tahiti and Mooréa on up to Hawaii, through the Tuamotus and the Fijis and Samoa, on across to the Marshalls and the Gilberts, once even as far as Rabaul. Where there were resorts she stopped for a while and earned her keep by taking tourists for day sails or picnics with maitais on deserted motus or for morning outings to dive over some safe reef. Where there were no resorts she hauled freight, as Taka had taught her to do.

Most of her crew and all of her mates, over the years, were island boys. She found them harder working, better sailors, and more fun than Americans or even Australians. She could learn from them— local languages, like the *beche-de-mer* of the Solomons, or pidgin, which changed almost island by island, or the dark, staccato French of Polynesia; the lore of shark gods and kahunas and the Great World-Builder, Maui, who yanked the islands one by one from the bottom of the endless sea with a bone fish-hook; and practical fishing as well, like how to bend a mullet or a flying fish to a long-shanked trolling hook of stainless steel so that it wouldn't slide off; or the best way to cook pig in an *umu,* the oven dug into the earth and lined with hot stones and taro or plantain leaves in which island chefs steamed their suppers and, not so long ago, their enemies. That dish was called *pua'a oa*—long pig. The best parts of a human being, an old Tuamotuan mate of hers named Jean-Claude Marama had told her, were the buttocks and the soles of the feet. *"Vraiment,"* he said. *"Très agréable."*

"How do you know when they're done right?" she'd asked him.

"When ze steam comes out from ze eyeballs."

Some of the mates became good friends. There was Charlie Tehare from the Tubuais, who could free-dive sixty feet on one huge lungful of air and stay down three minutes to clear a fouled anchor or spear a supper of grouper; and Heinzelmann, the wisecracking Samoan from Apia who could strip, repair, and reassemble any engine known to man in a matter of minutes; and Effredio Pascal from Negros in the Philippines, who taught Miranda everything she wanted to know about sea crocodiles and knife fighting. Pascal was a short, wiry man covered with scars. Didn't talk much except when he'd been drinking; then you couldn't shut him up. He'd tell you all about the war and MacArthur and the Moro *juramentados* of the insurrection, who bound their testicles in wet leather so that when it dried and shrank, the pain would drive them on to commit murder and face death willingly, who when bayoneted would grab the rifle barrel and drive the steel deeper so as to get at the man at the other end. Drunk, Pascal would describe to her the Balbal, a giant flying squirrel from Palawan with the body of a man and long, curved claws with which he loved to rip the thatch from a nipa hut and, with his sticky, snakelike tongue, lick up the people sleeping within. When he'd gotten her all spooked and goose-pimply, he'd suddenly jump to his feet and stare at her with wide, mad eyes. "I'm Effredio!" he'd scream. Then, subsiding to his heels with a warm smile, he'd ask, "Are you effred-a me?" At times like that, she was.

Some of the mates she slept with, some not. It didn't really matter. They were all good shipmates. All except the last, an American named Curten. She'd slowly been working her way back east by a series of charters that just happened to break in that direction—from the Marquesas to Pitcairn, then to Easter Island, then up to the Galápagos. Having come that far, she single-handed northward to Mexico, flush now from the earlier charters, to see what the coast had to offer.

It offered disaster in a smart-ass package. He'd come ankling down the marine dock where she was moored, at Cape San Lucas, a tall, skinny, loose-limbed guy with a dog at his heels. He wore sloppy, salt-bleached canvas Topsiders with spliced laces, denim cutoffs faded almost white, a rigging knife in a scuffed leather sheath at his hip, a blue chambray shirt worn so thin by saltwater soap that she could see his dark nipples through it, and a sun-bleached bandanna that had once been red, knotted pirate-fashion on his head to contain a sprawl of curly black hair. Boat bum if she ever saw one. She noticed all these details to avoid his impudent grin and the hard, frank stare of his blue eyes. She returned to the job at hand—polishing brightwork on the binnacle.

"So you're Captain Bloodblister," he said finally.

"What?"

"That's what they call you out in the islands," he said. "Or so I hear. A hard driver. Runs a taut ship. Lady Doom. Admiral Grief. I've never been out there much, mostly in the Caribbean and Colombia, but guys I've shipped with told me about you."

She grunted.

"Nobody messes with you."

She grunted again.

"I like a driver. I like a taut ship."

"So what?"

"So I need work," he said. "They said at the office you needed a hand."

She put down the rag and screwed the cap back on the can of polish, flipped her hair out of her eyes, and took a pull from a Dos Equis. The beer was warm. She spit it over the side and then spit again after it.

"That dog come with you?"

"Brillo?" he said. "Sure. He's a sea dog. Born in a boat, grew up in a boat, fully boat-broken. Hunkers over the gunwale to do his business and never wee-wees to windward." He leaned over and scratched the dog's ears.

Brillo was as curly haired as his master, and nearly as big. He had hard, yellow wolf's eyes that gave the lie to his happy, doggy grin.

"He earns his keep," the man said. "He's a guard dog, the best I ever saw. I picked him up as a puppy over in Colón from a guy who said he was descended from a long line of guard dogs—from the famous Bercerillo of Ponce de León, who could sniff out bad Indians from a crowd of good ones. Balboa had one of Bercerillo's pups, and that's how the line got established in Panama. This guy's official name is Bercerillo, too, but I call him Brillo for short."

"What make is he?"

"Beats the hell out of me. Must have some wolfhound in him, judging from his size, and probably some Chesapeake, from the coat. He's terrific in the water. Here, toss me that beer bottle."

Miranda tossed up the empty, and the man threw it far out into the anchorage. The dog watched it splash but didn't move. He quivered, though, waiting.

"Fetch it, Brillo boy."

Gone like a shot, the dog launched himself from the end of the dock in a flat, hard racing dive that must have carried him nearly thirty feet, then swam to the spot where the bottle had sunk. With no hesitation Brillo surface-dived, his tail wagging briefly. He was down for a full minute, then emerged with the bottle firmly in his jaws. He paddled back to the beach and shook himself dry, dropping his catch at the man's feet.

"Okay," Miranda said. "I'm sold. Now if he can hand, reef, and steer, tell good sea stories, and polish brightwork during the off watches, I'll hire him."

The man laughed, and she laughed, too.

"Come on aboard and have a beer."

His name, he said, was Hugh Curten—Curt for short.

They worked the Baja and the Sea of Cortés for most of that year, carrying whale watchers to Magdalena Bay and Scammons Lagoon to see the gray whales rolling and mating and calving, their big barnacle-crusted hulks as long as, or longer than, the ketch itself. They had an inflatable—a twelve-foot Avon Redshanks—in which to run alongside the whales and surf on their bow waves, veering off only when the wide flukes rose to smash at them. The whales retaliated by spouting to windward and drenching them with spray that reeked of rotten fish, but the passengers loved it. They wanted to pet the whales and got huffy when Miranda wouldn't let them. She soothed their feelings with ice-cold cerveza and fiery tequila.

In other seasons they cruised the Sea of Cortés from La Paz north to Mulegé, stopping to skin-dive among the sea lions on rocky reefs eerily sculpted by the waves or to spend the night on an empty beach, the passengers sleeping in tents after an evening of song and chitchat around a roaring driftwood bonfire, Miranda and Curt sharing the wide bunk in the master's cabin aboard the ketch. Curt proved a charmer with the customers, far more tolerant of their lubberly ways than Miranda, and the money was good.

From what little he revealed of his shadowy past, she came to realize that he'd run contraband in the Caribbean—marijuana, cocaine, automatic weapons and ammunition now and then—making small fortunes from time to time and just as quickly blowing them on cards or poor investments. For a while he'd owned a bar called the Cockleshell in Christiansted, down in the U.S. Virgins, but that had gone up in smoke, literally, when he crossed a Bolivian cocaine supplier on a run to Bimini. "The DEA was watching me," he told her. "I could just feel it. So I deep-sixed the load in a thousand fathoms off Turks and Caicos. I tried to explain the bit about discretion and valor, but the Bolivian didn't buy it. I'm lucky he didn't waste more than the Cockleshell."

"Did you have insurance on the place?" Miranda asked. They were sitting on the sea-lion rocks of Isla de Santa Cruz, north of La Paz, on a leisurely cruise to Loreto, while the passengers snorkeled in the shallows. Frigate birds swung overhead on crooked black wings.

"Yeah," Curt said. "All in a phony name. I had to beat it fast. Never collected a penny, and I guess I never will."

"Sounds like a loser's game, the smuggling trade."

"Tell me about it. I used to tell myself I was doing it out of contempt for society, that the money didn't really matter except as a way to keep score. Curt, fifty thousand; yuppies, zip. All I needed was to hit a cool million, and I'd be out of the game. Well, if I ever show my face down in the Caribbean again, I'll be out of the game all right, for keeps. Even this side of Mexico is scary."

"I know some nice islands out thataway," Miranda said, pointing west. "In the Cooks or the Tongas, or up around Kosrae in Micronesia. No fortunes to be made out there, but a good life anyway. And nobody to recognize you."

"You figuring on heading out that way again?"

41

"Maybe. It depends."

She could see in his eyes the fear that had driven him across the isthmus and up the coast to Baja. She could see, she thought, that he'd learned his lesson. She could sense that deep down he was a fairly decent man. She was wrong.

A month later they were back at Cape San Lucas, doing day sails around Los Friales, the twin rock-spires near the tip of the Cape, awaiting the start of the whale-watching season. Curt seemed more nervous than ever—too many wealthy gringos who might recognize him, she thought. If he were spotted and word got back to the bad hats—either his Bolivian nemesis or the DEA—both of them might be killed. But she could not betray a shipmate, couldn't leave a buddy in the lurch. She liked Curt. Well, maybe she even loved him. It hurt her to see him so frightened.

Had Miranda known the truth about Curt, she would have been even more hurt. Far from being a dope runner, he was an undercover agent for the U.S. Drug Enforcement Administration, one of their best. Over the past eight years he had infiltrated half a dozen South American and Caribbean drug networks, posing as a hard man with a heavy hand on a fast boat's throttle. But the longevity of deep cover is like that of the mayfly—ephemeral in the extreme. He was lucky to have survived this long, and when it became evident in Saint Croix that the ruthless barons of the cocaine empire were getting wise to him, his superiors had sent him to Baja, out of harm's way. He was merely marking time, awaiting orders to a new scene of action.

The orders came care of a small, potbellied, bright-eyed man named Miller Grilse, ostensibly the American manager of a Baja resort hotel but actually a DEA station boss. Grilse arrived at the dock where they were moored in San José del Cabo while Miranda was in town cashing some traveler's checks and buying supplies. He gazed deadpan at Curt for a few long moments, then winked broadly, and stabbed his thumb shoreward. They walked up the esplanade toward a cantina.

"Out in the southern Philippines," Grilse said softly, "there seems to be a major relay station for Golden Triangle heroin. Run by a renegade gringo named Millikan. Maybe not a renegade, though. Maybe a U.S. Navy type. Why, we don't know. Very little communication these days between agencies. You know how it is."

They stopped at the cantina and bought a couple of bottles of Tecate, then walked on. Grilse drank left-handed. His right biceps had been slashed by a Japanese samurai sword during World War II, out in the Philippines where he'd organized guerrilla bands for the OSS. He'd been a tough little guy then. He was even tougher now.

"Millikan's got his own private navy there," Grilse continued. "Local pirates, what they call *mundo*. Moslems, most of them. They bring the shit out of Thailand by fast boats, then funnel it east through contacts in the Philippine Navy. We want you to make your way out there, casual-like, as if you were on the run still from the Caribbean. Cover your tracks as well as you can. Steal a boat or something. Then ease on up to the Millikan operation and wangle a ride with them. You've got a good reputation as a fast-boat driver. Hell, you know what to do, you've done it often enough the past few years."

"What kind of boat?"

"Sail," Grilse said. "Something you can handle by yourself. Why not steal that ketch you're in right now?"

"No," Curt said. "That gal's okay. I wouldn't want to do a number on her."

"You sweet on her?"

"I guess so."

"All the better. More convincing that way if Millikan checks you out."

"I don't know," Curt said.

"Well, get yourself a boat one way or another. Your old pal Phil Chalmers is in Manila now, with Military Air Transport. Crooked as ever. We could have taken him out any time we wanted since the two of you did that job in Panama, but we've let him dangle out there and kept a close eye on him. He seems to be cozying up to Millikan. If you need help making contact with Millikan's outfit, Chalmers might be able to help you."

"What do I do once I've joined up with Millikan?"

"Get the details of the operation. Find out if they really are ONI. Or whatever. Then ease on out and get the word back to me. We'll take it from there." He finished his beer, belched like a foghorn, then flipped the empty over the seawall into the milky surf. He winked again, glum-faced but happy. He loved his work.

"Wish I was going with you," Grilse said. "That's my old stomping grounds out there. Great place, the PI. The men are bastards, wicked as sin, but the women are the best-looking babes in all Asia. *Suerte,* sailorman. And look out for the Benny boys." He winked again, cryptically, turned on his heels, and waddled up an alley toward his pickup truck.

When Miranda got back from town, Curt was gone. Brillo was gone. *Seamark* was gone, too.

At first she couldn't believe it. Maybe while she was in town, she told herself, some tourists had come by demanding a sailing trip—now or never. People from the States like to demonstrate their power by making spur-of-the-moment decisions like that, changing plans or directions at the snap of a credit card. But she knew she was kidding herself. They were gone. One evening, sitting on a bollard at the end of the dock, she started cursing—every salty phrase she'd learned in half a dozen languages. A potbellied little gringo stopped to watch her. He had a crippled arm, she saw, poor fellow. He winked at her clownishly, gave her a crooked thumbs up, and walked on.

Later that week she signed on as mate of a forty-one-foot Morgan beating its way back north after a race. In Ensenada she asked for her pay and with it bought the catboat. It was a seagoing Hyundai compared with the solid workmanship of her ketch, but it was seaworthy—twenty-four feet long, beamy, with a deep center-board and a new mast. In it she sailed north to the land of her birth. Up there maybe her wounds would heal. Years ago, when her parents were still together, they had all gone to visit her dad's folks at their house near Port Albion. She'd loved the house—big, warm, and shiplike, with lots of pictures and books on the walls. There were old harpoons, and guns and swords and old steering sweeps leaning every which way, and model ships swinging from the rafters, sea-shells that hooted ghosts in her ears. She remembered a big brass kettle the size of their Volkswagen, it seemed, that her grandfather said he'd used in the olden days to boil down blubber for whale oil. His own father had found it on a cannibal island out in the South Seas. "Why, Miranda," he'd told her one day, "you could cook a whole missionary in this pot—two if they was little fellers."

Every day, back then, they had gone sailing up and down that cold, bright, piny-smelling coast. Her dad let her take the helm of the old family schooner, and for the first time she felt the strength of the wind thrumming down through canvas, and watched the water boil closer and closer along the gunwales as they heeled to its might. "Spooming," her granddad called it in old sailor talk. Right then, she realized, with the wheel kicking under her hands, she was seeing the entire course of her life unreeling ahead of her.

Now she'd strayed off course through no fault of her own. Maybe her father could steer her back. Maybe.

45

SEVEN

~~~~~~~~~~~~

"Viv?"

At first she didn't recognize him. The man who came down the broken stone steps to the dock looked old enough to be her grandfather—white hair, slouched shoulders, the whiskers on his mottled face grown out in uneven patches, as if he'd tried to shave a week ago, then given it up halfway through, then picked up again on the other side a few days later, then quit for good. But it couldn't be her granddad. He'd died long ago. This man must be her father.

"No," she said, forcing a smile. "Miranda. How you doing, Dad?"

His eyes were murky green, the whites gone a curdled yellow, gummed at the corners of the lids as if his head leaked phlegm. Dim, slow eyes. Then they lighted up for a moment. But it was a weak spark, what you might expect from a corroded plug in a junkyard engine.

"Miranda?"

"Yes."

Now he tried to smile. Cracked lips, yellow teeth. The skin around his eyes creased into a million tiny white ridges that crawled across his cheekbones like albino wireworms. An old cut on his eyebrow popped open and beaded with blood. Even the blood looked pale, but maybe it was the light.

One pocket on his dark-blue wool CPO shirt was ripped and dangling. The other bulged with a dingy handkerchief crusted with dried blood. His khakis were worn through at the knees, stained and rumpled. Even his shoes were falling apart—old navy dress shoes, cracked from want of polish, and so worn at the heels that when he turned to lead the way back up to the house, she could see the brads gleaming through the rubber.

The house was a mess, too. Dust lay thick on the shelves and tables, clothes were scattered and crumpled like disaster victims on the bare, dull floors, plates, bowls, cups, and cutlery left wherever they'd last been used, unwashed, caked with mummified food and the dusty corpses of flies. The house smelled of garbage and stale coffee. Impossible. He'd always been a stickler for neatness. "Ship-shape and Bristol-fashion"—if she'd heard him say it once in her childhood, she'd heard it a thousand times. Home from the sea, he would spring surprise "white-glove inspections" on her mother, finding minuscule smears of grease or infinitesimal deposits of dust in the hardest-to-reach places, then issuing demerits in a voice that was only half-kidding. His khakis were always pressed to a razor crease, his shoes spit-shined to a mirror gloss.

He'd shaved every morning without fail, even on leave. They had a routine when she was a little girl: once he had lathered up—he used a brush and a shaving mug, she remembered—she would demand a kiss. He'd stoop down and grab her to him as if to smear her with the hot, white lather, then stop her just millimeters from collision and brush the tip of her nose with his cheek. It left a feathery blob there, which he would then—very cautiously, as if the act entailed great peril—remove with his straight razor. "Don't move now, Miranda, or I might slip and shave off your whole nose." But of course he was using the blunt back side of the straight razor. She knew that, but she didn't know it—or chose to pretend not to know it. The thrill was delicious. At her demand, when the whole hazardous operation was complete, he would apply a dab of Old Spice to the tip of her nose. It tingled, ice-cold and burning, and for hours afterward she could breathe its exotic, dangerous reek.

Now, as he moved to grab a pile of dirty clothes from the armchair by the front window, she heard his foot kick something that clunked like hollow glass. It rolled away under the chair and tinked against a chair leg. A bottle.

"Have a seat," he said at last. "I haven't been much of a housekeeper. Can I get you something? Uh, coffee? I think I've got some wine around here somewhere. You want a glass of wine, maybe? Homecoming and all that?"

"No," she said, trying to smile. "Nothing right now. I want to get my land legs back. I haven't been ashore since below Dana Point." She hope that might draw him out, get him asking about where she'd been, where she'd come from. But his eyes remained vague, unwilling to look straight at her.

"Well," he mumbled, "I could use something." He walked toward the kitchen. She heard him clanking around, muttering to himself. She stooped down and reached under the armchair. It was a wine bottle. Gallo Thunderbird. Empty.

Now he was cursing in the kitchen, his voice at first low and monotonous, then rising toward the timbres of hysteria. She went in. His eyes, when he turned to her, were red and full of tears. "Fuck it!" he screamed, then turned and smashed a cupboard door with his fist. He was shaking all over, his hands especially. "I can't find it, I know I had it somewhere in here. Where is it? I wanted to give you a drink for your homecoming. Where is it? I can't see it . . ." He stood looking at her with his broken hands clenched in lumpy white fists, tears dripping raggedly through the white stubble of his whiskers. His panic reached her like an airborne virus.

"Wait right here," she said, shaking. "I think I saw it."

She ran back to the living room, to her seabag, unzipped it, and pulled out the liter of José Cuervo she'd bought in Tijuana on her way north, before clearing Customs and Irritation. It was untapped. She'd meant it, after all, as a house gift.

"Here it is!" He was standing in the kitchen doorway, not looking at her. But still shaking. "Here, Dad, let me pour us one." Avoiding looking at him, she poured a couple of heavy slugs into two glasses on the coffee table. The glasses were filthy, but the tequila would kill any germs.

He grabbed his glass—"Here's how"—and belted it back, gagged, shuddered, coughed once, dropped the glass with a clatter back on the table, then launched into a coughing spasm that turned his face red, almost purple, saliva sputtering from the corners of his mouth, eyes watering, sweat starting all over his face. He bolted, hacking, for the kitchen sink. She heard him gag again and again, dry retchings with something gluey rattling at the bottom of them. Then he hawked it up, wet and heavy, and she heard it splat in the sink.

When he came back, the shaking had stopped, and his eyes were back in focus. He smiled crookedly and raised an eyebrow at her. "Cuts the fog, sure enough," he said, and poured himself another dollop. "Let's go topside."

They spent the rest of the afternoon out on the veranda, overlooking the sunlit, rolling sea. While Culdee sipped, slowly now, retopping his glass from time to time and diluting it with water, Miranda told him of her track since they'd seen each other last, trying not to brag of her adventures—storms, lee shores, tight corners—but aware, in her telling and by his few questions, of his growing pride in her seamanship. His eyes glowed whenever she described some smart bit of action. The way she'd rigged and deployed her ground tackle during a big blow in the Tongas. The time she'd given the French patrol boats the slip near Mururoa, where she'd hauled a gang of Greenpeacers to protest the nuclear testing there; the careful piloting, through fog-shrouded coral heads with her kicker crapped out and only the lightest of airs—contrary at that—to bring her safely through the dogleg channel at Nouméa.

But when she came to the part about Curten and the loss of *Seamark*, he began to glower. "So I bought that little catboat and headed up here, to see if I could find you," she concluded.

He was out of his captain's chair now and stalking around on the deck, his glass sloshing over at his ripping turns.

"The bastard," he grumbled. "The rotten cocksucker."

She looked out to sea. Well, Curt was anything but that.

"And you don't know where he went?"

"No."

.

49

"Those drug guys must have some idea. I wouldn't trust those fuckers—"

"Dad, he could be anywhere. He might already have made a big coke run in my boat and scuttled her somewhere. With what he scored off that, hell, he could be living it up—I don't know—in Paris or Papeete or, or Montevideo. Anywhere."

"Or he could be dead."

"Anyway, I'm not going to worry about it," she said. "It's not the end of the world. Right now I just want to get my bearings for a while, up here, and then see what I can do to get back out there." She gestured to the southwest—the great, rolling, cold blue sweep of the Pacific.

He sat watching her closely, smiling.

"What happened to your nose?"

"Got broke," she said, embarrassed. She covered it with her hand. "I bobbed when I should've weaved."

"Someone coldcock you?"

"No." She laughed. "It was my first race to Fiji. The man said 'Ready about.' I said, 'Ready about when?' " They both laughed.

"Why did you run away in the first place?" Culdee asked suddenly.

Miranda could have given him an hour's worth of reasons—teenage rebellion, counterculture peer pressure, child of a broken home, the only alternative to bulimia, a rampant Electra complex, penis envy sublimated to the imagery of masts and spars. . . . She'd thought about it often enough.

"Hey, look," she said at last, "every pimply shoe clerk and check-out girl in the world's got a degree in pop psych. Let's just say I had to go to sea. Anyway, what about you?"

"Well, nothing much," Culdee said. "The navy dumped me, you know." He took another long swallow of the Cuervo, then topped it up neat. "I tried the merchant marine for a bit—freighters, tankers, Ship-Land containers—but it was no good. You had to join a union. Can you believe it? Carpeting on deck, TV in the crew's quarters, even a swimming pool and a hot tub on one of the supertankers. You work an eight-hour day—one on, two off—and get overtime for extra duty. Up topside it was all SatNav systems and computers and autopilots. Muzak on the flying bridge, guys plugged into Walkmans running the winches in port. Anyway, the merch wasn't for me. I swallowed the anchor and came back here. With my pension check I have enough to keep me in booze and beans."

For supper that night they dined on saltines and Hormel chili. Culdee cooked on the grease-caked stove top and ate standing up at the kitchen counter because the table was too full of dirty dishes. Afterward he finished off the Cuervo and passed out on the couch.

Miranda turned to at daybreak the next morning. By the time Culdee had slept it off, she'd washed all the dishes, dumped the garbage, polished the kitchen floor. In the head, when he went for his wake-up puke, Culdee found the toilet bowl scrubbed spotless and the towels—fresh ones she must have located in some cupboard unknown to him—neatly folded on the racks. He staggered out onto the veranda and found her holystoning the deck. He hoisted himself into the captain's chair and stared, frightened, out to sea. Where had his energy gone?

In a week she had the place shipshape. At times he would hear her at her chores—hammering wind-skewed shingles back onto the roof, rehanging storm shutters, whisking great clouds of dust off the bookshelves; he'd hear the gurgle of linseed oil being poured out and the brush slap as spar varnish was applied. She sailed down to Port Albion in the catboat one day—Culdee's ancient Datsun pickup wouldn't start—and came back heavily laden with groceries, cleaning materials, hardware, engine parts. Then she fixed the car. But she hadn't brought anything serious to drink. His fear mounted. There was something awful in her energy, in the strong sheer of her jaw. By God, she was going to reform him!

Panic set his heart to racing. He was shaking again, all over. He slunk out the back door and down to the boathouse. In there, he now remembered, he'd stashed a jug of rum, stowed under tarpaulins. It was still there. He broached it and drank. Two hours later she found him flaked out on the dock and snoring in a halo of fumes.

Stalemate.

EIGHT

~~~~~~~~~~

And so it went for weeks, for months—Culdee either drunk and voluble or comatose in his captain's chair. The more he wasted himself, the harder Miranda worked. As if they were on a kind of seesaw, she thought. The lower he sank, the higher she flew. How long could he last? He was killing himself.

"Why do you drink so much?" she asked him one morning. He was at the bright, gabby stage of his lopsided cycle—twenty minutes of rum-fueled pep followed by a day and a half of the dead-eyed sulls.

"Doctor's orders," he told her slyly. "If I don't put away at least a fifth a day, I'll croak. So will the sawbones."

"I never heard anything so ridiculous. Who is this so-called doctor?"

"There's two of them, actually. Mine's the good doc. If I don't do what he says, the bad one will kill us both."

"What are their names? I want to talk to them."

"You won't find them in the book," he said. "But they call themselves Doctor Igor and Doctor Superigor." He laughed and raised the bottle.

Another time he told her about the hook rats. They were big, ugly things with thick tails. The tails had barbs on them like fish-hooks, and when you were asleep, they crawled up on you and stuck their tails in your chest. Then they started chewing into your belly. You couldn't pull them off. They had scales on them like sharks, razor sharp. Grab hold, and you'd rip your hands to ribbons. They burrowed in fast, and you could feel them tugging your guts, gobbling them like long, soft sausages. Scream, and they'd only chew faster, wagging their tails with joy. But they didn't like booze. If you could get to a bottle quick enough, all it took was a couple of long, strong slugs to make them scuttle away. For a while at least.

Now and then he could quit for a week or two at a time. Then he was fun to be with. He worked alongside her at the chores, cooking and cleaning and washing the dishes, fixing the pump when it broke, polishing brightwork or painting the hull of the catboat. He told her sea stories about WestPac and his old shipmates, memorable cruises and epic liberties. But he never talked about the scars. She'd noticed them, like bracelets of old coins around his wrists and biceps, shiny and concave, and when he worked shirtless in the sun, she'd see the deep, glossy hole in his shoulder. He had small round scars on his chest and back, and more of the coin things around his ankles. One day she asked.

"Got caught in the shit storm," he told her. "Shit burns deep."

They worked on for a while in silence. His face grew hard in the weak California light. They were caulking the catboat, paying cotton and oakum into the seams and pounding it deep with caulking irons. The air was sharp with the reek of creosote. Culdee hammered the oakum viciously with the heel of his fist, muttering to himself. Then he stood up and slammed the iron on the deck.

"Shit burns deep," he said. "But payback is a motherfucker."

He stared out to the far southwest.

Miranda was trying, long distance, to collect the insurance on *Seamark.* If she got it, she thought, they could afford help for Culdee—not a shrink, he wouldn't stand for that, but maybe a long trip somewhere, a sea voyage, something to put him back in touch with life. The insurance carrier was the Bank of Polynesia, in Papeete, and weeks passed between letters. The bank always wrote in French, in language so arcane and convoluted it took weeks more for Miranda to decipher them. They wanted proof that her vessel had indeed been stolen, not lost through some act of criminal

53

negligence on her part, some *fait maladroit* that would exonerate them of responsibility.

The few Mexicans she knew in La Paz and Cabo San Lucas pleaded ignorance of the affair, if they answered her letters at all. In despair, she wrote to all her former mates in the wide Pacific—Heinzelmann, Taka, Effredio, the lot of them. No answer. Then the bank, too, fell silent. She began to understand about payback.

Up the coast from the house a creek cut its way through the foothills and spread, behind the dunes, to form a small marsh. Below the marsh was a tidal outlet. Steelhead ran up through the channel to spawn far upstream, and in spring and fall ducks fed in the pickleweed of the brackish water. One day when Culdee was sober he took Miranda up there. They brought along a picnic lunch, a double gun, and two flyrods.

They hiked up through the dusty hills, spooking deer from the manzanita thickets. Valley quail whistled from the old, rotting fence posts, in fields where wild cattle once ran. Then they dropped down a rain-rutted draw to the creek. It was cold in the shadow of the madronas, and the boom of the surf, masked now by hills and dunes, was hollow in the distance. The creek was clear, with deep green holes beneath the fast falls. Culdee pointed out a dark, long shadow finning in one of the pools—a steelhead trout fresh in from the sea—but they continued on down a goat trail beside the creek until they broke out on the edge of the marsh.

"Quiet now," Culdee said. They left the rods and hamper beside a rock and crept, crouching down into the reeds. Culdee had the gun. They worked along the edge, slowly, in hip boots. The water was cold. Ahead Miranda could hear the throaty chuckling of ducks and see the circles of their dabbing. Then the ducks got up off the water with a sudden splashing racket, their green heads brilliant in the light, and Culdee shot twice. Two of them folded and fell. He turned and smiled. He'd shaved and brushed his teeth that morning, and for a moment, looked almost boyish.

Later he taught her to shoot at the birds that came swinging in over the floating bodies of the ducks he'd killed. He coached her in mounting the gun solidly—keeping both eyes open, her left hand far out along the barrels, then swinging smooth and fast and steady along through the swift, low shape of the bird until she saw, down the plane of the barrels, the black, glittering eye. That was the time to hit the trigger. She killed the third bird she shot at—a pintail, it turned out. And the fourth as well. That was enough ducks for one day.

They lunched in the warm lee of the dunes, sharing an abalone salad, the main ingredient of which Miranda had personally dived for from the offshore rocks, along with her own home-baked rye bread. Then Culdee took her to a big, cold blue pool where the creek met the brackish water. He pointed out the shimmering shadows cast on the rocky bottom by the newly arrived steelhead. He worked some line off the flyrod and with one quick, low backward cast laid it out, quartering upstream of the rearmost shadow. The fly—a Humboldt railbird he called it—lighted on the water without a splash and disappeared into the current. A moment later the shadow flickered and was gone. Culdee raised the rod, and it bent almost in half. A long, silver shape exploded into the sky, loud as the morning's mallards. The reel screamed. He handed Miranda the rod, smiling again, his eyes bright and happy. The fish was strong, as strong as the wahoo she'd often caught in the islands, as strong and acrobatic pound for pound as the blue marlin she'd hooked and lost off Kona. The steelhead broke off on its tenth or twelfth jump. She turned crestfallen to her father, but Culdee told her not to worry, there were plenty left where that one came from. Then he taught her to cast.

Later, as they hiked up the trail toward home, he stopped and looked back down at the marsh and the creek. His eyes were dark now, and the smile was gone.

"That was my heaven," he said. His profile to the sunset, Culdee's face was half red, half black.

While the good weather lasted, she hunted and fished on her own. She grew proficient at it, deadly enough when she wanted to be, but it could never be her heaven. She'd found that already, and lost it: the freedom of the seas. Now she was on the beach. They were both on the beach. That was the hell of it. She let her hair grow long. She'd only kept it short so it wouldn't foul in the rigging.

With the winter rains Miranda looked indoors for work. The old family schooner, *Caprice,* rested on blocks in the boathouse, high and dry and shrouded in canvas since her grandfather's death fifteen years ago. She was forty-eight feet, two masted, and although her rigging was rotten, the oak-ribbed hull was still sound—even if great gaps showed daylight through strakes where the caulking had dried out. Her masts of Douglas fir seemed strong enough. Crawling around the forepeak and lazaret with a flashlight, Miranda found a shipwright's treasure trove—blocks and shivs; snap rings and eye-bolts and spare pelican hooks; gallons of litharge and red lead; Stockholm pine tar for the rigging; coils of Manila, cotton, and hemp rope in diameters varying from three-inch hawsers to small stuff; shackles, thimbles, cringles, sail twine, and needles; bolts of heavy canvas stowed airtight and safe from rats and rot; reels of wire cable and shots of anchor chain (rusted by time but needing only the touch of a wire brush and some fresh paint to be young again); even two spare anchors, Danforths, just in case.

Miranda turned to. All winter long the boathouse rang to the chime of her caulking iron while rain drummed on the roof. At night, in the house, she sewed new sails by hand until her palms were sore, then soothed them by smearing warm tar into fresh rigging. She carved trunnels of locust wood to replace the few that had split, worked hot oil into frozen blocks until they hummed, cut chafing gear from an old cowhide. She wire-brushed and painted, rasped and splashed, until she was permanently spotted, like some gaudy reef fish—red and yellow and black. There were rats in the schooner's hold. She stalked the dumb ones and killed them with a marline-spike. The smart ones she smoked out with a slow fire of rags soaked in fuel oil and Raid, then shot them with the 12-gauge when they abandoned ship. Finally there was only one left, a grizzled old

56

graybeard wise to her every trick. One day she cornered him up in the forepeak. He reared back in the beam of her flashlight, glaring at her down the long, scarred reach of his snout, whiskers bent and twitching like frayed wire. He smelled horrible. One ear had been chewed to a stub in his lifetime of mating and fighting. He's ready to die, she thought, but he's not afraid. Ah, well, what's a ship without a rat? And she crawled away without touching him.

Topside at the house Culdee sat in his chair, staring out to sea. Now and then he'd catch a whiff of hot tar or red lead, and his nostrils twitched. Vagrant breezes brought him the rasp of Miranda's saw or the bang of a hammer. He got out of the chair and rummaged around the house until he found a coil of clothesline. He tried to cut off a length of it with his old rigging knife, but the blade was too dull. He sawed it through with a bread knife instead. About six feet ought to do it. He whipped the ends neatly with waxed wrapping twine so they wouldn't unlay and went back out onto the deck.

When Miranda came up for lunch, she found him at the edge of the deck, by the railing. He was throwing knots. Simple ones at first—Kelligs and beckets, buntlines and bowlines, timber hitches and Magner's hitches. He took them slow and easy, and when he tied them right, he almost smiled. Then he moved on to more difficult ones—the sailor's cross and waterman's knot, the lover's knots (true and false), lanyard knots, sheepshanks, a double crown with single loops.

On the difficult knots his hands sometimes cramped, and she would find him cursing, tears in his eyes, banging the hand on the deck. It resembled the monkey fist he was trying to tie. Before she could stop herself, she was telling him that if he ate better and didn't drink so much, he wouldn't cramp up like that. He just stared at her, not trusting himself to talk.

"Aw, this is just kid's stuff," he said finally. "I don't know why I mess with it. I used to tie these things in the dark. I used to could tie them in my sleep."

But the next day he came down to the boathouse and searched

through the old line until he found a coil of worn, two-and-a-half-inch hemp. He carried it back to the house, and she heard him chopping at it with an ax. On her visits to the house she saw him unlaying the rope lengths into their individual strands, then into their separate yarns. He checked them through for strength and began retwisting them. A week later he presented her with half a dozen neatly tied fenders, each grommeted perfectly at either end. "Keep you from taking splinters out of the dock when you come alongside," he said.

Now instead of just staring out to sea, he would stare out to sea and throw knots, blindly, all the time.

By winter's end, as the rains grew intermittent and the weather warmed, Miranda opened the boathouse doors. Through most of the afternoons the sunlight reached the schooner's stern sheets, and she began replacing sections of taffrail that had weakened or rotted out over the years. She found some old teak among the sea stores, lathed round and the right diameter, but it was straight. She rigged a steam box and softened the wood until she could warp it to the proper contours. It was pleasant feeling the sun again. One afternoon she felt she was being watched. She had stripped off her paint-stained canvas shirt and was working topless. When she looked behind her, she saw the rat's eyes gleaming in the companionway hatch.

Every day he watched her. She began leaving crusts of bread and hunks of cheese rind for him. Gradually she began working closer to him. Finally she was able to feed him from her hand. But when she tried to touch him one day, he crouched back, hissing, and flashed his long, yellow teeth at her.

He scuttled away and didn't return for three days.

She called him Rance the Rat. Rance, short for Rancid.

NINE

~~~~~~~~~

The letter was addressed to "Señorita Capitán M. Culdee, Port Albion, U.S.A." It had been battered, bent, smudged, spindled, and mutilated in the course of its passage through half a dozen post offices from Honolulu to Kentucky to Oregon to northern California. The cancellation mark across the gaudy alien stamps read "Siquijor, P.I." Of course, Miranda thought, the Philippines. Her hands began to shake.

"Dear Srta. Capitán," the letter began in a spiky, old-fashioned script.

I am a friend of your former shipmate Sr. E. Pascal, who has asked me to write to you. He had indeed seen your vessel THE SEAMARK in Philippine waters, at Puerto Princesa on the island of Palawan. Sr. Pascal was there on seamanlike business but four months ago. The vessel, he tells me, was taking on stores and water. When he approached it, a fierce Dog would not permit him aboard but rather attacked so as to bite him. Sr. Pascal inquired of persons at the dockside and was pointed at a young man of American persuasions who Sr. Pascal has asked where are you? The young man said you were drowned dead overboard in Mexico many months since. Sr. Pascal was very much saddened at this evil report but when the young man bought him beer to drink Sr. Pascal must wonder if this news is true. The young man was very much vagrant (¿muy vago?) on this news and hasty for his

59

departure so when Sr. Pascal received your mail message inquiring as to SEAMARK he was very lucky, contento. Please excuse my badly English but I am working long years here in Siquijor and Sulu Sea mainly among Moros and Sea Gipsy Badjaos who speak not your felicitous tongue. Sr. Pascal sends you his fond love and much affection and wants much to see you once more and help you in recovering your fine vessel SEAMARK. Sr. Pascal would write you by his own hand but has forgotten how to do it. God be with you.

It was signed "Padre Bartolomeo Cotinho, S. J., Misión San Ignazio, Siquijor Island, P.I."

So there is was. Effredio Pascal had come through.

Miranda went first to the attic and opened her grandfather's old sea chest, packed to its macramé-studded lid with charts and sailing directions covering the entire Pacific Ocean. They were hopelessly out of date, the most recent one published in 1938, but Miranda dug out a chart of the Philippines and carried it downstairs. Earwigs scuttled as she unrolled it, and the chart was badly gnawed around the edges, but she quickly found Siquijor. It lay due east of the south end of Negros Island, where Effredio had been born. Palawan, she saw, was a long, narrow island shaped like a dented, upside-down rifle. It lay, northeast to southwest, across the Sulu Sea less than four hundred miles west of Siquijor. Puerto Princesa appeared to be the island's largest town, overlooking a wide, well-protected harbor on the island's east coast. From there Curten could have gone north to Manila, or southwest to the tip of Palawan, then across the South China Sea to the Golden Triangle of Southeast Asia. Or he might have stayed in the Sulu Sea. It was full of islands—hundreds, thousands of them. Or he could have . . .

She stopped and smashed an earwig. Her heart was pounding. She had to slow down, think it through. She saw Culdee watching her from the deck.

"What is it?" he asked.

"*Seamark*," she said. "A friend of mine—an old mate—he's found her. Or seen her, anyway. Curten was still aboard her, and that dog of his, too."

"Where was this?"

"Puerto Princesa. In the Philippines."

Culdee turned away from her, back to his knots. He was laying up robands for the schooner's yards and staysails. But his hands trembled. He got up angrily and headed for the kitchen. He had a bottle of rum in the reefer, she knew. He pulled away on it in there for a minute. Then he came back out to where she sat looking at the chart.

"The Philippines," he said in a flat voice. He was looking down at her. He began humming an odd little tune. "What are you going to do?"

"Get out there," she said. "Get my ship back from that bastard."

Culdee started whistling the same tune, whistling up a wind she knew.

"What's that song?"

"An old one from the Philippine insurrection," he said. " 'I wanna go to the Filla-Pie-Neens, fight for my country and live on beans. I wanna go to the Filla-Pie-Noons, fight for my country and live on prunes.' It goes on and on from there, however silly you want to make it."

"Are you coming with me?"

"How?"

"In the schooner. She's nearly ready now. I ran her down to the boatyard in Port Albion and stepped the masts yesterday, and I've got most of the rigging rove. She's good as new. Shipshape and Bristol-fashion. You coming?"

"Christ, no," he said. "My sailing days are over. I'm too old for that shit. No way. I hate that part of the world. Forget about it."

That evening, toward sunset, Miranda rowed the dinghy out to where the schooner lay at anchor in the bay. Bare poles swung slow and naked against a red and black sky. The little ship lay trim on the water, her bowsprit raked sharp from the long, clean sheer of the main deck. The hull looked black in the failing light. Miranda tied up to the taffrail and rigged a bosun's chair. With a brush and a bucket in hand, she hoisted herself and painted over the schooner's name, *Caprice*.

Culdee watched from the captain's chair.

When she finished and lowered herself back into the dinghy, he could make out the ship's new name, in bold white capitals: VEN-GANZA.

"Vengeance," he thought. "Payback," but in Spanish. Appropriate. He uncorked the rum bottle, put the neck to his mouth, and tilted it toward the stars.

TEN

~~~~~~~~~

If Miranda had so far blown through the old estancia with the verve of a force nine gale, she now hit typhoon velocity. She hanked the schooner's new suit of sails and ran out for sea trials, discovering that although it made her hustle like a Honolulu hooker, she could indeed single-hand the ship if she flew only the main and a headsail. That would cut her speed some, but once she got down to the trades she could hunt up a few deckhands. In the PI, Effredio was waiting and maybe some of her old shipmates would be on the beach somewhere along the way. She called the Philippine consulate in San Francisco and learned that as a U.S. citizen she didn't need a visa, so long as she stayed in the Philippines only three weeks. Later, if need be, she could extend it.

Provisioning was a problem. She didn't have much money—a little over twelve hundred dollars from the sale of the catboat, and most of it would go for diesel fuel to drive the Graymarine auxiliary—there were doldrums down that course. She invested more than she cared to on canned meats, flour, and baking soda, then baked up a supply of hardtack and stowed it in the old ship's biscuit tins that she found in the schooner's galley. Not enough to last the voyage, but maybe she'd get lucky along the way. Her luck seemed to be turning now.

Antiscorbutics? With fair winds and a boost from the currents she was only a few weeks from Hawaii, where guavas rotted in the gutters, but she laid out a few more bucks at the health food store in Port Albion for a brown-glass bottle of generic Cs and two gallons of fortified lemon juice. It would go well with the tea she'd already stowed.

Pubs and charts? In a used-book store near Vallejo she found the U.S. Defense Mapping Agency's *Sailing Directions (Enroute) for the Philippines,* volumes I and II, all updated through the previous year, along with matching charts. After long hesitation, she sunk another three bucks on a coffee-stained, rat-chewed copy of *The Philippine Pilot.* Thank God she was born to a seagoing family: she had salvaged her grandfather's old sextant, barometer, and stopwatch while cleaning house last winter. The schooner's old brass-plated clock kept accurate time if you wound it regularly—she checked it against a time hack on the marine band. Anyway, she knew the wind and stars down there.

A barrel of kerosene (for the stove, the lamps, and the running lights), a cask of heavy cod-liver oil (to calm both her bowels and storm waters—just a tablespoon or two would solve either problem), three quarts each of marmalade and red-current jam (to go with the hardtack—she boiled them down herself to save expense), a dozen tins of butter and Crisco, dried veggies (mummified in a drying box she built from a foil-lined cardboard carton and a two-hundred-watt lightbulb), stainless-steel fishhooks and heavy-test monofilament (half a mile of it, for trolling once she got offshore)—on and on and on, until her head was spinning with the fun of it all. Fitting out, fitting out, make all preparations for getting underway. . . .

"You'll never find him," Culdee said.

"How's that?" Miranda was curled up on the bunk in the master's cabin, her hair all over the place, working up a list of everything she'd stowed. In the light of the kerosene lamps her eyes glowed red out of black and blue circles. A wild woman with a pencil in her mouth.

"Well, look at it. According to that padre fellow's letter, your old shipmate saw the boat a week before he wrote. But the letter didn't get here for seven weeks more. You've been another four weeks getting your gear together—that's three months already since the sighting. By the time you get out there, it'll be six months."

"Five. I worked it out on the charts already. Five tops, maybe less if the trades are steady."

"You mean you're going to cross the Pacific in a sailboat in only two months?"

"Look, it's 6,223 nautical miles, Great Circle, from San Francisco to Manila. At eight knots—"

"You can't go Great Circle. You'd be bucking the westerlies most of the way."

"Well, if I drop down quick to the trades, I'll only add a couple thousand miles more. At eight knots—"

"It's more like three thousand. And I've been watching you. You can't push that schooner flat out. You—even you—haven't got hands and feet enough to bend on full sail. You'll creep along at five knots tops, and even then you'll be lucky not to get knocked down, the first big blow that hits you."

"Then come with me."

"No way."

She grew sullen. He stood there in the hatchway, bleeding for her. He didn't want her to go. He needed her. Without her he'd drink himself to death in a month. There was nothing he could do about it. The hook rats would get him. But he couldn't go back. The rats out there were even worse.

"Anyway," he said, "what's the rush? You're driving yourself too hard. You're driving yourself nuts. Take a look in the mirror. Piss holes in the snow."

She looked, and he was right. Then her face in the mirror started to blur: images through saltwater. She blew out the lamps and went up to her room.

Late that night, prowling around the house dead sober, Culdee heard her tape deck playing behind the bedroom door. A tinny little Japo tape deck, all she could afford. She was playing songs from the sixties, songs she had to tape herself off the FM band because her old boyfriend Curten had stolen all her tapes along with her boat. The songs didn't mean anything to Culdee—he'd been out of circulation when they were popular—but they meant the world to her:

"Paint It Black," "A Whiter Shade of Pale," "Baby Love," "Me & Bobby McGee." Suddenly he could see her as she was then—a sad, skinny teenybopper whose daddy was in the big joint up north because he'd been a bad boy fighting in a bad war. Even her mother says so. Even her best friends say so. But she doesn't believe it, doesn't believe, and she sinks into the beat. "Nothin' left to lose."

Well, you better believe it. Culdee shaped his course for the reefer and the rum jug.

For three days, four days, she was down. She slept until noon, danced for a bit on the rocks above the surf, slept some more, played her tapes. She sat next to Culdee on the deck at sundown, looking southwest. Then she went in and slept some more to the music.

On the fifth day another letter arrived from Padre Cotinho. It was short and sweet. He had discovered the magic of the zip code, so it had only taken a week to arrive this time. In it he enclosed a clipping from the Zamboanga *Times,* dated just three days before he mailed the letter.

PI DOG BITES AGAIN!

BATARAZA, Palawan (AP)—The infamous Pi Dog of Bugsuk Island claimed more soft-hearted victims yesterday. Reports from Rio Tuba described how the Piratical Pooch lured another outrigger load of wealthy tourists to penury and embarrassment.

The curly-haired canine corsair appeared once more—the third time in as many weeks—swimming apparently exhausted in the high seas near Ursula Island, a noted bird-watching Mecca for which the outrigger was bound. Tourists with tears in their eyes begged the boatman to bring the dog aboard. "No sooner did he shake himself off, all over our camera, than he bared his fangs and cornered us in the bow of the boat," said shutterbug Toribio Banag of Davao. "I made a move at him, and he nearly took my hand off."

A few minutes later a high-speed inflatable—allegedly

an Avon Redshanks 12-footer, according to witnesses at the scene—raced alongside, and the Maritime Mutt's pirate master leaped aboard. Masked and silent as always, he relieved the passengers at pistol point of an estimated P50,000 in traveler's checks, cash, cameras and jewelry.

Then cur and cohort reembarked, and the raft sped off in the direction of Bugsuk Island, south of the crime scene.

Cave canem, especially at sea!

Miranda jumped and whirled, grabbed Culdee by the shoulders, and kissed him beard and all. "He's there! They're both there! That's my raft and everything, and that's the sea dog's style if I ever saw it. Curt used to leave him on guard when we were in port. One night we came back from a pig roast at the hotel in Mulegé and found Brillo with three Mexican kids cornered in the head. One of the kids needed stitches and a tetanus shot. He'd tried something with a knife. That's Brillo all right."

"Surprised no one's shot him yet."

"He's bulletproof," Miranda said. "Curt swears he can dodge bullets. He's uncanny."

"Sounds like you're more in love with the dog than you are with your boat."

Her smile faded.

"I'll get them both back," she said.

The next day, after stowing ice for her fresh stores and topping off the water tanks, Miranda was ready to sail. Culdee wandered around the house, wanting a drink badly but not enough to let his daughter's last sight of him be that of a falling-down drunk. Time enough when she was gone. He couldn't stop her now.

"Tide turns at 1800 or so," Miranda said after she'd run through her checklist for the last time. "Come on down and help me with the mainsail. Wind ought to be offshore by that time, and if I can sail off I can save some fuel."

"I don't know."

"Aw, come on. I'll buy you a drink."

"Well, maybe just one."

They sat in the schooner's cockpit, watching the sunset and waiting for the tide. Miranda opened a bottle of medicinal rum and poured Culdee a water glass full. No ice, no mix. He drank it down, in his sadness unable to talk.

"I'll work well off tonight and catch the current," she said. "Marine weather says strong northwesterly breezes gusting to thirty knots, so I ought to make good time. It's part of a big front. Maybe I can get clear of Reyes before it comes around to the south."

"Mmmnh," Culdee said.

"Here, let me top off that glass."

A string of pelicans lumbered past, heading out to the anchovy grounds. High overhead a wedge of geese moved north, yapping like distant beagles and catching the late red light.

"Remember to go shopping tomorrow," Miranda said. "I took the last of the fruit and vegetables and that package of hamburger."

"Mmmnh."

"Hand me your glass." She refilled it.

"I wrote Washington a couple weeks ago to deposit your pension check in the bank at Albion," she said. "Here's a checkbook I got for you." Miranda handed it to him, and he tried to stuff it into his shirt pocket. She put it in for him. "It'll be easier for you this way; you won't have to wait in line at the bank to cash it, and you won't be so likely to forget you even got it."

"Yeah."

"The Datsun's low on gas, so get some tomorrow. I covered it with that tarp last night to keep the salt air off it. You ought to do that every night you've used it. It's starting to rust out back there by the tailpipe.

"Mnnmph."

"Give me your glass. This is good rum, isn't it? They don't make rum like this anymore."

"Nuh."

"Hey, hand me that screwdriver over there next to the binnacle. I forgot to stow it."

He got up, staggered heavily to starboard, overcorrected to port, and sprawled against the cockpit coaming. Then he lurched toward the binnacle, and Miranda stuck her foot out. He hit the deck limp, rolled on his back, and started snoring. She looked at the chronometer on the bulkhead in the companionway: 1805. The tide was sucking weakly at the schooner's hull. She dragged Culdee down the ladder and into the mate's cabin, rolled him into the bunk, pulled the checkbook from his pocket, took off his shoes, covered him with a blanket, then stepped out and locked the door behind her. She went quickly up to the house, shut off the main fuse switch, tightened the water taps, left a forwarding address for the mailman, and then secured the heavy shutters over all the windows. She locked the doors. That was it. Tomorrow the sheriff would begin his watch, checking the place randomly three or four times a week to guard against break-ins. She'd had to pay him extra for that, but it would be worth it.

When she got back to the dock, the tide was drawing strong, black water racing seaward and straining the mooring lines. She ran forward and cast off, then ran back and loosed the mainsheet. The schooner groaned and shivered as the mainsail filled, the stern line grew taut and throbbed. She threw it off the mooring bit and jumped with it into the cockpit, grabbed the wheel, and spun it amidships as the dock dropped astern. *Venganza* heeled sharply to starboard as the wind caught the full reach of main and jib. The bowsprit bucked and soared to the lift of the first offshore waves, and the wake lined out astern, ghostly white in the evening gloom. She could hear Culdee snoring over the hiss of the sea. The whole ship seemed happy.

By God, she'd done it! How many daughters ever shanghaied their own father?

ELEVEN

~~~~~~~~~~~~

Sometimes the water gods smile on even the vilest of sinners. By the time Culdee sobered up, he was well past the point of no return. When he crawled up the companionway ladder that morning and the warm wind struck him flush in the face, he knew they were in the trades. Miranda was asleep in a corner of the cockpit, one bare foot on the lashed wheel. Overhead the mainsail bellied full on the port tack. Her face was sunburned, her cheekbones blistering, and she'd painted her nose with zinc oxide, an odd contrast to the purple half-moons under her eyes. He hauled himself upright on the coaming and stumbled to the leeward taffrail. Dry heaves, his stomach sore and pumping, bile in the back of his nostrils . . .

Up forward, a flying fish skimmed off the top of the bow wave; another two followed it. When his eyes cleared, Culdee looked at the binnacle: south and a half west. The wind was strong and steady, and he figured they must be turning eight knots or better. He had noticed the logbook on the bulkhead in the saloon, but he didn't want to read it. He slipped back behind the wheel and unlashed the tie-down. If he jibed her hard over and came about . . . But that would wake Miranda; she'd fight him, and he didn't have the strength for it anyway. The kick of the king spoke in his hand felt good. He let it pound through him, shaking loose the crud and cobwebs that clogged his body. All the booze he'd drunk all these years must have eaten a tunnel through his brain, earhole to earhole, and he imagined the filth blowing out, trailing like frayed commission pennants from his ear-lobe. He focused hard on the lubber's line of the compass, trying to hold the helm steady on course. *Venganza* could fly.

Miranda's foot was threatening to slip off the wheel. He lifted it gently and swung it over onto the banquette. She rolled on her side and mumbled something, then curled up tight and dropped back to sleep. He had to laugh, and would have if it didn't hurt so much. She'd really impressed him, in the seventeenth-century sense of the word. A one-woman press gang. Damn her—but he'd figure a way to escape.

A flying fish hit the leech of the mainsail and bounced clopping into the cockpit. Culdee scooped it up and brained it on a wheel spoke, then laid it out in the portside shade. When Miranda opened her eyes an hour or so later, he had three of them there, cool and fading and neatly lined up.

"There's breakfast," he said. "If you haven't eaten yet."

She got up, yawned and stretched, checked the binnacle and the telltales, then looked at him warily.

"You aren't mad?"

"What could I do about it if I was?"

"Okay," she said. "I'm going forward and set the mizzen. Time's awastin', and so's the wind. Hold her steady. Then I'll get us some breakfast."

They ate in the wash of the wind, fried flying fish, hardtack, marmalade, and steaming black tea. But he was coming around, the molecules of his brain close enough together now to wave and yell "Hi!" In a little while they'd be quarreling, though, and next he knew, throwing punches. That would hurt, and after the pain came the hook rats. What he needed now, before it was too late . . .

"Maybe a slosh of rum in this tea to choke it down easier?"

"All gone, Boats. You swallowed the last of it day before yesterday."

"Shit."

"There it is."

"When do we hit port?"

"A long time from now. Too long for it to make any difference."

He started cursing in a low, deep rumble, and Miranda went forward to fake down some lines and trim the headsails. After that

71

she pumped the bilges—anything to keep her busy, out of his range. She didn't want to resort to the belaying pin, but she would if she had to. It was a dirty trick, all right, and she knew she'd been lucky so far. The worst was yet to come—in a week or so, when the booze had really worn off. Cold turkey was tough meat. She'd eaten it once herself, two weeks of hell in the Pacific—on a little motu off Upolu in Western Samoa, where Effredio found her stash and sixed it.

"Coke is bad stuff," he'd said.

"Not if you can handle it," she'd replied.

"Nobody can handle it; all they can be is handled."

"But you didn't have to dump it," she'd said.

"Fuck I didn't."

"What about the fish? Isn't it bad for them?"

"There's more fish than there is Mirandas," he'd said.

"Fuck you," she'd said. "You're a fucking Commie."

He'd thrown her overboard and kept her swimming around for two hours, fending her off with a boathook every time she tried to come aboard. Finally she swam to the motu and crawled ashore over poisonous coral. She swelled up like an elephantiasis victim, lived on coconut milk and land crabs for the next two weeks, tried to hang herself from a palm tree with her T-shirt, but it ripped, and then all she had was a sore neck and a sprained ankle for her troubles. But Freddie brought her back aboard in the Avon and fed her vitamins and OJ and spent a lot of time just holding her close until she was straight.

Well, there were no motus around here. No Freddie either.

The hook rats came in the midwatch. Culdee could hear their scales rattling as they slid down the ladder, the drag of their barbed tails on the risers. He couldn't go aft and he couldn't go forward because they'd already set fire to the engine room, and when he tried to yell, Major Bui would tell Puddles on him and the B-52s wouldn't make it to the checkpoint. Now he could hear them knocking on the stateroom door. Maybe it was just room service, but he knew it wasn't. He reached for the buzzer to call the nurse, but he couldn't find it in the dark. The pistol was under his pillow. He grabbed it, but it went soft and sticky, Silly Putty covered with floor hair.

They were in the room now, snuffling and scratching, hunting him like retrievers through the tules looking for a wounded duck. All he could do was lie quiet, but his sweat would give him away. It didn't help to scream. That only made them hungrier. But maybe Miranda would hear. She was up there on the deck, at the wheel, singing her songs, oblivious . . .

One of them found him. He felt it climb up on the rack, scaly nose touching his toes, checking them out. He could smell it, foul as the bilges, then feel it crawling up along the blanket until it reached his chest. Its eyes glowed like Saint Elmo's fire, tiny at first, piggy, then growing, ballooning until they filled the darkness—like blazing sewer gas. The heavy weight was crushing his chest.

He screamed.

Then Miranda was there with a lantern.

"Get out of here, Rance!" she yelled and swung the lantern at the rat. It lurched off the bunk and pelted through the hatchway. Not a hook rat at all, just a common ship rat. A big one, ugly as sin, but not a hook rat. No barbs, no scales. Culdee couldn't stop shaking.

"You gotta get me a drink," he said.

"There isn't any."

"That thing'll be back. He'll bring the others."

"He won't," she said. "He's the only rat aboard. He's a pet. He just wanted to say hello."

"I'll kill the bastard next time I see him."

"No, you won't. He's too quick for you. And anyway, he's my friend. He keeps me company during the night watches." She lit Culdee's kerosene lamp. "He likes my singing, and I tell him sea stories. Now why don't you read awhile, and maybe you'll fall asleep. I'll check on you now and then. There's nothing to worry about. No hook rats. Rance won't stand for competition."

Each day, at noon and sunset, Miranda broke out her sextant and shot the stars or the sun. Culdee helped her with stopwatch and star tables. Then they bent over the chart table and corrected their dead reckoning track. The wind held strong, twenty to thirty knots during the day, sometimes falling off after sunset. Once they had to run the engine, but only for ten hours. They were reeling off close to two hundred miles a day, a fast passage.

Rance spent the nights now in Culdee's cabin, curled up at the foot of the bed. Kind of a guard rat, Miranda said. His presence helped Culdee sleep. The more they fed him, the tamer he got. Finally one day Miranda had him sitting on her shoulder while she steered. The only problem was his dreadful smell, but as he spent more and more time topside, sluiced by the odd wave and washed by the trade wind, the stench began fading. Either that, or Miranda and Culdee were getting used to it.

One morning Miranda noticed a flock of small white terns working furiously, low over the water ahead of the schooner. They dipped and soared, backed their wings, dipped again. The sea beneath them churned and boiled.

"*Ahi* birds," she yelled and raced below, emerging moments later with a heavy, twelve-foot bamboo pole. It was rigged with an equal length of thick monofilament, and she quickly tied on a mother-of-pearl lure she'd cut and finished from an abalone shell. The lure had tufts of white mono projecting on each side like the wings of a flying fish. "Yellowfin tuna," she told Culdee. "They're moving from right to left. Try and run down through the school, and steer to stay with it if they don't sound. Sashimi time!"

The school was dead ahead now, and Culdee could see the baitfish breaking and jumping, the flash of heavier bodies beneath them. The water glittered with hundreds of tiny loose scales. Miranda slung the lure into the boil, skittering it over the surface with the rod butt braced hard against her hip. Something big flashed green and gold, and the bamboo bent nearly in half. Miranda heaved and swung the fish aboard. It thumped heavily on the cockpit deck, drumming spray from its tail. The barbless hook fell free, and she flipped it overboard again.

74

"Coldcock that sucker with a belaying pin," she yelled over her shoulder to Culdee. "Don't worry about blood." Culdee whacked it twice, three times. Then Miranda swung another aboard. Then a third and a fourth. The school sounded.

"*Ahi,*" she said, breathing hard. "Small ones, thank God. Twenty, thirty pounds. They run up to two or three hundred. But this is plenty for us. *Ahi* means "wall of fire" in Hawaiian. Taka said they call it that because in the old days the Kanakas used to handline them from their canoes. They'd bend the line over the gunwale to brake it, and the yellowfin would pull so hard that the wood started smoking. The wall of the canoe caught fire."

She filleted one of the fish, skinned it, and sliced a fillet into thin, long strips. From the galley she brought up two roots. "*Wasabi* and *shōnzu,*" she said, grating them into a dish. Then she poured dark soy sauce over the shavings. "Horseradish and fresh ginger. Dig in."

The dark red meat was cold as the sea, fiery with the bite of the sauce. Miranda found some cold rice in the evaporator cooler she'd rigged from coarse-woven canvas and kept wet with seawater in the wind and shade. "Now we're in my part of the world," she said.

Two weeks out they raised Mauna Kea. At first it was just another cloud mass on the western horizon, but the clouds hung steady. An hour later, through the binoculars, Miranda could make out the purple of solid rock, and as the day wore on, the big island of Hawaii slowly heaved itself out of the sea. There was traffic now, liners, tankers, another schooner—the first ships they'd met since California—and half a dozen times they saw jet contrails creeping across the sky. Culdee was acting uneasy. He wouldn't look her in the eye, hardly talked all afternoon. She heard him rummaging around in his cabin, muttering to himself. Then he came topside.

"Where's that checkbook you gave me?" he asked. "We're going to need it once we get ashore. I can't find it in my clothes or anywhere."

"I don't know," Miranda lied. "But don't worry. I'll write the bank for more, and I've still got enough cash to top off the fuel tanks and buy any supplies we need. We'll anchor out so there won't be any docking fees, and I'm bound to find some people I know in Honolulu. I'm good for a touch with them."

The checkbook was hidden up forward in the lazaret. She knew he was thinking about giving her the slip and hightailing it to the airport. Tough luck.

They shot through the Alenuihaha Channel on a broad reach with the big island to port and Maui sliding abeam to starboard, its beaches and slopes studded with condos. Then Kahoolawe on the starboard bow, bare and pockmarked from the megatons of explosives that had pounded it since the navy took over the island in 1953 as a gunfire and bombing range. Culdee remembered how it smelled, the drift of burned powder over the water mixing with the aroma of flowers on the offshore breeze from Maui, cruisers and cans puffing perfect smoke rings as they heeled to their broadsides, plumes of fire and dust where the shells slammed the island. He liked it best when the LSMRs went into their act—a column of the little rocket ships scuffling past like empty gray combat boots inshore of the heavies. When they unloaded, they disappeared in a hissing white cloud. Instant sea smoke. The whole battered, knobby island jumped upward as the five-inch rockets hit, and the roar of the explosion shivered signal flags a mile to seaward . . .

No more LSMRs in the navy now, and he'd read somewhere that native Hawaiian activists wanted the island back. They'd found rock drawings, fishing shrines, and even a temple—what they called a *heiau*—on Kahoolawe, and the navy was shaking up the ghosts of their ancestors. That would be some war, Culdee thought, the ghosts of the old time Kanakas against a ghost squadron of rocket ships. No telling who might win.

Lanai and Molokai fell astern, and Oahu rose dead ahead. A million memories. By midafternoon Culdee could make out the spume from the Halona Blowhole, under Makapuu Point on the east end of the island. Looking closely through the glasses, he thought he could make out the steep stairway that led down from the highway to Halona Cove. He'd snorkeled there often in the old days. They'd rent masks, fins, and girls in town, buy a bottle of rum and a can of pineapple juice, then take a cab out to Halona. You had to stop to buy ice in Hawaii Kai, because if you brought it all the way from Pearl, it would be melted by the time you got to the beach. Cabs weren't air-conditioned in those days. You would take the girls out in the water to boff them if there was a crowd on the beach. He remembered one afternoon—right after Korea it must have been—when he took a hot little *hapa-Portagee* out there on the reef, and he looked down and saw her foot near a sea urchin. He yelled something and grabbed her away, and she nearly climbed up on his head.

"Did you step on it? Did you step on it?" he yelled.

"What? What?"

She was squirming all over his chin.

"The urchin."

"Oh," she said, and slid back down into the water. "I thought you said shark."

Miranda shortened sail as they neared Honolulu, and Culdee unhoused the anchor. Helicopters scuttled back and forth against the Pali, shiny as tropical bugs. They whiffed the land smell as the wind bounced back from the island—sweet and heavy, blossom and mud. As the harbor opened up, Miranda took bearings—Diamond Head, Fort DeRussy, the Aloha Tower—and shouted course corrections to Culdee at the wheel. By the time she lowered the sails and anchored off Ala Moana, the sun was down.

"I'll take the dinghy ashore and handle things," she said, walking aft. "Harbor master, stores, and I want to see if any of my old shipmates are in town. If not, I'll try to hire some kid for an extra hand. Watch and watch is a killer."

"Mmmnh."

They swayed the dinghy over the side, and Culdee watched her row toward the yacht basin. Lights glowed along Waikiki, and the land breeze brought him the sound of honky-tonks. In it he imagined he could smell whiskey, women, and fresh blood. Damn her! He brought a book and a lantern up from the saloon and tried to read. From the yachts anchored nearby he could hear laughter and the clink of cocktail glasses. He got up and went forward to check the anchor. They weren't dragging. He'd known it before he'd gone. He grabbed a hunk of small stuff and threw some knots, but it didn't help.

He'd never once missed a liberty in Wahoo, even if he had to swap a month of midwatches for a standby from one of the choirboys in the crew. It was a great liberty port, one of the greatest in the whole wide watery world. Back in the whaling days they'd called the red-light district Cape Horn, because the old-time white hats hung their consciences on the horn when they came around her. With Cape Stiff behind them and two or three years on the offshore grounds to look forward to, they had their work cut out for them in Honolulu. When the missionaries went to translate the Ten Commandments into Hawaiian, they got stuck on "Thou shalt not commit adultery." There was no such word in the Polynesian language. The best the long necks could come up with was "Thou shalt not commit mischievous sleeping." But that was the best kind.

Over on the beach Culdee heard the whoop and howl of men raising hell.

Okay.

Liberty call.

He stripped off his shoes and clothes, rolled them into a bundle, and was about to slip over the side when he remembered his hand. He ran below and came back with a long Ace bandage and a roll of tape. Then he swam breaststroke to the yacht basin with his clothes bundle belted to his head. He dressed quickly and wrapped the bandage tight over his many-times-broken right hand (a souvenir of too many drunken liberties), taped it down, then hiked west along Ala Moana toward Chinatown. Fuck Waikiki—too rich for his blood, with its tourists and gay bars and hundred-dollar hookers. Hotel Street was home. He could find it blindfolded just from the smell of Chinese herbs, rotting vegetables behind the open-air markets, dried shark fins and sea-slugs and sailor puke. He turned *maiku*—"toward the mountains"—up Nuuanu Avenue, crossed King Street, with the Iolani Palace and the gold statue of King Kamehameha lighted up to starboard and the reek of Nuuanu Stream to port, and there it was, just like he'd left it—scuzzy, shopworn, dimly lighted except for the neon of the dirty book stores and "hostess bars" lining both sides as far as the eye could see.

Some things don't change.

Drunken white hats and dogfaces staggered blindly, warily past one another, expecting a sneak attack at any minute. The Glade was gone, where all the faggots used to hang out, poor cocksuckers, but Wo Fat's was still in business, the oldest restaurant in the islands, 106 years old, the sign said, twice as old as Culdee (a dismaying thought). If he'd had any money, he would've ducked in for a bowl of *ja jeung mein*—old sailors swore that noodles and *hoisin* sauce limbered the joints for love. But he had harsher business pending.

He went into the first bar he came to. Hilo Fattie's, the sign said. Rock pulsed from the juke, colored lights through the smoke. B-girls sinuated through the crowd like destroyers through a wolf pack. He found a spot at the end of the bar and bellied up. A girl eyed him, but he shrugged her off.

"What'll it be, Pops?" The bartender, a plump young *hapa-haole* with a scraggly Yasir Arafat beard and a ring in one ear, smiled at him with the easy contempt of the young for anyone over forty. Culdee pretended to study the bottles ranked behind the bar, then stepped back frowning and hitched mock-painfully at his groin, as if he had the clap and wasn't allowed to drink.

"Better make it da kine ice-water," he said, slipping automatically into Hawaiian pidgin. "Gotta take it easy awhile yet. Otherwise it's auwe when I go to take a leak."

The bartender laughed. "Then, what'd you come here for, Pops? The ambience?" No pidgin for him, he was too hip for that crap. But he brought Culdee a glass.

Culdee studied the faces along the bar, then the hands. Over near the door sat a guy about forty, crew cut, eyes flat as razor blades, half-loaded already, it looked. He was wearing a flowery Harry Truman aloha shirt, and his bare forearms were braced across the bar, a glass of what looked like straight rum cupped in his hands. He had a globe and anchor tattooed on one forearm. Sure enough a jarhead. Culdee drank down his ice water and eased over.

"The Crotch sucks," he whispered.

"Wha'?" Razor Eyes focused on him. "Aw, fuck off, Gramps."

"Whatsa matta, brah?" Culdee leaned over even closer, eyeball to eyeball. "You get stink ear? Not hear so good no more? I said the Marine Corps sucks."

"And I said 'Fuck off, Gramps.' So fuck off."

"Come outside and say that, you jarhead *mahu*." *Mahu* means "faggot" in pidgin. That did it.

In the rain-swept alley beside the bar, Culdee faked a right, slipped the marine's counterpunch, left-hooked the man to the belly, and followed across as he folded with a sharp left elbow to the marine's jaw. When your hands are busted, you use the next best weapon. The marine fell and got right up again, blinking his eyes against the rain. He waded back in, head low, all shoulders and thumping fists.

Culdee bounced against the brick wall and slid left, but the marine caught him with a wide flailing right that stung. Culdee tasted blood. He tied the marine up and tried to knee him in the nuts, but he swung a hip around to block it. He pounded Culdee over the heart. Culdee swung around and bounced the marine's head against the wall, making a hollow, thumping sound, like kicking a pumpkin. The marine's eyes went blurry. They were both breathing rough. It was raining hard now, a deluge. The pavement underfoot was slippery, glinting cold; hard lights glared from the passing cars. Culdee thought Shore Patrol. This was taking too long. He measured the marine up against the wall and hit him with a solid right that, despite tape and bandage, sent fire racing to his shoulder.

The marine went down along the wall. Culdee kicked him in the jaw. Then he took the wallet from the man's hip pocket. It was fat with twenty-dollar bills. Enough maybe to buy a plane ride back to the mainland? Culdee riffled the bills with his thumb. His right hand was already puffing up, and his knees were shaking with adrenaline. All around and through him he could feel the singing: rain on cobbles, tires on asphalt, pulsing jukes and the song of strong drink in young blood, the silky hiss of women moving in the warm, wicked dark. Back on the mainland there was nothing but booze and bad dreams. West and south, though, far over the ocean, the song of this moment grew stronger. He took a bill from the wallet and pocketed it. Then he placed the wallet under the marine's head, like a leather pillow. He left by the back end of the alley.

By midnight Culdee was back aboard, sitting in the stern sheets in a pool of lantern light. The rain had stopped. A bottle of Philippine Tanduay rum stood on the chart table. He was listening to the boom of the surf and soaking his right hand in a bucket of seawater. He heard Miranda's oars creaking in the dark, the bump as the dinghy came alongside. Someone in the dinghy started handing up bags of groceries and cardboard boxes of hardware, then slung a heavy seabag after them. A man climbed up behind Miranda—a dark, wiry, frizzy-haired Filipino with a foxy face and a wry, slightly mad grin. He was wearing a cheap aloha shirt with the price tag still dangling from it and a pair of ragged bell-bottoms.

Miranda's face jumped from Culdee to the rum bottle, then back to Culdee.

"Did a little shopping of your own?" Then she looked at the rum bottle again and saw it wasn't opened. Her face relaxed.

"I had to see if I could do it," Culdee said. "I could." He pulled his hand from the bucket and showed it to her, puffed and purple.

The Filipino in the aloha shirt was Effredio, Miranda's old pal from the PI. He'd wangled a deadhead flight to Honolulu to meet them, knowing Miranda would be shorthanded. A good shipmate, Culdee thought. And another watch stander, thank God.

"All right," Miranda said, "let's get this stuff stowed. I want to sail at dawn."

Culdee slung the bottle over the side and turned to. He was on for the passage.

81

Part Three
LÁZARO

TWELVE

~~~~~~~~~~~~~~~~

The straight-line distance across the South China Sea from My Tho in the mouth of the Mekong River to Balabac Strait in the Philippines is a little more than six hundred miles. A well-found ship encountering no hazards and averaging a speed of six knots should make the passage in just over four days. It took the Vietnamese junk *Happy Life* nearly six weeks, and then her troubles had barely begun. But trouble was nothing new to this voyage.

Since slipping out of the Mekong Delta on a squally moonless night in early May, the fifty-foot trading vessel had encountered one disaster after another. Her rotting cotton mainsail blew out the very first night, its battens cracked by sudden gusts that howled like sea devils from every quarter. Near Con Son Island, as the ship staggered around at the wind's whim, crying babies and squealing pigs nearly betrayed her to a government patrol boat. Only another squall's blinding descent saved the ship that time. But the squall exacted tribute for its mercy: three women were swept overboard with infants at their breasts, and the foremast was carried away, sail and rigging with it.

Off Investigator Shoal a month later, the junk's worm-riddled hull touched coral. Holed in three places, she settled rapidly, increasing her draft enough to hit another coral head, which snapped the prop from her ancient French engine. Not that there was much fuel left. Half a dozen drums of diesel, bought at peril on the black market in Ho Chi Minh City, proved mostly water (salt at that) topped with a deceptive two-inch skim of oil.

85

But the hull had been patched, the bilges bailed—with buckets, cook pots, rice bowls, even tea cups—and the voyage continued. There were still fifty-seven persons aboard, mainly women and children and a scattering of older men—former officers and noncoms of the defeated Army of the Republic of Vietnam, a few prematurely retired businessmen from Saigon and Vung Tau, and the elderly sailor Tho Van Huong, who owned the *Happy Life* and served as her captain.

Most of the pigs and chickens that began the voyage had already been eaten or lost overboard in one storm or another, along with two of the three monkeys smuggled aboard as pets. The surviving monkey, a fierce, pregnant female, took refuge atop the mizzenmast, where her long, quick teeth fended off all attempts to recapture her. At night, especially in bad weather, she descended the rigging to steal food and water from the most unlikely and carefully protected places. Early one morning, before first light, Captain Tho had seen her loot a bag of sticky rice and a full gourd of *nuoc mam* from between the legs of the fat one-time banker, Nguyen Tran Le, then urinate on his pillow before scampering back aloft. Captain Tho had the only weapon aboard the junk, a rust-pitted American M2 carbine dating back to the days of the French, and could have shot the monkey from the rigging anytime he chose. But he admired her courage and contempt. Besides, he told himself, if I shot her as she huddled on the mizzenmast, she might fall overboard, and we wouldn't be able to eat her. I would only have wasted a bullet—I have just twenty rounds for the carbine, and those I must save in case of pirates.

It was more than that, though. Twenty rounds would not go far against the pirates on the South China Sea—Vietnamese, Cambodge, Thai, and the even crueler Filipino *mundo* they were bound to encounter as they neared their destination—all armed with automatic weapons and even (he'd been warned) rapid-fire cannon. Twenty rounds would barely suffice for the suicides he planned to recommend to the men and old women in his charge in the event they were taken. Horrible as survival might be for them, with its promise of rape and slavery, the young women and children had a chance, but the old, the ugly, the male—they would surely be slaughtered. No, twenty rounds was nothing. In the end, he would not shoot the monkey simply because he had seen too much death already.

His mother, father, brothers, and most of his sisters had died at the hands of the Japanese during the Pacific war, or under the martial ministrations of French and Viet Minh soldiery in the decade before Dien Bien Phu. His own wife and two sons—mercifully, he had had no daughters—were killed later by forces as random as a napalm cannister, a Viet Cong bicycle bomb, and a U.S. Marine Corps hand grenade.

The grenade had taken his wife—and two young water buffalo grazing nearby—as she planted rice shoots one foggy morning in a paddy near Phu Loc, up the coast from Da Nang. At Captain Tho's urging she'd gone north to the supposed safety of Da Nang, where her sister lived. Too many VC in the delta, he told her. Go north. The marines will protect you. They are the best of the *My*—the best of the Americans. Then one morning a truckload of drunken long-noses, red-faced and roaring with laughter, had driven past the paddy, heading up to the fighting around Hue in that bloody Tet of 1968, and one of them had thrown the grenade. The marine's friends congratulated him on his accuracy, Captain Tho's sister-in-law said later. She had witnessed the murder from the far side of the buffalo, which absorbed most of the fragments from the blast. Captain Tho's wife lay dead, a bundle of black and red rags sinking into the mud—just another wasted slope, as the *My* would say.

Another wasted slope. Not many years ago the phrase would have enraged him, or at least brought a bitter twist to his smile, but now he knew the words applied to him as finally as they did to his dead wife, and to all the dead of his lifetime. His passengers, at least, had hope. Most of them had relatives already in the United States—the World, as the *My* called it, the Land of the Big PX—and those who did not at least had friends in America who would swear to blood ties. The former ARVN officers would be welcomed, out of *My* guilt if nothing else; the businessmen, for their money, of course.

Captain Tho had no one to vouch for him; he had only the worthless Vietnamese piasters his passengers paid him in advance, some of which he had converted to a few ounces of gold—but not enough to bribe even the lowliest of those Filipino officials whose appetite for palm oil was legendary, even so far afield as Taipei and Singapore, themselves mythic capitals of corruption. Captain Tho knew his best chance lay in delivering his human cargo as secretly as he had loaded it, under cover of darkness on some lonely beach, then disappearing into the maze of islands—more than seven thousand of them, and few with any governmental presence at all—that constituted the Philippine archipelago. His gold and the pesos he might realize from selling the *Happy Life* could be enough to last him the few short years that remained to him. If not, there was always the carbine—or his knife, a razor, a short length of rope . . .

But now, as Captain Tho stood at the tiller, his legs braced against the first swells of the Sulu Sea, even those prospects seemed unlikely. Last night, with the southwest monsoon filling his one remaining sail, he had slipped the trawler between the Philippine islands of Palawan and Balabac, through the narrow Balabac Strait into the Sulu Sea. Other delta fishermen who had made this passage warned him that the southern coast of Palawan was infested with *mundo.* He must pass it with the utmost stealth, then turn northeast with the monsoon winds at his back and run as fast as he could for Puerto Princesa, far up the inside coast of Palawan. There was a Philippine naval station there, where his passengers could turn themselves in for temporary internment at a refugee camp until further passage to Manila and the United States could be arranged.

As dawn broke, with a high green island called San Lázaro dead abeam to the west, Captain Tho saw what he had dreaded throughout the voyage. Three small, speedy boats appeared through the break in the island's fringing reef and raced toward the *Happy Life,* their engines throwing rooster tails high in the red dawn light. Captain Tho checked to see that the carbine was loaded, with a round in the chamber. Then he hid it again beneath the straw mat beside the wheel. These would be the *mundo.*

Yet as the boats raced nearer, he felt a flicker of hope. The *mundo,* he'd been told, used what the Filipinos called pump boats, knife-hulled outriggers powered by big Japanese outboard engines. These boats looked more like military vessels. Their flat, wide hulls, on which he could see machine guns mounted forward of the gleaming glass windshields, were painted a dull dark green, the color of mangrove swamps, and all of them had long, whippy radio antennae. Perhaps this was a Philippine Navy patrol. Perhaps he wouldn't need the carbine.

As the sound of the boats reached the *Happy Life,* women and children awoke and scrambled on deck, lining the rail and chattering in high, tense voices. The men took their time appearing, trying to look brave and unconcerned, but Captain Tho could feel their fear as clearly as one feels heat from a bomb crater. They all kept glancing at him, there at the helm, and he tried to smile back reassuringly. The pregnant monkey at the masthead was screaming furiously.

Then the boats were alongside, idling down to take station astern and on either beam of the *Happy Life.* Some of the crewmen were dressed in navy-style fatigue uniforms, baseball caps, light blue shirts, dark blue dungarees. Others, though, had their heads wrapped in bandannas and were bare-chested or wearing dirty T-shirts with slogans written on them in *My,* the language of the long-noses. These men preferred greasy tan shorts or sarongs. All of them, regardless of dress, were heavily armed.

"Where are you bound?" A man on the boat to Captain Tho's right was speaking on a loud-hailer in Vietnamese.

"Puerto Princesa," he yelled back.

"What cargo?"

"Nothing. Just passengers and their personal effects."

"Heave to and stand by to be boarded. We must search your vessel."

Well, it was to be expected. Captain Tho put the helm over and luffed up into the wind. The *Happy Life* slowed and stopped. The boarding party scrambled over the rail. The man who had spoken on the loud-hailer came aboard and stood beside Captain Tho. He was a wide, thick, dark man with a face like a scarred slab of mahogany. A heavy pistol was holstered on his hip, but he bore no insignia on his fatigues. His eyes were an odd, flat green color, like that of the boats.

"Are you of the navy?" Captain Tho asked.

"You need not worry," the man said. He smiled with his mouth but not with his eyes. "A routine search, nothing more."

But it was a strange routine.

Down on the deck one of the searchers grabbed a chicken and yanked its head off. Then he threw the flapping body into the cockpit of the boat alongside, yelling something to those in the boat that made them laugh uproariously. One of them picked up the bird and pretended to copulate with it. They laughed even louder.

Another caught a pig after a brief chase and cut its throat with his bolo knife. The blood sprayed out over the women and children nearby, and they started to scream. The man raised his bolo, and they quieted. The pig lay bleeding into a bundle of clothes.

Other men were looting the passengers with easy efficiency, taking transistor radios, cook pots, items of clothing, wallets—whatever of value they could find. Trinh Van Suu, a trim, straight-backed old man who had been an ARVN colonel, stepped forward and remonstrated with one of the looters. His eyes flashed, as did the gold in his mouth. The looter drew a pistol and shot Colonel Trinh through the chest. Then he hammered the gold teeth from his mouth and pocketed them.

Looters were raping young women right there on deck. Children looked on, fascinated.

"You are not of the navy," Captain Tho said.

The wide man laughed.

Nguyen Tran Le, the banker from Cho Lon, waddled aft to the wheel, furious. He stopped just below Captain Tho.

"Traitor! Pirate! You betrayed us, you led us to these devil-bandits, you're in league with them! Deny it if you can!"

The monkey was screaming on the masthead.

"I deny it," Captain Tho said. The wide man laughed again.

Nguyen Tran Le had turned purple with rage. He fumbled under his shirt and drew out a small silver pistol. He pointed it, shaking, at Captain Tho, and the wide man ducked as the bullet whistled past. Nguyen Tran Le fired again.

Captain Tho pulled the carbine from under the mat and shot Nguyen Tran Le in the throat. The monkey screamed louder.

The rearmost fast boat suddenly shot forward and came up alongside. A *My* stood in the cockpit, a tall blond man turning gray, with the look of an officer about him. He wore a billed blue cap covered with gold leaf and a short-sleeved khaki shirt. Light glinted on odd, lozenge-shaped scars around his biceps.

"Goddamn it, Billy, what the fuck's all the shooting? I told you once, I told you a hundred times—fuckin' ammo don't grow on trees!"

"Not our shooting, Commodore," the wide man yelled back. "One of the passengers took a pop at the captain here, and the captain popped him back."

"Well, goddamn it—"

Just then the monkey let out a horrific scream. She squatted on the cross yard and crapped in her hand, then threw the handful at the *My* in the gold hat. It hit him on the shirtfront.

"Waste that monkey!"

The wide man drew his pistol and shot the monkey out of the crosstrees. She fell heavily onto the deck, still screaming. A tiny bloody monkey head popped out between her legs. The wide man shot her again.

Captain Tho fired the carbine from his hip. His bullet knocked the wide man's head sideways, and the captain saw the groove it had left along his cheek, blood dripping suddenly from the wide man's torn ear. The wide man shot him in the face. Then he emptied the pistol into Captain Tho's head.

The *My* in the fast boat threw up his hands in exasperation. He threw his hat on deck.

"All right then," he said. "Waste the fucking lot of them."

* * *

91

An hour later, and some twenty miles north of San Lázaro, Curt Hughes saw the smoke from the burning junk pall over the horizon. His dog stood on the cabin roof, growling toward the smoke. Curt wondered what it was. None of his business whatever. He was headed north toward Manila.

"Probably just those nasty pirates, Brillo," he said to the dog. "Don't get your bowels in an uproar."

Too damned hot around here, he thought. On his chart he circled San Lázaro in red pencil, then wrote beside it, "Bad news."

The *Seamark* ran north on the wind toward Manila.

THIRTEEN

In addition to *Venganza*'s deck log, Miranda kept a personal log of each day's major developments, along with her ongoing impressions and speculations. She'd developed this habit in her earliest days at sea, when she discovered that if they found her scribbling in a book during her off hours, her hornier shipmates would leave her alone. But journals are addictive, and even when she became master of her own vessel, she kept it up. She wrote in ink so she wouldn't be tempted by personal historical revisionism at some later date; she struck through her errors or those words she suddenly wanted to amend with a single line, ship's-log fashion, so that the original remained legible. She wrote in a long, green-covered logbook of the sort used by mariners for ages now, brass-bound at the corners and authoritative in its heft.

An excerpt:

> Underway 0620, Honolulu to Philippines, rhumb lines via Majuro in the Marshalls. Trades steady, NE to ENE; seas moderate. Having Effredio aboard is a great boon. Not only cuts the work- and watch-load by a third—more than a third, thanks to his energy—but gives me someone to talk to, a mooring line to my past. Says Curt has left Palawan—friends of Freddie's saw him briefly in Manila talking to some air force officer, other friends spotted *Seamark* later in Zamboanga, on Mindanao. Freddie sent his friend Padre Cotinho down there to watch him. Freddie's sister, who works for Pan Am in Manila, cut him a

free ticket to Honolulu, where he knew I must stop to replenish stores. Freddie well connected.

Shot noon sun—made good 48 miles since departure, solid 8½ knots—just before brief squall blew down from N. Reefed main and mizzen. *Venganza* heeled sharply to first gusts but kicked up her heels when I payed her off a point to leeward. Good seaboat. I love the sound of a wooden boat in a storm. She flexes like a strong man's dick. Rain felt good—collected 20 gallons in wooden casks from leech of sails. Next time we see one coming must remember to bring dirty wash topside and do some laundry. Hate a smelly seabag.

Dad still fit and clear-eyed following the Rum Bottle Test. Can't call him Dad anymore. He's a hand like any other. Will call him Culdee or Boats henceforth. He's been civil enough to Freddie so far but watches him like a seahawk. Checking him out. Saw him testing knots on Freddie's reef points when the rain hit, later watching the compass over Freddie's shoulder while he had the helm. Freddie knows what's up. Without looking back he said, "She keeks, Boats, don't she? Leetle beet, anyway." Culdee just grunted and went forward.

Checked caulking after the squall. No oakum spewed. Rance still hiding for fear of the Stranger. Saw his beady eyes peering at me from sea stores in the lazaret when I went forward to check for leaks. Warned Freddie not to kill him if he shows during his watch.

Shot evening stars—51 mi. made good since noon. At this rate we'll reach the P.I. in three weeks. (Don't count your landfalls before you raise them.)

Fresh mahimahi for the evening meal, the fish caught on trolling line by Freddie just as I was about to open a can of beef. A good omen?

Culdee's ghosts began to surface as they passed the entrance to Pearl Harbor. In the old days, when you cleared the dogleg at the inland end, the first thing you saw was the hulk of the old *Arizona* rising out of the dirty blue water. Now there was a museum there, he knew, shining white in the sunlight and dwarfing the sunken battlewagon. He didn't want to see it. Years ago he'd served in a destroyer with a mustang—an ex-gunner's mate elevated to officer grade by the war—who'd been in the *Arizona* back then. He'd been part of her company for eight years, since leaving boot camp. He was on leave, heading back to the States, when the Japs attacked on December 7, 1941. The ship that was taking him Stateside turned right around and steamed back.

Dan—that was the mustang's name—was a qualified navy hard-hat diver. He had to dive into the hull of his own dead ship. There were twelve hundred bodies in there, shipmates. "Some of them I knew when I found their bodies," Dan said one night on the mid-watch. "Some I didn't know. Some you really couldn't tell either way."

The images came back to Culdee when the *Venganza* shot past the entrance and broke toward the open sea—the darkness there in the ripped hull, weak light from waterproof lamps, and brighter stabs of light from the acetylene torches cutting through warped bulk-heads; fish darting in and out of the light; torn bodies floating, stuck like balloons to the overheads by the gas generated within them by death, some of the faces clear and recognizable—pale, slack-jawed, vaguely surprised by how easily it had taken them—others bitter at the knowledge, and others already eaten by fish; bits of old shipmates drifting here and there, arms sunk by the weight of a wristwatch, a Negro mess boy buried by the spill of blue-rimmed crockery that fell from the wardroom pantry shelves, and enginemen boiled the color of shrimp by the high-pressure steam of burst pipes. Dan had taken him clear through the *Arizona* that night, stem to stern, main deck to keelson, on the midwatch.

"After a while it wasn't so bad," Dan had said. "I'd pull one down off the overhead and say, 'Oh, yeah, that's Horns Gearhardt, whose old lady run off with the shoe clerk in Shit City.' Or, 'that's Old Chief Merriman, the practical joker,' and I'd remember the night we pulled liberty down in Tijuana and let the bulls loose from their pens behind the bullring up there on the hill and they charged down through T-town and chased all the whores ahead of them down the Avenida de la Revolución. But then I found my best buddy's head— Mike Powers, another gunner. How it got down there from the number one turret where he was a gun captain, don't ask me. It had rolled into a corner by the ruptured boiler. I couldn't send it topside with the rest of the body parts, not my best friend. I picked it up and put it into the boiler. As far as I know, it's down there still."

"Why'd you do that?" Culdee had asked after a while.

Dan laughed, briefly and bitterly. "I knew his immoral soul was for sure in hell. I guess I figured the boiler of a sunken battleship was the closest thing to that for the rest of him."

Sea stories. The old navy had a million of them.

FOURTEEN

~~~~~~~~~~~~~~~~~~~~~~~~

Curt tied off the Avon to a cleat at the head of the pier and walked toward the harbormaster's office. The wind was down and big, blue-black rain clouds were piling over the mountains to the east. He turned and looked out to the *Seamark,* where she rolled sluggishly at anchor. Will one hook be enough if it comes on to blow? Maybe he should run back out and drop the other anchor. But the holding ground seemed good—thick mud and sand. To hell with it. She looks nice out there in her new blue hull paint and yawl rig. Her new name shone in gold on the transom—*Sea Witch.* Memories of Miranda.

He could see the dog standing on the wheelhouse. Please release me, let me go. . . . It was the first night in port after the long run up from Palawan. But Curt didn't trust the harbormaster. He didn't trust the harbor. He surely didn't trust the Philippines. The whole place breathed a kind of ball-stomping menace—the heat, the tattered palms, shit and oil on the water, the dead-meat stink of flowers mixed with wood smoke and burning garbage and traffic exhaust. It's like Colombia all over again, or Panama, or Jamaica. Better to leave Brillo aboard to guard the boat. He might even get a chance to bite someone—his favorite sport.

There was a kid in the harbormaster's office, lying back in a rickety card chair and scratching his balls through his cutoff Levi's. He kept on scratching while he stared up blankly at Curt. It was as if Curt had walked into the boy's bedroom and caught him jacking off. He wasn't about to be interrupted.

"Can I use the phone?"

97

"Five peso," the kid said. He smiled wide. Filipinos smiled a lot.

Curt gave him five pee. He thumbed through the metro Manila phone book on the desk and dialed a number on a wall phone that looked as though it had been used to beat a carabao to death.

"Military Air Transport," said a chirpy voice that sounded almost American.

"Major Chalmers, please."

"Who calling Major Chalmer, please?"

"Tell him it's Mr. Curtis. Jim Curtis from, uh, Phisohex in Barranquilla."

"You call long distance, please?"

"No, I'm here in Manila, please."

"Just a moment, please?"

Curt flipped a Filipino Marlboro from the pack in his shirt pocket—awful smokes, they burned as hot and fast as a firecracker fuse. He lighted it with a nicked old Zippo, one of the chrome jobs that clanked when you snapped back the lid. The paint was nearly worn off the etching of a battleship on the lighter's front: the USS *Wisconsin* BB-64. It was an old lighter of Miranda's, or rather her dad's. Miranda was a good chick. Damn shame to fuck her over that way. Still, chicks are cheap.

"Mr. Curtis? Major Chalmer busy right now, please. He would call you soon. Where is your number?"

"How long will that be?"

"I'm sorry, please, we don't know already?"

Curt looked across the road. Beyond the whizzing traffic there was a neon sign on a low, tin-roofed stucco building: BE-BOP-A-LULA BAR & GRILL. He looked up the number in the phone book and gave it to the Please voice. He still wasn't sure whether it was a boy or a girl.

"Where is that, please?"

"Ermita, I think. Near the yacht basin there."

"Major Chalmer will call you certainly I think, Mr. Curtis, please."

The kid in the chair was still scratching. By now he'd gotten half a hard-on under the denim, fat as a Polish sausage. How's it comin', kid? Mostly by hand.

All the waitresses and most of the hookers in the Be-Bop-a-Lula Bar & Grill were wearing red jeans. Very tight red jeans. It was cool in the bar, dark and funky with the smell of stale beer and tropical dry rot, all blended by the big wood-bladed whap-whap fans on the ceiling. The bar was real wood, too—rich, dark, fine-grained wood with a lot of oil rubbed into it. Philippine mahogany, right? Right. The Filipino bartender had very square shoulders under a faggoty embroidered shirt and scars like thick white worms around his eyes, the kind of scars fighters or kick-boxers get. His grin was about as wide as his shoulders.

"What'll it be, Joe?"

"I'm new in town. What's your good beer?"

"San Mig. Made right here in Manila-by-da-Sea. MacArthur's old brewery, hey? San Miguel. Old Dugout Doug. He mighty rich guy."

"Gimme a San Mig, then." Curt looked at the glasses standing upside down on a shelf behind the bar. A cockroach about the size of a Havana cigar was crawling over them. "No glass."

But it was good beer, all right. Curt nodded his approval to the bartender.

"How's come all the ladies are wearing red pants?"

"From da song, Joe. You know da song?" He sang it in a wobbly falsetto, grinning. " 'She da gal in da red blue jeans, Be-bop-a-lula she ma queen.' Someting like dat."

"Yeah, sure, I can dig it. They work for the bar. But what about the ones in skirts?"

The bartender laughed. "You try one in skirts, Joe, you find out quick enough."

He spun away like a *karateka*—pow pow kick pow—and battled his way down the duckboards laughing.

It was a challenge.

Curt sipped his beer and sized up the girls. Cute, the lot of them—some in a darkish, peppery Mexican way, some longer-boned and darker still, with a hint of Africa in their frizzy hair, others delicate, hollow-boned like birds, almost flat-chested but not quite— tiger-eyed Asia in babydoll faces. Buy me one of those, Mommy.

He nodded to one in a slinky black dragon-lady skirt. She smiled, tiger-eyed, sultry, and snaked her way to the barstool with a fanny waggle that was bound to leave her in a wheelchair with lumbar arthritis by the time she reached twenty.

"Hi, Joe," she said in a throaty voice. Eyes up from under, lashes like spider legs—what you'd find in a load of bananas. "You wanna good time? Buy me a drink."

"What's your name?"

"Carlotta, but you can call me Lotta." She leaned back and licked her lips, slow and juicy, eyes locked with Curt's. "Lotta *Tung*. I'm Eurasian girl, you know?"

Curt laughed and bought her a drink—bar Coke and two ice cubes, eighty pee. That was four bucks American, twice as much as the San Mig. Ah, well. He gave her a Marlboro and lighted it with Miranda's dad's Zippo. She dragged deep, leaned back again, and started blowing smoke rings—red lips, wet tongue, perfect circles. The famous Tung Sisters. You find them in every bar, all over the world.

"Hey, Joe, you wanna dance? Come on, let's dance."

They went over to the jukebox in the far, dark corner. It was an old Wurlitzer, like from the fall of Corregidor, all pulsing pastel lights, throbbing round curves. Curt handed Lotta a fistful of change and leaned over her shoulder while she made her selections. Bent over, she pushed back against him and worked a slow, hot, silky fanny waggle against his crotch. The juke was a time machine—a monument to the fifties—Buddy Holly, Little Richard, Jerry Lee Lewis, the Platters, Dion and the Belmonts, Ritchie Valens, the Chantels. Lotta picked something slow—Patsy Cline, "I Love You So Much It Hurts Me." She turned and smiled. "Or, 'Who Put the Sand in the Vaseline?' " Lotta laughed . . .

They danced in the dark corner, belly to belly. Or rather, Curt's dick against Lotta's belly—she was tall for a Filipina, but still pretty short. In the light of the jukebox her lipstick looked almost black. She stared up at him breathing hard, moaning, doing her tongue number. She picked the wrong song, Curt thought. Sheb Wooley's "Purple People Eater" would have been more like it. It was all so false, it was almost true. He wanted to laugh and get out of there, but his dick'd been at sea too long, it had a mind of its own.

He glommed Lotta Tung's left tit. A falsie! Wait a minute—Asian girls are notorious for that. Titless wonders, but they make up for it in other respects. He slid the hand down over her butt. Real enough at that end. She was breathing harder, panting—another minute and she'd hyperventilate, or die of terminal dry throat. Curt grabbed at her pussy. She pulled away with a gasp before he could touch her.

"Hey, Joe, no! We go back here." She pulled him toward a doorway beside the juke. "I'm *hot!* I suck you off, right?"

Curt pulled back on her hand, slammed her against the juke. He socked his hand between her legs.

Jesus Christ! There was a cock and balls under the dragon-lady skirt!

"Tah-*dah!*" A spotlight from the bar flashed on the two of them. The bartender was laughing his ass off. Everyone in the bar was looking and laughing—GIs, airmen, hookers, B-girls, sailors, Flips in business suits and those faggy embroidered shirts. . . . Lotta Tung was laughing, too, in a much deeper voice than before. In the light it was easy to see she was a guy—five-o'clock shadow on the upper lip, a frigging tent pole under the skirt.

"I tole you, Joe!" the bartender yelled. "Da ones in da skirts, hey? Dat's da famous Pilipino Benny boys, Joe! Welcome to Manila, where da sun never sets and da cock always crows!"

Curt blasted out of there in a hurry.

It was dark now and raining like a bastard—the rain of the thousand fire hoses. Curt had been soaked in it from Haiti to Hawaii. It falleth on the just and the unjust alike, he mused, absolving all sins, cooling all passions. He danced in place, soaked and laughing. The traffic roared past unbroken, throwing oil spray as high as the Be-Bop's thundering roof. Then a car peeled out of the mainstream and splashed to a halt in front of him. A white man's face leaned out the back window. It was Phil Chalmers.

"Pile in!"

Curt piled. Chalmers yelled something to the driver, and they hydroplaned back out into a sea of spume and blaring horns.

"Goddamn it, Curt, don't ever call me at the office." Phil was pissed. *"Ever!"*

"Good to see you, too, old buddy."

"Well, goddamn it, I mean it. There's CIA all over the place. And other initials, too. You shoulda—"

"The only address I had for you was MATS," Curt said. He was whispering, but there was no need to. The driver had the tape deck on full blast—sounded like Jan and Dean's "Deadman's Curve." Appropriate.

Curt pulled out his Marlboros. Brown slush. Chalmers gave him a Benson & Hedges and a light from his gold Ronson. Just like downtown. They both cooled off.

"Where we going?"

"A little place up the way a bit."

It was a dark, loud little place on a dark, quiet street, full of diddy-bopping Filipinos. But Chalmers found a booth in the back where they could talk. They ordered a couple of beers—Chalmers drank 33, smuggled in from Ho Chi Minh City, he said. He was hooked on the formaldehyde, he added, kept him youthful. Curt stuck with San Miguel.

"Whatta ya got?" Curt asked.

"Not much," Chalmers replied. "It's tight as a spinster's pussy right now, has been for the past year or more. Worse than it ever was in Panama. Not just the drug guys, either. Actually DEA's a minor nuisance since Marcos left. The whole place is crawling with spooks—round-eyes, Chi Coms, even some Japanese. There's a spook under every toilet seat, under every manhole cover. They're scared of a Commie takeover. Dominoes again. The same old paranoia—who knows? They could be right. Aquino's weak. The government's full of the same brand of crooks that ran it under

Marcos. Only the names have changed. Trouble is, nobody knows which way to jump just yet. There's a million deals being cut every minute, and another million welshed on. The bottom line is, with all the spooks in the country, you can't get anything in or out. Certainly not from Manila."

"Well," Curt said, "looks like I came a long way for nothing."

"Looks like you did, pal."

"You said Manila. Anyplace else where it's looser?"

"I don't know," Chalmers said. He sucked on his 33. When he belched, it smelled like a funeral parlor. "Taiwan, maybe. Bangkok? Hong Kong? Singapore? I just don't know, I've been keeping my nose clean for so long now."

"I mean in the Philippines. There's a lot of islands in the PI. More than they got spooks to cover each one of them."

"Don't count on it," Chalmers said. "What kind of boat you got?"

"Small yawl with a kicker, not much for fast. Seven knots tops. But it's beamy. I could carry a lot, and nobody's gonna mess with a mere sailboat."

"Oh yeah? I'd sell it and buy a Pan Am ticket Stateside," Chalmers said. "Cut your losses."

"No way. I'm on everyone's computer by now."

"You got a problem, all right." Chalmers sucked down the last of his beer and socked the bottle down on the table. It sounded final. His eyes were remote, a man listening to a disaster report from a minor-league country. "I just can't help you at the moment, Curt. Maybe Bangkok, I don't know . . ." His voice trailed off, and he started to stand up.

"Hey Phil," Curt said quietly. "Remember Colón? Remember Port-au-Prince? I made you a lot of money, *pal.*" He didn't want to say the obvious: he could blow a whistle on Chalmers that would be heard clear back to the Pentagon. "We had some good times."

Chalmers sat back down and signaled the waitress for more beers.

"Yeah," he said wearily. "Good times. Okay. This is just hearsay, let me warn you, but I've been getting stuff on a guy down south of Palawan. Round-eye, calls himself Commodore Millikan. He's supposed to have his own private navy of fast boats down there and run a lot of stuff out of Thailand. He's got the *mundo*—the pirates—" Chalmers winced at the word—how hokey can you get? "He's got them eating out of his hand. I don't know what this is—Millikan is what they call any American down there, like Joe up here—but it smells kind of strange to me. Maybe a DEA scam, maybe Langley, or the mob, I don't know."

"That would count me out."

"Not necessarily. They take all kinds in that church nowadays. And you're good in a fast boat. I can vouch for that."

"So what do I do?"

"I've done business with one of his people, his CEO I guess you'd call him. Strictly on the up-and-up. They've got a shipping line down that way as a kind of front. Millikan Shipping. The exec's name is Torres, Billy Torres. He's got an office in Zambo City—that's Zamboanga, nice town, on Mindanao. Sometimes he's there, sometimes he's out at Millikan's private island south of Palawan. I gotta call him tomorrow anyway on some machinery he's got coming in from the States. I'll make an appointment for you."

"Fine," Curt said.

"How long will it take you to get down there?" Chalmers asked.

"I guess a week or ten days."

"I'll ask Torres to look you over, or one of his people. I'll give you a good introduction. That's really all I can do, pal. Right now, anyway . . . no, no, I'll buy the beers. You need any money? I'm about tapped out, but I could spare you a couple a thousand pee. Just don't stop along the way to rescue any drowning dogs. You read about that in the papers? Guy uses his dog as bait to rip off tourist boats. These Flips have got initiative, all right."

"That was me," Curt said. "Me and my dog, Brillo."

Chalmers stood up, half-laughing. He checked his watch—a Rolex, the platinum one. He peeled off some pesos from a wad in his pocket. He was shaking his head in admiration. True or bullshit? Then he remembered the dog from Colón.

"I should've known. That dog of yours. Good times, all right. Now listen, let me know what's happening. Don't be a stranger." He headed for the door. "Keep in touch. Take care. Have a nice day." Then his eyes went scared for a moment. *"But don't call me at the office."*

"Hey, Phil, what's the name of that island down there, the one near Palawan?"

"San Lázaro," Chalmers said.

FIFTEEN

~~~~~~~~~~~~~~~~

From Miranda's log:

Better than halfway there now. Still making good time, nearly 200 miles a day, but the wind's suddenly shifted to the SE. Some glitch in the trades, I guess, maybe El Niño's doing, who knows? If it continues this way, we might make better time by heading up to Wake Island for a midpoint landfall rather than proceeding to Majuro in the Marshalls. Suggested that to Freddie and Culdee this afternoon. "Whatever you think, Skipper," Freddie said. Culdee disagreed. "If we head NW at this point, we'll probably pick up the NE trades when we're only partway there. Better stick to your original plot. Anyway, Wake sucks. Nothing but thornbushes and coral. No fresh water there except what they ferry in. No fresh fruit. Just fucking navy types who'll treat us like spies."

Makes sense. We're holding our track for Majuro. Odd, though, how Culdee loves the navy and hates it at the same time. Usually he can't say a good word about anything but the navy—the old navy he knew, I guess—and certainly nothing good about civilians. What does he figure he is if not one or the other? Just some Flying Dutchman, I suppose. No, Flying Irishman is more like it. The apostate heir of Saint Brendan, maybe. Culdees were unordained priests of the old Scotch-Irish Church, I read somewhere. After the Vikings invaded Ireland, many of them sailed off to Iceland, and some disappeared to the West. Maybe they reached America?

106

* * *

Flying west to Japan many years ago, Culdee's plane—a prop-driven Boeing Constellation—had put down at Wake Island to refuel. Culdee was on his way to join a new ship in Yokosuka. He'd read about Wake's valiant defense in the early days of the war, seen the movie four or five times—big Bill Bendix skewering cowardly Japs on his bayonet, tough marines in World War I tin-pot helmets and puttees, courageous civilians grabbing up old Springfield bolt-action rifles to do their bit. Culdee was only seven or eight years old when he read that series in *The Saturday Evening Post*, "The Last Man off Wake Island." It and the movie brought the war alive for him for the first time, thrilling, horrifying, the most exciting thing imaginable to a small, immortal boy. Now here he was, a jaded, salty young white hat with his own war wounds still red from Korea, about to land on Wake a full fourteen years after it had fallen. He was as excited as ever.

From the air, as the Connie swept in to land, Wake looked scruffy—no waving palms trees, just dusty desert scrub and huge masses of bone-white coral rubble. Surf crashed high on the windward reefs, turning the brilliant blue of the lagoon to a milky green. The rusty bow of a sunken Japanese maru stuck from the shallows near the boat channel like so many red bones. Be interesting to dive from that hull, good spearfishing in wrecks. There was no air-conditioning in the bar adjacent to the airstrip, just slow old ceiling fans stirring the hot, humid salty-tasting air. The Connie's passengers bellied up to the bar. At least the beer was cold. One of the passengers, a civilian hard hat enroute to a job at Atsugi Airfield in Japan, wiped his sweating forehead and chugged down can after can of Blatz.

"Never thought I'd live to see this fuckin' rathole again," he told Culdee.

"You been here before?"

"Here when the fuckin' Japs took the island."

"Navy or Corps?"

"Neither. I was driving a Cat on a government contract. Straight up and down civilian, this fella." He ordered two more beers and slid one to Culdee.

"You guys fought alongside the jarheads, didn't you?"

"Fuck," the hard hat said, and laughed bitterly. "Hell no! We hid out in the puckerbrush, most of us. Lived on land crabs and rainwater while those jerks tried to hold off the whole fuckin' Jap Navy."

"But some of the civilians fought, didn't they?"

"Just the stupes. Got killed for it, too. Ten in the first Jap air raid on December eighth—same day as Pearl Harbor, but we're across the date line here. Then fifty-five more when the Japs bombed the hospital the next day. There were about twelve hundred civilians on the island when it started. Only about a dozen, maybe fifteen, were nutso enough to work during the fighting. Mainly PanAm mechanics who helped with the marine Wildcats while they lasted. Some of them joined the gun crews, too."

"Didn't they sink some Jap ships, those guns?"

"Sank a destroyer I heard, shot up a couple or three more. A leatherneck pilot sank another destroyer. But that just made the Japs madder. They went away and regrouped. That was on the eleventh. Ten days later they came back and kicked ass."

He flagged down two more beers. Culdee was about to refuse his, or at least insist on paying for them. This civilian wasn't telling him what he wanted to hear. Then he thought, fuck it. If he's fool enough to buy them . . .

"Our so-called government had no right to keep us there," the hard hat said. "No right to have hired us for that job in the first place. Don't tell me Rooz-veld and those Yid advisers of his didn't know what the Japs were up to. They just wanted to get the U.S. into the war and save their Jew-boy relatives in Europe from Hitler's soap works. Needed a couple of sacrificial lambs to get America fighting mad, to shut up the isolationists. So they gave the Nips Pearl, Wake, the whole fuckin' Philippines to boot."

"So what happened when the Japs came back?" Culdee asked. He couldn't look at the man now.

"Shit happened," the hard hat said. "After they'd pounded us flat with dive-bombers and cruiser guns, they sent a couple a thousand Jap marines ashore—big guys, mean as hell, the Maizuru Second Special Naval Landing Force. The marines killed a bunch of them on Wilkes Island, where I was hiding out, just across the boat channel from Wake proper. But the Japs kept coming. Wave after wave. Even when one of the guns on the airstrip hammered a transport and set it on fire, the troops still came ashore. They killed all the fighters on Wake, then rounded up the rest of us. Tied us up with wire. They were pissed that there were no women to fuck on the island. So they took it out on us—boots, rifle butts, whips made of bob wire."

"I don't believe Washington set you guys up as sacrifices," Culdee said at last. "Just doesn't make sense. Lose those places on purpose and then have to fight for four years just to get 'em back?"

"Bullshit!" the hard hat yelled. "It was a setup! Hell, the navy had a relief force under way from Pearl—carriers, cruisers, oilers, destroyers, the works. Then at the last minute the brass in Honolulu called them back. They were just over the fuckin' horizon all that time. We'd even sent a message—'issue in doubt.' One air strike might have turned it. But they called them back. Rooz-veld and them." He shook his head and spit between his boots.

"So what happened then?"

"You don't wanna know, kid. Just pray you're never a prisoner of war. Not a prisoner of the slopes, anyways. But we got Uncle Sugar back for it, after the war. Those of us who survived the camps, that is. About twelve of us—civilian working stiffs—we sued the contractor who'd hired us for half a million in back pay and fuckin' damages." He cackled happily at the memory. "We had 'em by the balls, and they had to cough up."

"How much you get—I mean, you personally?"

"Not a fuckin' lot, after the lawyers' bite was took out of it. About enough to buy a little cracker-box house in Levittown, out on Long Island. But then my old lady divorced me and got the house. So here I am again, a working stiff for Uncle Sugar."

About then their flight was called. As they shuffled to the door of the bar, a marine who'd been listening caught Culdee's eye. He was a real jarhead, this one, with a shaved skull like Yul Brynner in the movies and gunny-sergeant stripes on his khakis. The gunny nodded toward the hard hat's back. Culdee nodded back. When they got out the door, the marine shouldered the hard hat around the corner, and Culdee grabbed his arms. They hustled him behind the Quonsets and took turns pounding him. They left him unconscious and bleeding into the coral dust.

"Where's Mr. Krieger?" a flight attendant asked, counting noses before takeoff.

"His orders got changed," the gunny said. "His company needed him there on Wake." They took off.

Later, in his own POW days and often afterward, Culdee thought of the hard hat and what he'd said—government setups, sacrificial lambs. Now, as the *Venganza* left Wake squatting scruffily in the sea far to the northwest, he thought of it again. Turner and the abortive break at Brigadune. The shit the navy'd dropped on him when he got out later. Maybe the whole thing had been a setup—a North Vietnamese massacre of brave American sailors, unarmed and subject to torture as POWs, just at the time when the new isolationists—the long-haired antiwar protesters—were about to turn all of America chicken. By God, they had, hadn't they?

Suddenly he wanted a drink, wanted one bad. Instead, he threw knots, faster and faster, deep into the night. There on Wake, he thought, that was the first time I ever fought side by side with a jarhead, not against him. And the last.

Freddie, at the helm, heard Culdee laughing up on the hatch cover, under the stars. Crazy old coot, he thought, and laughed along with him, not knowing why.

SIXTEEN

~~~~~~~~~~~~~~~~~~

GOD IS MY COPILOT read the plaque above the jeepney driver's head. Let's hope so, Curt thought. He was hanging white-knuckled from the overhead grip as the vehicle careened north from Pershing Square, quadruple horns blaring, bald tires screeching, narrowly missing trishaws, carabao, bicycles, pedestrians, free-ranging chickens, and what seemed like a million other equally suicidal jeepneys. A tape deck in the dash was blasting "My Little Deuce Coupe." Curt leaned forward and yelled—shrieked—to the driver to stop at Pasonanca Park.

"You got it, Joe!" The driver turned to grin—a wild golden glare—and sawed the wheel's necker knob blindly. Curt slammed his eyes shut and gulped hard. Judging by the clench of his butt muscles, the pucker factor must have been well off the scale.

By the time the jeepney squealed to a halt, Curt's knees were guava jelly. He reeled like a drunk as he grubbed through a wad of pesos from his pocket. He peeled off the fare and noticed that the big chrome stallion on the jeepney's hood was literally prancing in place, eager to be off again. Puffs of steam spurted from its nostrils. But it was just engine knock and a chronically overheated radiator. The driver grinned his double-wide thanks and burned rubber back out into the traffic without checking his side mirror. Horns blared louder for an instant, then muted to the incessant din that shivered every Filipino thoroughfare every moment of every day and night, lacquered steel roosters crowing from dawn to unconsciousness. The charm of the islands.

It was quieter in the park, though, cool beneath the banyan trees, with bougainvilleas in perennial flame and the smell of blossoms thick on the silky air. Little kids of all colors splashed happily in the self-proclaimed wee-wee pool. Zamboanga was a fragrant city.

"Psst, hey Milikan!" At first Curt thought the kid in the bushes was calling someone else, and he looked around. Then he remembered what Chalmers had said—*Milikan* means American down here. The kid stepped out, looked around furtively, then flashed a small cardboard container. REGULAR GUY INDUSTRIAL-STRENGTH SUPPOSITORIES, it said on the box. What was this? The kid opened the box and shook out the ends of four thick hand-rolled cigarettes.

"Zambo Zowie," he whispered. "You like? Only a hundred peso apiece."

Zambo Zowie, Curt thought. Bombers at five bucks each. They ought to grow some potent grass in this climate. He hadn't smoked in a long time—when you're in the business, it isn't a good idea to enjoy the product—but out of professional curiosity he took one and sniffed it.

"What the fuck is this, cloves?"

"No, man," the kid said, "Zambo Zowie. Big bruddah to Maui Wowie, daddy to Matanuska Thunderfuck."

"That's cloves, kid. And I don't have a toothache. But keep up the good work."

He tousled the boy's hair and walked on. Then he heard a click—switchblade?—but it was just an old priest taking his picture. The kid straggled along after him, at a distance. Curt waited at the crosswalk while a caravan of Philippine Army deuce-and-a-halfs rolled past, the soldiers leaning bored on their M16s on the plank seats in the beds. Then he crossed over to the Zamboanga Plaza Hotel.

Plenty of time in hand for the appointment. The barter market on the hotel grounds was open, and he strolled slowly through its clamor. Wheeler-dealers gabbled in every tongue known to East Asia. Smuggling had always been a way of life on the Sulu Sea, the glue that bound Mindanao and the southern Philippines to nearby Borneo, Sabah, and Sarawak more tightly even than Islam. For a long time the Manila government fought against the smuggling, then realized it was hopeless and recently had legitimized the barter markets. There was another one, even bigger, down by the Hotel Lantanka, near the docks where Curt's boat was moored. You could trade anything there, from pigs and poultry and rare Gloria Maris seashells through antique Moro brasswork and Chinese porcelain to Volvo Penta engine parts, Mitsubishi air conditioners, and Thai opium. Provided you greased the right palms.

Curt bought a bowl of the spicy noodles called *sotanghon* from a vendor, then sat on a bench in the shade and washed them down with cold beer. He flirted briefly with a pretty Moro girl, until her father, or maybe it was her husband, gave him a dirty look and shifted his bolo higher on his hip. A church bell pealed from a distant tower. Four o'clock.

"Captain Hughes?" A short, wide-shouldered Filipino in white duck trousers and a long, loose barong tagalog shirt smiled as he rose from a couch in the lobby and stuck out a hand. "I'm Billy Torres. It's crowded in here. Shall we go out to the pelota court? Or would you prefer the casino? It's quite a good one—air-conditioned and strictly legitimate."

Curt glanced around the lobby. There were perhaps half a dozen people in what looked like a parquet-floored acre, listlessly reading the Zambo *Times* and sipping beer or coffee.

"I'm no gambler," he said.

"Then we'll just watch the jai alai," Torres said, and they headed out the door. Torres had a long red scar across his cheek and a piece of his ear missing. The stitches still showed. His eyes were flat and green, odd in a Filipino.

Two of the men in the lobby got up and followed at a distance. Big Filipinos, all muscle and a yard wide.

"Yours?" he asked Torres, nodding back at the followers.

"I'm no gambler either, Captain," Torres said. He smiled up at Curt and took his arm at the elbow, as if they were on a date.

The bellow of the jai-alai crowd, louder even than the traffic or the barter market, hit them as they entered. Great fistfuls of pesos changed hand with every smack of the ball on the backboard. The bodyguards pushed ahead and cleared space at the top of the stands. Billy Torres sat on Curt's right, a bodyguard on his left. The other one stood spraddle-legged behind them, watching the crowd.

"Major Chalmers tells me you're fluent in Spanish," Torres said. "It's better we talk English here. Most Zamboangans speak Chabakano, a kind of bastardized Castilian without the grammar and mixed up with maybe half a dozen other dialects, but they can follow Spanish without any trouble."

"Your English is very good."

"I was born and educated in Manila," Torres said. "And I served for many years in the U.S. Navy." He shook a cigarette from a pack and offered it to Curt.

"What is that, cloves or something?"

"Kretek cigarettes, from Djakarta," Torres said, laughing apologetically. "Yes, cloves. You get quite fond of them."

"Some kid in the park just tried to sell me some as marijuana. Five bucks apiece."

"The ripoff is the great folk art of these islands, perhaps of all Asia. 'Here lies a fool who tried to hustle the East.' "

Curt laughed politely.

"You didn't bring your dog with you today, did you?" Torres sounded almost playful.

"Chalmers tell you about that?"

"Please." Torres turned sideways on the bench and looked straight into Curt's eyes. That was the most disconcerting thing about Filipinos. Curt had noticed it everywhere. They watched you so closely while you were talking, sometimes even moving their lips as if they were ventriloquists speaking your lines for you. You could feel them inside your mind, poking around in there. Comfortably. Without a condom. It was a kind of supreme other-directedness, the exact opposite of Western individualism, and it sucked at the soul so that you could not tell them a convincing lie. Malays call this quality *lata,* and all of them possessed it to one degree or another. Torres had plenty of it.

114

"Back on the boat," Curt said at last. "He doesn't travel well on the beach. I can't take him anywhere."

Torres laughed and broke eye contact.

"That was a nice little business you had going off Palawan. Why did you give it up?"

"It was getting a bit old. You can't work the same scam too often in the same place, and besides, I only did it to get a few bucks ahead. Enough to get me up to Manila and see Phil Chalmers."

"And why did you come here in the first place—to the Philippines?"

"Well, I was heading farther west, actually. I have some friends in Bangkok"—a bald-faced lie, but Torres wasn't watching—"and I'd missed out on the great cut-rate cultural tours of Southeast Asia our government offered its young folks back in the sixties and early seventies. Wanted to mesh gears with my peers, you might say."

Torres chuckled, then bit it off. "You know that your little *scam* as you call it was conducted in another firm's sphere of influence? You seem like a bright young fellow. Didn't it occur to you that by drawing attention to the area through the newspapers, you might force the government to send its navy in after you—start it poking around in the South Sulu? Screw things up for others who might have bigger fish to fry?"

"Well, actually . . ."

"I'm a partner in that firm, *Captain* Hughes. Frankly, we were very cross with you. We sent out boats to look for you. There are fortunes at stake here that go beyond petty piracy. If we'd found you, you wouldn't have been eating *sotanghon* and chatting with baby-faced dope peddlers in the park today. Fortunately for us, your friend Major Chalmers happened to call." He said something sharp and guttural to the bodyguard at the top of the stands.

Curt felt his scrotum shrink.

"It's about forty feet from the top of this grandstand to the pavement below," Torres said. "Be a damn shame if you slipped and fell."

115

"Look, I didn't know," Curt said. "How could I know there was something else going on down there? I never been here before."

"Well, then, you're dumber than you seem," Torres replied. "But fortunately for you, you have other talents. Chalmers said you're a good man in a fast boat. I checked on that. You're well known to certain parties back in the States. You seem to have compiled an impressive offshore racing record, in Cigarettes and Apaches and suchlike, on the Bimini-to-Florida run. A lot of our firm's business requires swift movement of men and materials from port to port. We deal in perishables."

"You're offering me a job?"

"On a probationary basis."

"Pay?"

"One percent of the cargo value on every successful run. Your room and board will be taken care of."

"Benefits?"

Torres laughed, slapped Curt on the knee. "An excellent health plan for a man in your enfeebled condition. No physical required. And the best life insurance you could ask for in the Sulu Sea."

"Okay," Curt said. "When do I start?"

"You could sell your boat—we'll handle that for you—and start today."

"I'd rather hold on to the boat. In case the economy turns down, and anyway, it's got sentimental value."

"Up to you. Do you know San Lázaro? It's on the charts—about two or three days' sail southwest of Jolo, call it five days from here. I'll provide you with a crew—Tausuqs, good sailors, nominally Moros but faithful employees of our firm. They'll keep you clear of the minor-league *mundo* along the way. You'll need an advance to top off your fuel and replenish sea stores." He thumbed an inch of hundred-peso notes off a stack handed him by one of the bodyguards and passed them to Curt. "You ought to realize, of course, that if our board chairman, Commodore Millikan, doesn't approve of you, the

116

deal's off. But he usually trusts me on these things. See you next week."

The three of them pushed down through the milling crowds, with the bodyguards running interference. Curt slipped the money uncounted into his pocket.

San Lázaro bound . . .

SEVENTEEN

〜〜〜〜〜〜〜〜〜〜〜

From Miranda's log:

    Put into Majuro today—a gunkhole in the true sense of the word—just long enough to top off fuel and water. While Culdee and I did that, Freddie found a phone and tried to raise Padre Cotinho in Zamboanga. Took him half an hour to get through; Padre not there. Had moved on shadowing Curt to some small island group in the SW Sulu Sea—Efemerales, he said, major island, San Lázaro. (Will look for it on the chart tomorrow.) Freddie gave Zambo contact our ETA Philippines. Someone will meet us in Surigao Strait or beyond with latest word on Curt's track.

    Refueled and watered alongside public dock in Majuro's Old Port—a graveyard of unemployed tankers. Depressing, all those dead ships, all those sailors on the beach. Culdee seemed delighted. "Those bastards will run you down at night," he said. "They don't bother to post a lookout, or if they do, he's probably stoned and freaking to the rock beat on his headset. They're not ships, they're oil spills packed in giant sardine cans just waiting to happen. I hope they turn all of 'em into razor blades." What about the sailors? "They're not sailors, they're union members. The only sailors are in small boats like this, or the navy. And there's not many left in the navy, either." Some old song. So much for pity.

    Cast off last line at 1642, motored out of harbor into stiff onshore winds. Hate to burn fuel but glad to be clear. *Venganza* smells foul—there's an oily bathtub ring around her waterline—opened all hatches and aired her out as soon as we made sail. Food prices in the supermarket outrageous, but we bought some fresh fruit from a bumboat—bananas (red and yellow), guavas, papaya, lemons, grapefruit the size of cannonballs. Also a big slab of turtle steak, so fresh it was still twitching.

Wind almost due E tonight. We're angling back up to 10°N lat., dodging atolls along the way. Among them Bikini—bomb tests, partial freedom for the female mammae—Eniwetok and Kwajalein, where Culdee says you'd better not even get onto their radar scopes or the navy will blow you out of the water. Still some top-secret shit going down out there. Once we get to 10°N, it'll be latitude sailing the rest of the way to Surigao Strait.

Freddie seems very relaxed and happy tonight—loose-jointed, almost slack at the hips, grinning a lot. Probably got laid in Majuro. There's teenage hookers all over the place, some of them in cribs that look like chicken coops, others balling their johns in the rubbish-filled ditch behind the shopping center parking lot. All clapped up as hell, no doubt. Hope Freddie didn't get the drips. Ah, youth, said the old whore with the heart of gold.

Relieved Freddie at the helm shortly before midnight, and he swaggered below, humming some sugary ditty in Filipino. When my eyes adjusted to the night, I saw Culdee hunkered in his blanket up on the main hatch cover. He was throwing knots and staring steadily southward. "What do you see down there?" He didn't bother to look around. "That's where the Fat Lady died," he said at last. The Fat Lady? Probably one of his old girl friends.

The *Fat Lady* was a bimbo all right, but a tough one. Wake Island's ghosts were fading as the *Venganza* moved west, their signals breaking up, garbling, growing dimmer and dimmer with each noon sun line. Now Culdee heard other ghosts calling, from far to the southwest. He knew their voices from of old. They were the dead men of the U.S.S. *Neosho*, an ugly, ungainly fleet oiler whose nickname in the prewar Pacific Fleet was the Fat Lady.

Culdee's great mentor in his younger days had been a warrant boatswain named Will Boyne. They'd served together in three ships, from Korea on up until Boyne's retirement just before the Vietnam buildup. They'd pulled countless wild liberties together over the years, and even more midwatches. Boyne had been in the old *Neosho*. (In Culdee's time there was a new *Neosho*, but she had no legend; when a sailor mentions the old *Whatever-She-Was*, you can be sure a sea story's in the offing.) Boyne was in her from Pearl Harbor to the Coral Sea. It was there that the *Fat Lady* died.

"We'd been lucky at Pearl," Boyne told him one night. "We'd just finished pumping avgas and tied up starboard side to, heading seaward, at the head of Battleship Row, when the first Jap wave came in. Kates and Vals—torpedoes and bombs. We were out of there before they could hit us. That was the end of our luck. Early the next May we were down in the Coral Sea, south of the Solomons and east of the Aussie coast as part of Fletcher's Task Force 17. Once again we'd just finished fueling, and Fletcher detached us to keep us out of harm's way. The Japs were hunting his carriers but hadn't found them yet. They found us instead.

"That was the next day, the seventh of May. We had a single can for escort, the *Sims*. A Jap scout plane spotted us just after morning chow. At first they sent over high-level bombers—three waves of them. But their bombs fell wide. Then came the Vals—a whole skyful of dive-bombers. That was about noon. They clobbered the *Sims* on the first pass, three direct hits with five-hundred-pounders. Broke her back. She started going down stern first, and when the water hit the top of her stack, she just went kaboom. Jumped ten, twenty feet out of the water. There were parts of guys all over the place. Only fifteen survivors.

"Meanwhile about twenty Vals hit us. I saw in the action report later that they scored seven direct hits and eight near-misses, but nobody I knew was counting. One of the Vals—maybe a suicider, even that early in the war—plowed right into the number four gun mount on the port side, killed all the guys there and hosed burning gas down the deck where they were treating the wounded. The CO passed the word, 'Make all preparations to abandon ship.' Some people thought he just said 'Abandon.' They started dumping life rafts over the side, even lowered two whaleboats from the davits before they were stopped. But plenty of men had already gone over the side. After what they'd seen happen to the *Sims,* they didn't want to be on the *Fat Lady* when she blew. They climbed into the rafts and watched.

"We'd pumped out the day before, fueling the task force, and we wouldn't sink—we couldn't sink. A lot of us wished we could. The Japs kept coming in, again and again, and when their bombs were gone, they strafed us—dead in the water. That was terror. A talker on the bridge got so petrified he kept the button pressed on his sound-powered phones, and we could hear him babbling up there, praying, telling how the XO was burning to death right there on the bridge, a Jap tracer had set fire to the kapok in his life jacket, and he was burning up there. I was the talker on the five-inch mount. There was a big-bellied, tough old first-class in the gun crew who'd been telling us all along what chicken-shits we were and how brave he was. After about the third or fourth strafing run he broke and dived under the gun mount. But because of his big gut, he was crammed in there pretty tight. When we trained the mount around to track the next target, the gun-platform ground him to bellyburger.

"Most of our people took it pretty well, though. During a lull in the bomber passes, some gunner up on another mount started a carnival spiel. 'Oh, come, come, come in and see the *Fat Lady!* See her quiv-v-v-er as she laughs. See her boobies bobble like washtubs. Count her double chins! Come one, come all! Come in and see the *Fat Lady!* Bring the missus.' Some guys were actually laughing. It gets that way.

"Then the Japs went home. We drifted for four days, patching up the wounded, burying the dead. The men and the life rafts that had gone over the side early in the fight disappeared during the first night. There were sixty-eight of them. Only three lived through it. Finally, on the fourth day, about noon again, another plane came over. That was the ultimate moment of woe. We knew it had to be another Jap. But it was a PBY—one of ours. A Catalina. That afternoon another can—the *Henley*—came over the horizon and found us. We scuttled the *Fat Lady* right there, in the middle of the Coral Sea, and watched her go down. There were a hundred and twenty-three of us left."

"Tough duty," Culdee said finally, wondering where he would have hidden when the Vals came down.

"Tough duty," Boyne agreed. He grinned at Culdee in the tropical mid-Pacific dark, out there on the wing of the bridge. Out there on the hatch cover, forty years later . . . "That's why I quiver when I laugh."

EIGHTEEN

~~~~~~~~~~~~~~~~~~~~~~

Commodore Millikan was the fourth of that line in these troubled waters. The first, and certainly the best (since it was he who gave the name its magical resonance), was a vengeful, tightly wound young ensign fresh out of Annapolis whose PT boat was sunk off San Lázaro during the Japanese takeover of the Philippines at the outset of World War II. His real name was Edgar L. Downes, but in the Sulu Sea the locals called him Milikan, as they did all Americans. The extra *l* slipped in there thanks to a yeoman's typing error at the Office of Naval Intelligence. No harm done. It sounded more American spelled that way. It made for better cover.

The original Millikan organized a ragtag fleet—hence the title commodore—of local small craft—the slim, fast outriggers called pump boats, heavier trading vessels known as *kumpits,* and long-hulled, brightly clad sailing canoes called vintas. He armed them with weapons stolen from Japanese bases at Jolo and Tawitawi in the Sulu archipelago and wrought great havoc among the enemy. His sailors for the most part were Tausuq Moslems, a warlike, freedom-loving, seagoing people who had dominated the Sulu for generations—pirates, slavers, smugglers, afraid of nothing.

At night they slipped aboard Japanese vessels where they lay at anchor in the islands and cut the crews' throats, taking their testicles as trophies. They mined harbor entrances with stolen Japanese contact mines. They wiped out whole garrisons of Japanese occupation troops on the smaller islands. They sank a Japanese troopship carrying reinforcements to beleaguered Leyte in the fall of 1944,

123

using a twenty-four-inch oxygen-propelled Japanese torpedo taken from a light cruiser, the *Abukuma,* that with fitting justice had been crippled by a U.S. PT boat in the Battle of Surigao Strait. The seas around the wreck boiled with feeding fish for weeks afterward. When the Japanese withdrew from the Philippines, Commodore Millikan's sea guerrillas combed the evacuated islands mercilessly, killing every Japanese straggler they found. And they found them all. The stragglers did not die swiftly.

Commodore Millikan rejoined the U.S. Navy. As Lieutenant (j.g.) Downes, he was killed at Okinawa the following year, when a kamikaze hit the gun mount he commanded aboard an attack transport anchored in Buckner Bay.

But the ONI, recognizing the value of the Millikan legend, reactivated the title after the war, when the pro-Communist Hukbalahap movement flared in the Philippines. Another commodore was dispatched to San Lázaro and welcomed with great warmth. The Tausuqs had enjoyed the war. They'd never had so much fun before, at least since the Spanish left.

The Huk movement died down. Southeast Asia flared up. The southern Philippines, always rebellious, never totally under Manila's control even in Spain's long day, lie close to the Asian mainland, a natural and political soft spot in the flank of America's most prized Pacific ally. A third Commodore Millikan replaced the second, just to make sure the Commies didn't try any cute stuff down there.

Men age and die; bureaucracies live forever. When the U.S. pulled back from Vietnam in 1973, there was no need to maintain the Millikan force in the Sulu Sea. But you never can tell. The operation, after all, was inexpensive, self-sustaining in large part through the very institutions that sustained the Tausuq. Smuggling really hurt no one but the Manila government, and the U.S. was already pumping millions into the Malacañang Palace, anyway. Slavery was a way of life among Moslems that would continue regardless of a Commodore Millikan's presence. And what the hell, a little piracy never hurt anyone. The commodore remained on station.

When Magellan first spied the archipelago that would be named the Philippines, on March 15, 1521, Islam was still moving northward through the islands. Though Spain stopped that movement, she never quite quelled it. From Mindanao south through Basilan and the Sulu archipelago, and through all of Palawan below Puerto Princesa, Moro insurgency continued to smolder, but at low heat, localized, endemic. Then, when Ferdinand Marcos imposed his arbitrary but Draconian martial law on the nation in the early 1970s, the insurgency flared to real rebellion. A Moro National Liberation Front was formed, well organized, armed with modern automatic weapons and explosives, demanding an autonomous Moslem nation for the southern Philippines and willing to wreak terror to win it.

Grenades blew at night, then in restaurants at sundown. Sugar plantations controlled by absentee landlords out of Manila flared sweetly under the pirate wind. Small-town alcaldes woke briefly in the hot, dark, insect-singing night to find their throats cut ear to ear. Army convoys never reached their new posts, and sent their oily, flesh-scented smoke to mix with that of the plantations and restaurants and movie houses. Sulu Sea *mundo* grew bolder, attacking even tankers and freighters as they steamed slowly up the Sulu toward Manila. Planners in Washington began muttering the unholy litany—Qadafi, Arafat, Khomeini. It couldn't be local, it made no sense, how could a cluster of scruffy islands with little or no mineral wealth, oil, or industry hope to forge a self-sustaining nation?

Well, what if the rebellion succeeded? The Moro nation could never last. Its very existence would demand aid from the rest of the Moslem world, especially those parts of it most troublesome to American interests. Let Qadafi, Khomeini & Co. bleed themselves even paler into the wide, blue Sulu Sea. The real importance of the Philippines lay to the north—strategically with the U.S. strongholds at Subic Bay and Clark Air Base, economically with the markets for American trade in populous Luzon and the other big islands. Marcos would keep them in line.

Then Marcos fell.

The faint click of dominoes was heard once more in the corridors of Washington. But this time they were falling from different directions. Certain thinkers at certain agencies suddenly remembered the Millikan force. It might be well—a kind of insurance—to strengthen that little operation. Always good to have a foothold, small as it might be, deep in enemy territory. From tiny beachheads whole reconquests grow . . .

Commodore Millikan IV thought of all this as he lay in a hammock one hot, humid morning under the nipa roof of his veranda. An ice-cold bottle of San Miguel stood balanced on his flat belly, puddling coolly into his naval. It was the hour between the land breeze and the sea breeze, and though he was wearing only a sarong, he wished the sea breeze would hurry up. In the still air he could hear church bells pealing from the ancient stone cathedral in San Lázaro City. The fifth Sunday of Lent was fast approaching, the feast day of Saint Lazarus, the island's patron. Like many a Commodore Millikan before him, he thought of the irony—or perhaps it was a historical portent—implicit in that name.

Magellan had discovered the Philippines on the Feast of San Lázaro. In keeping with Spanish nautical custom of the day, he'd named the entire archipelago for Lazarus. It was not until 1542, fully twenty-one years later, that the islands had been renamed for the infante of Spain, Don Felipe—*las Islas Filipinas*. As far as Commodore Millikan knew, his little island deep in the heart of Asian Islam was the only one that still bore the original European name of the place. Perhaps though, in the months and years to come, the name might once again reverberate with geopolitical significance throughout the Indies, symbol and tocsin of a new resurrection. And he'd be the man to arouse it.

The Catholic population of San Lázaro was small—there was a tiny Buddhist colony on the island as well, along with a dwindling population of pagan animists on nearby Balbal—but like all Filipino Catholics, the Lazareños were very devout. Passing the cathedral on his way to or from the Millikan Shipping offices, he sometimes saw *penitentes*, grown men, not your usual soft-minded old women or pubescent boys confusing religious ardor with sexuality, stumping

126

across the crushed-coral square and up the stone steps on their raw, bleeding knees to pray at the statue of Lazarus in the cathedral's gloomy nave. He'd gone in there once to look at the statue. It was carved of wood and painted a ghastly, bilious blue-green, a scrawny, limp, dead old man in the last stages of rot, his skin—his very flesh, it seemed—flaking away onto his winding sheet. Yet the old man's eyes (they must have been carved of some local semiprecious stone) were alive, a bright, sparkling, almost vengeful sea green. The rough coral prie-dieu before the statue was worn smooth by the knees of past penitents. The grooves were brown with the blood of stale sins.

This Commodore Millikan was nominally a Protestant of the Congregational persuasion, but he hadn't been to church since he left the naval academy, except when duty required it. Over the years he'd prayed, or pretended to, in Buddhist temples, Jewish synagogues, Moslem mosques, and even, once—ironically—in an austere Dutch Reformed chapel in the Namib Desert of South-West Africa. That wasn't long ago, and he'd prayed sincerely that white-hot morning. He was on his way north from Windhoek to the Angolan border.

He couldn't pray in this cathedral, though. His men wouldn't approve. But Billy Torres, his exec, prayed there every Sunday, prayed there sincerely, humbly, from the depths of his black Filipino heart. He was as cruel as he was pious. Perhaps the two went hand in hand. At least here they seemed to. Torres had told him the other day that on Good Friday there would be three crucifixions in the city—voluntary crucifixions, like the ones you could see for the goodness of your soul every Holy Week in that rice paddy in Barangay San Pedro, outside San Fernando de Papanga on Luzon. "Ours are better than that," Torres assured him. "Last year one of the men died. Actually bled to death on the cross from the holes in his feet. The spike nicked an artery. Bled out before they could pull him down. You ought to come along with me this year—the Tausuqs think it's the only worthwhile rite in the whole Catholic religion. Put you in good with the men."

"Why don't you be my surrogate, Billy?" the commodore said.

"You really seem to enjoy it." Torres had laughed in that way he had. Like when he gunned down boat people, or even his own countrymen. Torres pulled it all together, every sadistic trait of the three cultures that made up his background—every Filipino's, for that matter—Malay, Spanish, American. Along with a few tricks learned from the Japanese during the war. Wicked mean cultures, sure enough. Still, for all that, Torres was a sissy compared with some of the men the commodore had known in the course of his career. On a scale of one to ten, Afghans ranked at the top; the Reclamos in Mozambique, the Simbas in Kivu (what remained of them), the Somalis in Eritrea—all black Africans rated right up there. Brits, Boers, and Rhodesians barely got on the scale, at least those he'd known. They didn't really enjoy it. Not like the Koreans, or the Vietnamese, for that matter . . .

His beer had gone warm, but the sea breeze hadn't come up yet. He didn't want to get all sweaty climbing out of the hammock. "Rosalinda!" he yelled in to the housekeeper, warbling it almost playfully—Rrrosa-*leen*-dah! "Could you bring me another San Mig, *por favor?*" He loved to twit her with the odd Spanish phrase now and then. Though Rosalinda Aguinaldo-Musa (what a name) was from Luzon, where Spanish was almost as prevalent as English, she knew barely a word of the language. Her English was slangy and fluent. A nice old bag, Rosalinda—Christ, she was probably younger than he, but it was different with a woman—and a damn hard worker. Millikan III had hired her after laying her a few times up in Subic, swore she was stone loyal—he'd had Washington run a security check on her. "Throw her a screw now and then," III had advised him, "and she'll follow you anywhere. She'll die for you." Well, IV didn't value life quite that highly, though he didn't tell his predecessor in so many words. She must be getting it someplace else, he thought now, as she brought him the beer and went back to her household accounts, because she's certainly happy enough.

Down on the beach a group of naked children were dancing and skipping in a cluster, laughing as they pointed to something on the sand. He took up his binoculars and focused in on them. They had caught a large crab and torn off one of its legs. It was scuttling in backward circles, its claws raised in futile protest. A little boy reached down, quick as a snake, and yanked off another leg. The circles got tighter. The children's laughter quickened, musical as church bells at dawn. Cruelty, the commodore thought. It's as natural to us as breathing or sex or eating.

He hadn't always felt that way. As a young line officer, newly hatched from the academy, be firmly believed he was defending a better, gentler way of life, a seagoing crusader for the unfettered pursuit of happiness. He'd always had the gift of tongues, and when he applied to the Monterey Language School to study Vietnamese, he was quickly accepted. On graduation (at the top of his class) he was tapped for the ONI. Then began his postgraduate studies in the field—Cruelty 101.

He was shocked at the joy the torturers took in their work. It was the same on both sides, everywhere. Of course he was naive. He hadn't learned much yet about human potential. He'd even felt guilty about his first mission in the north. He'd been planted in a POW camp on the coast to foment a breakout while at the same time ensuring that the American prisoners would be massacred when they tried it. The hope, as he understood it, was that when word of the slaughter leaked out Stateside, it would turn the tide of anti-war protest and somehow stiffen the American will to win. Kind of a cross between the Malmédy Massacre and the old movie *Brute Force*.

It almost worked. He'd drummed up enthusiasm for the break surreptitiously, using the tap code when his cellmate was out, leaving notes in the head or the shower, and meanwhile brownnosing the camp commander and his swishy assistant. In the end his cellmate queered the deal. He had to get himself tortured to prove he wasn't slimy—a collaborator. But the damage had been done. Only four men—all enlisted—made the break finally. Only one of them was killed. It was not his cellmate, who was in solitary when the break failed. Too bad for the poor sap. Had he died, they wouldn't have had to deep-six him from the navy when he was finally released. There'd been talk of arranging a convenient accident for the man in Manila or

Subic Bay, but the bastard had won some kind of medal in Korea, and the black-shoe line types wouldn't hear of it. Instead they busted him back a notch and discharged him. "You won't have to worry about him crossing your track anywhere down the line," they assured the commodore. "He won't be able to get there. Couldn't afford it on *his* retirement pay."

Culdee. Sure, that was his name. Typical old bosun. Dead stupid. Crusty on the outside, mush at the core. Had the look of a Mick boozer about him. A brawler and a sentimentalist. Wooden men in iron ships. Well, he was probably dead by now.

A sail showed on the horizon and beat in on long reaches toward Lázaro Harbor. The commodore watched it through his glasses—yawl-rigged with a blue hull and high sheer forward, a pretty little vessel. The sea breeze had finally kicked up, and the boat had a bone in her teeth. The commodore couldn't make out the man at the helm, so he swung from his hammock and walked down to the beach. The angle was better there. It was a round-eye in a pirate bandanna, with two of Billy's Tausuqs on deck. Appropriate. Must be that kid Torres mentioned, from Zambo. The dope-running boat bum who'd worked that drowning dog routine up near Bugsuk Island last month. The commodore's first inclination when Billy told him about it was to dust the kid. He could only be bad news. But then the commodore realized it might be good to have a bad news round-eye on tap. That way if Manila or some rival agency in Washington ever started snooping around, they could throw the boat bum to them.

Something nipped his foot. He jumped back and looked down. It was the crab the children had been torturing. Legless now, it had nonetheless managed to crawl over to him on its stumps and pinch him with its one remaining claw.

The commodore stomped it flat with his bare heel.

NINETEEN

~~~~~~~~~~~~~~~~~~~~~~

"Ever driven one of these, Cappy?"

They were standing in a big, shedlike boathouse that covered a complex of rickety piers. From the sea or air its thatched roofs and roughly finished mangrove supporting poles would make it look like a crude structure slapped together by Third World carpenters with hangovers, a lot of palm fronds, a coil of binder twine, and about six nails. The sort of *mañana* architecture that blows off to Bolivia in the first strong breeze (HUNDREDS DIE!) or collapses in a loud fart. But Curt could see that the thatching overlay a smoothly finished and probably steel-reinforced concrete roof. The corner posts were most likely disguised the same way. And certainly the six boats that lapped at their moorings alongside were top of the line.

"Blue Thunder," Curt said. "Built by USA Racing on Northeast 188th Street off Dumbfoundling Bay in the North Dade section of metropolitan Miami. Don Aronow's far-famed Fleet Street. His last design. Not the quickest fast boat ever launched—sixty or seventy miles an hour tops—but very stable in open water. It won't kick your kidneys to hash in an hour of heavy seas." He turned and grinned at Torres and the commodore. "No, I've never driven one. The only folks who do are the Coast Guard and U.S. Customs."

"Civilians own them, too," Torres said. "Prince Rainier has one. King Hussein of Jordan has a couple. Plenty of Arabs whose names escape me."

Some civilians.

Curt knew the Blue Thunder. The Caddy—no, the Rolls—of

131

offshore powerboat work. He'd known Aronow, too. A big, strong, swaggering man, good-looking despite those bushy eyebrows that crouched above his hard, brown seaman's eyes like a couple of porcupines touching noses. A *shtarker* in the Yiddish of Aronow's coreligionists. But smart. He'd built Fleet Street practically single-handed. The names of the boat-building companies he'd founded, made famous, then sold lined the street—Formula, Donzi, Magnum, Cigarette (his masterwork), Squadron VII, USA Racing. He was the latter-day king of that dangerous world, the Mickey Mantle to Gar Wood's Babe Ruth, a helluva racer. Sixteen deep-sea victories—a record. Two world and three U.S. championships in the late sixties. 'Fraid a nothin', as the saying goes—hell or high water. Back in the old days guys used to walk in off the street like Curt did, scruffy hippie boat bums, and slap down a Ziploc plastic bag full of thousand-dollar bills, buy a Cigarette right off the floor. Don would pour them an Amaretto from the big swivel jug on his desk and stuff the dough in his pants pocket, then walk around with it for days, they said. No one was gonna rip him off . . .

He should have been afraid, though. In the end some dude just pulled in off Fleet Street in a big vague car, walked over to where Aronow sat in his Mercedes coupe, and pumped him full of lead. On a work day, too, with loads of potential witnesses. Stole his Rolex right off his wrist as the final indignity. Miami Metro hadn't arrested anyone for that one yet, and it was a couple of years ago. Claimed they hadn't the vaguest idea who did it. Neither did Curt. In that crisscross world, it could have been anybody. Curt was lucky to be out of it.

He walked out to the end of the dock and looked down into the crystal-clear water. Bright fish circled the pilings, and deep in the shadows he saw the mottled backs of dozing barracudas. Their baleful yellow eyes looked up at him, unafraid. One of them yawned. There was no wire-mesh net protecting the entries to the slips, nor could he see the pilings for one farther out in the bay.

"No net," he said.

"We don't really need one," the commodore said. "Who'd want

to steal or sabotage our boats around here? We're the island's economy."

"What kind of paint is that?" The boats were painted green or dull black.

"Stealth stuff," Torres said, after looking for the commodore's nod. "It absorbs radar signals where the angles of the hull don't deflect them."

"Pricey boats, pricey paint jobs," Curt said.

"Our firm is amply capitalized," the commodore replied, and laughed. "Our stockholders earn good dividends on their investment. We hope you'll help us add to our profit margin."

"The best I can, sir," Curt said.

"Do you shoot, Captain?"

"I've been off the hard stuff for years," Curt answered. "Never really cared for needle drugs."

"I meant wing shooting. Game birds—pheasant, quail, doves, ducks."

"Oh, you mean like skeet? But on live birds, those pigeon shoots in Caracas or Bogotá? Up one goes, and bang, bang!"

"No," the commodore said. "Bang."

Curt laughed. "Never tried it. I'm fair with a handgun, though. Or an Uzi."

"Too bad," the commodore said. "Billy doesn't care for the sport, and it would be nice to have a shooting companion. There are jungle cock over on Balbal. I like to run over there when things are slow and enjoy a few hours of sport."

"Jungle cock? I thought they were illegal. I mean, you can't even bring a few feathers, much less a skin, into the U.S., can you? Endangered species, or something."

"Not here. They're abundant on Balbal. The feathers are very valuable, almost priceless, and the best kind for tying salmon flies." The commodore had many friends back in Washington who appreciated his gifts of carefully dried jungle-cock necks, salmon anglers all in the corridors of power. Venial sins in a diplomatic pouch.

"Well, heck, sir," Curt said. "I wouldn't mind learning. I'm not

133

one of your bug-fucking hippie nature boys who wouldn't swat a housefly. Wing shooting, hey? A real gentleman's sport."

"Good," the commodore said. "We'll run out there this afternoon in one of the Thunders. Later, when it cools off a bit and the birds are moving. You can show me how well you drive a fast boat, and then carry my game bag. Two birds with one stone." He chuckled.

Pain in the ass, Curt thought. Now I'm this fucking gun-bearer. But he chuckled right along.

They drove back to the bungalow in Billy's dinged-up GMC Jimmy. It was painted gray, like a navy carryall, the kind you see around the whorehouses in Old San Juan when a carrier or cruiser's in port. Curt liked what he'd seen so far of Lázaro—the wide, stone seafront embarcadero with its huge old flamboyant trees in blossom, coco palms tossing in the trades that washed it most of the day, little cantinas and shops lining the shaded paseos, a spindly towered mosque in town, and the big, square-spired cathedral overlooking the sea. It was like the Caribbean before it got nasty down there. Here people actually smiled at a white face, doffed their hats and called you Don.

Lunch was cold roast beef—a bit stringy, Curt thought—and chicken salad with chopped coconut, grapes, and bits of what looked like mango or papaya mixed in. The crisp-crusted rolls were from the *panadería* on the waterfront. They ate on the lanai, to enjoy the sea breeze, and were served by little brown barefoot Tausuq boys in starched whites. Rosalinda, the commodore's housekeeper, kept a watchful eye on the boys. She was a handsome woman, in her fifties, Curt guessed, and he wondered if the commodore or Billy was doinking her. There was a hint of the whore about her, the kind that really loves her work. A rare breed, indeed.

"How do you like the roast beef?" the commodore asked.

"Flavorful but a bit chewy," Curt said. "What is it, carabao?"

"Close, but not quite. Tamarau. A wild buffalo from over on Balbal. There's a good-sized herd of them there still. Used to be abundant here on Lázaro as well, in the Spanish days, but the dons liked to ride them down on horseback and spear them. Tough customers, the dons. At least in their heyday. A tamarau's no sissy, not like his poncey water buff cousin, the carabao. Sharp horns and a strong life. Took two rounds from a .375 Magnum to stop this guy, didn't it, Billy?"

Torres laughed.

"Another one not so long ago killed a well-to-do Filipino client of ours from Davao. He'd knocked it down with one shot, walked up to have a look, then, when he turned away, it stuck him right up the backside. Like a *toro bravo* might an incautious matador."

Torres laughed again, with his mouth full, then patted his lips with the linen napkin and kept on chuckling.

"Balbal, hey? Where we're going to hunt birds this afternoon?"

"That's right," the commodore said. "They're often in the same cover together."

"A little bit hairy, isn't it? Shouldn't you bring a rifle?"

"Just adds to the sport, Captain. Adrenaline's good for the circulation. A healthy shot of it now and then reams out the blood vessels like Drano in a clogged sink. I'm sure it just gobbles up the cholesterol. How's your cholesterol, Captain? Mine's a bit high, but I think it's in control now, out here."

"I haven't had a physical lately," Curt said. "Billy told me I didn't need one to get this job."

"True," the Commodore replied. "But we care about our employees' health and welfare. Don't we, Billy? Anyway, you won't be getting much cholesterol from that chicken salad, in case you've been worrying. It's jungle cock."

"Delicious," Curt said.

"Siesta time, gentlemen," the commodore said.

Billy Torres woke Curt from a restless sleep a little after three. Curt's pillow was sweat-soaked despite the air-conditioning in the little stucco-walled guest house they'd assigned him. The commodore was waiting on the dock at the boat shed. One of the green-painted Blue Thunders rumbled and blatted beside the pier, its engines already warmed up. The commo stepped impatiently down into the boat and gestured at the gear piled on the dock. Curt handed it to him—a scarred pigskin gun case, a canvas game bag from which a few gaudy feathers flew, an El Al flight bag heavy with what felt like a case of shotgun shells. He cast off the bow and stern lines and jumped in.

"Take her out, Captain Hughes."

Curt engaged the drive, crimped the leather-padded wheel, and touched the throttles. The Thunder spoke, the boat leapt forward.

"Easy, Captain."

"She's sensitive."

He took her out the channel blasted through the inshore coral, following mangrove pole markers, until they were in blue water. Balbal lay to the northeast, a high, darkly forested wedge-shaped island wearing a cap of afternoon rain clouds. He could see surf creaming on the beaches to Balbal's windward side.

"Straight for the centerline of the island," the commodore shouted. "It's ten miles to the near shore. I make it just three-sixteen P.M. Now two-block them, and let's go. All ahead full." He gripped the holds on the padded dash and spread his stance. Curt nailed the throttles.

The Thunder shot out like a dragster, up on the step in an instant. She rode straight, smooth, and bounceless despite the trade wind's rough chop—as if she were on rails. When they'd run about half the distance, the commodore leaned over and yelled into his ear, "Now cut me a doughnut. Don't touch the throttle." Curt obeyed, his stomach suddenly clenching. Well, she was the commodore's boat . . .

The Thunder turned on her own tail in a smooth, tight, perfect circle. She scarcely heeled at all to the maneuver, but Curt's instinctive lean into the turn almost threw him off balance when it didn't happen.

"Incredible," he yelled.

The commodore looked into his eyes and grinned happily. A

great, big forty-year-old rich kid showing off his toys to the poor boy on his block.

"Now to starboard," he yelled.

Curt cut another doughnut, then wheeled back around and had a run at the Thunder's steep wake. The boat skipped over it as if it were a crack in the sidewalk. She wasn't much for fast—just a touch over sixty-five m.p.h. at red-line revs, ten slower than an Apache or even a well-tuned old Cigarette—but she was heaven for smooth.

He throttled down as they neared the Balbal shore.

"Six minutes and change," the commodore said proudly. "With time out for coffee and doughnuts."

They anchored, bow to seaward, off a pink-flour beach and waded ashore, Curt lugging the gear. "Empty a box of those shells into the game pouch," the commodore ordered as he assembled his shotgun. "Make it two boxes. Hand me those chaps." He pulled a pair of green nylon tubes over his bare legs, securing them at his belt with snap straps. "There's another pair in the bag," he said. "You'd better put them on."

"What're they for? Snakes?"

"They wouldn't turn a snake bite," the commodore said. "But there's other things in there that bite."

"I hate anything on my bare legs," Curt said. "If it's all the same to you—"

"Your legs," the commodore said. "Your funeral." He dropped two shells into the slim, double-barreled gun, then snapped the breech closed. "Let's kill some birds."

He pushed into the jungle.

Back on Lázaro, Billy Torres walked casually out onto the dock where *Sea Witch* lay moored. He was whistling softly to himself, soothingly, trying to walk as nonchalantly as a tourist on an afternoon stroll. Torres did not like dogs.

Brillo watched him from the shade of the wheelhouse, head between his paws. Silent.

Why do I always draw the shit duty? Torres asked himself. I could have taken Hughes out in the boat, checked him out and all, while the commodore searched Curt's sailboat. Dogs love the commodore. They're always coming up to him to be scratched behind the ears. They don't like me. They *know*. And I can't even shoot the fucker if he comes for me. Then the kid would know someone's been aboard her. Why shouldn't he know? He's working for us, isn't he? We could say some Tausuq thief did it.

He stopped at the gangway leading onto the cockpit. The dog was still silent, not even watching him now that he was behind it. One ear was cocked back at him, though. He put a foot on the gangway. The dog didn't move. "Good boy, hey, you're really a good doggy, aren't you boy?" Nothing. No movement, no growl, just that ear, twitching once as Torres spoke. He took a step. Another. Watching closely.

"You're a good pooch, aren't you, boy?" Torres lied. He knew the dog knew he was lying, even though it still hadn't moved.

He was across the gangway, onto the main deck, at the head of the companionway. "Good boy, atsa good doggy!" He was onto the ladder. Piece of cake—

Then the dog was there—so fast that Torres caught only a red-brown blur—there at the head of the ladder. Filling the sky. All eyes and hair and teeth—very long, white, sharp teeth. The dog growled once, low and ugly, deep in its fire hose of a larynx. Torres bolted into the cabin and slammed the door, shot the bolt, staggered back and jabbed his kidney hard against a sharp edge of the mess table. He was hyperventilating, his heart pounding like an M60 machine gun with an endless belt of ammo. . . .

But he was there, down in the cabin, where the commo said he had to go. Plenty of time for a thorough, leisurely search that would leave no traces. Plenty of time to take rolls of film with the Minox, if there was anything to photograph. More time than he could ever use.

How the fuck do I get *out* of here?

* * *

138

It took Curt only five steps to realize he'd made a grave mistake. He should have worn the brush chaps. Thorns, nettles, vines that sucked at his legs like leeches even as they bit—he was ripped and stinging from his shorts clear down to where his Topsiders were filling with blood. Maybe it was just mud—there was plenty of that. And leeches, too. Real ones, not lianas. The commodore snapped them off his own arms and neck as he strode along, breaking trail. He was chattering away a mile a minute, asking Curt what he thought of the Thunder, how he liked Lázaro so far—he hoped Curt would be happy in his job; it's a nice, friendly little island once the people get to know you. Hard to get laid, though, almost impossible, the way these Tausuqs guard their daughters. But Billy'd brought in some girls from Angeles, clean girls, all tested negative for AIDS, though it's rampant there and at Subic as well. Inexpensive, too, in fact, he could have a freebie courtesy of the commodore—at least the first night.

Every now and then something roared up from the green jungle gloom, and the commodore killed it before Curt could even react. The light little double was at his shoulder before the bird was off the ground. Pow! Pow-pow—nailed two that time. Pow! Pow! Each time he killed one, he looked back at Curt, puzzled at first, then exasperated.

"Look" he said after he'd picked up two or three of them. "*You're* supposed to be the retriever. Next one, you fetch it."

Aye-aye, sir. Or should it be woof-woof?

Pow! "Fetch it, Captain!" Curt fetched. It looked like a Technicolor chicken, only smaller, harder-bodied, kind of like a banty cock, with long, sharp spurs.

Pow-pow!

"Double! Fetch 'em up, Cappy! Fetch dead!"

The commodore shot one that fell and then took off running.

"After him, Cappy! He's a runner! Go fetch him up, boy—go, he's getting away!"

Curt finally grabbed the bird by its tail feathers, and when they pulled out, threw himself on top of it like a lineman on a fumble. It

139

squirted out from under his chest and raked him down the cheek with one of its spurs. He grabbed it by the neck. It beat him and gouged his arms with its wings and legs.

"Bite its fucking head off!" the commodore advised.

Curt chomped—crunch. Blood and feathers . . .

"Good boy, Cap!"

On and on they pounded, with Curt beating the thick covers now at the commodore's behest, arms, legs, neck, face ripped raw by thorns and stinging with acid sweat. He didn't even bother with the leeches anymore. Maybe they'd kill him before the jungle did.

"What's the bag limit on these birds?" he finally asked the commodore. The commodore looked at him quizzically. Whoever heard such a dumb question?

"Why, whatever I make it," he said. "What's the matter, game bag getting too heavy? You're not wimping out on me, Captain, are you? Not turning into, what did you call them, a bug-fucking hippie on me?"

"No, sir."

"Good."

A while later—ten minutes? An hour? Who cared—something dark and heavy went crashing off through a bamboo thicket to their right. The commodore looked at the ground, wrinkled his nose, sniffed the mildewed dead air. He touched his toe to what looked like a cow flop. Curt saw the deep indentations of cloven hooves in the mud.

"Tamarau," the commodore said. "Well, we're almost back to the boat. They won't bother us now." And sure enough, a hundred leaden steps later Curt popped like a champagne cork out onto the beach. The brilliant light brought tears to his eyes. There was the Thunder, bobbing at her anchor line just ahead of them on the water. Curt could have sworn they were miles away from it.

"Just bring the boat in here, bow first, while I take down this gun," the commodore ordered. "And put those birds in the cooler under the console till we get back. Rosa will clean and skin them."

The saltwater stung. Small fish nibbled on Curt's torn skin.

* * *

It was hotter than the proverbial hinges down in *Sea Witch's* cabin. Billy Torres lay on Curt's bunk, feeling the sweat roll down his ribs. He'd shot all his film, emptied a jug of warm water (nothing to drink in the reefer, which had no ice in it, anyway), tried to read one of the hundreds of books and diaries he found in the cedar chest at the foot of the bunk but found them all too arty (he was a Mack Bolan fan; even Louis L'Amour was too rarefied for his taste), and studied all the tapes and records without finding one C & W album. Then he heard Curt coming along the dock.

"Hey there, Brill. Coulda used you this afternoon, boy. Balbal's a ball breaker—your kind of country, Brillo boy. Hey, what you got down there in the cabin, boy? Good eats, hey? Okay, let me get past you now."

The hatch was bolted from the inside. Then it slid back and the door opened.

Billy Torres was glowering at him.

"Oh, hi, Mr. Torres," Curt said, smiling. "Find what you wanted?"

"What did you tell him?"

"The only logical story," Billy Torres said. He and the commodore were on the veranda, sipping their sundown stingahs. "I came aboard to check his mooring lines, and the dog chased me into the cabin."

"He bought it?"

"What else could he do? Remember, he works for us. We could off him in a minute if we wanted, and he knows it. Anyway, it's credible enough."

"What did you get?"

"I shot the log page by page, the books—just the covers, titles, like that, but the books are legit. I don't know about the records or tapes, he's got no fresh batteries for the machine. A wad of old pictures of some broad, a hard-looking bitch with a crooked nose, and of what I guess is her as a kid, with her folks. And what looked like the broad's diary, written in some old logbooks. I copied as much of that as I could before I ran out of film. Pretty boring stuff. Like the books."

"Where's the pictures of the pictures?"

"In the lab, drying still."

"Let's go." They walked across the wet lawn to the casita that was the photo lab. The door was unlocked, and Torres turned to the commodore, eyebrows up. Rosalinda was in there, dusting and emptying the trash cans. It was okay—III had cleared her and given her the key along with the job.

"Could you come back later, Rosa?" the commodore said. *"Gracias. Muy bueno, chicita."*

"I'm sorry, Commodore Millikan," she said, a bit miffed. "I wanted to clean up early so I can go to confession tonight at the cathedral. It's Lent, you know, and we—"

"Yes, yes, Rosa. Good thing there's still some Christians among us. I count on you to keep the faith for this household."

"What would she have to confess?" Billy asked when Rosa had left. "Old lady like that."

"Plenty, Billy," the commodore said. He was studying the contact prints where they hung from clips on the drying wire. "Ever notice how she smiles some mornings when she's serving breakfast? Hand me a loupe."

He studied one strip of contacts closely with the magnifier, then unclipped it and took it over to a table with a strong overhead light. He looked closer still.

"Weird," he said. "Have a look."

Billy saw a girl—the crook-nosed one, but still a kid in this picture, her nose still short and unbent, like a proper human being, not a round-eye. There was a round-eye woman with her, kind of prim-faced. And a guy in a Donald Duck suit. Navy blues. The sailor wore crossed anchors above his three chevrons. Four hash marks on his sleeve. Mean-looking fucker, with a bent nose like the girl when she grew up. BM1—a deck ape. Torres had been an ET—an electronics technician—before they sent him to OCS. Operations sailors hated deck apes. Deck apes hated everything but other deck apes, and they didn't even like many of them that much.

"What do you see, sir?"

"That white hat. I know that man. I knew him on another assignment, long ago. Thought about him just the other day, matter of fact. I figured he was long dead. Now here we get a new recruit— a dope runner you tell me, an outlaw from the word go—and he just happens to be sailing a boat that is carrying pictures of this old, well, *shipmate* of mine. I call that weird."

"The file we got says this Curt guy stole the boat from some girl he was working with. Broad named Dundee, it said."

"Not Culdee?"

"Dundee, sir, I just reread it this morning."

"Some fuckup in the office. The white hat's name was *Culd*ee."

"That's an old photo, sir," Billy said. "The white hat might very well be dead. The file said the broad is in her thirties. She's only about five or six in that picture."

"I still don't like it," the commodore said. "The Brits have a saying, Billy. Once is happenstance. Twice is coincidence. Three times is enemy action. This is a very strong once."

143

TWENTY

~~~~~~~~~~~~~~~~~~~~

Curt came down the esplanade with Brillo at heel. It was dark now, and the cobbles glinted under weak lamplight. Rock music blared from a few honky-tonks and from the transistors in the open-air barter stalls. Turbaned old Tausuqs glowered at him and fingered their cutlery. The dimly lighted pawn shops, packed with all manner of goods from ship's clocks to golf clubs, seemed empty of life, save for the inevitable Chinese pawnbroker who inevitably beckoned with a wide, warm smile.

He wants a piece of somebody, Curt thought. So do I, but different. We all do. The commodore's right—no streetwalkers in this town. He passed another pawnshop with golf clubs in the window. Golf clubs? The nearest course was probably no closer than Zambo or Davao.

A mongrel came down a side alley and trotted over stiff-legged to check out Brillo.

"Easy, boy." Brillo would break its neck with one snap. That might piss off some bolo-man, and they'd both be shish kebab. Brillo looked up at him with a cutting, pissed-off look of his own. Curt saw a stairway leading up the bluff toward the cathedral. Might as well check it out. No Tausuqs up there. They climbed. Down in a workyard lighted by torches, Curt saw carpenters planing and chiseling away at what looked like three very large wooden crosses. They worked solemnly, with none of the chatter and laughter Filipinos bring to most jobs. The wood shavings smelled musky, almost like incense, as the breeze spun their odor up to him. Church music played softly from a transistor—Gregorian chants.

No music sounded from the cathedral when they reached it, just the mutter of old women praying their penances in the rearmost pews, and the occasional growl of a priest in the one working confessional. It was dark in there. Red candlelight, the stale smell of holy water and the distant seafront. Christ hung bleeding and twisted from crosses all over the walls, the same long, black-bearded agonized face at every turning, like that of crazed dopers Curt had seen as they checked out after an inadvertent hot shot. Or a planned one, for that matter. He winced at the sight of the realistic thorns on Christ's crown, feeling again his own experience of them on the commo's mad bird hunt. Never again, if he could help it.

An old woman in black shuffled out of the confessional, her face as doleful as Christ's, except for the lack of a beard—she had only a white, potato-sprout mustache. Another woman got up to go into the box, and Curt recognized Rosalinda, the commo's housekeeper. A bit long in the tooth, he thought, but sexy in a hot, smutty way. Maybe he ought to stick around and buy her a drink down in town when she came out. Maybe he could give her some more ammunition for her next confession.

Padre Cotinho sat behind the confessional screen, sipping something from his chalice. Rosalinda sniffed—tuba asesina, the wicked local toddy that was said to corrode the brain more than absinthe. What are the Jesuits coming to? Not long ago they were like other priests, righteous supporters of the status quo and whatever regime was in power. Then suddenly they were out on the streets with the opposition coalition, Bayan, the enemies of Macoy Marcos, the movement that had brought Cory Aquino to power. Even priests had been salvaged by the Marcos goon squads—that is, they'd achieved salvation by knife, gun, or electrode. Their bodies would be found along with those of suspected Communists, New People's Army sympathizers, election workers, and anyone who took part in Aquino's Laban campaign, the bodies smoldering on Smoky Mountain, that giant garbage dump in Manila's Tondo section, where the poor scavenged their miserable livings. Most of the salvage victims were beheaded, the women raped for good measure, usually beforehand. *Laban* was a Tagalog word meaning "battle" or "fight." Rosalinda was fighting still. So was Padre Cotinho.

"Bless me, Father, for I have sinned," she said. "The Milikan hijacker Hughes showed up today. In fact, he's at the back of the cathedral right now. I saw him just as I entered the confessional."

"Did he follow you?" The priest's voice was husky with assassin's rum.

"I don't think so. He probably just wandered up from town to look around."

"You're sure it's the right man?"

"Look for yourself, Padre."

The priest rose quickly and leaned out the back of the screens. He was quiet and steady enough on his feet despite the chalice.

"Yes, the very one," he said. "I photographed him in Zamboanga the day he met with Torres. *Bueno*. Effredio and his lady friend will be here soon, and the seafighters from Tawitawi with their boats. What else?"

"Hughes has the big dog with him, the one you mentioned. With him even now, in church." She laughed quietly. Rum and killer dogs in San Lázaro's holy of holies. "Torres went aboard to search the sailboat this afternoon while the commodore took Hughes out hunting on Balbal. The dog trapped Torres in the cabin. If only he'd torn him apart and eaten him."

"In time, *compañera*. What did Torres find in the boat?"

"He made many photographs with the small camera. Some were photographs of photographs themselves. Of the girl of Effredio and her father. I saw three pictures. The father wore the uniform of a chief petty officer in the U.S. Navy. Boatswain's mate. He looked, how do they say, salty?"

"Good," Padre Cotinho said. "He may prove of more value than we thought."

"Orders, Padre?"

"For your penance, my child, get close to this Hughes man. Whatever you need to do. You are practiced in those arts. Get him to anchor the sailboat out in the harbor, away from the fast-boat basin. Suggest it might make your rendezvous with him less publicly embarrassing to you. Study the boat carefully. Disarm all weapons—break firing pins, defuse hand grenades, even dull the edges of his knives when you cook for him. Make friends, if you can, with the dog. When we move, we don't want any alarms in the night. Again, if you have something important to tell me before your next confession, attend the early mass and leave a message in your missal. I will find it and return it to you. Now go in peace, my child, and Christ be with you."

As she rose, she saw him lift the chalice.

Curt took her the first time less than a hundred meters from the cathedral, on the wet grass beside a crypt in the graveyard. He was easy. She had smiled, taken his hand as they walked into the dark, leaned against his shoulder, tickled his palm with her middle finger in the universal let's-fuck manner, then led him grinning ear to ear down the pathway to the tombs. His urgency was that of a schoolboy.

"How long has it been since you've had a woman?" she asked him as he slumped, finished, onto her belly.

"Too damned long."

"But there are many in the Philippines."

"Not so's I could find them," he said. "All the ones I tried were hung with the same gear I've got. What do you call them? Benny boys?"

"Yes." She laughed. "Very bad for business, in my former profession. Unfair competition."

"Especially to the prospective buyer," Curt said. They both laughed. "How much do I owe you?"

"Why, nothing!" she yelped. Offended pride was the ticket. "I am a proper working woman now, with a salary. I am the commodore's private secretary." She turned her hips and shrugged him off onto the grass. It was wet and cold on your back down there. She rose huffily and straightened her dress, then stuffed her panties into her handbag. She felt his come creep down her leg like a cold garden slug. The dog was watching her from the darkness. Unsmiling. She waited, rather than walking off in pretended outrage.

"Hey, sorry," Curt said. "I just thought—"

"Is okay," she said. "Let's go."

They passed the carpenters, still busy at their crosses.

"What's that?" Curt asked. "New shrines in the works for the cathedral?"

"Not really," Rosalinda said. She hooked her thumb back over her shoulder toward the graveyard. "Gólgota. The crosses are for the crucifixions on Good Friday."

"You mean real people are going to get nailed to that wood up there?"

"Certainly," she said, as if to a backward child. "We are a very religious people."

Curt stopped and stared back up the hill toward the graveyard. It lay just under the bare, rocky crest. Moonlight made the coral blocks of the crypts look white as marble against the dark, kneelike thrust of the hilltop, and looking closely he could make out the shapes of three—no, four—no, half a dozen or more—crosses tilting crazily against the tropical stars.

"Gólgota," Rosalinda said again as she took his hand in hers. "The Place of the Skull." She tickled his palm again.

With the island of Negros abeam to starboard and Mindanao slumped black against the southern sky, *Venganza* plowed her way into the Sulu Sea. Culdee was at the wheel, watching for the dim lights of fishing boats off either bow. Surigao Strait had been thick with them, none paying the least attention, of course, to any known rules of the road. They'd stayed to the centerline of the broader Bohol Strait to avoid inshore boat traffic, and now, with the vast Sulu opening out dead ahead, the piloting would be less hazardous. Miranda came up from the galley with three mugs of coffee. Tonight they all had the midwatch. Freddie was up in the masthead watching for hazards and for the boats from Tawitawi that were to meet them.

148

"Hey, Freddie," Culdee yelled up into the dark. "You want some jamoke?"

"Not now already," the voice came back. "I got da lookout. You drink it for me, Boats."

Culdee spun the wheel to meet a following sea, kicked up by a warm, steady northeast trade that smelled of fire and jungle. Loggers were burning slash high on Negros, and they could see fires flaring and guttering on Mindanao as well. Freddie said the Mindanao fires might be the work of the NPA or the MNLF, the two rebel groups working together in these mountains. To Culdee it all smelled of Vietnam.

"Last leg, Boats," Miranda said.

"How far do you make it on the chart?"

"A little over six hundred kilometers, rhumb line from here to San Lázaro. That's about three hundred twenty or thirty nautical miles. If this wind holds, we'll make it in well under two days at eight knots. Did you read what the entry in *The Philippine Pilot* had to say about Lázaro?"

"Yeah."

"Pretty freaky down there."

"Flips are great bullshitters," Culdee said. "If you thought Mark Twain could spin a tall tale, just ask a Manila jeepney driver about the dent in his front fender or the Band-Aid on his knuckle. You'll hear a yarn that'll turn your hair green."

"But there must be something to it. All the other entries sound legitimate."

"Well, if it was printed by any government printing office, especially one connected with navy brass anywhere, you can bet it's hiding something. They've probably got some big top-secret military installation down there, covert operations up the ying-yang. They don't want tourists hanging around, clicking cameras and talking to the hometown newspaper when they get back to wherever. Even the snoopiest American reporters didn't see half of what went down in Vietnam."

"I don't know," Miranda said. "Some of these far-out corners

149

can be dangerous. We don't even have any weapons aboard to speak of. Just the 12-gauge and that .30/30 of yours."

"That's all the blackbirders needed in these waters," Culdee said. "And if it gets tougher, there's that old punt gun of my granddad's up in the fo'c'sle. It's a 0-gauge—shoots a half-pound of shot with a load of black powder behind it. He called it Whiplash Willie, because that's what you got when you fired it. Said he killed two hundred and nineteen sprig with it one night, with one shot, down in that little delta where I took you. Part of the loading instructions is to swallow two headache powders before you shoot, and two right after. A gun like that ought to scare these outlaws off."

"Flashing light on the port bow," Freddie yelled from the masthead. "Three short, two long, one short. They're repeating it."

"That's the signal," Miranda said. She grabbed a flashlight and ran for the rigging. "Bring her up into the wind, Boats."

The outriggers roared out of the dark, then throttled back. Wiry brown men swarmed over the gunwales, all of them hung with bandoliers and automatic weapons. Some in sarongs, some in ridiculous double-knit Ban-Lon bell-bottoms, stained and ripped and garish in the running lights—electric blues, puke greens, dog-shit oranges—must've been some kind of special at the Sulu Sea K Mart. They were tough-looking little men, though, wiry as VC, but darker. Their weapons gleamed rustless, well oiled, when they caught the light. An older man stepped up to the helm and saluted Culdee.

"Permission to come aboard, sir," he said in unaccented English. Then grinned in amazement at his success with the phrase.

"Granted," Culdee said.

"Are you Captain Culdee already?"

"No," Miranda said, coming up behind him. "I'm the skipper. What can I do for you?"

"I have these communication from Padre Cotinho," he said, looking up at her with the same surprised grin. "Advising me to divulge to you anyway. Also many boxes of things for the storing of them in your ship's belly." His men were already swaying heavy

150

crates onto the foredeck from a *kumpit* that had wallowed up behind them. The crates clanked faintly, with the heavy, businesslike sound of weapons, and Culdee smelled Cosmoline grease as they came aboard. Miranda took the canvas envelope from the little man's hand, and he saluted smartly. She squared her shoulders, half-smiling, and saluted him back.

"Let's look at these in the chart room."

Freddie came in with a basket of melons, oysters, and what smelled like a rich fish stew. The *mundo* had given it to him.

"Okay," Miranda said, after reading the brief note from the padre. "Curt's there, all right." She flipped quickly through the sheaf of photographs enclosed with the letter. "And here's *Seamark*—shit, he's repainted her and rigged her as a yawl! And Curt and Brillo and some guy he says is Commodore Millikan." She handed the photos to Culdee. "Cotinho says Curt is working for this Millikan, running dope in from Thailand. It's a big operation, he says. Fast boats and lots of guns. I don't know what this means to our plans."

Culdee had been staring long and solemnly at one of the photographs.

"I know what it means," he said. He slid the snapshot across the chart table to Miranda. She saw a middle-aged man with a handsome but rather weak face. Like the faces of the yachtsmen she'd crewed for so long ago. He seemed to be giving orders to someone out of the picture, and his face wore a look of weary petulance. He had on a dark blue baseball cap over his close-cropped hair. The cap bore no slogans or insignia, but there was gold leaf on its bill. Underneath, in a cramped, spiky handwriting—Cotinho's fist, all right—it said, "Commodore Millikan, U.S.N."

"Millikan, my ass," Culdee said. "I know that guy. He's the fucker who jobbed me in North Vietnam, who got me kicked out of the navy." He grabbed an oyster from Freddie's gift basket and shucked it with his rigging knife. The juice ran down over his scarred, lumpy knuckles. "What it means," he said, "what it means is that

151

this boat has the right name for both of us. *Venganza,* hey? We've both got a shipmate to kill down there."

He slurped the oyster and grabbed another, his knife wet in the lamplight. Freddie, watching, smiled.

As dawn broke behind them, *Venganza* made all sail and squared her yards for San Lázaro.

Part Four
THE DANGEROUS GROUND

TWENTY-ONE

The last pickup was scheduled for sunset at a small dirt airstrip on a Thai island called Ko Kut, just across the Cambodian border. The planes would be old ADs, the prop-driven Spads from the early days of the Vietnam War, now foisted off on the Thai Air Force by the U.S. They'd be coming down from Ban Sattahip, via Chanthaburi and Trat, loaded with smack. Curt glassed the island from a mile offshore, scanning the 'groves until he picked up the jetty he'd been told to look for. Its pilings were spiky with barnacles now that the tide was out. A trail from the red smear of the runway atop the bluff led downhill to it. There was a tin-roofed hut at one end of the runway with a radar mast and a wind sock on opposite corners and a jeep parked near the door. The radar dish was looking northwest. Then it swung due north and locked there, quivering. Curt was about to put down the binoculars when the door of the hut burst open. Two men ran out and jumped into the jeep. They disappeared in a cloud of red dust. A moment later he heard the planes. They were jets.

Billy Torres, in the other Thunder, heard them, too. He looked over to Curt and shook his head. A definite no. Billy grabbed a flak jacket from the gunwale and put it on. Then he put on a steel helmet. Then he picked up the rocket launcher. Well, Curt thought, when in Rome. . . . But he couldn't find his Kevlar vest. Or his hard hat. Or the fucking Redeye missile unit, either—too late now, anyway.

The jets, two of them, droop-nosed F-4 Phantoms, swept in low from the north in echelon, so low over the backbone of the island that their exhaust swirled in the thorn scrub. They broke right and left and bored in on the Thunders. The cannon flashes started when the jets were still half a mile away. Curt jammed the throttles forward and felt the Thunder leap out, straight toward a column of geysers spouting and collapsing where the cannon shells had hit the water. He spun the wheel hard right and shot inshore, along the reverse line of the cannon fire. He could taste salt spray hanging in the air when he bounced over the seething holes in the water. The jets had passed overhead by now and were sweeping at wave-top level in opposite circles. The Phantoms were painted brown and green, but they bore no numbers or national markings. Their low speed caused them to wallow in the heavy, wet air. They had his range now. . . .

Out of the corner of his eye, Curt glimpsed a brilliant flash. Billy had the Redeye tube at his shoulder, he saw. Smoke trailed lazily downwind. The Phantom on his left suddenly disappeared in a boil of white light. Bits of it rained down, pocking the sea, and one hunk whined over Curt's head. Another splatted hard against the gas drums stored aft, but nothing blew up. He ducked, about half an hour too late, as usual. The remaining jet kicked in its afterburners and climbed steeply toward heaven. Curt saw Billy tracking it with the rocket launcher, but he didn't fire a second round. Maybe better that way: let the survivor go home and think about it. Billy looked over to Curt again and pumped one fist, up and down, rapidly. Make tracks. Then he pointed toward the Ko Kut shore. Follow me.

They lay inshore among the mangroves until it was dark. The mosquitoes were fierce."

"What the fuck was that all about?" Curt asked.

"Who cares?" Billy said. "Happens sometimes. Always has, always will. Somebody didn't lay the right number of bahts on the right colonel? Or maybe the wrong general. Or maybe it's just some old-school Thai who refused to play the game." He pulled a San Mig from his cooler and popped it, then took a series of long, noisy swallows. "You see that mother go boom, though? I love that, when that happens. Thank Christ these Thais can't shoot worth shit."

Billy finished the beer and threw the bottle over the side. Crabs scuttled in the mangrove roots. He stooped over and lugged something limp up to the gunwale. It was a Tausuq with no head, Billy's crewman. His T-shirt had said something witty, Curt remembered, but now it was obscured by blood. Billy slipped him over the side. Blood washed away as the body wallowed in the shallows. The T-shirt said, NO PAIN, NO GAIN. Not so witty after all. The crabs hit the water running and headed toward the Tausuq. Chow time.

"You got a beer to spare?" Curt asked Billy. "I'm fresh out."

"Tough luck," Billy said. He popped himself another and chugged it down. "You shouldn't drink so much on duty." He tossed the bottle at the dead Tausuq. It bounced off his chest. Curt's Tausuq hissed and looked away.

"Okay," Billy said. "That's it. Let's blow this pop stand."

They headed back east toward Lázaro. Curt's Tausuq was sulking in the rear of the cockpit, squatting back against the reserve gas drums.

"Easy, Abdul," Curt told him. "It's over now."

"Never over," Abdul said. "Always just beginning already."

Every week, usually on a Thursday, a Philippine Navy PBM-3 Mariner flew in to Balbal and landed on the water off the lee shore. The commo had another installation there, top secret, with radio masts and concrete bunkers. It was hidden back in the jungle, up a narrow but deep channel through the mangroves. You couldn't see it from sea or air unless you knew it was there.

The weekly Mariners had no markings on them, but Curt knew from talking to the flying boat's crew that they were Flip navy. "You come Davao-side sometime, Joe," a friendly first-class aviation machinist told him. "I make nice party for you. We got pretty girl Davao-side. We eat *kilawin*, raw fish with soy sauce put lead in your pencil, drink lotsa tuba wine, fuck them Chinese and Hapon girl plenty. Make 'em go *ee-tai*, hey? Ouchy-ouchy, hey! You and me, we eat durian for dessert."

"What's durian?"

"Durian better than Hapon girl for dessert," the first-class said.

157

"Smells like shit, tastes like heaven." He stooped back into the plane and threw a mango-like fruit to Curt. "Try it," he said, "you like it."

The first-class was right on all counts.

After loading their cargo—scag, opium, bricks of Thai hash—the Flips took off and shaped a course to Mindanao. Curt checked their flight log once when the crew was ashore. Davao, all right. Just the facts, ma'am.

After the first run Billy stayed on the beach. "He's trigger-happy," the commodore told Curt. "He thinks ordnance grows on trees. He thinks its like Chinese firecrackers. Redeyes cost money—a fortune! You should be able to dodge those dorks when they shoot at you. This is a high-tech boat, capable of incredibly evasive maneuvers."

"How come they shot at us?" Curt asked.

"Somebody blew it in Bangkok," the commodore said. He threw a piercing look at Curt. "Why?"

"You ought to get rid of that Bangkok dude."

"Maybe I did."

"Who was he? Just for my own curiosity."

"Yours not to reason why, Cappy," the commodore said. "Leave that part to me."

The *Sea Witch* was anchored out in the roadstead now. Two or three nights a week Rosalinda came aboard after dark, from a bumboat, and she and Curt made love in the wide bunk in the captain's cabin. Curt had been right about her. She was hot. She had a mouth on her like sizzling liver. Brillo seemed to like her, too; he always got on well with women. Rosalinda cooked good chow—a hot coconut soup she called *binakol; dinengdeng,* which she made from eggplant, squash, and the leafy green lettucelike *kangkong* and splashed heavily with *bagoong,* a spicy sauce of fish and shrimp fermented in brine; and *adobo* stews of chicken and pork spiked with vinegar, soy, garlic, chunks of liver, and—sometimes—chilies as hot as anything Curt had blistered his tongue on in Mexico. These fires were duly extinguished with fruit salads chilled in shaved ice—papaya, mango, tart little red bananas, guava, lanzon, chico, rambutan, and—of course—the malodorous, melt-in-your-mouth durian. "We call this *halo-halo* in Tagalog," she said as she dished up the salad. "Means 'mix-mix.' Good eats, hey?" Curt could only groan and grin. Christ, he was getting *fat!*

One night soon after the Phantom attack at Ko Kut the crewman Abdul came alongside in a pump boat. Rosalinda ducked below as he roared in from the dark. The Tausuq tied up and jumped aboard the *Sea Witch*. He had something wrapped in a hunk of canvas and, he chunked it down on the chart table.

"You been notice dat bad smell on da Tunder?" he asked. "Gets worse and worse each days. Been making sick, me. I look, I poke, I hunt it down. Find it already back among da gas drums."

Curt unwrapped the canvas and the smell hit him hard. It was a human head, rotted from the heat and covered with a writhing mass of red ants and maggots. He quickly covered his mouth and nose with a bandanna and brushed the insects away. A white man's head—the one remaining eye was blue, the mustache on the ragged upper lip a reddish blond. There was something familiar about the bloated face . . .

He remembered the Phantom's blowing up on impact with Billy's rocket, the bits and pieces whizzing through the air, the thing that splatted against the gas drums but didn't blow them up. This must have been it. Jet fighter. White man. Then it came to him. Phil Chalmers, Major, U.S. Air Force, currently assigned to Military Air Transport but formerly a fighter jock in Vietnam. This thing was Phil's head.

"Okay, Abdul," he said. "Well done. It's probably from the pilot of that plane we blew up last time. Nothing mysterious about it."

He chucked the head, canvas and all, over the side.

"Not show Mr. Billy? Not show commodore?"

"Not while they're eating, Abdul," Curt said. "I'll tell them in the morning."

Abdul went back ashore, shaking his head gloomily. Rosalinda

159

waited until the sound of his Suzuki 25 faded away completely before she came topside again.

"What was that?" she asked.

"Abdul found a hunk of rotten meat on the Thunder. I deep-sixed it. How come you're so afraid of him seeing you?"

"I'd lose face," she said. "Sleeping with a white man. I've got my position to consider, you know."

Later, after she'd done the dishes, they made love on the cockpit deck. He saw Brillo watching them from the cabin roof. The dog looked envious. Too bad, old pal. We've got her *position* to consider, you know.

"See you again tomorrow night?" she said when the bumboat returned for her.

"Afraid not, Rosa," Curt said. "We've got another run laid on. Duty calls."

"Not Ko Kut again?"

"No," Curt said. "Too hot there last time. The commo won't decide on the place till after we're under way. He'll radio us at the last minute with the rendezvous coordinates. Less chance for double-crosses that way."

Later, when she'd gone, Curt lay topside under the stars and thought about Phil Chalmers. Why in the hell would his old business buddy try to wipe him out? They'd never really been friends, of course. As far as Phil knew, Curt was just another minor-league dope runner, hardly worth killing if to do so required wiping out part of an outfit Phil himself wanted to do business with. But, of course, in the dope trade it always paid off to eliminate anyone who could tie you to the business, and Curt had, after all, made a veiled threat against Phil back in Manila that night. Probably he'd signed on with another of the many organizations in Southeast Asia that were channeling heroin from the Golden Triangle back to the United States. Or maybe Phil wasn't really as corrupt as he seemed. Maybe, like Curt himself, he was working under cover for some government intelligence outfit. That would really be ironic. Mysterious East, hell. The mysterious West was more like it.

160

In the morning, when Abdul brought the Thunder alongside fueled and ready for the run, Curt looked over the side for the head. It rested like a huge sea slug on the coral rubble near the anchor. Already the crabs and reef fish had been at work on it. Parrot fish nibbled at the mustache.

TWENTY-TWO

The sun was already on its downward slide when *Venganza* raised the Flyaways. Miranda, halfway up the ratlines, could see a plume of smoke from a volcanic cone off to the southwest, trailing low and blue under the trades, then the peak of Mount Haplit itself, a broken, lopsided blue-black lump just breaking the horizon's rim. That was San Lázaro. The Moro lookout in the mainmast's top shouted something and pointed ahead. She trained the binoculars in the direction he gestured. Low, dirty white waves surged and chopped as far as she could see, and occasional flashes of brown coral or yellow sand showed through the sea spume. Reefs. Lots of them. Coming up fast.

"Dangerous ground!" yelled the old *mundo*, whose name was Kasim. He seemed delighted.

"Strike that mainsail," she said when she hit the deck. "Scandalize the bastard, fast! The mizzen, too." Freddie jumped, yelling to the other Moros. "Bring her up into the wind," she told Culdee at the helm.

"No, no," the old *mundo* said. "I know way in. Take off speed, yes, but no come up to wind. We be fine." He took the helm from Culdee and yelled something to the lookout. The lookout pointed off the port bow and sinuated his hand like a snake. "Channel lie there," Kasim said. "We follow."

They eased with bare steerageway through the winding channel. Occasional coral heads rose suddenly to within inches of the keel, and twice they scraped them—ugly, hollow, rasping sounds that

162

caused Miranda to bite her lips. She had Culdee light off the engine. That way she could back down fast if they began to run aground. It was the only insurance available, beyond faith.

"*Putas,*" Kasim said, frowning. "These rocks, whores? That is how we name them here. What you name them by your homeplace?"

"Whores," Culdee said. "At any rate, that's what they call them on the charts off the Maine coast. *Putas.*" They laughed. The sea is the same the world over.

It felt like an hour at least, but by the time they cleared the reefs, Miranda saw that the sun had sunk only an inch or two toward the western horizon. She shook herself to relax as they entered blue water. Her lips were raw and numb. She'd hate to have to run that channel alone. On both sides, all the way through, they had seen what looked like wrecks shifting in the surge. Broken masts and bowsprits, covered with gull guano, protruded into the salt haze over the reefs—like *punji* stakes, Culdee said. Big, dark, hawklike birds swung, stiff-winged, low over the water as Freddie's boys bent on more sail. Bird cries cut the wind, at once mournful and contemptuous. "Gallows bird," Kasim said. "Eat people."

The lookout yelled again. He pointed to the south, off *Venganza*'s port beam. Miranda returned to the ratlines with the glasses. At first she saw only the dark bulk of San Lázaro and the lesser dark green of what must be Isla Balbal. Then she spotted two wakes—rooster tails from fast motors—cutting toward them from the south. As they neared, she made out two pump boats bouncing on the chop.

"*Lázareños,*" Kasim said. "*Mundo. Muy malo.*" He yelled again to his men. Weapons suddenly appeared—ugly, wood-stocked guns with long, curved magazines. Even the lookout in the mainmast had one, concealed in a furl of sailcloth.

"AKs," Culdee said. "Good medicine."

"We cannot let them escape," Kasim said. "Capitán Katana very strong on that. *Sorpresa,* how you say, 'surprise'? *Muy importante.*"

"Who's Capitán Katana?" Miranda asked.

"Padre's navy adviser," Kasim said. "Chinee, I think, him."

Now the two pump boats lay off, paralleling *Venganza*'s course

163

out of gunshot range. There were three men in one boat, two in the other. One of the three climbed up on his engine cover to get a better look at them. He danced slightly, as if on coals.

"Must be scorching his feet," Culdee said. "They've been running wide open."

"Tausuq, hard feet," Kasim said. He slapped his own soles—hard and hollow-sounding, like old leather or horn. "*Muy calloso.*"

Culdee slipped below for a moment. When he returned, he had his .30/30 case, with the butt of the oiled walnut stock just showing through the unzipped fleece of the lining.

"You watch," Kasim said. "You must look frighten of us." He widened his eyes and drooped his mouth in mock fear. Then he jumped up onto the cabin roof and waved to the pump boats. He yelled to them in Tausuq. The two boats began to converge on *Venganza*. But slowly, slowly.

"They sniff crippled meat," Kasim said softly. "They would pick the bones." He waved and yelled some more, laughing happily. He pulled his bolo and gestured fiercely at Miranda and Culdee. They cowered convincingly.

While the boat with two crewmen lay off, the other came alongside. Two Tausuqs in baseball caps and ripped sarongs swung over the taffrail. They were young and carried bolos. As they steadied on deck, Kasim grabbed one and cut his throat. A Moro rose from beside the mainmast and shot the other as he turned. From the main top, a long clattering burst chopped down the two in the boat lying off before it could get under way. Empty brass clanked down and bounced off the deck.

The pump boat alongside burst away in a great horrified roar, throwing oily spray across Miranda's face. She heard a loud, heavy, single bang beside her, and as her eyes cleared, saw Culdee crouched against the taffrail, the .30/30 out and tracking. Another bang. He worked the lever, brass flew. He shot again. She saw the escaping pump boat suddenly buck and swerve sideways. Its engine died. Pale blue smoke . . . The Tausuq at the tiller—an old man with wild gray hair—tried to leap overboard, diving low toward the

164

outrigger. Culdee fired a fourth shot. The Tausuq disappeared underwater, flailing.

Culdee was up, levering in his last round. "I don't know," he yelled, "did I hit him?" His face was pale under his tan, and his beard blew in the following wind. Kasim yelled up to the lookout. The lookout shouted back, nodding vigorously, his face in a wide, white grin.

"*Sí!*" Kasim said. "Suleiman say you kill him. Sharp eyes, Suleiman. *El águila.* 'Eagle'? Here." He poked a hard finger under Culdee's right armpit, then poked him in the lower left ribs. "Through and through," he said. "*Muerto!*"

Culdee turned and vomited over the side. He retched again and again, emptying his stomach. Then he sat weakly on deck with the rifle across his knees. "Too much adrenaline on an empty stomach," he said to no one in particular. His smile was weak and shaky, apologetic. Freddie came up to him.

"They would have done us worse already," he said in a soft voice. "They would be laughing now. You good man, Culdee."

Culdee turned and retched again.

"Okay," Miranda said quietly. She, too, was pale. "Let's get back on course."

Looking astern, she saw gallows birds already swinging over the sinking boats.

From his hammock on the lanai, Commodore Millikan watched Curt's Thunder and two others depart for their Thai run. A few minutes later he saw Billy Torres approach the *Sea Witch* in a pump boat. The big dog on the cabin roof studied him silently. Pure menace. The commodore watched Billy anchor near the yawl, then shrug into scuba gear and slide over the side. Good. That morning Abdul had come with Billy to the commodore and reported the severed head. The commodore was furious—"You should have told me about it right away!" he raged. "What did you think you were up to?"

"Obeying orders," Abdul said. His mouth wore a sullen twist, but then it always did. "You say many time, use chain of command, not bother you with stupid businesses."

"Well, damn it," the commodore spluttered. "Next time you find something like that, bring it to me or to Mr. Torres."

"You mean like another American head, or what?" Billy asked. All innocence, of course.

"I mean something important!" the commodore shouted. He saw the houseboys watching him fearfully. One of them, though, was hiding a grin. That was Daoud, the one with the good English. "Get out of here!" he yelled at them. "Go help Rosalinda pluck those chickens." They departed quickly for the butcher block, where the estimable Rosa was killing the evening meal.

"*Mr.* Torres," the commodore said, "you will go with Abdul out to that yawl as soon as Mr. Hughes has departed on his run. The two of you will dive up that head and bring it to me. On the double."

"So Abdul doesn't go along with Curt this run?" Torres asked. "Who do you want to replace him? And won't Curt get to wondering why no Abdul this time?"

The commodore hadn't thought of that. Get hold of yourself, he thought. He tried to swallow his fury. No, he realized, his goddamn embarrassment.

"You're right," he said at last. Calmly. "Abdul goes with Curt. You dive it up alone, Billy. You're scuba-qualified. Now . . . get to it."

While Billy dived, the commodore dozed. He hadn't been sleeping well lately. Not since the Phantom attack. There'd been fuck-ups before on the Thai end, always were in a business like this. But never before had such sophisticated aircraft been involved. Not that Phantoms were top-line planes anymore, compared with what the real navies and air forces flew. But for Southeast Asia? This was strange. And now a white man's head. . . . He dozed off into uneasy dreams of carnival sideshows, leering Asian magicians, severed heads floating in dusky air and flickering like old black-and-white movies . . .

He woke to the sound of footsteps on the crushed-shell walkway that led up to the lanai. A timid tap on the screen door. Ah, Billy! But when he swung from the hammock, he saw two Filipinos, a man

166

and a woman, standing at the door in their Sunday best. The man wore a pressed but shiny black suit, white shirt, and black tie; the woman, a lumpy gray dress and a silly straw hat with plastic fruit on it. They were gray-haired, solemn.

"What do you want?" the commodore snapped at them.

"We're from the gospel, sir," the man said. He gestured with a black-covered book. "Are you saved, sir?"

Goddamn it! Jehovah's Witnesses! You couldn't get away from them—not even out here, in this cannibal isle.

"Yes, I'm saved," the commodore said. "Now go away and save someone else."

"But what church are you, sir?" the old man persisted. The woman stared at him, smiling weakly but bravely.

"None of your goddamn business! Now clear out before I call the houseboys to drive you away with whips. As Christ scourged the money changers from the Temple."

"You are disturbed, sir," the old man said gravely. "If we could but speak with you awhile, perhaps—"

"No! Can't you see, I'm busy? Now scram, both of you!"

"We will just leave you a copy of this Good Book, sir, and some brief, simply written pamphlets with consoling words from the Prophets. If you care to keep the book, a small donation—"

But the commodore was advancing on them now with blood in his eye. The old man laid the book on the stoop, then he and the woman fled. Her high heels spiked the lawn, and she almost fell, but the old man caught her arm, and they redoubled their speed.

Billy, holding a heavy canvas parcel at arm's length, watched them pass.

"What was that about?" he asked the commodore a moment later.

"Religious freaks," the commodore fumed. "Born-agains. Witnesses. I don't know. But, Christ, they're persistent. You got it?"

"Yes, but you'd better put on a gas mask." Billy laid the parcel on the glass-topped table. Even tightly sealed it smelled disgusting.

The commodore took a deep breath and opened the canvas.

Hold on to your lunch, he ordered his stomach. He put on his half-glasses and bent over the thing. Most of the face had been nibbled away by reef fish, but the side that had lain on the bottom still bore large patches of skin. He fetched the magnifying glass that came with his compact edition of the *Oxford English Dictionary* and peered closely.

"Beats me," he said at last. "Round-eye sure enough, but he could be a Russian, a Brit, a Frenchman, even an American for all we know."

"He is," Torres said. "American, that is. He's a fly-boy from MATS in Manila, name of Phillip Chalmers. I did some business with him through the shipping line a while back. He was angling to get in on the heroin traffic, or at least he seemed to be. He's also the guy who recommended Curt to us."

The commo mixed himself a stiff drink at the portable mahogany bar—Glenlivet on ice, no twist—and gestured to Billy to help himself. They went out onto the lawn. The lanai would probably stink for a week. He lighted one of the five Manila cigarillos he allowed himself each day and paced the close-grown, dewy grass in the fading dusk.

"CIA?" he asked Torres at last. "Maybe DEA? We've got plenty of enemies in Washington."

"Could be," Torres said.

"Take that thing down to the photo lab and get some close-ups. Good ones, in strong light. Bracket the bastard. Get me some decent snaps, and we'll send them to ONI back home, maybe someone knows this guy. Then put the head in the freezer, double-wrapped. We may need it as evidence somewhere down the line."

"What about Curt?"

"He's no threat," the commo said. "There's no indication he's anything but a fast-boat bum, a runner. We've checked out his background, and he's okay. Small potatoes. This Chalmers probably fed him to us to improve his own image—if he *was* a spook, that is. He could just as well have been working for some other heroin conduit aiming to take us over. Keep a close eye on Curt, though. We can eliminate him whenever we feel it's necessary."

"Well, sir," Billy said, "if it comes to that, and I hope it does, I'd like to volunteer for the assignment."

It was dark by the time *Venganza* reached her destination—a long, low island enclosed by a coral reef on which the surf pounded in rhythmic, luminous explosions.

"What is this place?" Miranda asked Kasim.

"Isla Perniciosa," he said. "How you say, 'Island of Harms'? 'Of Dangers'? Not much here, just bad *culebras*, bad snakes, hey? And plenty mosquitoes." He whined like a million of them, then laughed for joy. "You bring down sails now," he said.

Kasim piloted the schooner through the reef and motored around to the northwest side of the island. The channel, in starlight, looked sharp-edged in places, as if it had been blasted by dynamite and shaped by capable engineers. A concrete and coral-block mole projected into the lagoon at the end of the zigzagging channel, and Kasim brought the schooner alongside it. Men waited in the dark for their mooring lines. The bollards on the mole looked sturdy, businesslike, not the usual makeshift mangrove stumps seen on other docks in this part of the world. They tied up behind what looked like a floating crane, its arm bent dark against the darkness.

"These men take care of ship," Kasim said, pointing to the hands at the mooring lines. "We go now, you meet Capitán Katana."

"Who'd you say he was?" Culdee asked. "Cotinho's naval adviser? I thought Cotinho was just a simple priest, a missionary kind of guy."

"*Sí,*" Kasim said, smiling happily. "*Misionario,* Padre Cotinho 'missionary'! Sure enough! Capitán Katana his good friend, his *ayudante*—'adjutant,' right? You meet now, we go."

"Chinese, he said before," Culdee whispered to Miranda. "Probably a Chi Com—Red China's everywhere out here, one way or another. You know him, Freddie?"

"Nope," Freddie said. He looked off into the night.

Kasim led them inland, along a narrow, winding path of crushed coral toward a low ridge that loomed dark against the stars. Sharp cactus thorns plucked at their clothes in the tighter corners. They were all wobbly-legged, still swaying from the sea. Land crabs scuttled noisily away. Once or twice swifter things slithered off into the cactus, thick and leathery. Snakes? Maybe just lizards. Kasim's mosquitoes were hungry, all right. Under the brow of the ridge they came to a heavy steel door set in the coral slope. Kasim banged on it twice, paused, banged once, then three times more. A slot opened in the door, and an eye peered out. What's this, Culdee thought, a pernicious Filipino speakeasy? The door opened.

At the end of a low corridor cut into the concrete they came to a second steel door, this one open and secured. Beyond it, a bunker. Sure, this must be the old Jap sub base the *Pilot* mentioned. The walls were hung with maps and charts—Culdee recognized a large map of Southeast Asia studded with red and blue marking pins, and a detailed chart of the Flyaways similarly marked. In the center of the room was a chart table, lighted by an old-fashioned gooseneck lamp. Moros stood around it, peering down at another chart. A taller man, Asian also, from the shape of his shaved, flat-backed head, stood with a pointer in his hand. He wore starched, military-looking khakis. The Moros looked up as they entered. The tall man turned, dropping his pointer. As it fell, he caught it on the toe of his shoe and flipped it, sending it spinning back up in the air. "Bloody hell!" he exclaimed, snatching the pointer. He faced them now.

"Ah," he said, a warm smile on his face. "The Yank battlewagon has at last arrived. Welcome, shipmates!" He stepped toward them. "I'm Captain Katana. But you may call me Sôbô."

Rosalinda came onto the lanai, her arms laden with dishes. She and the boys had cleaned the table thoroughly, and the stink of Lysol had replaced the other one. Dinner was already half an hour late, and she had yet to set the table. She looked around for the duty houseboy. The commodore stood at the far end of the lanai, sipping a cocktail.

"Where's Daoud, sir?" she asked.

"I sent him out to the trash barrels," the commodore replied.

"Some religious types brought me a bundle of their trash this evening and left it on the stoop. I told Daoud to dump it. And not to stop and read it along the way. That kid's always got his nose in a book, especially if it's written in English."

Not Daoud, she thought. Oh, Mother of God, not Daoud . . .

The explosion shivered the screens and set the lamps swaying. Rosalinda dropped the dishes with a crash that echoed the blast. Bits of shrubbery splattered against the porch as the flash faded to red and yellow flames.

By the time they reached it, the fire was already dying. Daoud lay on his back ten feet from the flames. His hands were gone. His face was black and red meat with a few white teeth stuck in it. His chest had burst open. He was dead.

Shredded paper drifted down from the dark, falling into the flickering light. For a moment the commodore thought it was snowing.

TWENTY-THREE

~~~~~~

They stood at the chart table while Captain Sôbô Katana explained the operation. The Moros had gone, and only Kasim remained with them, nodding and smiling gloriously at every stab of the pointer.

"Millikan has two bases here," Sôbô said. "This boat basin on San Lázaro itself, not far from his house, which also serves as a kind of headquarters. And a larger base on Balbal, right here." He tapped the chart. "The boat basin doesn't seem to be protected by an antisubmarine or -swimmer net, and apart from the Tausuq boat crews and Millikan's mechanics it appears only lightly guarded. There are at least eight, maybe ten, fast boats there. Blue Thunders, American-built, capable of fifty or sixty knots flank speed and armed with M60 machine guns—7.62 millimeter weapons with a rate of fire of six hundred rounds per minute, slow by modern standards—and some sort of antiaircraft missile system, shoulder-held. There are machine shops, barracks, a small armory, and a fuel dump associated with the boat-basin facility.

"We don't know much about the base at Balbal, though. It can be reached only through a narrow channel leading inland from the shore. Once a week a flying boat comes in from the east—looks like an ancient Mariner, no pun intended, a PBM of elderly aspect. Maybe Philippine Navy? No markings. The drugs Millikan's fast boats bring in from points west, Thailand mainly, are transshipped on the Mariner, probably to Mindanao. Where they go from there, we don't know. We do know, however, that the commodore has an old U.S. Navy river gunboat up at the far end of the Balbal channel. She's not much to worry about, though. That class was built around 1927 in Shanghai for patrol work on the rivers of interior China. USS *Panay* was one of them. You must remember her, Bosun? Japanese naval aircraft sunk her in the Yangtze, upriver from Nanking, on 12 December 1937. A famous incident at the time, but Washington preferred to look the other way. For that the imperial navy was always grateful. We weren't ready then. . . . But I digress. These river gunboats are 191 feet long, displace some 450 tons, and are armed with single-barreled three-inch guns fore and aft, complemented by ten .30-caliber machine guns at her waist and topside. They are shoal-draft vessels, potentially capable of eighteen knots. But we are told that Millikan's gunboat, the *Moro Armado,* is a bit wheezy in her old age. As aren't we all?" He smiled at Culdee and swung the pointer between them. "All she can do is an unreliable ten or twelve."

"That's still a lot more knots than our schooner can crank out," Culdee said.

Sôbô raised his eyebrows and smiled again, cryptically.

"In any event," he continued, "in order to retake Captain Miranda's vessel, which is anchored here"—he tapped the chart just off Millikan's house/headquarters on San Lázaro—"we must neutralize both bases. Though we have plenty of pump boats and adequate small arms, we are still outgunned, and we can certainly be outrun by Millikan's Blue Thunders. To stand any chance of completing this mission, we must make maximum use of the element of surprise."

"Like at Pearl Harbor," Culdee said.

"Precisely. And Savo Island, among other places. Yes, surprise—and temerity. With those factors in our favor, we can succeed. And we will begin early tomorrow with my plan, which I shall reveal to you in full later—on a scouting expedition to San Lázaro. I should like Captain Miranda to accompany Kasim here and Mr. Pascal"—he swung the pointer toward Efreddio—"in a pump boat to reconnoiter the boat basin and get an accurate estimate of enemy forces present. Also to study the *Sea Witch*'s anchorage, from a safe distance, and to see how many persons are aboard her. When we execute the

plan, which I have code-named Operation Seamark in honor of the
vessel's true name, the furor over our double attack on the two
bases will cover the cutting out and withdrawal of that vessel, our
primary target. Now I'm sure you're all tired from your long and no
doubt harrowing voyage. My, my, across the Pacific in just seven
weeks! Under sail! I've had quarters prepared for you on this station.
As you've probably guessed, this was an imperial navy submarine
repair and replenishment base in the late war. Your quarters are
officers' quarters. I hope you will find them comfortable. Any questions?"

"Yes," Miranda said. "Just why in the world are you and this
Padre Cotinho and all these men—Kasim and his crew—going to all
this trouble just to get a piddling little sailboat back for an American
woman you don't even know? What's in it for you?"

"A battle," Sôbô said, smiling. "A good, rousing sea fight for a
just cause. It's as simple as that, Captain."

And I'm afraid it's not, Miranda thought.

"Is all right," Kasim said, patting Miranda's shoulder. "Capitán
Katana good man. He my friend, I your friend. We all fight together,
kill unbelievers, all go to heaven in the end. *You* see."

Padre Cotinho sat in a faded canvas lawn chair under a flowering
hibiscus tree, looking down on the cathedral and, beyond it, on the
whole blue and green sprawl of the Flyaways. He was drinking tuba
asesina cut with papaya juice. He knew Padre Fagundes, watching
him from the window of the nearby rectory, would be shaking his
head sadly, as always. Rum from a priest's sacred chalice! At seven
in the morning! He and Diogo Fagundes had grown up together in
the slums of Lisbon, had attended the Jesuit seminary in Spain
together, had both been posted to the Philippines, where the Society
of Jesus traditionally served in the vanguard of missions to the Moros.
But while Cotinho had long ago grown disillusioned with the Church's
role in social reform, turning finally—reluctant at first, then with
ever fiercer certainty of its justice—to violent revolution as the
answer, Fagundes had remained complacent in the face of Macoy's

174

atrocities. A capon, Cotinho thought. But at least a loyal one. My capon. He sipped from the chalice.

Bees buzzed loud in the overhead blossoms, angrily almost, but not so furiously as Padre Cotinho. He had disapproved of the book bomb right from the start. Even if it had worked, it would have alerted Torres at least to the fact that something was going on. Now the bomb had merely killed Rosalinda Aguinaldo's most trusted messenger. Millikan was not even wounded. He would certainly react. He would certainly redouble his watchfulness, alert his men, take radical measures to ascertain who was trying to kill him, and why. But the revolutionary powers in Mindanao had approved the bomb plot. In fact, it was their idea. Better to kill the American commander in one stroke, they caviled, than risk defeat with Katana's plan. Nonsense. All they knew was bombs and knives in the night. They'd been reluctant to undertake the destruction of the Millikan operation right from the start. Cotinho had been watching it for more than a year now.

"Let us expose American corruption here in the Sulu Sea," he had argued in their councils. "The American press will love it. It will discredit the U.S. once and for all in Philippine eyes—in the eyes of all Asia, and the world. The American navy running drugs in from Thailand to further debase the American people—American youth in chemical chains forged by the U.S. Navy! And at the same time preparing a stronghold for the subsequent reconquest of the Philippines once our revolution has succeeded."

"They will deny it," the leadership replied. "They will maintain that the proof we provide is faked. Besides, the American people are bored with saying no to drugs. It will only increase American jingoism and lead to a stronger American presence, greater American military aid to the puppet government in Manila."

But then, with a stroke of fortune that could only be God's hand at work, Effredio Pascal had received a letter from some American girl. By happy chance—again, God's hand?—Padre Cotinho was on Siquijor—hiding from government salvage squads—when Pascal got the letter. Pascal of course turned to his old confessor for advice.

Padre Cotinho saw the whole plan clicking into place: PHILIPPINE FREEDOM FIGHTERS AID AMERICAN GIRL IN REDRESSING GRIEVANCE AGAINST U.S. NAVY PIRATES. And not just the good-looking, clean-cut young American woman, but her war-hero father as well—a navy man who'd been injustly ousted from the service he loved and served with total loyalty, and who now was prepared to take vengeance on that same navy for crimes committed against his helpless daughter. . . . It was perfect. Even the leadership had, finally, to agree.

But they still had their doubts about Katana. So did Padre Cotinho, for that matter. A former officer of the Imperial Japanese Navy. Elderly (though he didn't look it), and perhaps slightly loco. Perhaps, even worse, with links to Japanese organized crime. Tough-looking Japanese men accompanied him everywhere he went in the Flyaways. *Yakuza?* The Japanese equivalent of the Mafia? Perhaps the *yakuza*, quite understandably, planned to take over the operation once Millikan was destroyed. So Padre Cotinho would see to it that not a single Japanese, Katana included, survived the forthcoming battle.

But certainly Katana had a keen tactical mind. He understood ships and weapons far better than Padre Cotinho could ever hope to, far better than the revolutionary leaders could—that was certain. And even if Katana's battle plan failed—which it well might: Katana intended, after all, to divide his forces, and even Padre Cotinho had read enough Clausewitz to know that that was the route to disaster— even if the plan failed, there would be survivors enough, with photographs. It might even be better that way. BRAVE AMERICAN GIRL AND WAR-HERO FATHER DIE AT HANDS OF U.S. NAVY IMPERIALIST PIRATES. DESPITE AID OF FILIPINO FREEDOM FIGHTERS, RESCUE OPER-ATION FAILS. In a play on the phrase he had heard many Americans use, Padre Cotinho knew he couldn't lose for losing. He finished his drink—it had grown warm now, even in the shade—and rose from his chair. A short, lean, bearded man with a thick shock of white hair that still grew low on his forehead, Cotinho looked almost military in his long black soutane. The scars of many beatings crisscrossed his hard, brown face. Padre Fagundes, watching from the window of his study in the low, stucco-walled, red-roofed rectory, studied his friend's gait as he approached the house. Steady, erect, straight-backed, firm of tread despite his seventy years and that blasphemous breakfast of assassin's rum—like Saint Ignatius of Loyola himself must have walked, nearly half a millennium ago, before he was wounded and found God—and the Society of Jesus—in the blood of his wound. A soldier. Ah, but the cause?

Kasim woke them shortly before sunrise. Their rooms in the officers' quarters were spartan but clean and airy, with mosquito-proof screens on the windows. Miranda had slept well on the tatami mat and futon, enjoying the cool night breeze and the imagined sway of the land after weeks at sea. Japanese scrolls ornamented the walls of her room—scenes of samurai and doleful ladies, of Fuji and rearing blue seas. A portrait of Hirohito, looking incredibly young and garbed in full imperial robes, hung faded on one bulkhead. Chrysanthemum blossoms, floating in a bowl of water, graced the air with their delicate perfume. Kasim brought with him bowls of strong tea and a wicker platter on which rested a black, flower-patterned lacquer bowl of steaming hot water and rolled, hot towels. He told them, smiling as always, that the *capitán* awaited their pleasure in his *oficina*.

"Now then," Sôbô said when they had mustered. "Down to business. Captain Miranda, Kasim, and Mr. Pascal to their scouting mission. Bosun, you and I will be off shortly to the islands of Moro Armado and Balbal on work of our own. It will give us a chance to recall old times, tell a few sea stories, no doubt, and allow you to see the scope of these islands. Later, when we return, you may advise your companions about what you have learned. By the way, lunches and beverages have been prepared for all of us, and await us in our respective boats. Now, let's be having you."

"I thought Moro Armado was the name of Millikan's gunboat," Culdee said.

"Yes," Sôbô answered. "That class of gunboats was named for various Philippine islands. His is named for the island of Moro

177

Armado, right here in the Flyaways. You'll see it shortly. It's a prison island, political prisoners mostly—anyone who doesn't agree with the commodore's policies ends up there. It sometimes provides victims for San Lázaro's Good Friday crucifixions as well. Quaint custom, what? Tomorrow is Good Friday. But I'm afraid we'll be too busy to attend. Now let's be up and doing, shall we?"

Sôbô led them out a back exit from the bunker complex and across thorn-walled trails to the lee side of the island. Two pump boats lay beached on the white sand, their big Yamaha engines tilted up at the stern. At Sôbô's suggestion, Miranda hid behind the thorn scrub and replaced her work shirt and cap with an oversized yellow T-shirt and a bleached-out blue bandanna. "You're tall and dark enough to pass for a Moro," he told her. "This will complete the disguise." With the bandanna wrapped and knotted pirate-fashion around her pinned-up hair, she did indeed look like a *mundo*, Culdee thought. Especially with those green eyes and that hawklike profile. And with her arms folded across her chest.

"We go," Kasim said. Efreddio and Miranda pushed off, Kasim started the engine with one pull of the cord, and they were on their way.

Sôbô and Culdee headed out soon after.

The two men beached the pump boat in the near lee of Moro Armado. In the distance Culdee could see the blinding shimmer of salt pans exploding with mirages even in the low sun of morning. Huge, gaunt figures, warping in the wind, stalked the flats, then shrank instantly, becoming squat, black antlike dots. The growl of truck engines and dredges reached them through the wind. "Prisoners," Sôbô explained. "Mining salt. Those kennellike structures over there"—he pointed to some low, crusty-roofed lumps on the edge of the pans—"that's where they're housed. I think they market the salt in Zamboanga and Puerto Princesa, but of course it's just part of Millikan's shipping-enterprise cover. Those are the guard towers." He pointed to some tall, skeletal gantries that encircled the salt pans. "M60 machine guns, I'm told. Barbed wire around the whole place. Ah, here comes our man."

A jeep bounced over the salt slabs, squealed to a rusty-drummed halt, and extruded the tallest Arab Culdee had ever seen. He was clad in white from head to foot—turban, long flapping robes, even a pair of white sandals with turned-up toes. His face looked black by contrast, and, as he approached them, storklike in his stride, Culdee saw that he had one eye missing, with a white patch covering the hole.

"This is Balabatchi," Sôbô said, introducing them. "The One-Eyed Crocodile, some call him, hey, old man?" He clapped Balabatchi's bony shoulder, and the Arab smiled brilliantly. "Nominally, he's the island's sailmaker and foreman of the boat-repair yard at Narr Lagoon. In fact, he is superintendent of the guard force here. And he's with us. Now, old son"—Sôbô turned to Culdee and bowed apologetically—"if you'll excuse us for a few moments, Bala and I have some details to iron out. To 'finalize,' as you Yanks so delightfully put it."

Culdee walked the surf line, kicking seashells, while the two talked in Tausuq. Balabatchi looked like a slippery customer, all right. Never had Culdee seen a slier, more devious face. If there were two sides to any confrontation, you could bet that the One-Eyed Crocodile would not only play both of them but would also find a third and a fourth side as well, to make sure.

When Sôbô returned to the boat he looked worried.

"Blast!" he said. "Bala tells me someone made an attempt on Millikan's life last night. Some kind of book bomb. Didn't kill him, though, didn't even scratch him. But now he'll be on the alert. Stone the crows! These bloody Moros and that asinine old padre. . . . But let's get a move on. We've got business at Balbal."

"What about Miranda?" Culdee asked. He suddenly felt his heart beat double time.

Sôbô glanced at him, his black eyes glittering like go stones. "Out of our hands now, old-timer. You remember what Moltke said? 'No plan survives contact with the enemy.' "

TWENTY-FOUR

~~~~~~~~~~~~~~~~~~~~~~~~~~~~~~~~~~~~

Kasim slowed the motor as they approached the reef off San Lázaro. Miranda could see the big, low, stucco-walled house that by its size alone proclaimed itself Millikan's place. Following along the shore, she saw the fast-boat basin tucked in among the mangroves. The tin roofs of sheds flashed through coco fronds on the higher ground. Kasim cut the engine, and they drifted just inside the reef.

"We pretend to dive *conchas* here," Kasim said. "Seashell, hey?" There were face masks, snorkels, and swim fins in the bottom of the boat, the equipment all well worn and mismatched, typical island diving gear. "We work slow—*despacio*—to shallow water. Very easy. Never look ashore. Just peek. You look hard though later, hey? When you rest from dive on outrigger?" Miranda and Freddie nodded.

The reef was a ruin. Great screeslopes of dead coral scarred its inshore margin. Huge elkhorns lay toppled and shattered across the bottom, and a brain coral the size of a small sedan, white as something you'd find in a pickling jar, lolled stem-side up, where dynamiters had blasted it in search of hiding grouper. A few patches of eelgrass had managed to survive, or perhaps invade the devastated ground, and Miranda moved slowly over them picking up shells. She saw nothing of value—no Gloria Maris certainly, not even any conus shells or tridacnas, just horse conchs, or something quite like them.

Even the reef fish were few and far between—a few anemic-looking sergeant majors, a lone squirrelfish poking along as if in a trance, its colors vivid against the rubble. On one dive, Miranda thought she spotted the antennae of a rock lobster swaying at the mouth of a crevice, but when she checked it out, it proved to be nothing more than the wires of a rusted fish trap. She saw not a single moray eel. No wonder. The dynamiters had left nothing.

"This is no good," she told Kasim after half an hour. "No one in his right mind would dive this reef for shells. It's all dead down there. Anyone ashore who's watching us will know we're just pretending."

"You find pretty shell?" Kasim said joyfully. His eyebrows shot upward in delight. "Bring me, I sell, we make *mucho dinero.*"

Freddie blew his snorkel beside her and pushed back the mask. She repeated what she'd told Kasim. "He doesn't understand," Freddie said. "A lot of these old Moro, they don't swim, sure don't dive." He said something to Kasim in Samal, the old Moro's tribal tongue. "Okay," Freddie said. "Let's just move inshore steadily now, in the boat, make a slow pass. We check it out, then go."

As they neared the shore, they saw plenty of activity in the fast-boat basin. Men hustled from boat to boat, loading things, lugging oil drums and what looked like ammunition boxes. The ragged pulse of revving engines sounded like a swarm of hornets preparing for war.

"I count a good ten boats in there," Miranda told Freddie. "Maybe more; I can't see into that far bay. Too much shade. How many men do you make out?"

"Thirty, forty," Freddie said. "They run so fast, can't keep count."

Just then a boat idled out from under the shade and into the channel. Miranda saw machine-gun barrels sticking up at angles beside the windscreen. A man stood on the engine housing, glassing them. He was short but wide-shouldered, steady as a rock on the swaying deck, and he seemed to be wearing a navy fatigue uniform. He pointed to them and yelled something to the Tausuq at the Thunder's helm. She leapt toward them.

"We run?" Kasim asked. He looked nervous for the first time since Miranda had met him.

181

"No," she said. "Not fast enough, us. We wait, pretend we just fishermen." And lots of luck, she thought.

"Let me talk," Freddie said. "You go back by the motor, pretend you're fixing it. Don't let them see you face to face."

Crouched by the engine, Miranda heard them talking in Moro or some other language. The wide man had a hard, military-sounded voice, imperious. Freddie whined and faltered, obsequious as a frightened islander certainly would be in such circumstances. Kasim said nothing. Miranda cut one quick glance behind her. Kasim was up in the pump boat's bow, easing his way out of the wide man's line of vision. He was peering curiously, wide-eyed and simple seeming, into the Thunder's cockpit, where the driver stood watching the dialogue between Freddie and the wide man. The wide man had a big hunk of one ear missing . . .

Then everything happened at once. The wide man began to draw his pistol. Freddie dived toward him, they grappled and teetered on the Thunder's gunwale. Kasim was in the Thunder's cockpit, his bolo flashing bright in a downward arc. There was the bang of the wide man's pistol, the juicy thwop of Kasim's bolo. Freddie and the wide man toppled into the water. Kasim yelled something to Miranda, gesturing her into the fast boat. She jumped . . .

"God-*damnit!*" Commodore Millikan, watching the whole proceeding through his binoculars from the boat-basin dock, suddenly danced with fury. "Idiot!" He watched the Thunder race off in a boil of white wake. Torres and the man from the pump boat were still flailing in the water. "I'll shoot that stupid fuck!" he yelled. The crewmen around him edged away. "Billy Torres has the brains of a sea slug—no, less." He'd told Torres to bring the pump boat in, no fuss, no palaver, certainly no guns. The commodore wanted to talk to those people, at his leisure. If they were just innocent fisherman, all right, he'd let them go. No sense in alienating the locals any more than necessary. If they were part of this plot, whatever it was, he'd find out. So Billy gets into an argument and draws his fucking .45. . . . Trigger-happy Flips! Idiots, all of them!

The commodore waved a boat over, jumped in, and ran out to where the men in the water were still fighting. The islander, if that's what he was, had a knife in one hand. Billy had him by the wrist, trying to shake the knife loose. Both men were spluttering, coughing, blood dripping from their faces and diluting in the splash. Then Billy got the knife away from the islander.

"Don't kill him, Billy!" the commodore roared. "Kill him, and you're dead!" He had his own pistol out now, and he fired it into the sky. Billy was still trying to cut the islander. The commodore shot into the water beside him. He had to shoot twice more before Billy got the message.

He looked up at the commodore, rage still hot in his eyes.

"All right, Billy," the commodore said, trying to gain control of himself. It was hard, with the 9-millimeter Walther in his hand. "We'll take him ashore and ask him a few questions. *As I told you to begin with!*"

Two more Thunders were turning slow circles around them, awaiting orders. Only now did the commo become aware of them. His fury surged again.

"Get them!" he yelled at the boat crews. He pointed seaward. They stared back at him, stupidly. "The other boat! Our boat! Get it! Get it *back! But don't kill the people in it!*" Two Thunders roared out in pursuit of the first.

It was a hard climb through the Balbal jungle, but Sôbô seemed tireless. Culdee's legs were quivering after twenty minutes, and his breath came short, fast, and ragged. His mouth tasted of stale salt from the sweat cascading into it faster than he could spit.

"Hey, hold up!" he gasped at last. Sôbô turned, surprised. Culdee was slumped beside the muddy trail. "What's the hurry?" he puffed.

"Sorry, old man. Didn't notice. Here, have a swallow—it's just cool water, no whiskey." Culdee accepted the canteen gratefully. He washed out his mouth, spat, then swallowed two long pulls. His breath was coming back.

"Too long at sea," he said. "No exercise except steering and and hauling. Sorry."

"No problem. My fault actually. *Mea culpa,* old bean."

They were heading up a steep mountain trail that was leading them into Balbal's interior. Two short, dark, naked men with ritual scars on their faces and chests had met them at the beach. They had kinky peppercorn hair, black wiry beards, and carried spears. Negritos, Sôbô had explained briefly. He had to see their leaders this morning. It was vital.

"You're in pretty damned good shape," Culdee said when he could. "How the hell do you do it? You've got to be pushing seventy."

"Sixty-eight," Sôbô answered. "I was the youngest member of my class at the naval academy on Eta Jima. But I try to keep fit. Eat a lot of seaweed, that's the secret. Popeye the Sailorman. That wasn't really spinach in those cans—it was seaweed, old top. Make a lightfoot lad of you again every time."

"Well, I wish you'd brought a can or two along on this expedition," Culdee said.

It took them another hour to reach the Negrito camp, proceeding at a slower pace until Culdee's legs could handle a steady rhythm. At one point the two guides, who had been moving so silently and invisibly that Culdee had almost forgotten them, suddenly came darting back. They looked fearful and kept jabbing their spears toward the jungle canopy ahead. One of them was whispering to Sôbô.

"They say it's a *balbal,* the giant man-eating flying squirrel for which this island is named," Sôbô explained. "It swoops down out of the trees and licks up Negritos with its sticky tongue, then takes them off to tiffin. Actually, it's a *haribon,* a very large, monkey-eating eagle. One of the largest and rarest eagles in the world. The bird books say you'll find it only on Mindanao. Let them think so. I've seen them once or twice before, coming up here to chat with these fellows."

Sôbô withdrew a small automatic pistol from inside his shirt and gestured the guides forward. They moved cautiously. Then Sôbô crouched. "There," he whispered to Culdee.

The big bird stood erect on a limb, glaring down at them. Its hooked beak was red with blood. One great yellow talon was buried in the throat of a very dead monkey. The eagle rattled its beak and screamed—a long, metallic, blood-chilling scream. Then it flapped off into the canopy with the dead monkey trailing from its claws.

"New addition to your life list," Sôbô said, smiling back at Culdee.

The Negrito village was a small circle of huts surrounding a thatched longhouse in a clearing. Blue, sour-smelling smoke trailed listlessly up from cook fires and pooled under the jungle canopy. Small, dark women with breasts too large for their frail bodies darted away when they appeared. Their children toddled after them. Men came out of the longhouse to greet them. With them was a taller, lighter-skinned Negrito in what looked like an army jungle uniform. He carried a pistol holstered on his hip and wore a floppy-brimmed green jungle hat of the sort seen in old film clips of the Burma campaign. He strode crisply up to Sôbô and saluted.

"This is Grande," Sôbô told Culdee. "Crackerjack jungle fighter. Ex-Philippine Army Scout Ranger. Great record in the war. Killed more of my countrymen than the A-bomb. I don't for a moment doubt it. I've had him training these tribesmen for a little flanking attack I have in mind. Now, if you don't mind, I have details to work out with Sergeant Grande."

One of the Negrito guides brought Culdee a steaming calabash full of dark liquid. He sniffed it warily. Just coffee—and good coffee at that. The other brought him a platter of fried sliced bananas. When he had finished the meal, the two men invited him into the longhouse. It was dark and smoky in there, but the jungle light filtered through the plaited roof, and gradually Culdee could make out details. The most striking of these were the shrunken heads that adorned the roof posts—dozens of them, it seemed. And they were not the heads of other Negritos. Some had red hair, some close-cropped stiff black hair, others the black, curly tresses and long

185

noses of Tausuqs. One was blond. Culdee stared at them long and hard. One of the Negritos nudged his partner and pointed to Culdee, laughing.

"*Sí, hombre,*" he said when Culdee looked over at him. "*Como tú.* White Joe Milikan, hey?" The Negritos fell down laughing, tears streaming from their eyes. Culdee went out, trying to laugh along with them. Waiting on the longhouse steps, he noticed that many of the Negrito men carried rifles as well as spears. From old newsreels and books on the war he recognized the weapons as the standard broom-stocked Japanese 7.7-millimeter Type 99 infantry rifles. But these didn't look as though they dated back forty-some years to a war in a tropical jungle. They looked fresh out of the box, gleaming with oil, scarcely a speck of rust of them. And though the rifles were nearly as tall as most of the Negritos, the men handled them familiarly, almost as naturally as they did their spears.

Then Sôbô was ready to leave. He returned Sergeant Grande's salute, exchanged good-byes with the Negrito elders, and they headed back down the trail.

"Fascinating place, what?" he said to Culdee.

"Those heads are a bit spooky," Culdee replied. "Christ, they had white men in there."

"And plenty of Japanese, too," Sôbô added. "Don't forget that, old sport. These, by the way, are the fellows described in the guidebooks as kin of the 'gentle Tasaday.' If that's gentle, you have to wonder what the grumpy ones are like."

Kasim's maneuvers at the wheel of the Thunder sent Miranda sprawling onto the cockpit deck. By the time she found her feet and groped her way to the handgrips up forward, she saw they were not heading back the way they'd come, but south, toward San Lázaro harbor.

"Where we going?" she yelled to Kasim.

"You sailboat," he yelled back. He pointed ahead. She saw *Seamark* dead ahead, lying at anchor in the roadstead. "Capitán Katana, he say so. *Ordenes, no?*"

The sailboat grew larger as they approached. Miranda held on tight. The Thunder was flying, straight toward the ketch—no, a yawl, she thought inanely. That fucker Curt. . . . She saw Brillo suddenly stand up on the cabin roof, his ruff bristling. He was staring right into her eyes. They would hit the *Seamark* exactly amidships . . .

"Brillo!" she yelled.

Kasim cut the wheel hard left, and they whipped alongside her, not ten feet from collision. Brillo saw her and barked, once.

Then they were heading seaward, toward the reef. Behind, she saw two Thunders chasing them. Seeing their change of course, the Thunders had angled to cut them off at the reef. Combers broke over the coral. Kasim headed straight for them.

"You hold fast!" he yelled. "We jump!"

It was solid coral dead ahead, covered for a moment by the spilling waves, then bare and sharp-fanged again. They'd tear the Thunder's guts out . . .

Kasim's luck ran with them. He hit the reef just as a comber crashed over it. The Thunder leapt up, airborne and straight as an arrow shot from a crossbow, and they hit the sea smoothly on the far side. *"Allah akhbar!"* Kasim yelled. "God good fella!" Looking back, Miranda saw the first of the pursuing fast boats hesitate a moment, then smash the reef at some sixty miles an hour. Bad timing. Bodies flew through the air, along with chunks of the Thunder. Its gas tanks exploded in a great orange and black burst. The other chaser circled, then ran parallel to them inside the reef. But Kasim angled outward from it, rapidly widening the distance between them. The old man's eyes were sparking with joy. He turned and looked at Miranda and laughed aloud. "You take wheel awhile, hey? Good fight, hey? I clean up a bit."

Only then did she notice the dead Tausuq crumpled in the cockpit corner. Blood had pooled deep where he lay. Kasim lifted him by the shirt collar. The man's head flopped onto his chest. His neck had been nearly severed by the bolo stroke. Kasim shook his own head sadly.

"I grow old," he yelled to her over the engine roar. "My arm too—how you say—*débil? Flojo?* 'Weak,' hey?" In his younger days he'd have beheaded the man with one blow.

He heaved the body over the side and turned to with swab and bucket. The mess must be cleaned up—Capitán Katana was very strict about such matters.

Miranda hardly noticed what was happening. As the horror of the chase receded, the greater horror of the whole situation came into sickening focus. What kind of hell had she gotten them into? Five men dead yesterday in the Dangerous Ground—cut down by bolo and gunfire in a matter of moments. No hesitations. Now this morning, at least three more. Maybe four? What about Effredio? Her friend of so many years, the best mate she'd ever had. Even if he were still alive, what would they be doing to him?

TWENTY-FIVE

Okay, the commodore thought. Once is happenstance—the photographs in Hughes's boat. Twice is coincidence—the exploding Bible. Three times is enemy action—the incident off the boat basin. He'd lost two Thunders that morning. The one stolen by the people in the pump boat and the one that blew up on the reef. The crew of the second chase boat had brought back the boloed corpse of the Tausuq helmsman in the stolen boat. What was his name—Mustafa? If those pump-boat folks were just simple islanders, they were mighty damned tough.

He made his decision. The boat basin was the weakest link in his operation—no defenses to speak of, wide open to the sea. He'd withdraw the larger portion of his Thunders to the Balbal base, concentrate them there, take all his files and stores along with them. Leave four or five Thunders here with just fuel and ammunition enough to present a threat to the flank of any attackers who showed up off Balbal. But the main fight, if it came to that, would be in the waters off Balbal. That's where his strength lay.

There were still many things the commodore didn't understand about the situation. (Like all of the details, he thought wryly.) The MATS guy's head, for instance. Hughes's role in the equation, if any. The Bible-thumping man and woman from the gospel, though of course that was certainly just cover. Damn clever, though. Ironic. It indicated more subtlety behind the scenes than Culdee could possibly muster. Chi Coms? NPA? MNLF? Perhaps even some rival intelligence agency. The other side's or our own? Too early in the game to waste time figuring it out, though. The best bet, the commodore was sure, was to concentrate his forces immediately at Balbal, scour the islands, locate the enemy, then wipe him out.

He wondered how Billy was faring. Billy had the prisoner from the pump boat down in the little casita that served as the commodore's brig, interrogating the man. The commodore hated that end of intelligence work. Still, he'd better go down and have a look, make sure Billy hadn't killed the man out of sheer Filipino vengefulness without getting anything from him. God, he hated it! Maybe he'd better check first to see how the evacuation was faring . . .

"That's it," Billy Torres said. "You're for the cross, my boy." Effredio was already hanging, arms extended sideways, dripping with blood, but from manacles on the wall of the brig, not from a wooden cross. He watched Torres through eyes blurred with pain. Every bone, every muscle in his body ached, his arms worst of all.

"But the cross is for Christians," he croaked weakly. "I am, as I've told you again and again, a Muslim. My very name is a Muslim name. Kasim bin Musa, no self-respecting unbeliever would take such a name." They were speaking Samal. Effredio's fluency in the tongue was far greater than Torres's, and Billy was bothered by that. But not much. Most men in the southern Philippines spoke several languages, especially sailors, traders, and military men. And of course revolutionaries.

"So you insist," Torres said. He poked the joint of Effredio's shoulder with a Shore Patrol nightstick. The man on the wall grunted. That was one of the fine points about torture—once you'd softened your man up, tenderized him so to speak, you didn't have to hit him hard to make it hurt. By reducing the actual amount of force employed, you prolonged his life and thus his value. The longer he hung there, the greater the pain. To him, it seemed it would never end. Torres had seen men actually will themselves dead on the wall, but they always needed maximum agony to take them over the edge. This he would not provide. It was a hallmark of Billy's style, the signature of a master.

"But for a Moro, you look very much like a Visayan to me." Billy tapped an elbow. Effredio grunted. "Leyte, Cebu, Negros, Iloilo, Siquijor even. You look more like Samar than Samal." He laughed at his own word play—one was an island, the other a tribe—then tapped Effredio on the ribs. Effredio grunted.

"I told you," he said. "My father was Samal, my mother from Negros. I'm just a boatman. We were diving shell over on Palawan—good shell waters there, off Taytay. Also stealing birds' nests at El Nido, those cliffs of black marble where the swallows build their homes. Chinese in Manila must have their *nido* soup, their bird's nest soup. Good money there. But *mundo* robbed us near—" He coughed on a trickle of blood, and the very flexing of his ribs almost made him pass out.

"Yes, yes," Billy said impatiently. "Near Balabac Strait, on your way to Sabah, where you hoped to recoup your losses by smuggling cigarettes back up to Basilan. Your engine was making trouble, so you stopped here in hopes of repairing it. Then, cruising along the reef, you decided to see if you could dive up any worthwhile shells. You soon discovered the reef was dead, et cetera. I must say, you're consistent. But so am I. Persistent as well. So we'll give it one more try, then it's the cross."

"But I am a Muslim. The cross is for Christians—"

Torres rattled the nightstick against Effredio's rib cage. Hard.

"Listen to me," he barked. "This has all been preliminaries, a warm-up so to speak. Stretching exercises to limber you up for the workout. Now that you're strong, stretched, and centered, we'll begin."

"*Curt!*" Effredio yelled, his eyes wide with pain and fear. "That's the name you want. Take it! *Curt* is his name, a Milikan named *Curt!* I know nothing more, but he is the man behind us, the man who pays us." His head slumped down on his chest, and he moaned a long, gurgling moan.

Torres smiled and went out to fetch the commodore. On his way to the basin, he told the guards to take the man Kasim off the wall

191

and get him up to Gólgota. Things were begining to move in the right direction. They always did with Billy Torres at the helm.

Culdee lay chin-deep in the *hotsi* bath, steeping like a tea ball. The water was salt—Perniciosa's freshwater was precious, collected almost entirely by catchment and cistern from the brief, passing rainstorms that lashed the island nearly every day—but it felt damned good. Culdee ached all over from the hike. Two Japanese sat soaking at the far end of the bath, phlegmatic little men with graying hair and the hard gray-blue hands of laborers or mechanics. There were Japs all over the island, Culdee was learning. They'd *ohayo*ed him and bowed politely when he came in, but now they were pretending he wasn't there. That was fine with Culdee. He had things to think about.

Miranda had returned with Kasim at dusk, an hour behind Culdee and Sôbô. She was nearly hysterical. Freddie had been killed or at best captured. Kasim had chopped a man's head off. A boat had blown up, bits of guys flying through the air, great literal balls of fire, gunplay. Culdee's relief at Miranda's safe return had been nearly squelched by the news about Freddie.

"It's all a mistake," she kept saying when he met her on the lee-shore beach. "We should never have come. Too many killings, too much danger, too much death for everyone, we've got to clear out of here."

He'd tried to calm her and reassure her—maybe Freddie's all right, you didn't actually see them shoot him, or even see them capture him. Yeah, we'll think about getting out of this place. But Culdee knew damned well they couldn't. Sôbô had them now, for whatever end he had in mind, and he wasn't going to just let them go.

Sôbô, of course, was delighted with the capture of the fast boat. His black go-stone eyes shone like those of a kid with a new toy, or, more aptly, an admiral with a new addition to his task force. He promised Miranda that everything possible was being done—he'd already given orders to rescue Effredio. He had agents in Millikan's camp. And more such bullshit. If he had agents with Millikan, how come he didn't know about the book bomb until that slippery Arab on Moro Armado told him? But Culdee didn't mention that, certainly not to Miranda.

The funny thing was, Culdee didn't want to clear out. Not knowing, as he did now, that Turner was there, and that Turner was Millikan. And that Sôbô planned to kill Millikan-Turner as dead as those SEALS who'd died at Brigadune. Culdee wanted to be in on that, even if it killed him in the process. But he also wanted Miranda out of it, whether she got her boat back or not. Shit. . . . Salt water stung his eyes, and it wasn't from the *hotsi* bath. He ladled more of it over his head, to keep the Japs at the far end from noticing. She was his daughter, by God . . .

He found himself remembering something that had happened long ago, when Miranda was just a toddler. He'd been home-ported in Long Beach at the time, and one weekend he borrowed a car from a shipmate and drove Viv and the kid up to Marineland of the Pacific, in Palos Verdes. A family outing. Miranda would surely adore the porpoises exploding from the water in formation, the big black pilot whales suddenly erupting from the surface to take fish from a man's hand. Guys who'd been there said kids loved it. While they were waiting in line for their tickets, Miranda staggered around at their feet—she was still unsteady on her pins, just learning to walk and proud of it—and a man trying to cut into the head of the line bumped into her, knocking her flat on her diapered duff. Culdee had never felt any particular possessiveness about his daughter up to that point, just a gentle, pleasant fondness for her, a mild sort of love. But when the line-jumper knocked her down, rage ignited in him like a gasoline fire. Before he knew it, he'd grabbed the man by the shoulder, spun him, and coldcocked him—knocked him sprawling on the dirty asphalt. He was shaking with rage when the security guards intervened. Viv straightened it all out, as did the other bystanders, and no harm was done, except to the other guy's face and dignity.

It was a revelation. Culdee'd heard other men, tough old salts, officers and white hats alike, talk on the long night watches about how fiercely they loved their kids. He'd thought it was bunk. Then, he knew differently . . .

As he toweled himself dry on the steaming tiles, three more Japs came in. These were younger, though. Tougher-looking, or at least more swaggering than the older mechanic-Japs. When they stripped off their robes, he saw they were tattooed from their necks to their ankles, from wrist to wrist. Japs had to be crazy.

Sôbô sure was.

The two priests stood in the chancel, surveying the cathedral. Its santos, with the exception of San Lázaro, of course, were suitably draped in Lenten purple, as they had been all Holy Week. The patron saint's effigy was wrapped in wax-steeped cerecloths, like those that bind a corpse. Under the flicker of candlelight he glowed faintly yellow in the gloom of the nave. It is the color of pus, thought Padre Cotinho, as from a suppurating wound. Not Christ's wounds, surely, but those of a failing church.

An unearthly din filled the cavern of stone, the keening and wailing of old women—the *manangs*—as they chanted the *pasyon*, each in her own cadence. To Padre Cotinho's eye they resembled molting vultures gathered at the final agonies of a dying beast—a great, noble stag perhaps, foully wounded by poachers, gut-shot and waiting for them to follow up with their axes and spears. This *pabasa* of the old women, this endlessly repetitive recitation of the Passion of Christ, was their way of hurrying the glorious moment of His death and their salvation. Ah, what a fine irony, Cotinho thought. They have no idea how close at hand their true salvation stands . . .

"It's beautiful," Padre Fagundes sighed. "Each year it moves me more deeply, each Easter I love God the more. I only wish I were younger and could make some fine sacrifice for him."

"You could become a *flagelante*," Padre Cotinho said. "In your *kapirosa* they wouldn't recognize you, so your sacrifice would be all the more noble, all the less self-serving." The *kapirosa* was a hood the *flagelantes* wore, under a crown of thorns, to disguise themselves from their neighbors as they scourged their way up Gólgota behind the crosses with their flailing thongs of glass-spiked leather. On Lázaro they scourged the cross-bearers as well as themselves.

"Really, Barto," Padre Fagundes said, "you do have the most macabre imagination—"

"Excuse me, Diogo," Padre Cotinho interrupted. "I have a late confession to hear." He had seen Rosalinda enter the narthex. She looked distraught, on the verge of panic. Padre Cotinho hurried to the confessional.

"Bless me, Father, for I have sinned," she rattled as he entered and knelt behind the screen. "They have your friend, Effredio Pascal."

"Are you certain?"

"He fits your description, Padre, though he calls himself by a Moro name." She described the man. It sounded like Effredio, all right.

"Has he talked?"

"Not yet. Only that the man Curt Hughes is his leader." She paused, still breathing heavily from her run up the hillside. "I rather liked that part, about Hughes. Is that sinful of me, Padre."

Cotinho suppressed a laugh.

"I shall absolve you in any case, my daughter," he said. "But Effredio—he is still alive?"

"Yes. They plan to crucify him tomorrow with the others. Torres hopes the fear of that or, anyway, the bite of the nails, will draw more from him. I'm not sure they believe the business about Hughes."

"Where do they have him now, Effredio that is?"

"At the old *capilla* below Gólgota, Padre. There in the ruined garden." She waited. He was thinking. "He is heavily guarded," she added.

"Have we a man among the guards?"

"Yes, a Cebuano—stupid but loyal. His name is Candelario de Mactan. He is to be Longinus tomorrow."

Perfect, Cotinho thought. Longinus was the one-eyed centurion who, out of pity, delivered the spear thrust that put Christ out of His misery. According to the local legend, a spurt of blood from that sacred wound hit Longinus in the face and restored his sight. But spears can be thrust in more than one direction, and blood can cover whole islands. Once more, Padre Cotinho felt the hand of God moving in the night.

"The chapel at Gólgota, you say? I shall go there at once."

"And I, Padre?" Rosalinda asked.

"Wait for me beneath the hibiscus near the rectory," he said. "Padre Fagundes has the midnight mass. Pray for me, daughter. Pray for our cause and our mission. God is with us still. We will prevail."

"Curt?" the commodore said. "I don't believe it."

"Neither do I, sir," Billy agreed. "Curt's too dumb for anything this elaborate."

"My feelings precisely."

"But we've got this guy Kasim talking anyway. He'll give us more. I told him he's going up on the cross at noon tomorrow." He looked at his watch. "Today, actually."

"Oh Christ, Billy!" He stared at Torres. "The cross?"

"Well, it's got him thinking, and I'll bet he's thinking about talking. That's what you want, isn't it?"

The commodore nodded wearily.

"And don't worry. It's just nails and whips. I won't expend any ordnance, sir." Billy laughed.

The commodore looked up at him. He wouldn't be baited. The bags under his eyes felt full of sand.

"You're a cruel man, Warrant Gunner Torres."

"But good at my job, sir. Don't get upset—he won't die. At the touch of the first spike, he'll spill his godless Commie guts all over Gólgota. If it even gets that far. You going to be there to hear his confession, sir?"

"No, I've got to get things battened down over on Balbal. We may receive an attack at any moment. We've lost two Thunders already, that's a quarter of a million in U.S. dollars. Apiece. Our budget is stretched to the limit. Over the limit, come to think of it. What with the empty run you made to Ko Kut last week. I hope Hughes made the pickup all right this time. Any word from him?"

"No sir. Remember you ordered radio silence after I messaged him with the rendezvous fix? He's due back tonight, tomorrow morning at the latest."

"He'd goddamn well better make it," the commo said, "or I'll bust him back to—" Wait a minute, he thought.

"To what sir?" Billy Torres asked. "Civilian?"

Candelario de Mactan had the night watch, and he didn't like it. He was a big man. Big men get cold faster than little men. There was more of them exposed to the wind. He didn't like the wind blowing down from Gólgota. It blew through the ruined garden that surrounded the chapel and brought him the smell of dying flowers and cold marble. It brought him the smell of those crooked crosses on the hilltop. He didn't like to look up, unthinking, and suddenly see them there outlined against the cold moon. Yet he couldn't keep himself from staring up at them. He forced himself to look away, and then he was staring at the mask. He didn't like the mask at all. It was the face of the centurion Longinus, who had killed Our Lord. A cruel, black-bearded face with only one eye.

Don't be foolish, Candelario told himself. It's only a mask. The fact that it has only one eye does not mean it will take the sight from one of my own eyes. I am not a savage, I am a descendant of Lapu Lapu, the king of Mactan who killed the evil invader Magellan in the surf of the Mactan Sea. All men of Mactan are Lapu's sons. The mask looks like Magellan's face, on the monument at home. But Lapu Lapu stands as big as life, bigger than life, high above Magellan, whom he killed with one stroke of his bolo. Even though I must wear the mask tomorrow—today, really, in only ten hours or so—it will not make me Magellan. I am working for the men who will kill today's Magellans. Who knows, perhaps I myself will be the one to behead the commodore, Magellan's heir.

But still he was cold.

He could hear the padre inside the chapel, hearing the confession of the captured Moro. He had not realized Moros believed in confession. It was warm in the *capilla*. The padre had brought coffee. Candelario could smell it on the warm air from the chapel window. He stepped closer to breathe the coffee smell more deeply. A man could take sustenance from smells alone.

"When you sought me that day on Siquijor," the padre was saying, "you brought me fresh hope, my son."

"And I brought this upon myself," Effredio said bitterly. They were speaking the heavy Visayan dialect of Negros, which neither Candelario nor any other of the commodore's guards could penetrate.

"Don't despair, my son," Padre Cotinho said. "You'll be safe, as safe as any of us. I'll arrange it. It's all being arranged. But you must not talk. They will not harm you. The commodore will not permit it. Like all Americans, he is soft at the core. Torres for all his cruelty obeys the commodore's orders. He must obey them. He is a slave of the Americans. Never fear. There is always hope."

"Not on that, there isn't," Effredio said. He was staring out the lancet window at a cross on Gólgota.

"There is always hope in the cross, my son," Padre Cotinho said. "It is *my* hope—no, it is my *certainty*—that you will find it up there."

Effredio was quiet for a minute.

"I have sinned, Padre," he said at last. "Bless me."

Padre Cotinho embraced him, kissed him on both cheeks. Effredio's cheeks were wet. The padre poured him another cup of coffee from the thermos he had brought with him. Some slopped over, onto his hand. He handed the metal cup to Effredio, then with his wet thumb traced a cross lightly on Effredio's brow. He stood back, smiling, and traced a larger cross in the air.

On his way out a few minutes later he handed Candelario the last of the coffee, and took him aside.

"Today, as Longinus," he said, "you will place the lance deeply and accurately. The man within is a traitor to our cause. Yet though he has betrayed us, I do not want him to suffer. You will use the spear *before* they nail him to the cross. Make sure of your thrust, *compañero. Comprende?*"

Candelario nodded. He always obeyed orders. He appreciated the gesture of the coffee. The padre was a good leader.

TWENTY-SIX

~~~~~~~~~~~~~~~~~~~~~~~~

The old imperial navy submarine pens had been blasted out of dead coral and roofed with reinforced concrete, then layered with loose coral rubble and sand. Now, nearly half a century later, they were invisible from land, sea, or air. Cactus and wire grass covered them on top while clever jogs in the entrance channel disguised their hidden gates. Inside, though, they were brightly lighted by the power of generators, clanking and howling with activity. Sôbô had found a few of his old crew from the destroyer *Yunagi* to serve as foremen. The younger Japanese machinists and construction workers were the most skilled he had been able to locate. All were eager for the job— a chance to travel to forbidding but exotic tropical isles. Good pay, too. And plenty of cut-rate sex. They'd done a crackerjack job. Renovations on the schooner *Venganza* were nearly complete. Sôbô had thanked the men personally and distributed bottles of sake to the foremen for immediate (but moderate) consumption. He himself would not stay for the toasts—just for the first one—which he pretended to drink—Banzai!—but spilled on the floor instead. Then he went topside.

Cool and quiet in the sea air of the midwatch. He walked down to the mole, breathing deeply. The moon—just its last waning sliver—already touched the western horizon. A million stars. The respirating sea on the fringing reef sounded a steady thud and hiss. He sat on a bollard and reviewed his battle plan for the hundredth, the thousandth time. He told himself again it would work.

First, he would neutralize the San Lázaro boat facility by filling its channel with shallow-anchored contact mines—not the huge and obvious ones he'd found in abundance in the sub base's armory, but the small antiboat mines. They would be seeded from *kumpits* so as to be indistinguishable from the customary Lázaran harbor traffic. A few well-armed pump boats would lie off to destroy any Blue Thunders that might manage to escape.

Second, Balabatchi on Moro Armado would free the political prisoners, killing whatever recalcitrant Tausuq guards did not agree to his change of colors. Two *yakuza*, perhaps three of the six Sôbô had with him, would assist Bala. *Kumpits* and pump boats would ferry the freed prisoners—at least the most influential of them—to Lázaro City, where they would spread the news of the revolt. In concert with Padre Cotinho's agitators, they would provoke a rising on Lázaro proper. That rising need not necessarily prevail. The tumult it caused would be diversion enough for Sôbô's purposes, pinning down whatever land force Millikan had on the main island.

Third, and most important, Sergeant Grande's Negritos would assault the Balbal base from the rear. This attack would occur simultaneously with the San Lázaro rising, further confusing the enemy, getting him to look behind him rather than toward the sea. Pump boats and the faster *kumpits* would, at the same time, have landed men on the Balbal base's right and left flanks, attacking along the shore.

Once that preliminary phase of the Balbal assault was well under way, the real battle would begin. *Venganza* and her escort of pump boats would approach from the sea and take the base under fire. Millikan would of course retaliate with artillery and his fast boats at first, then, as they were destroyed in detail, he would be forced to sortie his gunboat. *Venganza* would look like an easy target—a flimsy wooden-hulled vessel that could scarcely move faster than a man walking at a brisk pace. Millikan was in for a surprise . . .

Sôbô heard footsteps in the crushed coral. It was Culdee.

"Couldn't sleep," he said. "Saw you down here and thought I'd join you." He had two mugs in his hands. "Want some jamoke? I went back to the galley and got you one."

"Thanks, old-timer," Sôbô said. He sipped the hot coffee—the U.S. Navy's fighting blood. "Beautiful night."

"Ugly day ahead," Culdee said. "Ugly *days,* I should say."

"I never could sleep, myself, when I knew it was coming," Sôbô said.

"You've seen more of it than I have. A helluva lot more."

"It's always the same, except for the details," Sôbô said. "But not to worry. Once it starts, you're into it, and you feel nothing but the weapons."

"What sort of missile system is that in the Thunders?"

"FIM-43A," Sôbô said. "American-built Redeye. Nothing to fear, really. It's a surface-to-air system, shoulder-fired and long since outdated. Both your Stinger and the British Blowpipe are far superior. I expect poor Millikan gets the scrapings from the bottom of the U.S. Navy's ordnance barrel."

"Redeye," Culdee said. "It's a heat-seeker, isn't it?"

"Infrared, actually. Its sensors lock onto the aircraft's exhaust emissions. I don't think a pump boat's engine would be hot enough to attract it, and anyway, an outboard's exhaust is at or below the waterline. Redeye's red eye would be stymied in any event. It couldn't see through waves even if it were sensitive to a Yamaha's exhaust."

"Redeye," Culdee said again. "I could use a slug of that stuff right about now." He took a long swallow of coffe instead. "So the missile system won't help him against us. So what do we do about the fast boats? About the gunboat?"

"Outgun them," Sôbô said. "Come with me." He led the way back into the submarine pens. Culdee saw dozens of Japanese in coveralls working under bright lights, heard the hammer of pneumatic wrenches and drills, saw the glint of gun barrels in the glare. Back at the far end of the pens a long, low, filthy, wooden-decked vessel of some sort was receiving a lot of attention. The boat looked like an outsized *kumpit.* It had no bowsprit or masts, just a series of sawed-off stumps where they once had been.

Walking past the boat, they came to a tunnel. Sôbô led the way past Moro and Japanese sentries to a huge steel door. It sighed as he turned the dogs securing it—airtight. Inside he turned on the lights. Culdee caught his breath.

The lights illuminated row on row of neatly stowed weapons— racks of gleaming torpedos; nests of spike-armed mines, some big enough to sink battleships; a whole wall stacked high with ammunition boxes; stands of rifles; fully assembled heavy machine guns, glowing on the concrete decks. All the boxes, all the gear for that matter, bore Japanese lettering.

"Who the hell financed this?" he asked.

"The emperor," Sôbô replied. "When he was much younger, of course. This is the old sub base armory, unseen by human eyes, untouched by human hands, unsullied by salty sea air since the day back in the winter of 1944 when the base was overrun by the first Millikan's guerrillas and abandoned."

"How come the guerrillas didn't get in here? They could've used this stuff."

"The base commander mined the entrance," Sôbô said. "After a few dozen Tausuqs flew off to join Allah, the rest gave it up. The war was winding down, anyway. We had to excavate tons of rubble ourselves before we found it. I lost some men in the digging. It was worth it, though. Now our small craft are armed with these—" He slapped a drum-fed machine gun with a big spider-web-shaped forward sight and a heavy water-cooled cylinder of a barrel. "IJN Type-92, 7.7 millimeter copy of the old Lewis gun. Five hundred rounds per minute at twenty-four hundred feet per second from the muzzle. Slow but steady. It's the old British .303 cartridge, probably the deadliest bullet ever manufactured, when you reckon all the wars it's been in. Very reliable. Some of the larger vessels will mount these." He had moved on to a shorter-barreled, air-cooled machine gun with a short wooden stock and knurled, straight pistol grip. It was mounted on an adjustable monopod that could be fixed to a deck. Its feed was a curved magazine that fit on top of the receiver. "Type 93, 13.2 millimeters—about .50 caliber as you people compute bullet diameters—well capable of chewing up a fast boat and spitting it out all over the sea. My gunners have trained our pump-boat crews on these weapons for more than a month now. They are handy with weapons, these Moros—with all deadly implements. And they are not afraid to die."

"Neither are Millikan's Muslims."

"Perhaps," Sôbô said. "But they are paid to die. Our men kill and die for love."

"We'll see," Culdee said finally. "But .50-caliber mgs won't stop that gunboat. She's got three-inch guns. If I remember correctly, a three-incher can hit up to three or four miles out. These guns can't."

"In the fullness of time, old chap," Sôbô said, turning toward the door. "All in the fullness of the time. Take my word for it, the Good Lord will provide."

Billy Torres stood near the top of Gólgota watching the procession approach. The doleful chant had been thrumming its way up from the harbor for nearly an hour now, the parade's caterpillarlike progress preceded by heady fumes of burning incense and the crack of leather whips. All around him old women wailed and swayed to the swaying of the crosses—side to side, up and down. He watched as the crosses jutted above the red hoods and rhythmically cracking whips of the flagellants and the bobbing heads of the crowd. There were four crosses, Billy saw. Three volunteers and the so-called Kasim. Kasim had joined the others under close guard when the procession reached the chapel in the garden, which the islanders called Getsemani. Billy had interrogated him just minutes before the procession arrived. The man had looked too weak to make a battle of it, but he wouldn't talk. Billy left him unmanacled during their little chat, and when he raised his SP nightstick, Kasim cowered.

"I'm afraid of you," he whimpered, his voice slurred and staccato. It sounded like "Effredio." Billy was just exulting in the fact that at last Kasim was talking English and had leaned in to give him a clout when Kasim suddenly stepped forward and kicked Billy square in the balls. As Billy buckled, Kasim pushed him over and kicked him again, in the ribs. "Are you afraida *me!*" he screamed. He got in a few more good boots before the guards pulled him off and clubbed him down.

"Don't kill him!" Billy yelled. One of the Tausuqs had drawn his bolo. The big Cebuano had a spear poised. "Later," Billy told them. His voice was choked with pain. "Later, and slowly, slowly."

Fuck the commo! Billy would get this guy to talk and then, when he was pinned and bleeding on the cross, flay him inch by inch. The crowd would love it.

Billy's balls were still throbbing when the Cristos arrived. The screams and chants of the mob had reached a level of lunacy. Women were fainting, men ripping at their own faces until blood flowed, children dancing and pummeling one another dizzy, dogs howling and darting underfoot . . . a madhouse on a hilltop, under the noonday sun. The *moriones*—the mock centurions with their round, roached steel helmets and cuirasses and greaves and those horrible fright masks—came in for the worst of the crowd's frenzy. Rotten fruit and dog turds bounced or splatted off their armor. Rocks clanked against their shields. Two of them broke from the circle guarding the Cristos and flailed the crowd with the flats of their swords, jabbed at its fringes with stiff, quick spearpoints that meant business. Men and women reeled away bleeding. A reek of pierced guts stung the air. The crowd retreated but redoubled its outcry.

Torres saw the town doctor, drunk on rum and staggering, watch bleary-eyed as the first Cristo took the nails—this one was a volunteer. The others waited stoically, their shoulders and backs rivered with blood from the flogging. The hammer clanged. The crowd howled along with it. Kasim stood straight, chin up, among the waiting Cristos. He had had the worst of it, despite his short walk under the scourges. Ridges of torn flesh striped his upper body, his mouth drooled blood over his unshaven chin. But his eyes were clear. Clear and hard. Torres made his way through the crowd to Kasim's front. Kasim watched him approach.

"What do you have to tell me?" Billy asked.

Kasim spat full in his face. Blood mainly, but plenty of saliva.

205

Kasim was not frightened. No man could spit that much if he were scared.

"Him next!" Torres ordered the *moriones*. "The dullest, rustiest nails you've got."

But he felt respect for this man now, felt it for the first time. The respect muted his rage. He wiped the spittle from his face and watched, fascinated. Two *moriones* threw Kasim down onto his heavy, blood-stained cross. Another spread his arms and held his hands down on the wood. A fourth approached with the heavy iron maul and a handful of spikes. Kasim stared up at him, grinning.

"*Cobarde,*" he said happily to the *morion* with the hammer. "Moro *cabrón. Maricónes,* all of you. *Sin cojónes!* Come kill me, you big, fat, brave fairies."

The crowd roared louder than ever as the first of the crosses went up. The volunteer Cristo sagged against the nails and fainted. Someone in the crowd threw a bucket of water on him. He awoke briefly, then fainted again.

"*Jesús, Jesús, Jesús, Jesús* . . ." The crowd began to chant in unison now. "*El Salvador! El Salvador! Hijo de Dios! Jesús! Jesús Rey!*"

The *morion* with the hammer placed the first spike point on Kasim's right palm. Kasim spit in his face. As the *morion* leaned back to wipe his face, another *morion* suddenly stabbed Kasim with his spear. It was the Cebuano. The spearpoint took Kasim in the chest—deep, to the bar of the crossguard—and the *morion* twisted it once, twice, thrice . . .

Kasim heaved his back clear of the cross, against the spear's thrust. His eyes went wide—focused on someone in the crowd. "*Traidor!*" he screamed.

Billy spun to follow Kasim's eyes. He looked amidst the crowd—red, wild-eyed faces; black, gaping mouths; yellow teeth, as yellow as a horse's, snaggled and flashing over glistening wet tongues; tears and sweat running thick and fast down a screaming wall of faces. . . . And a priest standing there, watching Kasim. An old priest, white-haired, white-bearded, his mouth a grim line, his eyes hard and brown. Soldier's eyes. A priest in a long black cassock. A priest making a cross in the air. A priest not sweating at all. Then a woman at the priest's side grabbed his arm and with it pointed to Torres. It was Rosalinda.

The crowd surged forward, knocking Billy sideways before he could move. The mob swarmed over the centurions, over the other Cristos, over Kasim, where he lay on his cross.

By the time the centurions had beaten the crowd back, Kasim was dead. So was the Cebuano. Someone had ripped his Longinus mask so that it lay crooked on his face. A knife had entered the eyehole and remained buried, to the hilt, in the spearman's face. A dozen bodies littered the hilltop, some still writhing.

The priest was gone. So was Rosalinda.

Curt was adrift on the South China Sea. Both Thunders were adrift, about a mile apart. There was water in the reserve gas drums. Now and then the two big engines would light off and run for a minute or two, but then—inevitably—they crapped out again. The batteries were growing weaker and weaker with each abortive start. And the sea was a mirror—practically windless, unbearably hot. What little wind there was came in cat's-paws from the northeast, pushing them back toward Cambodia when it reached them, eating up what little gains they had made. He didn't know whether to curse the breeze or bless it. When it blew, at least it provided momentary relief from the heat. The air was like wet, hot cotton wool, and the sun pounded down through it with a beat that stung his skin as sharply as any Portuguese man-o'-war would have.

They'd made the pickup all right this time, no sweat—a float-plane load of opium bricks, well off the Thai coast. The sea's calmness had been welcome then. Curt expected the roar of Phantoms every minute during the exchange. Of course, the Thunder engines had run beautifully during the trip across. It wasn't until they were halfway back that the trouble began.

Finally, though, after three straight hours of battery depletion, rising and crashing hopes, more curses in English, Spanish, and

Tausuq than the South China Sea had heard in eons of seagoing horrors, Abdul had found a chamois cloth down in the forepeak. They emptied one drum of the polluted gasoline and were now slowly, painfully straining water-mixed gas from another drum into the only container they had—a leaky Igloo cooler. So far they had collected barely two gallons, half of which Abdul wanted to give to the other Thunder.

"Fuck them, Abdul," Curt told him. "Let them figure it out for themselves."

"No," Abdul said.

Curt's head was reeling with the fumes he'd inhaled. His skin was on fire. He was about as strong as a soggy Kleenex. If only they could get under way, he'd be fine. Just fine.

"I order you, Abdul. I'm the captain here. Let's get going. Home."

"No," Abdul said.

"Goddamn it, Abdul. *Do it!*"

"Fuck you, you infidel dog turd."

Curt went for a wrench.

Abdul had it. He also had his bolo drawn. He started the Thunder's engine and drove west, back to the other boat. They shared the gasoline. It lasted barely half an hour. Then they began to strain gasoline again.

The sun did not seem to have moved an inch in the sky of molten brass.

"He *speared* him to death?" Commodore Millikan's voice, scratchy as it was over the ancient AN/PRC radiophone, came breathless with disbelief. "One of our guys *speared* him to death?"

"That's affirmative," Billy said. "Over."

Though the Commodore insisted upon correct voice-radio procedure within his command, and had indeed docked men a week's pay when they failed to comply, his own style on the airwaves was as sloppy as a civilian's. That's the way flag officers worked in this man's navy.

"Did you get anything out of him?"

"Just a kick in the nuts and a faceful of spit," Billy said. "Over."

"Say again. Anything?"

"Negative. Nothing. *Nada*. Zilch," Billy said. "Over."

"Goddamn-it-to-hell, why not? Why'd the guy spear him? What—" His voice was momentarily lost in static.

"The guard speared him because he was angry. Kasim made him very angry. Kasim would not break. Kasim would not talk. Kasim died right then. Over."

"Well, I'm very disappointed in you, Anvil Base. Very, very disappointed. Over."

"Armadillo, this is Anvil Base. You had to be there. Interrogative orders for me? Over."

Long crackling pause while the commo thought about it. Then the transmitter keyed again with a click and a roar like a full gale.

"This is Armadillo. Just stand by at base until Anvils One and Two return. Any word from them? Over."

"That's negatory. Over."

"Anvil Base, this is Armadillo. I assume that was you with the 'negatory.' The word is 'negative.' And use proper call signs from now on. Have you raised Anvils One and Two this channel? Over."

"I say again, that's negatory."

"Goddamn-it-to-hell . . . well, raise them. Find out what the fuck's taking them so fucking long. Then get Anvil One over here ASAP. You come with him. Out."

Billy flicked off the AN/PRC battery switch and returned to the lanai. He had three Thunders out searching for the priest and Rosalinda, a whole squad of Tausuqs scouring Lázaro City. He was damned if he'd tell the commo what he suspected. The asshole would only countermand his orders, chew him out for fucking up, go into an even worse tizzy than he was in already. Billy wouldn't try to raise Curt on the radio, either. That would be stupid. Curt's Thunder and the other boat were probably lying in pieces on the floor of the Gulf of Siam right now, blown to bits by more Phantoms. Good fucking riddance. Ever since that pissant boat bum showed up, there'd been nothing but trouble. Should have killed the fuck back there in Zambo, in the jai-alai court. But the commo didn't want that. The commo. That was the wrong name for him. It ought to be commode.

He laughed and poured himself a rum on the rocks. He deserved a drink. His balls still ached from Kasim's kick. Tough little fucker, Kasim. Maybe he was a Moro after all.

Out in the harbor and all along the Lázaran shore the evening paseo was shaping up. Pump boats and *kumpits* were returning to Lázaro City after a hard day at sea, fishing, shell diving, dynamiting the reefs, killing whatever helpless strangers happened to wander into view. The sun was over the yardarm now. The scene would continue all night. Billy had long since given up worrying about unchecked traffic. No way to control it anyway. As the commode said, Millikan Shipping was the entire Lázaran economy, every Lázaran's friend, the source from which all blessings flowed. The commode. Yeah. Billy laughed and poured himself another drink.

TWENTY-SEVEN

"How do you like her, old man?" Sôbô beamed proudly, eyes flashing, as he pointed to the old hulk tied up alongside the mole. Culdee looked again. What he saw in the red wash of sunrise was a scruffy island trading vessel, a cut-down schooner that was probably quite lovely before her owners sawed off her masts and bowsprit. They hadn't even squared them tidily. Ragged splinters spiked the stumps, gray and filthy, and a short, stubby foremast carried a sloppily furled gray canvas sail. The sail was poorly patched with mismatching dark swatches of fabric—hunks of old dungarees?—from which loose sail twine flapped in the dawn breeze. A crooked Charley Noble, soot black where it wasn't rusty, jutted up from her engine compartment, its guy wires frayed and sprung. Bald truck tires served as fenders where she wallowed against the mole. A true tramp, all right, Culdee thought, a seagoing textbook of nautical sloth, all Irish pennants, green-crusted brightwork, oil-stained deck planking, and rust stains like dead blood striping her sides. She carried a big piece of deck cargo atop her aft hatch, covered with a scruffy black tarp.

"What a piece of shit," Culdee said. Miranda had come up beside him with Kasim. The name on the vessel's stern read BLOEDIG-FEEKS, BALIKPAPAN, BORNEO.

"You'd never recognize her for the trig little schooner that sailed in here just the other day," Sôbô said, "would you?"

"What schooner's that?" Miranda asked. Then, as the truth struck her, she spun to face Sôbô. "Where's *Venganza*? You said you were going to hide her in a safe place so her masts wouldn't give us away to snoopers."

211

"No snooper would ever give her a second look now," Sôbô said, beaming even more happily. "That's *Venganza*, right there. And a damn fine job we did with her, if I say so myself."

"You bastard," Culdee said. He balled his fists, and tears came to his eyes. Miranda felt herself reeling with the enormity of it. "Why the fuck . . ." Culdee was spluttering with rage.

"Now, now, easy, both of you," Sôbô said quickly. "She is not as she seems. That's a disguise, and a damn clever one when you consider how limited our time was. My Nipponese crew has been working around the clock on this project. She's a Q-boat now, your *Venganza*. A killer in tramp's clothing."

"What's a Q-boat?" Miranda asked.

"During the war the Germans and Japs rigged beat-up old merchant ships with modern cannons, depth charges, machine guns, and new, strong engines," Culdee said. "They'd lure our subs to the surface for an easy capture, then sink the poor fuckers unawares." He recognized her now: the hulk the Japs had been working on down in the pens last night was *Venganza*, mutilated.

"There's no real harm done," Sôbô said. "We pulled your masts with our crane and stowed them in the pens, then stuck these rotten stumps in. We also pulled your rather puny old Graymarine and replaced it with a brand-new four-hundred-horsepower 6V-53TI built by Detroit Diesel back in the good ol' U.S. of A. Beautiful piece of machinery—a gift from some Japanese friends of ours in Honolulu. She'll push along at ten knots or better now, thanks to some refinements we made below her waterline. That'll put her at least in the same league as Millikan's gunboat." There were Japanese workmen still swarming over the hulk. Sôbô called to an older man in coveralls who was leaning on the after taffrail, wiping his hands on a wad of oily waste. The old man barked *"Hai!"* and swung down below, into the engine compartment.

"Takahashi," Sôbô said. "Damn fine man. My chief machinist on *Yunagi*, back in the good old bad old days." He hummed a bit of "Chicago," smiling wistfully. They heard the engine start up, a smooth, powerful, humming roar quite unlike the old auxiliary's

212

ragged rattle. Then a puff of sickly black exhaust belched from the Charley Noble.

"That's rotten-looking smoke," Culdee said. "For a brand-new engine."

"More of the disguise," Sôbô replied. "That's false smoke, from a generator at the base of the stack. The real exhaust is voided at the waterline, aft. You can barely see it." He pointed to the chugging bubbles and pale wisps of steam. "And it won't attract Redeye missiles, either."

Miranda couldn't look at the tramp any longer. She turned her back and stalked off the mole. But the more Culdee looked, the better he liked Sôbô's notion. Damned clever tactic. That old stinkpot would draw fast boats, fat, dumb, and happy, like dead meat draws flies. Maybe even the gunboat, if Millikan was sucker enough.

"What about firepower?" Culdee asked. "I sure don't see any yet."

"Watch." Sôbô called more orders to the Japanese workers. Four of them stripped the tattered black tarp off the deck cargo. Culdee laughed. Under the tarp was a long, gray-barreled naval rifle, bolted securely to the deck, with ammunition ready boxes close at hand.

"What is she, a five-inch?" he asked.

"Japanese 4.7-inch rifle," Sôbô said. "Standard on the imperial navy's earlier I-class submarines and the pre-*Fubuki*-class destroyers. Damned fine weapon. And this one's weight, complete with the mount and all necessary ammunition, just balances the weight of the new diesel. There'll be heavy machine guns on her as well—those 13.2 and 7.7 millimeters. She rides a bit lower in the water, but that's all right. She's faster than she was before, and she outguns Millikan's gunboat now." Culdee laughed again with delight.

Then Miranda walked back toward them, her heels thumping hard on the coral.

"Look," she said to Sôbô, "I don't like any of this, and I want out of here. This is all a mistake. A lot of men have died already, horribly, and you're planning to kill more. You've totally maimed a boat I worked long and hard to make seaworthy, a boat I love almost as much as I love *Seamark*. You say you're doing all this to get my boat back for me. Well, I don't want it back at that price. You're just using me as cover, too, in a way, so that you can knock over this man Millikan's piddling little dope empire and probably take it over yourself. I don't even know what's happening to Freddie, and he's the best damned mate I ever had." She looked at Culdee. "Yeah, and that includes you, too, Dad. You love all this war crap, I can tell just by looking at you now. Well, stay and die with these other saps, then. I dragged you up out of that lousy boozy gutter you'd found for yourself, wallowing there in self-pity and rum, uglier than this poor tramp here, and I made you back into a sailor. Now you want to be a naval hero and a killer as well. So, stay here and kill, or be killed, for all I care. I'm cutting out."

"I've got to stay here now," Culdee said quietly. "I've got to kill Turner. Or Millikan—whatever his real name is. He killed my shipmates in North Vietnam."

"Look," Sôbô said, "you don't have to fight, Captain. I'd hoped to send you with young Kasim here"—he slapped the white-haired Moro's thick shoulder—"to cut your boat out of that harbor tonight, under cover of our attacks. But he can do it alone, with a few of his men. Your boat will be back here sometime after dark. We can replenish her speedily—I have stores already marked and set aside—and have you on your way safely by midnight. With Samal crewmen to carry you as far as you wish. As for *Venganza*, as soon as we've defeated Millikan, my men will restore her to her original condition. Better than her original condition, in fact. The new diesel is my gift to you for your help so far. A new paint job will go with it, new rigging and new sails as well. I'll send it after you, later, to do with as you see fit." He stopped, standing erect and solemn in the land breeze.

"To hell with both of you," Miranda said at last. She turned on her heel and stalked stiff-backed toward the bunker. Kasim followed, grinning with amazement. The two men watched her go. Then

Culdee turned back to the Q-boat. He was reading the registry on her stern.

"*Bloedig-Feeks*," Culdee read off the stern. "What's that mean?"

"It's Dutch," Sôbô said. "Means 'Red Witch.' Did you ever read the book? The movie was terrible but the novel, by your excellent Mr. Garland Roark, was a crackerjack sea story. Almost Conradian, I'd say."

"Bloody Fix," Culdee said, shaking his head as he watched Miranda go through the bunker hatch. "We're sure as hell in one with my daughter."

Curt and the two Thunders arrived back at San Lázaro shortly after sunrise. The pilot of the second boat had finally found an unpolluted gas drum, and while they ran east on that one, the crews strained enough from the bad barrels to allow them an uninterrupted passage, but much slower than it should have been. As it was, both boats' tanks were beginning to suck air as they eased into the Lázaro basin. Where was everybody? While Abdul refueled, Curt went up to the commo's house to find out.

"He's on Balbal," Billy Torres said. "There's been a world of shit happened since you left. We might have a revolution on our hands here. The commode's holed up in his fort at Balbal with most of the boats. We're only leaving a few here to cover our ass. I'm heading over that way right now. You'd better come along."

"I've got to collect my dog from the yawl," Curt said. "I don't want these Tausuqs making *aso* out of him."

"Too bad," Torres said. *Aso* was a Filipino delicacy—dog-meat stew. "I'd take seconds and thirds if they did."

"You don't like my dog," Curt said.

"Damned right I don't. And you can take him in your own boat when you've got him. He's sure as shit not coming in mine."

Curt bummed a jeep ride back down to the basin. Abdul had finished fueling his Thunder, and the two of them ran out to the *Sea Witch*. Brillo looked gaunt, standing there on the cabin roof. Had Rosalinda forgotten to come out and feed him last night? His bowl

215

was empty, so Curt fed him a big double portion, loaded his loose gear, and led the dog, leashed, down to the Thunder. They saw Billy in another Thunder racing out of the channel toward Balbal and accelerated into his creaming wake. Revolution? What the fuck's all that about, Curt wondered.

He found the commodore inshore on Balbal, in a huge fake-thatched boat shed behind the headquarters. The shed connected to the channel leading in from the sea. Curt had seen the shed but never gone into it before. His eyes adjusted slowly to the green gloom, and then he saw Millikan on the forward deck of a long old-timey-looking ship moored to bollards at the dock. The ship bristled with machine guns and cannon.

"What the hell is she?" he asked when he'd come aboard.

"River gunboat," the commo said. "About sixty years old. Slow and rickety but loaded for bear. She's called the *Moro Armado*. The first Commodore Millikan arrived here on her early in the war. She'd pulled him out of the water after his PT boat was sunk. Apparently a survivor from Corregidor, she was. There were three gunboats still afloat there just before the island fell, in early '42, and all were reported to have been scuttled, but this one must have sneaked away. No one knows for sure. By the time the Tausuqs found her, the Japs had nailed her from the air. Only man left alive was Millikan, and he couldn't even recall being rescued. Her real name and numbers had been blown or burned off by the Jap dive-bombers, and apparently the crew had deep-sixed all her papers and records. Once Mill One came around, he renamed her after one of these islands down here, *Moro Armado*. She's kind of a talisman to the Tausuqs, magical because she brought them their great guerrilla leader, the commodore." He laughed wryly. "*Moro Armado* means the 'Armed Moor.' But Billy and the more cynical members of our little navy call her *Albino Armadillo* because of her white hull and her god-awful waddle. She only comes out, usually, for Commodore's Day—that's Easter Monday. The day Millikan finally emerged from his coma and the guerrilla war really got under way. A showboat, but we may damn well have to fight her."

216

"Can she fight?"

"Those are old three-inch guns, fore and aft," the commo said. "Reliable but slow. I've replaced her original machine guns with M85s; those are .50 calibers, fast and hard hitting. Ought to be able to handle any pump boats or *kumpits* that get uppity with us."

He looked Curt over, head to toe, with a doubtful twist to his mouth.

"Say, you're not the leader of these half-assed rebels who're making to attack us, are you?"

Curt laughed—a sudden, spontaneous guffaw.

"Fuck no," he said. "*Sir.* I don't know what you're even talking about. Rebels?"

"I didn't think you were," the commo said. "Yeah, rebels or something like that. Funny stuff going on around here. I don't have it all scoped out yet, but I'm taking no chances. Too damned many coincidences, all aimed in our direction. We'll fight from here if it comes to that."

"Well, this run went fine," Curt said, "except someone managed to water our gas reserve. That's why I'm so late getting back. No more Phantoms, though, thank Christ."

"Amen to that. Say, did you get any kind of weather report this morning? I don't like that sky that's shaping up out there."

Curt had noticed it, too, alto- and nimbostratus moving in from the northwest with what looked like big anvil clouds looming on the horizon. Weather on the way.

"The weather band out of Puerto Princesa forecast something they called *vientos azores* for this part of the Sulu, starting sometime this evening. That's 'hawk winds,' isn't it?"

"Shit," the commo said, nodding a gloomy yes. "They're supposed to be a bastard, according to Torres. Just what we don't need if it comes to repelling a sneak attack."

Torres came into the shed and up the accommodation ladder.

"Forecast of hawk winds on the radio, sir," he said, saluting the commo and grinning. "Probably *baba del diablo,* too, the men say. It's that time of year."

217

"What's *baba* whatchamacallit?"

"Means 'devil's drool,' " Billy said. He laughed. "They say you gotta be there to appreciate the full effect."

All through the day boats kept arriving at Perniciosa—outriggers, *kumpits,* the long, brightly sailed canoes called vintas—and debarking heavily armed Moros. Kasim's men met them in their own boats and guided them in through the Dangerous Ground. Culdee watched them for a while, then walked up the shore away from the landing. He felt awful about Miranda. He knew she was right, in her way, and he knew for sure that if she hadn't arrived at the house in California, he'd be a dead man by now. Dead of booze and despair, maybe with his head blown off by his own shotgun. Yet he had to stay, had to kill Turner—at least see him die. The whole business of Brigadune, of that entire war, of his naval career so stupidly terminated—by Turner, he was sure now—none of it would count for anything if he didn't see Turner die. There were ghosts out there, crying to be avenged. And ghosts inside himself as well, demanding that he be the one to do it.

Christ, he needed a drink. He'd come far up the shore by now, kicking broken seashells. Gulls were circling above, screaming in the strong sea breeze of midday. He knew he could get a drink back at the base. There were racks upon racks of bottles in the mess where they ate. Scotch, bourbon, gin, rum, brandy, sake—Sôbô's navy followed the British tradition when it came to drink. He could just ease back there, slide into the mess, pour himself one stiff one. Just one.

Sure you could, he told himself. He walked on. Ahead he saw something in the haze of the surf: animals milling in the wash of the waves, gathered around something there on the shore, fighting over it, driving one another away, then quickly turning to feed again.

As he came closer, he made them out. Island dogs. Mongrels. Skinny and scabbed with old wounds and touches of mange. Ratty tails, long snipy snouts, flashing teeth. He had heard them last night, howling in the dark. Now here they were. How long had they been

218

living on this island? Forever? They were eating something dead that had washed up from the sea, something gray and rotten—he caught the stink of death from a hundred yards off.

Then suddenly in his heart he was back at the shiplike house in California, drunk on the veranda, watching wild dogs tearing at dead things on the surf-pounded beach. He felt again the despair, the total, utter weakness of himself at that time. No. He would not take a drink when he got back. He would not take a drink. He would certainly not take a drink until the fight was finished. Until Turner was dead. Then he would take a drink. If he really felt like one.

He turned and walked back.

Sôbô called a meeting in the hour before noon. Culdee sat in the mess hall beside Miranda, who would look at him only with cold disdain. Sôbô was accompanied by a short, wiry man in fisherman's clothes, a cold-eyed man with a white spade beard, short, almost military-cut white hair, and hands that were not those of a fisherman. With him was a dark, handsome woman in torn but respectable clothing, Filipino, not Tausuq. The soldierly man looked Caucasian, maybe Spanish. The woman looked exhausted—angry, frightened but exhausted.

"This is Father Cotinho," Sôbô told the group. "He and Mrs. Rosalinda Aguinaldo have just arrived from San Lázaro. He brought news which I must with reluctance—with repugnance—pass on to you." He looked at Miranda. "Your friend and shipmate Mr. Pascal is dead."

Culdee felt Miranda stiffen; her eyes went wide.

"He was murdered by Millikan and his henchman, Billy Torres. But he revealed nothing detrimental to us in our upcoming fight while he was held by them. He died bravely, a shipmate to the end." ·

"How did he die?" Culdee asked. Miranda looked at him appalled, as if to say, How could you ask such a cruel question?

He'd had to ask it. Freddie was his shipmate, too.

Padre Cotinho made a cross in the air. Mrs. Aguinaldo looked down and away.

"They crucified him" Sôbô replied. "Yesterday was your Good

Friday. They crucified him on the Gólgota above Lázaro City. They lanced him to death on the cross."

Miranda's hands covered her face, and her head fell forward. Culdee could feel her shaking. He saw tears seeping through her fingers, down her forearms, pooling on her legs, sliding off. He put his arm around her.

Padre Cotinho nodded solemnly, confirming Sôbô's statements. "We see this, Señora Rosa and me," he said in a deep, heavily accented voice. A sad voice. "These bad mens. *Muy malo.* The Satan's own child, they are." He paused, shaking his head slowly from side to side. "I bless your *compadre* beforetime he die. I remove him his sins. He was my good *amigo,* my frien'. He is in heaven with Our Lord."

Miranda kept shaking. Culdee hugged her hard, and she leaned against his chest. Culdee's own eyes were wet now. He fought the sobs deep in his chest.

"Millikan has removed nearly all his fast boats to his base at Balbal," Sôbô continued. He would not look at Culdee. "That is to our advantage. For that is where our heaviest blows will fall. We can run with him now, and we outgun him. Our mines have been seeded in all channels Millikan's vessels might use to attack us. A special force of indigenous freedom fighters will assault the Balbal base from the rear. Flanking attacks along the shore from north and south will pin him in his fortress. Our Q-boat and its escorts will block any escape seaward. If he comes out to fight, we will destroy him."

Sôbô looked around the room. Culdee followed his eyes. Younger Japanese were translating for the older ones, gathered in a clique at one side of the mess hall. Kasim was translating for his own men. For a change Kasim was not smiling. The Moros half-drew their bolos and proved their edges against hard thumbs. The Japanese nodded gravely.

"We will destroy him," Sôbô repeated slowly. He pulled something from a sheath on the table before him. A katana—a samurai sword. It flashed in the stark light of the mess hall. "*Banzai!*"

The Japanese echoed the cry. Culdee stood and joined them.

"Banzai!" His fist was clenched, broken and dark, weathered by battles and sun and saltwater. He thrust it upward again and again.

"Banzai! Banzai! Banzai! May we live ten thousand years! *Banzai!"*

Now the Moros joined the chant, their bolos flashing bright as Sôbô's sword.

"Banzai!" Kasim screamed. *"Katana!"* He laughed and wept at once.

Then Miranda was rising, standing beside Culdee. Her square fist punched upward, slowly at first, then faster—a piston pounding toward heaven with the others. Her face was still streaked with the wet snail tracks of tears, her eyes green and flecked with motus . . .

Sea fire.

"Banzai!" she screamed. "Ten thousand years! Kill them! Kill them all! Burn in hell ten thousand years!"

Rosalinda was weeping. Outside even the dogs howled, the dogs of the barren shore.

Padre Cotinho, looking on quietly, held back a smile. Effredio had not died in vain.

TWENTY-EIGHT

Torres had left four Thunders at San Lázaro, all fully fueled and armed, their mooring lines singled up and their engines warm. The senior *mundo,* a middle-aged man named Siddi Ibrahim, kept his crew close to the boats. His father had served the original commodore, and Ibrahim took pride in that. He did not like the *kumpit* traffic that kept pouring past the mouth of the channel leading into the fast-boat basin. Too many boats for this time of day. He kept glassing them with the worn binoculars Torres had left for him, but they all seemed normal enough—a few crewmen lounging in the shade of the after awnings, the helmsmen, bored, smoking cigarettes or drinking from mugs. Double-dragon coffee, Ibrahim thought. A cup would taste good right now. It was nearly noon, and his men were making bets on which would sing first today, the minaret or the cathedral. They laughed and flashed rolls of pesos, staring eagerly back up toward the town. The imam of the Lázaro City mosque was in unspoken competition with Padre Fagundes to see which could proclaim high noon the quicker, the muezzin's hoarse yell from the minaret, or the great bronze bell of the cathedral.

Today the muezzin won. His deep, musical bellow had just begun *"Allah . . ."* when the vibrant peal of the bell tolled high above the town. The men were beginning to crow or protest the decision when a new sound joined the chorus. Ibrahim ducked flat on the dock. *Bap-bap-bap-bap-bap* . . . it came. A machine gun. He heard the rounds snap past, caught the flash of a tracer, brighter than the noon sun, and heard the smack of bullets hitting wood. Habib Amin, the

222

happiest of the gamblers a moment ago, stood still, a wad of pesos flapping in his hand. A bullet knocked him flat. His head exploded . . .

Ibrahim saw tracers pouring from two *kumpits* lying dead in the water at the mouth of the channel. Bullet splashes stitched the water, walked up to the dock, tore into one Thunder, paused a moment, walked on. Ibraham smelled leaking gasoline.

"Go!" he yelled. "Into the boats! Attack!"

The crewmen scrambled toward their boats, crouching low and weaving as they ran. Another man fell, knocked sideways clean over a Thunder and into the water. Ibrahim dived into his cockpit and reached up to start the engine. Hassan, his crewman, tumbled in and lay flat in the scuppers. "The gun!" Ibrahim screamed. "Shoot back! Make them drop their heads!" The engine roared and Ibrahim flipped the mooring lines loose, bullets whipping close overhead. Another Thunder was roaring, and another. Two leapt out ahead of him into the channel, and Ibrahim followed directly behind them—their bulk would mask him from the gunfire. Then his engine faltered. The reek of gasoline—sharp—danger. . . . He heard another boat roar up behind him and slipped his Thunder sideways to let it through. The first two Thunders were nearly at the mouth of the channel, veering out away from each other to exit at diverging angles. Good! Divide their fire! The third boat raced up behind them.

Then the Thunder to the right disappeared in a red and black burst. Burning gasoline spewed out over the water. The second boat dodged sideways, but then it, too, suddenly vanished in a great boiling weal of torn water. Debris and water splashed down. . . . Ibrahim cranked his engine, it coughed, then ignited, then stuttered again. He choked it, hard, slammed the throttle forward, and it roared clean again.

The third boat—fifty yards ahead now and opening fast—shot into the gap left by the two destroyed Thunders. Other *kumpits* had closed in behind those at the mouth of the channel. Ibrahim saw muzzle flash wink from their bows. The third Thunder—who was that? Hakim? *Yes*—began shredding fiberglass. It blew back in chunks, green and whizzing, and Ibrahim saw bullets rip the boat fore and aft, Hakim suddenly gone from behind the wheel, the windscreen starred and breaking up. Then there was a flick and a flash and a ballooning gout of blazing gasoline as the Thunder exploded.

Ibrahim steered for the flames, cut the wheel hard to the left, feeling the heat singe his eyebrows, stiffen his face, and he was through it—in the pall of the smoke, and racing seaward. Hassan had swung the M60 aft and was firing back at the *kumpits*. A good man, Ibrahim thought. He looked ahead and saw another Thunder racing up at an angle to join him. Who was it? Had one of his own boats actually gotten clear of the trap? Or maybe a boat sent by Torres or the Commodore . . .

Blood was blurring his eyes, washing down with the wind from a nick in his brow, and he wiped them clear, trying to see who was in the other Thunder. His eyes flickered clear. He saw the pilot—a white-haired Moro in a sun-bleached blue turban, his beard blowing back in the wind as he grinned at Ibrahim. There was another figure in the Thunder, behind the machine gun, long dark hair blowing wild, wide green eyes over the gun barrel, through the sights, close now, not twenty yards, fifteen, ten . . . it was a *woman* at the gun! A young woman with a face like a hawk . . .

The Lewis gun opened up at point-blank range. Its bullets smashed the Thunder's pilot into bloody rags, then leapt to the gunner and riddled him. The last burst hit the engine, and the Thunder blew up . . .

"Muy bueno!" Kasim shouted over the wind. *"Allah akhbar!"*

High above town the cathedral bell sounded the last stroke of noon.

Shortly before noon Balabatchi's jeep returned with the five guards he had summoned. Balabatchi awaited them in his sail loft. They looked puzzled as they entered the room, more puzzled when two wide-faced, pale-skinned, pockmarked men with crew cuts and the odd, flat black eyes of Hapon shut and bolted the door behind them.

"We are overthrowing the commodore," Balabatchi told them simply. "He is an enemy of our religion, our islands, and thus our people. Are you with us?"

"Who are these men?" a guard named Mufaddhi asked. He looked at the Japanese.

"Allies," Balabatchi said. "What is your answer?"

The guards remained stupefied.

"Make up your minds," Balabatchi said. "We must begin now. Friends or enemies, you?"

Three of the five, the youngest, quickly said, "Friends!"

Mufaddhi and another man, Haji Hassam, one of the most respected of the guards, were still silent.

Balabatchi nodded to the Hapon. They took Mufaddhi by the arms and frog-marched him to the big, black-and-silver machine that stood on a bench near Balabatchi. Haji Hassam began to edge backward, toward the door. Another Hapon was there. He had a machine pistol in his hands. The haji recognized it—an Uzi. Made in Israel, the enemy of all men.

One of the Hapon grabbed Mufaddhi's right hand by the wrist and forced it into the mouth of the sail-sewing machine. His partner stood by with a finger on the power switch.

"Friend or enemy?" Balabatchi asked again.

"Friend," Mufaddhi said, his voice cracking.

"You are lying," Balabatchi said. He nodded abruptly toward the man at the switch.

The machine thudded swiftly, loud yet muffled, like a distant machine-gun. Mufaddhi stifled a scream. The heavy-gauge needle slammed through his hand a hundred times, tearing it to pulp.

The haji had stepped forward again, involuntarily.

"Too late," Balabatchi said. He made a quick gesture across his throat to the Hapon, then led the three younger guards to the door. Looking back, they saw Mufaddhi and the haji slumping to the floor, their throats slashed from ear to ear by the Hapons' knives. One of

225

the Hapon jumped back to avoid the splash of blood. He cursed in a voice harsh as the sewing machine.

"Now we release the prisoners," Balabatchi told them as they climbed into his jeep. "The boats should be here at any minute."

They bounced out over the rutted track toward the salt flats through the shimmer of noonday mirages—afrits and djinns danced to the whine of the engine.

"So tell me," the commodore said, "just what *were* those thumps, then?"

"What I told you before, sir," Billy Torres replied. "Probably just some locals dynamiting fish."

"Probably? I told you to check."

"I *know* it was just dynamite," Torres said. "Why send a Thunder down there when we already have four of them at the basin?"

"Because they might have been attacking the basin!"

"Not enough explosions for any kind of serious attack," Torres said.

They were standing on the beach at the end of the Balbal channel. The commo had his binoculars to his eyes, trying to see around the southern bulge of the island all the way to the Lázaro boat basin. It couldn't be done. He jerked the glasses upward. Black clouds rose and thinned over San Lázaro.

"That's smoke," he said sharply. "Just about where those thumps were. Just where the basin is." He lowered the glasses and turned to Billy. "What did they say on the radio?"

"Their radio isn't working," Billy said. But he was worried now. That *was* smoke to the south. "I'll send a boat out."

He signaled the first of the eight Thunders moored behind a revetment in the channel, caught the pilot's eye, and pointed toward San Lázaro. The pilot nodded; he'd already been briefed.

The Thunder eased out into the channel, then speeded up a bit. But after only a hundred yards or so it backed down suddenly, its engine throwing blue smoke.

226

"Minas!" the man at the wheel yelled, pointing seaward. "Boat mines! Many of them there!"

"Oh, fuck!" the commo said. He started to throw his binoculars down, then thought better of it. "Goddamn it, Billy—"

Just then the sound of heavy firing broke out from the jungle behind them.

A high adobe wall topped with razor wire and spikes encircled the base from the rear and down both sides to the beach. Loopholes pierced it every few yards—firing slits for riflemen. Curt was walking in the shade, whistling for Brillo. He'd ordered the dog to sit and stay while he talked with the commo, but he was gone now. Ahead Curt saw Tausuq guards suddenly crouch and duck away from the grilled rear gate. One of them fell over on his back, kicking. Something stuck up from this throat. Another guard raised his M16, then snapped backward like the first. An arrow? Sticks clattered against the far side of the gate, and one wobbled toward Curt, bounced sideways off his shoulder to the dust. He picked it up. Bamboo fletched with jungle-cock feathers, a long, hand-forged iron head spiked as with the barbs of a stingray's whip and covered with sticky black tar—*poison.*

Gunfire exploded all around, from both sides of the gate. Guards crumpled and crawled. A bright flash—the gate toppled on one hinge and lay askew. Little black children came pouring through the gap, naked kids, carrying spears and long-barreled rifles. Kids with beards? Pygmies! A pygmy saw Curt and cocked his arm. Something dark and long and heavy flew past his ear. Other pygmies raced toward him with bolos in their hands.

Brillo slammed past Curt, dodging as he leapt, growling deep in his throat. A pygmy went down beneath the dog, and then Brillo was up. The pygmy kicked once. He had no throat left. Bolos whirled. The dog was everywhere, a red-brown blur, slashing white teeth. Pygmies screamed.

"Brillo!"

Curt was running back past the gunboat shed, the dog loping

beside him looking back, snarling. His muzzle was red. Tausuqs streamed past Curt, running toward the gate, firing from the hip as they ran. Brass spun through the noon dazzle. Curt turned a corner of the shed and collided with the commodore. They both lay sprawled on the ground.

"What . . ." The commo swung a .45 wildly in one hand as he scrambled to his feet.

"They've carried the gate," Curt shouted over the clattering gunfire. "Pygmies! Hundreds of them!"

The commo looked ahead—to the flash and crump of grenades behind the boat shed. Smoke. More *mundos* were running past them, slowing as they recognized the commodore. Torres ran up with an M60 machine gun in his hands, its belt draped over one shoulder. He was breathing hard, his eyes were ablaze.

"There's boats all over the place out there," he shouted, pointing seaward. "Some kind of a big old island schooner with no masts chugging up behind them, covered with goddamn Moros. Should we hit them? Sortie the Thunders?"

"There's Negritos coming through the rear gate," the commo said. He sounded calm, white under his tan, but composed. "Get back there and organize the perimeter. Get more of those M60s back there. Cross-fire on the gate." He looked around. "*Here!* You men!" A dozen *mundos* racing toward the rear gate skidded to a halt. They all carried M16s and bolos. "Come with me." He turned back to Torres. "I'm going out the side gate, if it hasn't been taken yet, and try to flank these Negritos. Hughes, get a weapon and come with me. We've got to take the pressure off our flank before we can tackle those boats out front."

One of the Tausuqs ran up to a pile of bodies at the corner of the gunboat shed and came back with an M16. He slammed it into Curt's hands. He smiled grimly—it was Abdul. Then he slung a bandolier of magazines over Curt's shoulders. The commo was already running. . . .

* * *

Sergeant Grande watched his troops fall back as planned, still throwing poison arrows and stick grenades through the gate. The satchel charges had blown it open as he'd hoped they would, and now the enemy was looking to its rear. Grande had two Lewis guns sited to keep the gate under fire as long as necessary. Negritos waited beside him for orders. Some carried heavy, conical bundles—shaped charges of the sort the sergeant had used in the war to shatter the walls of Japanese bunkers. He sent the four men with the charges to their assigned positions. The others—a dozen of them—he ordered on another mission, back into the jungle to round up his secret weapon. They smiled happily and trotted off, silent as stalking hunters. Some, he noticed, had severed Tausuq heads swinging from thongs across their shoulders. Sergeant Grande checked his wrist-watch: 1235 hours. Right on schedule . . .

Kasim slowed the Blue Thunder and idled by the edge of the reef, just off the boat basin. Miranda had changed the drum on her Lewis gun and was leaning back against the cockpit's after coaming. The sound of gunfire from the boat basin had at first frightened the gulls and shorebirds into loud, wheeling flight. But now she saw that the gulls at least had returned. They circled and screamed near the mouth of the channel. She watched one land in the water, peck cautiously at first, then with rapid gluttony, at something floating on the waves. Her stomach heaved.

Kasim handed her a cup of cold, tart fruit juice. She took only a swallow and set it aside.

Well, she'd made her own decision. Now she'd have to live with it. She thought of radioing *Venganza* on the small Japanese-built handset Sôbô had given them, but the thought of having to talk that stupid military jargon was too much for her. Anyway, they were busy down there. She could hear dull, thudding explosions and the occasional rattle of machine-gun fire on the weakening northwest wind. To the west she noticed big anvil clouds shaping up on the horizon. Mares' tails preceded them like silver-gray banners. Battle flags torn by some war in the sky. Weather on the way.

More gulls were on the water now, tearing at long, limp hunks of red and khaki-colored meat, screaming and slashing at one another with their beaks whenever intruders came too near. Her stomach heaved again, and she had to put her head between her legs. What had Culdee said? Too much adrenaline on an empty stomach? That's not the half of it, she thought.

"Okay Kasim," she said when she'd gained control of herself, "we might as well get on out to *Seamark*."

He looked at her with concern in his eyes, then nodded and pushed the throttles forward.

Crouching, the commodore led them up a gully overhung with spiny lianas. Two Tausuqs were out front on point. Curt could hear the stutter of machine guns ahead to his right, and the quicker chatter of other weapons from where the wall ran across the rear of the base. They were moving toward the slower guns. Moss-covered rocks filled the gully's bottom, and twice he turned his ankle. Brillo padded beside him, his coat stiff with blood. It looked as though the dog had been nicked across the left shoulder. Christ, not one of those poison arrows I hope, Curt thought. But Brillo showed no signs of poisoning. His eyes burned hot yellow through the green gloom.

Millikan raised his right arm behind him, palm toward them—stop. Then he signaled Curt to come up beside him.

"Okay, we're right on their flank now," he whispered. "The guns can't be fifty yards from us. I think there's a clearing ahead—see how the light brightens out there? Maybe another ten yards. I want you to take half the men and spread out along the lip of the gully. I'm going to take the rest and cup them in to your left. Give me five minutes, and then move out when you hear my first shots. Get in on them, keep low, and lay it on 'em. We'll push these bastards to the wall. Let's synchronize our watches."

"I don't wear a watch," Curt said. "No use for 'em."

"Christ," the commo moaned. He banged his head lightly against the barrel of his Armalite. "Hippies. Okay, just wait for my shots and then open up. If they start pushing you back, make your stand here in the gully. It's good cover, and you can stop them." He sniffed and wrinkled his nose. Brillo was breathing in his face. "What a breath on him," the commo said, pulling back. Then his eyes lit up. "Say, can he retrieve?"

"Damned fine retriever, sir," Curt said. "Everyone says so."

"Well, we'll take him with us next time we go out to pop some birds. I saw three coveys running ahead of us back there a ways. Ought to be a good season."

He got back into his crouch and moved out, up the gully, with his six men.

Curt called Abdul over to him and explained what the commo had said. Abdul nodded and began dispersing the men. Curt looked at the M16. All the Filipinos called it an Armalite. How did you work the son of a bitch? He'd had one down in Colombia, in the boat, but he'd never fired it. He began fiddling with levers. He was still fiddling when he heard a burst of shots from the jungle to his left.

Abdul and the others were up and moving, crouched low, weapons pointing ahead. Brillo whined eagerly and glared at Curt. No, he thought in a flash of panic. I'll just stay here in the gully, back them up. . . . Then he thought, What if those pygmies are circling us? If they've gotten behind us, like we did to them? Visions of swinging bolos. He got up and followed the others.

The jungle ended abruptly a short way ahead. The light in the clearing was blinding after the gloom. Bullets slashed through the greenery, twigs flew and fell, whole branches sagged, twisted by the fire. Curt saw muzzle flashes at the far end of the clearing, more flashes from the jungle to his left. A grenade whirled their way and exploded, throwing dirt and moss over them. Two Tausuqs were down, groaning. He saw Negritos running toward them, dodging, crouched nearly to the ground. Arrows whizzed up from their bows, traveling among the winking muzzles, and whipped close to Curt's head. He tried to raise the Armalite, but its front sight was caught in a vine. The vine stuck him with thorns when he tried to clear it.

He saw the commo, kneeling beside a tree stump, rifle to his shoulder, blasting away, reloading, blasting again. Negritos screamed and charged, then fell to the commo's volley. More grenades, from both sides. Gouts of black and green with fire at their heart.

The commo was up and running forward, his men with him, four of them, anyway, firing as they ran, kneeling to reload, then running forward again. Then Curt heard a weird drumming sound. The ground under his belly started to shake. An earthquake? No. Those Phantom jets again? He looked up at the cloud-ripped sky.

Out of the corner of his eye he caught a glimpse of something black and wide and spewing dust. Turning to look, he saw them coming—Christ! Stampede!

The jungle at the far side of the clearing erupted into a herd of charging cattle, small black wiry animals with steeply veed horns. They pounded into the clearing at full speed, bellowing and screaming and tossing their heads. Pygmies came behind them, firing long, broom-shaped rifles into the air, whooping like tiny buckaroos. Curt saw a thick-necked little bull catch a Tausuq on its horns. The horns punched through the man's chest and stuck out his back, red and jerking. Other Tausuqs were knocked down and disappeared under the slashing hoofs. The commo stood his ground, firing single shots into the arrow-shaped phalanx of the stampede, well-aimed shots, dropping an animal with each one. Then his Armalite must have gone empty. Curt saw him fumble for another magazine. The herd was coming fast, it was on him, he disappeared in the dust cloud that swelled from the racing hoofs.

Abdul and the others were gone.

Curt turned and ran.

Behind him the charging tamarau herd swung left under Negrito control and headed straight for the gap in the tall, pockmarked adobe wall. Sergeant Grande let them pass, then ran, with his men in their wake, through the gates of the fort.

Curt found a pump boat beached on the shore, far south of the fighting. He saw other boats pulled up and hidden in the jungle's edge. The tracks of many barefoot men led away from them, toward the base. This boat would do. He ordered Brillo aboard—the damned dog wanted to go back and fight some more, at least take on one of those goddamn cows. They must have been those buffalo the commo talked about, Curt thought. Tamaracks? No, those were some kind of trees.

The outboard started at the first pull. The housing was still warm. Curt swung the boat seaward and ran back toward San Lázaro. No more commo, he thought. Billy would be happy. The commo wasn't such a bad guy. He sure was brave enough. But no more commo—not if one of those tamaracks skewered him the way they skewered those others. Tausuq shish kebab. He shuddered.

He headed back toward the *Sea Witch*. She was fully provisioned, he knew, her tanks topped off with diesel and water. This isn't my fight, he thought. I'm damned well out of it. Pygmies. Buffalo. Screw it. With the wind dying from the northeast, I ought to be able to work well offshore by nightfall. Don't like that weather to the west, though. Hawk winds? Devil's drool? Well, it was better than what lay behind him, anyway.

He approached the *Sea Witch* from her starboard side. She was tugging at her anchor chain on a weak outgoing tide. Good, even a weak tide would help him. He tied off the pump boat and swung aboard. Brillo jumped up after him, stopped for a moment, then gave a yelp and sprang for the companionway. His tail was wagging madly. What?

Curt heard a thump alongside, saw a bowline hitched on the portside rail. He looked over. A Thunder was tied there, empty, bobbing. Where was the M16? He'd left it back at the gully. He heard footsteps on the companionway ladder and turned around.

It was Miranda Culdee.

TWENTY-NINE

~~~~~~~~~~~~~~~~~~~~~~~~~~~~~~~~

No wind now. The air was hot and heavy. All around them the sea rolled slow and clear, thick as molten glass.

Culdee and Sôbô sat in the lee of the deck gun, their backs to the action. Sôbô thought it best that they not disclose themselves just yet. Bullets buzzed overhead now and then, but the fire from Balbal had shifted from the schooner to the pump boats closer inshore. Culdee had watched the pump boats for a while, crouched behind the tarp-shrouded gun. They raced at speed toward the beach, bow on, then cut hard over and ran parallel to the reef, guns blazing. Like Indians attacking a wagon train, he thought. A bullet spanged on the deck gun's barrel, then rattled around inside the tarp at random, ticking and clanking until it hit the deck. The schooner's Moros crouched behind bales that lined the gunwales, firing back and whooping as the mood struck them.

Culdee turned and sat down beside Sôbô.

"Nothing much happening," he said.

"It will, old son," Sôbô said. "And soon." He checked his watch. "At 1330 precisely—only five minutes more." He hummed something tunelike under his breath. "Only five minutes more. Remember the song? Back during the war? Tokyo Rose played it all the time. Good old Rose. I hear she's alive and well in the United States now."

"Beats me," Culdee said. He was watching Suleiman the Eagle, up on the foremast. *El Aguila* was spotting for the guns on deck. He sat in a tatty-looking crow's nest atop the mast. It was built of old barrel staves on the outside, but inside was a curved shield of boilerplate that rang like a steel drum when bullets hit it. There were boilerplate shields inside the schooner's hull as well, clear down to the waterline. Heavy enough to stop machine-gun bullets all right, but how about three-inch shells? They'd soon see.

A tendril of smoke wafted across the deck from the bales. Culdee sniffed at it. A tracer must have set a bale on fire.

"What the hell is that stuff? The bales, I mean."

"Marijuana, I'm afraid," Sôbô said. "One of the *kumpits* from Basilan had a load aboard, and I commandeered it. Adds to the allure, what?"

"Weird-smelling stuff."

"Don't inhale too much of it, old man. It's called Zambo Zowie, and I'm told it's quite potent." He sang quietly to himself—"Only two minutes more, only two minutes more." He laughed. "I loved that old Yankee dance music back then. Great tunes. Hate this music they play nowadays. Beastly stuff. Too loud for these old ears. Rock 'n' bloody roll." He sounded a creditable Bronx cheer.

"Miranda loves it," Culdee said. He wondered how she was faring.

Seamark, once *Sea Witch,* pounded north into the chop, running on her engine. Kasim followed in the Blue Thunder. Miranda, with a stubby AK cocked on one hip, kept a close eye on Curt where he stood at the helm. Brillo sat at her side, leaning against her legs. Now and then she scratched the dog's ears and he mumbled. But her eyes didn't soften.

"This is stupid," she said harshly. "I really ought to, you know."

"Ought to what?" Curt asked. His knees were shaking. He was scared. He was more than scared. He was downright fearful for his life. He'd never seen her look like this before.

"Just blast you where you stand, you son of a bitch. If it weren't for you, none of this would have happened."

He couldn't believe it. She'd followed him clear across the Pacific, tracked him down. Vengeance. He hadn't thought she'd had it in her. "Hey, wait a minute!" he said, trying to keep his voice steady. "I'm

235

on your side. Maybe you don't know it, but I am." His mind was working wildly, looking for a story. "Why do you think I'm here? Why do you think I was working for Millikan? It's not sheer coincidence. . . ." He'd been about to add "baby" but caught it in time. "No way. I'm working for. . . . Well, I can't tell you, but it's the good guys."

"Oh, come off it," she said. Her eyes were even harder now, and she shifted the gun on her hip, dropped the barrel lower. Toward him. "You must think I'm the most gullible woman walking. Cut the bullshit."

"Dead straight, Miranda," he pleaded. "No lie. They sent me here under deep cover to penetrate this outfit. Report back what's going on down here. And I've been doing just that. Hey, it's not easy, either. I've been shot at by pygmies and jets, damn near chopped in half by bolo knives, nearly flattened an hour ago by a herd of stampeding tamaracks. Or whatever they call them. Those black guys with the long horns? Buffalo."

"Tamaraus," Miranda said. "And you're full of it." Her thumb was on the AK's safety.

"Millikan's dead," he said. His voice cracked this time. He checked it with an effort. "I killed him. Back there in the jungle. Drove him in front of that herd of . . . those things. And they smashed him flat. That's when I decided to split. Come back to the boat, get across to Mindanao, report the whole damn deal."

"Ha."

"But Torres is still alive," Curt almost yelled. "Millikan's right-hand man. A mean bastard, worse than Millikan even. They've got a big ship back there, behind the beach, up the channel. I know what Torres's plans are. Just get me to your people, and I'll tell them how to stop him. I'll help you beat him."

Miranda shook her head slowly from side to side. She was smiling, but there was a bitter twist to it. When it came to hogwash, Curt could swill it with the best of them. But there was just enough truth in what he said to make it remotely possible. The gunboat, for instance. And the Negritos, those indigenous freedom fighters Sôbô

236

talked about. She wondered about Millikan, though. If he really was dead, maybe this killing would stop. Without a leader the Tausuqs might fall apart, or even join with the MNLF revolt, which was certainly more in their interests than serving some off-island underling like this Torres. Maybe Sôbô ought to know about this, question Curt himself. *Venganza* couldn't be far ahead. She didn't dare look around to estimate how far, though. The cockpit was small, and Curt could easily jump her. She felt a knot of anger and indecision tighten suddenly in her stomach. She made up her mind.

"Kneel down," she told Curt. "Behind the wheel. Good. Now lash the wheel on this course. That's right. Put your hands on top of your head. Okay, now walk forward slowly on your knees, over to the lee gunwale."

Oh, God, Curt thought. She's going to do it. His vision started to blur, thin out in quick, white starbursts. He thumped forward on his knees. He heard her walk up behind him, barefoot, the muzzle of the AK cold and round on his neck.

"Lean your chin on the gunwale," she said.

"Miranda, don't. Please don't."

She laughed, and he heard something click. He passed out.

Miranda tied his hands behind his back with a length of small stuff, then his ankles, then cinched both ties together so he couldn't move. She went aft and unlashed the wheel. She steered for *Venganza*, only half a mile ahead.

"What the hell happened to you?"

"It was just like the movies, Billy." The commodore laughed happily. His khakis were ripped, splashed with blood, and a deep slash on his chin showed a glint of jawbone. Blood dripped from it down his chest. Dirty red knuckles were scraped ragged. But his eyes sparked bright as a little kid's.

"Like those old Saturday-afternoon Westerns with the cattle stampeding and the cowboys caught in front of them. Those Negritos ran a whole herd of tamarau down on us, just when we'd started to hurt the guys at the gate. I killed three or four buffalo, Billy—pop,

pop, pop, right through the eyes. Pretty shots, Billy, pretty shots. Then the gun was empty. They hit us. I dived into the lee of a bull I'd dropped, right at my feet, Billy. I tucked in tight against his back, and the ones behind came crashing over him. One of 'em kicked me, here, on the button. . . . Get a corpsman over here, Billy. Sock some stitches in this thing. . . . Then the tamarau swung toward the gate with the Gritos behind them. I cleared out with what men were left." He stopped, took a bottle of Scotch from the table in the boat-shed bunker where they stood, and swallowed a slug. He poured Scotch from the neck of the bottle over the slash, winced, cursed, then drank some more. He sat down.

"You stopped the charge, I take it."

"Just barely," Torres said. "I'd rigged claymores either side of the entrance. Machine guns through the firing slots. Must be ten, twenty dead buffalo out there, and quite a few Negritos."

"Pity to lose the buffalo meat," the commo said. "Good heads out there, too—those ones I shot. That's war, though. So what's the overall situation?"

"Bad," Billy said. "We've held the Negritos for now—I blocked the gate with that old backhoe we use to dredge the boat channel, but there's heavy fire coming in from all sides now."

The commo could hear it.

"There's Moros in close on our left and right flanks, the Negritos behind us. Dozens of pump boats and *kumpits* out to seaward, laying it on us nonstop."

"Anything heavy?"

"Just machine guns—.30 calibers, nothing more."

"What about that old tub that came in with the pump boats?"

"Just that—a beat-up island trader they must have captured on their way here. There's a slew of Moros on her, using her as a fort. But they're only firing light stuff." Billy paused. "You know, the more I think of it, the more this looks like a big pirate raid. Nothing political—not MNLF. They'd have mortars at least. And RPGs. These guys are just *mundos* from east of here, Jolo or Tawitawi.

They probably heard there was good pickings over this way and took a shot at grabbing it away from us."

"What about those Negritos, though?" the commo said. "They're damned well organized—good weapons, and they know how to use them. You ever hear of Negritos cooperating with Moros? And these Gritos are certainly local, from right here on Balbal. I've seen sign of them plenty, out hunting in that backcountry."

"I don't know," Billy said. He hadn't thought of that. "What do you think?"

"I think this isn't the time to puzzle over stuff like this. We can't hold here. I hate sieges, anyway. We've got to sortie—Thunders and *Moro Armado*. Get some sea room where we can maneuver and put our speed and firepower to work."

What I told you a long time ago, Billy thought. But aloud all he said was, "Good. I've got the engines turning over in the gunboat and swimmers out in the channel clearing those mines. We can send unmanned pump boats through ahead of the Thunders to blow whatever mines they miss." He checked his watch: 1329. "We can be ready to roll in twenty minutes."

"Where's that corpsman with the surgi—"

Heavy explosions boomed from the wall outside the boat shed. Gunfire rose to a crescendo. They ran for the gunboat.

Sergeant Grande lay stiffly behind a downed tree trunk, one leg crooked and swollen, leaking blood through the field dressing that covered a cannister wound. The claymores had scythed through his attack like the strokes of a bolo. He'd hoped to carry the gate behind the tamarau and not have to rely on the war-era shaped charges or the vague time sense of the Negritos lighting their fuses. He watched the wall a hundred yards ahead of him closely. Any second now, he thought. . . . Then they went off—four ragged blasts—and through the red dust cloud of the shattered adobe the holes from the blasts came clear, the wall itself teetered above the holes, crumbling, falling with a great clattering roar. As it died away, he blew his police whistle. But the Negritos hadn't waited—they were into the wall through the reeking smoke fumes, spears and bolos flashing, into the sudden rising burst of uncoordinated gunfire, stick grenades spinning ahead of them. And a contingent of Moros from the flanks was pouring in after the Negritos. Listening to the screams and explosions, Sergeant Grande opened his canteen and swallowed a mouthful of warm water. Cannister shot left big holes in a man. Big as ball bearings. He felt water dribbling through the second hole, the one in his stomach. It was cool on the hot edges of the wound.

"Here they come," Sôbô said. He had the glasses to his eyes, watching the plume of steam from the *Moro Armado*'s stack creep slowly seaward through the treetops lining the channel. A half-dozen pump boats, unmanned and engines at top revs, had raced out first. Four of them hit mines and blew to splinters. After them came the green-hulled Thunders, hydroplaning already so that they would run as shallowly as possible through the mined outer channel. Their guns blazed ahead of them. Two Thunders hit mines and slewed onto the reef, burning, then exploding. That left six. They flared to engage the Moro pump boats. Tracers streaked both ways, rooster tails rose and fell, leaving wakes in crazy crosshatched patterns on the sea. The bow of the *Moro Armado* emerged, then her long white hull. Her pilot house, Sôbô could see, was protected by armored side plates. She bristled with machine-gun barrels, and the long muzzles of the three-inchers on her bow and stern cranked around to engage the slow-moving Moro *kumpits*. Flame spewed from the forward gun mount, and a *kumpit* suddenly lost its bow in the black burst of a hit. Another shell took it amidships, sending a geyser of water and shattered planks up and astern. The *kumpit* capsized and broke in half. The cannon banged again . . .

"Christ," Culdee said, his voice choking. "Here comes Miranda."

Sôbô saw the yawl close alongside, the stolen Thunder behind it. Kasim leapt up on *Venganza*'s deck, tied off the Thunder, and ran forward to help the sailboat. He reached down and came up with a limp, hog-tied bundle—a white man with a sick grin on his face and glazed eyes. Miranda followed.

"You must get clear of here," Sôbô said to her. "We're about to engage the enemy."

"This is the guy that stole my boat," Miranda said, not moving. She kicked the man on the deck. "This is Curt. He's been working with Millikan. He says Millikan's dead. Maybe you've won already. Maybe you can get them to quit."

Sôbô swung his glasses onto the gunboat's pilothouse. He saw a blond-haired white man in ripped khakis on the wing of the bridge. A short, dark, wide-shouldered man, also in khakis, stood beside him, directing fire from the gun mounts toward the remaining *kumpits*.

"Then who's that?" Sôbô handed the glasses to Miranda. She looked. It was the man in the photos Kasim had showed them, so long ago now. She turned and kicked Curt again.

"You lying bastard! I should have shot you like I wanted to."

"He's alive?" Curt said. His eyes looked wide, hopeless. "He can't be. The tamaracks . . ."

"No time for this now," Culdee broke in. "Miranda, please just get back in the boat and clear out of here. It's going to get damned hot in a minute or two."

"What about him?" She booted Curt again.

"We kill him?" Kasim had his bolo out, grinning eagerly at Miranda.

"Wait a minute," Curt pleaded. "Let me fight for you. I can help you. I can run a Thunder better than any of Millikan's guys. I can fire that Redeye that's on the boat. You need all the men you can get, don't you?"

"Not that badly," Miranda said.

Another *kumpit* lurched to a three-inch hit. Her crew dived overboard as heavy machine-gun fire from the gunboat lashed her decks.

"Put me in the boat with this guy," he nodded at Kasim. "I'll drive, he can shoot. If I try anything, he can kill me. I promise. I'll fight for you."

"Can the Redeye help us at all?" Culdee asked Sôbô.

"Possibly," Sôbô said. "If Millikan has any aircraft available. We don't know if he has, but I don't know how to fire that system. None of us does."

Moro pump boats lay awash, dead in the water, sinking under the superior firepower of the Thunders.

"I leave it up to you, Captain," Sôbô said to Miranda. "But we must start fighting this ship soon, right now in fact, or we won't have anything left to fight with."

"Okay," Miranda said. Over Sôbô's shoulder she could see the *Moro Armado* turning her bow toward *Venganza*. Smoke and fire erupted from the forward gunmount. A shell screamed overhead and ricocheted off the water a hundred yards beyond them. "We'll let the battle decide it. Throw him in the Thunder, Kasim. Let him drive. You shoot. If he does not fight—" She swung an imaginary bolo.

"Aye aye, Capitán," Kasim said. His mouth drooped in disappointment, but he slung Curt down into the Thunder. Miranda paused at the rail.

"Get clear of this place," Culdee said. He stepped over to her. "You're right, we never should have come. But we're here now. You've got what you came for, so please, please get clear of here."

"Come with me, Dad."

He took her in his arms and hugged her. She was strong. His own flesh, but stronger than he had ever been. He smelled gun smoke in her hair.

"I can't," Culdee said. "Turner's over there. Alive. I haven't gotten what I came for yet. And this ship needs me." He kissed his daughter and turned her toward the sailboat. She dropped over the side, and he cast off her line.

She gave me back my life, he thought. Now I can throw it away.

THIRTY

~~~~~~~~~~~~~~~~~~~~

Following the initial raids, ground assaults, and small-boat actions that provoked it, the Battle off Balbal (as it came to be known) evolved in four distinct phases: Sortie, Pursuit, the Duel of the Heavies, and Mop-Up. Commodore Millikan's main force—gunboat *Moro Armado* and six Blue Thunder fast boats, on reaching the open sea, proceeded to destroy the enemy's small craft and transports. *Moro Armado*'s main battery of three-inch guns, accurately directed by her exec, Warrant Gunner's Mate William Torres, sank *kumpits* almost at will, while the fast boats, with their superior speed and maneuverability, easily shot up or swamped the attacking force's outboard-powered pump boats. At this point Commodore Millikan did not yet recognize the threat posed by the attack force's Q-boat. He ignored the pleas of Gunner Torres to take her under fire, arguing that the conservation of his limited supply of three-inch ammunition was of greater importance in the long run. This was the first of his mistakes.

"Goddamn it Billy! Don't waste ammo on that floating junk heap! We can take her later with a boarding party, for Christ's sake."

"I don't like the looks of her, sir. And there's lots of men on that trader. All of 'em have guns."

"Popguns! To hell with them. Get those pump boats."

"Aye, sir."

"What's that on her deck? Those bales?"

"Look like bales to me, sir."

"Take a closer look with your binoculars. Is that marijuana?"

"Hard to tell, sir, but it could be. Color's about right."

"All the more reason not to shoot her up, Billy. We can use that stuff—help pay for some of this damage at least. Six Thunders blown to hell! God knows what these Commie terrorists have done to the boat basin and the Balbal fort. Washington's gonna be pissed, Billy. Mightily pissed."

Shortly after Sortie, heavy weather, which had been building throughout the day, descended on the embattled vessels. Icy winds poured down at gale-force velocities from the white-edged, black-bellied anvil clouds gathered over the islands. These winds, which resemble Aleutian williwaws, are known locally as *vientos azores* ("hawk winds"), because of the speed and ferocity of their assault. Under their blast on this day, seas rose instantly in great, churning, conflicting surges, swamping pump boats and fast boats with impartiality. Two of the Millikan force's Thunders went under with all hands. Many of the attacking pump boats survived, however, drifting awash with crewmen clinging to wooden hulls and outriggers until the winds moved off to the east. Fortunately, the yawl *Seamark*, making her way north out of harm's way, was proceeding on engine power—had she been under sail, she would have been knocked down and swamped instantly. These winds, though, were just what the attack-force commander, Captain Katana, had been hoping for. It gave him the opportunity to lure the Millikan force farther to the north.

"Why the hell didn't you open up on him when we had the chance?"

"The time wasn't right, old man. If he'd seen we outgunned him, he'd likely have made tracks out of range. I want him well away from San Lázaro, up in the reefs of the Dangerous Ground, where he can't turn tail and run from us. We'll—ah, there he is, see him? He sees us, too. Yes, he's coming on, old son. Just the way we want him."

* * *

Nonstop lightning, thunder as loud as naval gunfire, sheets of rain and seawater slashing ships and men with the impact of chilled bird shot, seas moving at speed in all directions, colliding, erupting in bone-white bursts that stood frozen in the lightning glare, taller than mastheads; sudden rifts in the swirling black clouds, blue sky, hot sunlight turning the water milky green where it wasn't white, glimpses of Balbal emerald-green and silver with the flailing undersides of coco fronds. *Seamark* tossed, bucked, rolled her masts nearly to the wave tops, throwing Miranda to the bitter end of the lifeline she'd tied to the rudderpost. The harness bit deep into her back, but she kept her grip on the helm while the big dog crouched with wide-planted paws on the cockpit's leaping deck, his eyes grave through wet-matted hair, riding it out, weathering it. To the west the *Moro Armado* rolled rail to rail, her blunt bow scooping green water and catapulting it aft, over the pilothouse, where Millikan stared through binoculars into the chaos ahead . . .

"There they are, Billy—030, about five hundred yards, maybe seven hundred. Right standard rudder."

"In this sea, sir? We're damn near on our beam ends now."

"The sea's coming every which way, I don't see it makes any difference how we steer. And stop questioning my orders. Right standard fucking rudder!"

"Aye, sir. Helmsman, right standard fucking rudder. Steady on fucking 018, if you can hold her there."

"Aye aye, *sir!*" Smirks in the gloom . . .

"Watch your language on my bridge, Billy! Goddamn it, that's the third time we've seen them in the past half hour, and we're not closing on them. What're we making?"

"Turns for ten knots, sir."

"That shit box can't make ten knots. It can't make five knots from the looks of her. What's going on?"

"It's these seas, sir. Maybe moving her along quicker than us? Who knows in seas like these."

"Well, let's get her. Now! Ring up all ahead flank."

"Sir, this old engine, sir. She'll tear herself apart at flank speed. We'll—"

"Don't question my orders, Gunner Torres! All ahead flank!"

"When's the last time you pulled sea duty, Commodore?"

"None of your goddamn business. Just ten years ago, you insolent, mutinous son of a bitch."

"Well, I refuse to destroy this vessel unless you put the order in the log, sir, and in writing to me personally."

Millikan laid his hand on the butt of the .45-caliber model 1911A1A Colt automatic pistol holstered at his right hip, then saw that Torres had his own hand on a similar gun butt. A great following sea crashed over the gunboat's fantail, and the ship shuddered, faltered, squatted scupper-deep in the confused and roaring combers. Her bow lifted skyward, corkscrewed sharply to starboard, her keel screaming. . . . Slowly she regained her feet.

"You have the conn, Mr. Torres," the commodore said when the gunboat had struggled back to equilibrium.

"Aye, sir. Helmsman, I have the conn. Boatswain's mate of the watch, enter that in the log. Time: 1523."

As the first wave of hawk winds moved off to sea, small craft that had survived its fury began rejoining their mother ships. Those swamped but not sunk pumped their bilges or bailed by hand. As they did so, a predator in false colors moved sharklike among the disabled Thunders of the Millikan force. It was the Blue Thunder fast boat stolen early in the operation by Katana's competent subordinate, Kasim Ali of Jolo, the Samal sea raider whose men comprised most of Katana's pump-boat fleet. His pilot was the renegade American known as Curt Hughes, late of the Millikan force. Kasim sought out those swimming Tausuqs and crippled Thunders that lay helpless in the water, pumping out or trying to start their water-logged engines. He destroyed them without mercy.

"A la derecha, Brusco. Pronto, pronto. Más rápidamente." The Thunder spun to its right, and Curt saw the target—another fast

246

boat spewing white gushers from its bilge pumps, the two-man crew emptying buckets of water over the sides, oblivious of approaching danger. Kasim was calling him Brusco and it took Curt a while to figure it out. Then he got it. *Brusco* is Spanish for 'abrupt'—or 'curt.' They found they could communicate okay in Spanish. Kasim was all right. But Christ, what a killer . . .

"Despacio, mas despacio. Sí, bueno," Fifty yards now, forty—the crewmen still unaware. Then one looked up. He smiled first—a helping hand!—saw the truth. Horror widened his eyes. He jumped for the M60, but before he could reach it, Kasim's Lewis gun was hammering him, hammering the Thunder, chopping it to pieces. Curt brought their boat alongside the other, Kasim emptied the drum into the cockpit, then popped a stick grenade—smoky sizzle of the fuse—and tossed it into the enemy boat.

"Adelante!" Curt nailed the throttle, and they leapt ahead just as the grenade exploded. Behind him he saw the other Thunder break in half, explode as fire hit its fuel tanks.

Kasim laughed uproariously, then spotted swimmers in the water ahead—Tausuqs from a sunken boat. Dead meat before they knew it . . .

Only two Thunders made it back to the *Moro Armado.* They reported another fast boat still afloat behind them, pumping out when they last saw it, and possibly a fourth heading up from the south to assist it. *Moro Armado,* known irreverently among the saltier members of the Millikan force as the *Albino Armadillo,* was gaining now on *Bloedig-Feeks.* Seas were settling fast, but occasional gusts and swirling low clouds still swept down from the heights of Balbal. That island now lay astern on *Armadillo's* quarter, and the eponymous prison island of Moro Armado dead abeam. It appeared deserted from the vantage point of *Armadillo's* bridge, no boats at anchor or alongside in Narr Lagoon. But the commodore did not have much time to reason why. (He did not know as yet that the camp commander, Balabatchi, had defected to the "other side" and removed the healthier, more combative and influential prisoners from

247

the island, taking them to San Lázaro itself to provoke a popular rising.) The commodore was understandably concerned: each time a squall blew through, obscuring *Bloedig-Feeks* from his sight, she seemed to leap far ahead of him. At one point, toward the end of the main storm, he had her within half a mile's range. Now she was at the very limit of his three-inch guns' reach—nearly four miles. Then he would close again, to three miles, two and a half. Another squall. Back out to four miles. Now, though, with sunset only an hour or less away, he had her within the grasp of his guns.

"Put a shot over her bow, Billy."

"Aye, sir. I'll get the crew to the gunmount."

"They're not at their stations? Goddamn it, Billy, we're at general quarters! Where the fuck are they?"

"I sent the crew below in shifts, sir, for a hot meal. We may have a long night ahead. You know what they say, sir. A stern chase is a long chase."

"Bunch of goddamn pogy-bait pansies you're making of them, Billy. Let 'em eat horse-cock sandwiches at their battle stations. Hot joe's hot chow enough when you're going into combat."

The gun crew raced to its mount, trained out on the wake of the *Bloedig-Feeks*. Torres, down at the gunmount, cranked in some more elevation. Shell loaded, breech closed and locked. Fire. The splash fell astern of *Bloedig-Feeks*, a bit to the left.

"Add fifty, right seventy-five," Billy told the trainer.

Fire again. Still short, but on line this time.

"Add twenty-five."

Fire. Over, about five yards. The splash threw water back on *Bloedig-Feek*'s bow.

"Drop ten. Fire."

This time the splash was fifty yards astern of the trader, fifteen yards to the right.

"What the hell's going on? You had her bracketed! Now get on her, Billy, and pound her. To hell with that marijuana—I want that cracker box in slivers. Now!"

"I think she speeded up, sir. Just before we fired that last time."

"Just shoot, Billy. Hit her!"

And so it went for half an hour—*Moro Armado* expending ammunition in a futile attempt to lay just one round on the fragile wooden hull of its jinking, stutter-stepping, seemingly helpless target. Each time Katana saw the gunboat's forward crew loading, he increased or reduced the Q-boat's speed. His exec, former Chief Boatswain's Mate James Francis Culdee, USN, had the helm. An accomplished ship handler and Korean War Bronze Star winner, Culdee managed with each change of speed to slip *Venganza* subtly to starboard or port. This totally confused Gunner Torres and his crew. As for Commodore Millikan, never a calm man at best, it reduced him to a state approaching apoplexy.

With dark fast approaching and the radar he'd ordered from BuOrd in Washington still not installed, he knew he must make use of the remaining daylight or run the risk of losing his prize. As this game of ducks and drakes proceeded—*Armadillo*'s three-inch shells skipping futilely off water where the enemy should have been but wasn't—both ships were fast approaching the reef-studded waters of Dangerous Ground, just east of Perniciosa Island. The sun was settling fast on the horizon. Captain Katana excused himself from the schooner's fantail and went below to the cabin. Boatswain Culdee conned the ship into the entrance of Dangerous Ground's tortuous channel.

When Katana returned, he was dressed in the crisp, high-collared whites of an officer of the late Imperial Japanese Navy. The crest on his cap was the gold, sixteen-petal chrysanthemum of the emperor. From his left side swung a long, sheathed samurai sword.

"Now, my old friend, we are ready for battle."

"And about time," Boatswain Culdee replied.

The sun hung red and fat, shifting shape as it dropped toward the horizon. No wind. Heaving seas. The evening star, to the east, was green. *Seamark* lay beyond the Dangerous Ground, hove to while Miranda pumped her bilges. She could not bring herself to leave just yet, not until she knew the outcome of the battle. All day she'd heard the booming of Millikan's guns. No reply from *Venganza*. She had navigated the nightmare channel through reefs and coral heads with infinite skill and every bit of seamanship she owned. Checking the bilges, she found no leaks, just the water laid there by the hawk winds. Coming topside she stared to the west, back into the channel, into the setting sun. Two black shapes were moving slowly, twisting and turning through the ball-peened glare of sunset. Smaller, quicker shapes accompanied them—the Thunders. One was definitely with *Venganza*—Kasim and Curt had lasted. The first of the larger shapes was certainly the *Venganza:* Miranda recognized the low schooner profile and high sheer as the boat turned into the widening exit of the channel. Then *Venganza* heeled sharply to port. Rounded up. And stopped. She saw men pulling the tarpaulin from Sôbô's gun. And suddenly she saw what he had been aiming at all along.

"Why the hell we stopping here?" Culdee asked. "We're barely out of the coral."

"Surely you know why, old man?" Sôbô smiled, but his eyes were hard black stones. "Surely you recognize the beauty of it, the classic structure, the wonderful inevitability? We've crossed his bloody T! All of our guns bear on him. Only his forward guns bear on us. Togo at Tsushima! Oldendorf at Surigao! Classic!"

Culdee looked, smiled, and laughed out loud. "You have. Let's hit 'em now. Hard."

"Keep the conn if you would, Boatswain. I'll serve the gun. Just hold her on the engines, right here, across the channel mouth."

Sôbô walked forward, no haste, his whites almost phosphorescent in the eerie light of sunset.

Beautiful, Culdee thought. There's three vengeances at work here. Miranda's on that guy Curt. Mine on Turner. And Sôbô's on the whole U.S. Navy. This is Surigao in reverse. Miniaturized, sure, but the same setup. Only this time Sôbô is Jesse Oldendorf. And Turner is Admiral Nishimura. Beautiful . . .

Two Thunders shot forward through the last light, away from *Armadillo*, up the last hundred yards of the channel. The schooner lies broadside, their intent is obvious. Hit her hard, rake her fore and aft with machine-gun fire, with 40-millimeter grenades from the stubby M79 launchers. Then board her and bolo what's left of the crew.

Flames leapt from the forward hatch of the schooner. A great white-hot gout of water threw one Thunder's bow sideways. Her motor overrevved and exploded in a chuff of white smoke. Dead in the water. The Tausuq crewmen stared at one another, mouths gaping. The second round blew the fast boat to bits, the Tausuqs along with it . . .

"What's that?"

"A gun, sir. A big one. Up there on the forward hatch. It was under that tarp."

"That sneaky bastard! We—"

"Won't help to bitch, sir. We'd better get out of here. He's got more gun than we've got."

"What do you mean? We can't get out of here! Back down through this goddamn channel? What makes you think he's got more gun?"

"That's a five-inch, sir . . . I know the sound."

"Well, *hit* him, Billy. That's a wood hull. Hit him with the three-inch. Hit the sneaky yellowbelly before he hits us."

Here it comes, Culdee thought. He flinched involuntarily at the flash from *Moro Armado's* bow. The shell exploded on *Venganza's* fo'c'sle, starting fires and sending splinters flying. Sôbô fired from up forward again—good, the gun's okay. Sôbô's round smashed the gunboat's pilothouse, taking off half of it in a great blinding flash.

Moro Armado's second round hit the schooner's cabin roof. Gone. Splinters stung in Culdee's arm.

A Thunder bellowed out of the dark, machine guns winking. Bullets ripped along the schooner's gunwales. Bales of marijuana jumped at the impact. Men screamed. Small-arms fire stabbed at the Thunder, but she was gone. A grenade blew on the ruined bow.

Sôbô's gun fired, the flame ten feet long. The *Moro Armado* was slewed half-sideways now, nudging toward the coral, and the 4.7 round smashed her after gunmount. Culdee saw it wrench up and backward in the flash, the gun crew in fragments.

He couldn't see Millikan's remaining Thunder, but their own fast boat was alongside, under the lee of the schooner, away from *Moro Armado*'s gunfire. Kasim was yelling to Sôbô. Sôbô leaned down toward him, pointed toward the *Moro Armado*, chopped the air. Kasim nodded, grinning. Boarding party! Culdee saw Curt, dull-eyed and white in the glare of the fire now blazing on *Venganza*'s bow. Then they were gone . . .

Then they were back—no, it was the other Thunder, Millikan's, loaded to the gunwales with Tausuqs off the *Moro Armado*. Culdee ducked away from the muzzle flashes of their guns. The Thunder thumped alongside. Tausuqs over the rail—bolos flashing—another boarding party. Theirs.

Culdee saw a Tausuq swinging at him. He ducked, and smashed the man with his right fist, felt bone snap, then drew his pistol with his left hand. An awkward cross-draw. Shot Tausuq in the face. Splat. Red hole.

Sôbô fired . . . a hit between wind and water. Red flames shot from *Moro Armado*'s engine room.

The *Moro Armado* fired again. Culdee felt the deck lift under his feet, then sag. *Venganza* lost way. Her engines, too, were gone now. A fire blazed down below, flames licking through the companionway hatch. He used the last of the schooner's way to nudge her bow well up on the coral berm of the channel. She ground up over it, growling deep in her guts, her timbers yelping like a pack of hounds. She stopped, aground. But the channel was blocked now. There was no way out for either boat.

The two heavies lay not a hundred yards apart, exchanging gunfire.

Culdee, crouched low, played a fire extinguisher on the flames from the companionway. He moved down as they died down, forcing the fire back deeper, deeper, until rising water from the shattered hull killed it altogether. Then he crawled back topside. An AK from one of the dead Moros was lying nearby. He checked it—loaded, intact. He rested it over the body of the Tausuq he'd killed and began firing single shots at the burning *Moro Armado*. Something roared out of the dark—Kasim's boat. Curt was slumped in its cockpit, blood dark on his face.

"I take him to Captain Miranda," Kasim yelled up to him. "She out there somewhere. I see before sunset already. Then come back, we fight them together."

Culdee nodded vaguely. Miranda? She's safe, though. Do what you want, old man, he thought. I've got my hands full. He looked up to take aim. Something sticky hit his face. Then another sticky thing. His eyes were sticking together, and he blinked, then blinked them clear. He looked up into the dancing firelight. The sky was full of gossamer scarves, drifting down on the light land breeze from the islands—*baba del diablo*—spiderwebs on the wind. They were sticking on everything. The two guns—Sôbô's and the *Moro Armado*'s—fell silent. The gunlayers couldn't see to shoot. Culdee ducked down the charred companionway. Up in the forward cabin he groped in the dark until he found the punt gun. Powder—yes, right here—and shot pouch. He dragged the gun back on deck and began loading it.

There might be more boarders . . .

Seamark stood on and off the Dangerous Ground as the battle neared its climax. Miranda's hair was stiff with spiderwebs. She wanted more than anything to wash it, at least to pour a bucket of seawater over her head. But if she left the helm in these random winds, she might capsize. Flashes of gunfire lighted the dark to the west, yellow behind the filaments of the *baba*. She kept the helm, on and off, off and on, a broad reach outbound, making short tacks back in toward the battle.

An engine rumbled toward her out of the booming background of surf and gunfire. She allowed a gust of wind to lay the boat over on its port side as black water hissed at the lip of the coaming. The engine came closer—she could not hide the sailboat's profile. She took the AK and held it ready. The dog, warm against her feet, suddenly rose and stared toward the sound of the engine.

It was a Thunder. She saw its bow, shattered by gunfire, move toward her. The dog growled. Miranda held the wheel with a tight-pressed hip and raised the rifle. She lowered the barrel until its forward leaf sight disappeared into the denser blackness of the approaching boat. She didn't want to shoot, but she would . . .

"Not shooting now, please."

It was Kasim.

She shivered and put down the rifle.

Kasim brought the Thunder alongside and slung something heavy and limp into the cockpit. It was Curt. In the flare of a gun blast she saw he was cut across the top and side of his head. Brillo licked at the blood, looked up at her, licked again.

"Maybe dead already," Kasim said. "Or not. I go back. You go away. Zamboanga, Hawaii, America."

"Don't go back into that hellhole," Miranda said. "Stay here. We'll get out of this, go together."

The dog growled. He leapt into Kasim's boat.

"Is a fighter, the dog?"

"Yes," she said. Kasim laughed—the most amazing thing he'd ever heard.

Kasim waved, smiled, and rumbled away into the darkness, toward the flash of the gunfire.

Padre Cotinho stood at the door of the cathedral. Below him the town was burning. He could hear the pop of gunfire, louder than burning timbers. Looters whooped their owl song amidst the ruined shops. He stared to the north.

"Do you see it?" he asked Rosalinda.

"What?"

"The gunfire."

She followed his gaze and saw it, pale blooms of light behind the devil's drool.

"Let them kill each other," she said. "What about these people?" The cathedral was full of women and children, praying in the dark, under the smile of Saint Lazarus.

"They will survive," he said. "Only the town is dying."

Balabatchi came up from the town. He had the *yakuza* with him. The six Japanese looked pleased with themselves, strutting and laughing, hung heavily with weapons and loot.

"*Que va?*"

"*Bueno,*" Balabatchi said.

"Then now is the time," Padre Cotinho said.

Balabatchi nodded. He beckoned to the *yakuza* and walked briskly toward Gólgota. They followed, laughing. They died in the shadows, under the flash of many bolos.

"You are no man of God," Rosalinda said.

"No," Padre Cotinho agreed. "Just a man."

He stared to the north, watching the slow flares of gunfire.

THIRTY-ONE

~~~~~~~~~~~~~~~~~~~~~~~~~~~~

"I think that does it," the commodore said. He had his binoculars to his eyes, the flare of the other ship's fires dancing on the lenses. Billy Torres fed another shell into the gun, slammed the block closed, and fired again, for good measure. The round smashed into the schooner's bow, sending splinters high into the night. "No movement," the commo said. "Just dead men, Billy. She's burning from stem to stern."

I can see that from here, you asshole, Billy thought. Without binoculars.

"Get on over there in a boat and blow her up," the commo ordered. "Take a couple of satchel charges."

Billy slammed another three-inch shell into the receiver, slammed the block, fired again. Chunks of burning wood spun off crazily at the hit.

"Do it now, Billy," the commo said. "You're just wasting ammunition, and you know they don't make that kind of three-inch any more."

"You go," Billy said.

"What?" The commo turned, his face redder than the light of the fires. Both ships were burning, and to Torres it was only a question of which would sink first.

"I said, 'You go.' " Billy fed the gun again.

"You fire that thing one more time, and it's a general court," the commo said.

"Then you go over there, sir. I'll cover you."

256

"This sounds a lot like mutiny to me, Billy."

"*Fuck* mutiny," Billy said. "Fuck *you,* sir." All of it came surging up now. "Yeah, fuckin' aye, mutiny! Why don't you go over there, you round-eye pussy? Why's it always me?"

"Mutiny!" the commodore screamed. He slammed his binoculars onto the deck, kicked them into a fire.

"Mutiny," Billy agreed. His *lata* told him the commo was scared. It was there in his eyes. Billy had a .45 Colt automatic pistol on his hip, and he pulled it now. There was a round already chambered. There was always a round chambered. "Get off this goddamn tub, or I'll blow you off."

The commo stepped back. He didn't know what to say now. Billy reached into the wheelhouse and pulled out a heavy canvas packet. A satchel charge. He tossed it to the commodore.

"Move it," he said. "I wanna see this. And don't try to run. I'll take you out with the three-inch."

"What do I—"

"Blow her up. Then you can go to hell as far as I'm concerned." The commo went.

Culdee had slipped below, in the shadows, to check the bilges. There was a fire in the engine compartment, and he could see Takahashi's body sizzling over the flames. He flashed a light down through the scuttle. A lot of water down there. No power. No pumps. Timbers overhead cracked and crackled. Something rustled behind him. The engineer's assistant, a wiry little man with gray hair but no face, twitched in the far corner of the engine compartment. Culdee looked down into the bilges again and swung the beam forward as far as it would reach. Firelight flickered on the oily water, and he saw bodies floating face down, toward the bow. Sparks and burning embers fell through a hole in the main deck and hit the water with angry hisses. Some fell on a dead man. They burned on. The *Arizona* . . .

Topside again he saw Sôbô crouched by the gun. He motioned Culdee to lie flat on the deck. It was hot. Sôbô pointed toward the

257

Moro Armado. Culdee heard the revving engine of a fast boat. Someone was coming over. Where was the AK? He couldn't remember where he'd left it. Fire. Flying splinters. Another hit from the *Moro Armado.* Kasim's Moros slumped dead over the wrecked Lewis guns. The smell of burning flesh . . .

Culdee saw the Thunder now, silhouetted against *Moro Armado*'s fires. There was one man at the tiller.

The *Moro Armado*'s forward three-inch banged again, and the hit came on the fantail this time. Bodies spun off into the water. No one was left alive there, or dead either. Except Culdee. The *Moro Armado* was still moving, slowly, on the night wind—but moving, right to left. *Venganza* was dead in the water.

Culdee felt a body shudder against his elbow. It was a dead Moro, still kicking. No rifle, though. Culdee took the man's bolo. The fast boat loomed close aboard. There was a man at the helm, scared—a white man at the helm. He wore no hat. His khaki shirt was torn. His hair was blond, blond going gray. The man looked up as he cut the motor. He threw a line over the taffrail, looked up again. He heaved himself aboard the schooner. He had a pistol on his hip, a satchel charge in his free hand.

Culdee stood and faced him. They weren't a yard apart.

"Turner."

The man stepped back, went for his pistol.

"Culdee?"

He slapped at the holster flap, his pale blue eyes red with the smoke, that weak chin, wattles along his jawline. Turner, sure, but old now.

"Goddamn right," Culdee said. "Culdee, J. F., Chief Boatswain's Mate, USN."

He swung the bolo. Turner ducked. The blade clipped his left arm, and the satchel charge dropped. He had cleared the holster flap now, he had the pistol coming out, coming up. Culdee moved in and chopped again. Again Turner dodged. The gunbarrel was up now. There was the close slam of the .45. Culdee dodged sideways, swinging the bolo. Fire flashed from the pistol, whined, smacked. Culdee reeled to his left—shit—the bullet. . . .

My right hand, he flashed. That's the one that's busted up the worst. He shook it. Two fingers were gone. Where was the bolo? Turner fired again . . .

Another shell from the *Moro Armado* smashed home, amidships this time. Turner was lost amidst the flash and the flames, smoke heavy and choking all around him.

Culdee saw the bolo, crawled toward it. He heard the near, loud crash of the 4.7, saw its shell smack the *Moro Armado* at the waterline. A perfect smoke ring blew from Sôbô's gun muzzle. Then smoke blinded him again. Must have been like this then, on the *Fat Lady* . . .

Sôbô opened the gun's breech block, and the brass clanked out in a bright yellow whirl, thumping on the deck behind him. Ghosts of white smoke rose up, acrid from the plug. He groped for another shell, grabbed it by the ogive curve, swung it up, and slapped it into the receiver tray. And rammed it home. He closed the block. Easy now, easy now. He looked hard through the smoke and saw the *Moro Armado* close aboard, broadside to him. He sighted down the barrel of his gun. He cranked in some deflection, cranked the muzzle down until it was smack on the gunboat's pilothouse. He fired. Another hit. The pilothouse exploded in spinning fury. But the three-inch barked back at him. The shell whined overhead. Sôbô opened the breech block. He reached for a shell . . .

Culdee hunted Turner through the smoke. On his hands and knees. Slipping in blood, his own blood. Splinters bit when his shoulders moved. He was spiky as a porcupine—wooden ships . . .

Turner was hiding beside the stump of the mizzenmast. Flames licked behind him. He flattened himself on the deck. Too much, too much—they can't ever pay me enough for this shit duty. . . . He saw Culdee briefly through the smoke, angling toward him, left to right. He leveled the .45 and slapped the trigger. Bang—gone wild. . . . No, dork, it's not a shotgun. . . . The receiver locked open. It was empty. He reached into his hip pocket for another magazine. No hip pocket. He felt his shirt pocket. No more ammo. Billy'd blown it all away . . .

Sôbô hit the *Moro Armado* again, at the waterline. Billy fired back at his muzzle flash. The shell flew high once more, loud and almost visible in the dark. Sôbô swung the breech block open, grabbed another round. He saw the flash of the *Moro Armado*'s muzzle. Splinters skewered his face. His right eye went dead. He pulled himself up, his hand sizzling on the gun barrel. He cranked the muzzle down again, point blank. Yes, he'd chambered the round just as the three-inch hit. He fired. In the afterimage of the flash he saw the gunboat shudder, spew gouts of smoke, list heavily to port. The gunner would have to correct now, maybe he couldn't correct enough, couldn't depress his muzzle quite enough to hit the schooner. Diagrams flashed through Sôbô's mind—he smelled the Inland Sea, the chalk on the instructor's blackboard, Eta Jima, Gunnery 101. . . . He reached back for another shell as he opened the plug . . .

Culdee's legs were broken. His shirt was on fire, flapping against his back with its own self-inspired wind. Fuck it. He rolled over onto his back, squelching the flames. Blood welled from his belly. He looked down, wished he'd hadn't. There was a big frag from that last one, in his belly. The blood was slow and dark, and there were pieces of crud in it. He could smell shit along with the blood. "Shit!" he yelled. Then he laughed. You heard about it on the midwatches, your shipmates had seen it, and here it is. No pain yet, though. Thank Christ for that.

Where was Turner?

He heard the dead cranking of an engine. That nagging, sullen whine—Viv carping about payday, about shore duty. Turner was over the side, in the fast boat. Culdee could hear him muttering down there in the dark. Abandon ship. The *Fat Lady*. They all died, didn't they? Or most of them, anyway.

Sôbô fired again. Culdee saw the hit, again at the waterline. Then he saw a flash from the gunboat's forward deck. Not a gun flash, a grenade launcher. Like in the delta . . .

The grenade hit Sôbô in the chest, blew through him, exploded against the gun. The round Sôbô had just chambered went off, but the barrel was bent now. The gun exploded. It shredded Sôbô like raw meat in a whizbang.

Surigao autumn . . .

Culdee's head clanked against something hard and metallic. He could hear Turner cursing as he turned the starter again and again. Culdee reached behind him, felt the metal. It was the punt gun, where he'd laid it before the fight started. The weapon was already loaded with half a pound of black powder, a heavy charge of cannister. He began pulling himself toward the taffrail, hauling the punt gun beside him every few drags of his elbows. Caps? He slapped what was left of his shirt. Yes, right there in his pocket, where he used to keep his smokes. He could see the *Moro Armado* listing dangerously to port now, her nearside scuppers dipping close to the sea every time a wave reached her. He saw the grenade launcher flash again, heard the grenade blow, back near the gun Sôbô was serving. He looked over toward the gunmount. In the flare of the fires he saw Sôbô dead against the smashed gun. Culdee's elbows skidded in the blood and oil on the deck. His face hit the planking, and two teeth splintered. Burning coals fell on his back and shoulders. He crawled on.

Turner was still trying—the engine had taken frags through its feed line. When he saw gasoline leaking, smelled it on his feet, in the boat's bilges, Turner pulled the gas line free. There was a spare tank. He pulled the sloshing steel tank aft and plugged it onto the tit. He pumped the rubber bulb, priming it. Then he cranked the starter once again. A choking splutter. The smell of gas fumes . . . flooded. He'd have to wait another minute.

But Torres was still lobbing grenades. The gunboat was quite close now, and Turner could see Billy on the fo'c'sle, the M79 stubby against his shoulder like a blunderbuss, thumb clear of the breaking lever, pop—flash—*bam*. This time too close.

"Cease fire!" Turner yelled. "Cease fire! They're done, you idiot! They're all dead, don't waste any more grenades!"

"Fuck you, sir," Billy yelled back. He popped a round at the commo, saw it burst on the schooner's cabin roof. Then he broke the launcher and slipped in another round. Turner crouched down in the Thunder's cockpit. Court-martial for that man, no doubt about it now . . .

Culdee reached the rail. He dragged the punt gun up and slid the barrel out over the side. Turner was just forward of him, cowering in the fast boat. But Culdee couldn't depress the muzzle of the punt gun enough to hit him. The barrel was too long, longer than a tall man is tall. He'd have to stand to do it, and he couldn't stand on his wasted legs. Turner was up again, on his knees. He was grabbing for the starter key. He was turning it. Culdee heard the engine fire. Then it died. Turner cursed. Culdee fumbled in his pocket for the box of caps. He got it open, took one between the thumb and forefinger of his right hand, the stubs of the last two fingers still leaking blood onto the deck, onto the gun itself. He felt a bone in his right thigh poke through his skin and the bite of the air on its marrow. He tried to cap the nipple of the punt gun. The cap slipped off, tinkled on the deck, bright and brassy in the firelight. He took another.

Culdee heard the engine light off. Turner was babying it with the throttle, letting it purge itself of fumes and smoke. Culdee knew he couldn't kill him with the punt gun, not this close. He looked around, saw a coil of Manila near his left hand. He grabbed it, his maimed hands working automatically now, and threw a hangman's noose in the line, fed the loop up, and shaped it. He peeled off some slack. Turner was ready to run. Another grenade lobbed over from the *Moro Armado*. Turner ducked. The grenade popped against the bow, wire frags whirring like cicadas. . . . Then he engaged the engine and pushed the throttle ahead. Culdee threw his loop . . .

Out of there! Turner exulted. Free at last. . . . Then the noose settled over his shoulders, slid down his arms, and locked where his throttle arm bent. He felt it tighten and looked back. He could see Culdee belly-down on the deck, the line paying out from his hands. Turner fumbled with the tightening noose. The Thunder went squirrelly, skewing sideways, until he kicked the wheel. He almost tumbled out of the boat. Turner screamed, fighting the noose . . .

A bitt! Where was the bitt? Culdee felt the Manila burning his palms, saw a bitt off to his right, rolled toward it. He could feel a bone scraping on the deck planks—his shinbone. The bone in his opposite thigh cut circles across his muscles. The blood pumped stiff into the frayed flesh. He threw two quick half hitches onto the bitt, then rolled back to the punt gun.

The line payed out to its hitch on the bitt. When it reached its stop, it tightened hard and fast, yanking Turner out of the boat. The coaming smashed him hard in the ribs, and he felt them snap. He was in the water, tied, kicking, the fires blazing all around him. Cold water, hot flames . . .

Culdee took the cap in his left hand. He still had all his fingers there, port side present and accounted for, sir. He thumbed back the stiff hammer until it clicked and locked. He stuck the cap on the punt gun's nipple. He raised the heavy wooden butt to his shoulder. The trigger, thick and cold, felt slippery—blood from his right hand. He put his remaining fingers on it and sighted down the barrel. Turner was thrashing in the glare of the burning ships. Culdee held on him. Something exploded up in the schooner's bow, and from the corner of his eye he saw the ship rat go over the side, swimming toward a smoldering spar. Sinking ship . . .

Turner was drowning. His lungs ached, his eyes stung from fire and salt. He couldn't loosen the grip of Culdee's noose. He kicked frantically, trying to keep his head above water. Then he heard Culdee yelling to him, and he felt his ears pop clear for an instant. He saw Culdee looking down the barrel of an immense gun, Culdee's eyes locked hard on him, the flicker of light on a cocked hammer.

"Turner!" Culdee's voice was louder than the explosions that racked both ships. "This is for the Dune!"

The hammer fell. The cap popped. The half pound of black powder exploded . . .

Turner screamed . . .

Through the smoke Culdee saw the charge slash the water all

around Turner's head and shoulders, saw Turner lift from the weight of fast-moving shot as it tore through his body. He saw the red and white lace of the shot against the black flickering sea, the sea red and yellow with the dance of flames, and the deeper red boil of water around Turner's shredded body. Ammunition was exploding all around Culdee now, skittering off at odd angles, red, white, yellow, hissing and roaring. He saw something dark flash fast through the boil of red water where Turner was. A hunk of wreckage? Too fast. It turned, returned. A triangular dorsal fin.

At that moment the flames reached the satchel charge. As it exploded, Culdee felt himself go off through the air, torn apart by its blast, a man in many pieces.

Billy Torres knelt in the gunboat's scuppers. He couldn't stand now, his legs limp from loss of blood. And around him were dead men, fire, broken weapons. His eyes wept from the heat of the flames.

The commodore was dead. Billy had seen him blown apart by gunfire from the sinking schooner. He felt guilty—he should have gone over there. The commodore wasn't a bad man. Just a fool.

The fires crackled louder, grumbling deep in the gunboat's innards, a ship of death, sinking.

Something growled, more ominous than the fires, growled in the dark behind him. Billy turned and stared. It was the horror of his life.

The dog came fast into the firelight, too fast for Billy to fire his pistol. It knocked him flat on the deck, ripped at his throat and face. Billy pressed the pistol against its hot belly and fired. The dog bit harder. Something ripped. He threw the dog from him, screaming.

Kasim stepped out of the dark and swung his bolo. The head rolled free, down the canted deck. It had no face. The dog had taken it.

THIRTY-TWO

Miranda heard the *Moro Armada* roll over. The groans and snaps and creaking of her final moments as she broke up came loud and clear over the water. She saw her fires disappear in the quenching wash of the sea. A great gulping belching sound followed, and one last fire on the gunboat's bow flared briefly, then died. But fires still raged on the *Venganza* as she lay mortally wounded in the dark. No one could live in that inferno. Miranda heard small-arms ammunition cooking off on deck and down below, then saw a great yellow-red flash as something powerful exploded. The roar hammered her ringing ears. Maybe Culdee's black powder cans? Whatever it was finished the schooner. The level line of the fires whose smoke and glare obscured her sight of the ship itself began to assume a stern-high angle. She was sinking at the bow, and as the fires died one by one at the touch of the sea, Miranda could just make out the huge ragged shot holes in her sides, the 4.7-inch deck gun lying smashed and barrel-bent on the forward hatchcover. Her whole stern section seemed to have been shot away, or was clinging to the remainder of the hull only by a few splintered deck planks. As her angle steepened, wrecked gear and bodies skidded forward, some toppling limply over the side. Something heavy broke loose below decks and grated forward, roaring. The engine. As the glare lessened, Miranda could see triangular dorsal fins circling at the wavery edge of the light. She had to look away.

When she looked back, the ship was gone. Only shattered flotsam bobbed in the dark, some wood, some flesh.

Her eyes stung suddenly, then blurred with the tears. She wanted to cry out aloud, but she wouldn't. If she let go now, she didn't know what might happen. She had to hold on. She had to get out of there.

Then she saw Curt lying smashed and limp on the cockpit deck. His head was propped against the gunwale and lay at an odd angle to his shoulders. At first she thought he was dead, but when she drew closer, she could see a pulse beating weakly at the root of his throat. She eased him out flat on the deck and propped his head on a life preserver. The sky was lightening now to the east, and she was able to examine his wounds. The most obvious was a long, deep gash across the side of his head that was still seeping blood through its dark clots. His hair was stiff and sticky with blood, and she could see the gleam of white bone at the bottom of the gash. A shell splinter? Who could tell? Who cared? She tore off the sleeve of his shirt and bound it tight around the gash.

Then she pulled off the rest of his shirt and cutoffs. He was studded with splinters all down his right side, and there were flash burns, puffed and watery, across his chest and stomach. Small dark-blue holes dotted his left thigh, but when she probed it, the bone didn't feel broken. Shrapnel. She'd have to dig it out with the forceps in her medical kit. She ducked down the companionway and found the kit after a brief search. Topside again, she opened it. Good. He hadn't marketed the morphine. There were half a dozen Syrettes nested in cotton wool. He'd need them once she turned to with the forceps. She found burn ointment and plastered his blisters with it, then squeezed some onto bandages and taped them down over the burns. With the forceps she began pulling splinters. She was careful, as gentle as she could be, but he began to moan, then twist away from her. His eyes popped open—wide, wild, out of focus. He tried to talk, but his mouth was like glue. He could only mutter a bit, still out of it. One particularly stubborn splinter brought a yelp from him, and he passed out again.

As the light strengthened, Miranda went to work on the shrapnel holes. That yanked him ragingly awake, screaming and fighting with an impossible strength. She slapped him hard and pinned him down on the deck.

"Stopping yapping, you shit heel," she said. "I ought to dump you over the side with the other stiffs. Don't give me a hard time."

He looked up at her, fully conscious for the first time. "Why're you doing this, then?" he said in a raw, croaking voice.

"Just shut up. I'm going to shoot you full of morphine now so I can get this metal out of you. Then I'm going to stitch up your head. What comes later, I don't know yet."

She uncapped a Syrette, checked to make sure there was no air in the hypodermic and popped it into his arm. Then she went below to boil up some water for tea.

When she came topside with it, he was asleep. Good. She'd made only tea enough for herself.

She was tying off the last stitches in his head wound, having cleaned it thoroughly with cotton soaked in hydrogen peroxide, when she heard an outboard motor chugging at low revs in the distance. When she looked up, the horizon had closed in to no more than fifty yards. Sea smoke lay thick and gray on the waves. The motor was closing on her. She grabbed the AK and ducked down behind the gunwale. When the boat sounded close enough, she eased her head up and stared into the fog. It crept out slowly, bow on in her direction. A pump boat. Ours or theirs? She slipped the safety off and checked to see that there was a round in the chamber. There was.

The pump boat plugged its way toward her, cautiously. She raised the rifle and slid it over the gunwale, sighting down the stubby blue barrel. Then she heard a bark. Brillo! The man at the tiller stood up. It was Kasim. She rose and waved to him with the rifle. Brillo barked twice more, his tail swinging hard and fast.

"Ah, you live!" Kasim cried. *"Milagro de Dios!* We both live is a miracle of Allah." He tied up at the taffrail and swung aboard. His shirt was holed and bloodstained, and his arms were blistered. Two fingers were gone from his left hand—just black stumps where he'd stuck them in hot tar to stop the bleeding. Kasim embraced her powerfully with his good arm, a double *abrazo*, his eyes gleaming with tears and his smile threatening to split his burned face open. Brillo went over and sniffed Curt. Miranda could see singed patches of fur along his back and down three legs, and already clotted blood on his neck and haunches. She'd have to patch him up, too. And Kasim.

"No," Kasim said when she reached for the burn ointment. "You must go now, not waste time here. Capitán Katana dead now. You father he dead, too. Millikan dead. Torres dead. Many my men dead. Many, many their men dead. But Padre Cotinho live still. *Un hombre muy engaño, muy perfidio*—very tricky. You sail east. Go home now."

"Come with me," she said. "I'll bring you back to Jolo."

"No, *gracias*. I must stay at this place, gather my few men, see to their hurts. I must make certain Padre Cotinho does no treacheries." The sea smoke was thinning. They both looked south toward Mount Haplit and the slopes of San Lázaro. "This place my home for a while now already," he said.

"I must search for my father," Miranda said.

"*Inútil,*" Kasim said. "Useless. He is *muerto,* dead with his ship. I see, I know. Capitán Katana as well. You must go now, go east, away, fast. Padre may want you dead, too. Newspapers like that much better, you dead. Let him even believe so already. I tell him you ship, she sink, too. You dead, that man—El Brusco—he too is dead." He gestured toward Curt. Miranda looked toward him.

"No, Brillo!" The dog was cocking his leg over Curt's head. He stalked stiffly away and lay down on the cabin roof.

Kasim laughed.

Miranda burst into tears. It all came pouring out now, all the awfulness, the fear and the anger and the unforgettable memory, images burned forever into her mind—shells bursting, boats exploding, great sudden gouts of flame, torn bodies sprawling like bloody waste rags—the horror. . . . Kasim embraced her with both arms, held her hard and tight against his chest. He was weeping, too.

"It is always forever ugly," he said at last. "But you must sail, *hija*. You are my daughter of battle now. *My* daughter, now. And you must live." He kissed her gently on the eyes. Then he was gone. She looked up and saw the pump boat disappearing into the last wisps of sea smoke, toward San Lázaro.

His voice came through the fog one last time. *"Allah akhbar!"*
She went forward to make sail.

By late afternoon the islands had sunk below the western horizon. Not even Haplit's blue volcanic banner could be seen on the wind. *Seamark* was making good speed across the Sulu. The hawk winds had abated, the *baba del diablo* blown itself out, and a freshening breeze from the southwest filled *Seamark*'s sails to a hard, muscular tautness. It was the southwest monsoon, Miranda knew, a bit early this year, but the sea and its weathers kept no firm schedules. The wind gods had blessed her, and she was grateful.

Then Curt awakened. She had dragged a spare mattress topside and rolled him onto it, rigged a tarp for a sunshade. He looked at her from his blankets, unsmiling, almost puzzled.

"Why are you doing this?" he asked at last. "You still don't owe me."

"Damned right I don't," she said. She eased the helm to a following wave. The seas were rising. "This yawl rig was a good idea," she said, looking back at the small triangular kicker sail. "She damn near steers herself now, if I tie down the helm at the right degree." She tied it down, then went below to make some tea. When she came back, she had two mugs. She handed one to Curt.

"Thanks." He tried to sip from it, and tea slopped onto his chest. He winced when the hot liquid touched one of his burns. He switched the tea to the other hand. The cup still shook, but less wildly now. "I don't get it," he said. "You could have deep-sixed me back there, and you'd have been within your rights."

She stared at him and took a swallow of her tea. Her eyes were hard, her mouth set firmly.

"I figured it out while you slept off the morphine," she said finally. "Four options open to me. I could have killed you right then when we took you—I know how to do it now, learned a lot about killing these past few days. But frankly I've seen enough death to last me the rest of my life. Don't think I wouldn't, though, if I felt I had to." She slapped the stock of the AK racked against the gunwale.

"Two, I could have taken you back to Lázaro, or had Kasim take you when he brought Brillo back. Let Padre Cotinho dispose of you as he saw fit. Or stayed on myself, and with Kasim's help become the new Commodore Millikan. Kind of a Pasionária of the rebel pirates. But that's not for me. I'm no revolutionary, whatever the cause. And it would tie me to the land. I'm for the sea, always have been. At any rate, Cotinho would have disposed of you for me in either case."

She drank some more tea. Brillo came aft at the mention of his name. Miranda scratched him behind the ears, and he grumbled happily.

"Look at that," she said. "Your dog loves me more than he ever loved you. I had to keep him from peeing on you this morning when you were out of it. That leads me to three. I could just drop you on Perniciosa, with your wounds, no money, no boat. Not even your dog for company. Very tempting. A nice unity to it. Turnabout is fair play, after all. It's just what you did to me in Mexico back then. I liked that idea very much, but even then it wouldn't undo all the hurt you've laid on me. And on my dad."

He wanted to tell her the truth—that he'd done all this under orders, for the good of mankind, that he was one of the good guys who'd sacrificed a normal, decent life to risk everything for his country. But he didn't really believe that himself—his motives were based more on excitement than altruism—and anyway, he'd tried to tell her once already, when he thought she was about to kill him. It hadn't worked then, and even if it did now, it wouldn't matter to Miranda. Nor could he really blame her.

"Where is your dad?" he asked finally.

"He's dead. Went down with his ship." She laughed bitterly, then lashed the wheel again and went below. He could hear the clatter of crockery in the galley, then the whistle of the tea kettle. Her eyes were red and wet from tears when she returned. "I don't know," she said, "it's how he wanted it, I guess. Fire and smoke. Kind of a Viking funeral. But he got what he came for. He got his revenge." She shrugged.

The sun was sinking fast now toward an empty horizon.

"So what's option number four?" Curt asked.

"What I'm doing," she said. "I'll carry you as far as Zambo or Davao. Get you to a hospital, where they can patch you up. Then you're on your own. Once you're all better, you'll find some scam to work, I'm sure. Some other dumb babe to mess up."

"Hey," he objected, "you're no dumb babe. Look, I really felt—"

"Oh, shut up! You're a lying, conniving bastard, and you always were. You always will be. Even if you are some kind of undercover cop, you're still a shit. I suppose it's the nature of the work, part of the job description. You're good at it, I'll give you that." She kicked him sharply on his wounded leg. He almost yelled out from the sharpness of the pain but bit it off, went bone white under his tan.

"Okay," he said after a while. "You're entitled. Can't blame you a bit. But whether you believe it or not, I *am* a cop. And you're right, camouflage is the most important part of the game. But I'm getting out of the game after this one. I don't expect you to turn cartwheels with joy at that announcement, but just consider this. I'm a quick healer. By the time we get to Zambo or wherever, I probably won't need a doctor. I could crew for you on the way back across. You'll need an extra hand to work your way north to the forties and the westerlies. The monsoon season's just getting started—heavy weather ahead. And you've always got option number one still open."

Miranda stared at him for a long time. "I don't know," she said at last. "We'll see."

The sun was nearly down now, an orange ball of fire balanced on the rim of the sea—a funeral pyre consuming the dead of the Flyaway Islands.

"I'll cook us some supper," she said. She lashed the wheel and went below.

* * *

271

Far to the west the sea lay littered with the wreckage of battle. Sharks tore at the few remaining bodies they found. Smoldering spars floated spluttering on the waves. Isla Perniciosa loomed dark against the sunset. A charred hatch cover drifted on the current toward the beach near the sub base. The ship rat perched on it, singed and bloody but still alive.

When the hatch cover neared the shore, the rat slipped off and swam through the chop. Ashore, he shook himself dry. Far up the beach wild dogs were eating something large and gray. The rat sniffed the air, then scuttled silently up toward the wire grass. He sniffed again. Yes. Another rat, a female, in heat . . .

He ran west into the night. Behind him in the seaward dark, gallows birds swung low on stiff wings above the waves, their cries wild and mournful over the thud of the surf.